VOICES

Angela Bier

Black Rose Writing | Texas

This is a work of fiction. Names, characters, businesses, places, events, and incidents are either the products of the author's imagination or used in a fictitious manner. Any resemblance to actual persons, living or dead, or actual events is purely coincidental.

ISBN: 978-1-68513-616-1
PUBLISHED BY BLACK ROSE WRITING
www.blackrosewriting.com

Printed in the United States of America
Suggested Retail Price (SRP) $22.95

Voices is printed in Minion Pro
Cover art by Patrick J. Bier

*As a planet-friendly publisher, Black Rose Writing does its best to eliminate unnecessary waste to reduce paper usage and energy costs, while never compromising the reading experience. As a result, the final word count vs. page count may not meet common expectations.

PRAISE FOR
VOICES

"A tease of the supernatural woven into a modern account of an anxious teen girl starting junior year at a new high school makes *Voices*, by Angela Bier an intriguing read. Full of girl power, you're rooting for the main character, Elena, and the young women around her with every turn of the page while being helplessly drawn into the secret that, in both large and small ways, impacts all their lives."
–Emily Refermat, author of *The Invisible War*

"Elena is a normal junior in high school. Until she's not. In Elena's world, some girls are…not quite what they seem… Angela Bier both manipulates and guides the reader through the maelstrom that is Elena, her family, and her friends, revealing, bit by bit, the secret of the Voices and the struggle to understand and use it."
–Mary Ann Noe, author of *Water the Color of Slate* and *Deserving of Murder*

"Elena will steal your heart. Author Angela Bier skillfully twists and turns the usual adolescent culprits of angst, questions, lack of confidence, too much confidence, wanting to scream when you look in a mirror. and that incredible first love... and then adds a dollop of something new. Ancestral magic. But magic that no one in her immediate family seems to know about. The only one who understands what's happening is the girl in high school who hates Elena the most. Find a cozy corner, pour yourself a tall glass of soda, add a plate of cookies, and settle in for the duration. You're not going to want to stop reading."
–Kathie Giorgio, author of *Don't Let Me Keep You* and *Hope Always Rises*

To Natalie and Evelyn

VOICES

CHAPTER 1
ELENA

<u>Worst case scenarios</u>
1. Flat tire
2. Can't find locker
3. Can't open locker
4. Can't find homeroom
    . . . 64. I lock my keys in the car and can't leave at the end of the day

Elena sat in her car, willing time to stop. If the clock never switched to 7:35, she wouldn't have to go to school. This being highly unlikely, she hoped that if she forced her logic to control her feelings, everything would be fine. She pulled the schedule from the front pocket of her backpack. She had already memorized the wrinkled sheet, but scanned it again.

Belvedere Senior High School
Elena Tannin—Class of 2019
2017-2018 Schedule (Junior)
Homeroom: Room 115

Calm down, Elena scolded herself. You're starting at a new school, not facing a firing squad. She closed her eyes and slowed her breathing, trying to emulate the guided meditation taught at her old school, St. Veronica's. Not that it ever really worked; Elena's hamster wheel of a brain rarely stopped spinning.

Eventually, she gave up and rubbed her sweaty palms back and forth along her shorts until a hangnail snagged against the fabric. She chewed down the offending cuticle, a destructive, but helpful coping mechanism. She changed the radio station and turned off the audio. She always flipped to an unremarkable Top 40 channel before leaving the car. Although highly unlikely, she feared a passenger accidentally being exposed to her preferred station. Elena was the only kid she knew who listened to *Morning Edition* on National Public Radio. She liked to feel intelligent, and she certainly liked being able to discuss current events with her teachers and other impressionable adults.

Elena was confident she would excel academically at Belvedere. She had dominated at her old school, which was highly competitive. She hoped that it wouldn't take too long to win over these new teachers. She considered her intellect and charm her armor.

Belvedere Public High School was in a small town of the same name. It had no church attached and no sidewalks out front. The most notable thing about Belvedere was the football stadium with names of local businesses emblazoned along the fences. Lit up on game nights, it seemed like a place of worship. The biggest sport at her old school was girls' lacrosse, and that paled in comparison to the performing arts department.

After her family's move out of the city, Elena had spent all summer both hyper-aware and stubbornly ignorant of the countdown to the first day of school. She skipped the open house for freshman and transfer students. She didn't want to go with her dad to a pre-season football game. She drove alone on the first day.

Maybe that was a mistake. Maybe she should have let Mom take a morning off and drive her. Elena could have leaned in for a final hug in the scent of almond lotion and fabric softener that was her mother. Maybe she should have let Dad drop her off on the way to the twins' toddler music class. Ava and Jacob's chattering would have drowned out the ever-increasing roar of anxiety in her brain. Too late now.

When she was little and feeling overwhelmed, Elena's mom taught her to break her worries down into smaller, more manageable chunks.

"Let's play the 'what's the worst that could happen?' game," she said. Then, Elena talked through the worrisome bits, itemized worry being preferable to a messy knot of anxiety. A list of worst-case scenarios constituted her previous night's list. Other girls wrote rambling journal entries about feelings and friends, if they wrote at all, but Elena's journal consisted of bulleted lists. Last night's took two pages.

An increasing stream of students flowed past her car toward the school. She knew there wouldn't be uniforms, but the jumble of variety unnerved Elena. What would it feel like to take that first step toward the sprawling brick building, surrounded by cornfields on one side and the edge of a new subdivision on the other?

At exactly 7:35, Elena opened the door. The cool air and teenage energy hit her like a tidal wave. Numbly, she locked the door, slammed it shut, and shouldered her backpack. The sum of her anxieties was reduced to a throbbing ache somewhere in her center. Her intellectual armor intact, Elena merged into the lane of student traffic heading toward the front doors. She focused straight ahead, at a pair of shorts that crept dangerously high on a non-uniformed girl.

"Hey, man!" she heard a boy yell. The owner of the voice cut across her path toward a thick-necked guy who must have been The Man. She slowed to avoid him. She stepped onto the school's wide steps and tripped, stumbling into The Man anyway. He didn't even notice the collision against his linebacker's build. Ugh. Tripping wasn't even on the list.

Elena found her red, scratched locker and opened it on the second try, despite the sweaty palms that the first try produced. She arranged her color-coded notebooks and binders and glanced at the guy to her left. He pried open a plastic container of pens, his only visible school supplies. He had one thing hung up in is locker: a picture of a car obviously ripped out of a magazine, held up with a magnet from Stefano's Pizza. Elena examined the car picture for clues about the boy. Without meaning to, she caught his eye and automatically smiled.

He paused with his hand on his shelf, midway between dropping his keys and grabbing a pen, and smiled back. He had crooked teeth and mild acne. "Hey. You're new," he said.

"Yeah, I just moved to this school this year. I'm Elena."

"Chris," he replied.

"I wonder if we have any classes together?" asked Elena, desperately trying to remember how to make small talk.

"I spend as little time as possible in this building," he said. "So, unless you're in welding or autos, I doubt it. In the main building, I'm doing business math and civics." Chris pulled his hoodie up and walked away.

Elena grabbed a binder, pencil case, and lip gloss; an electronic bell rang and she moved on to the rest of the worry list. Some of Elena's worries were reasonable. After all, there were many differences between the urban, all-girls, Catholic school and this rural public school. The biggest change was the boys and the side effects of their presence, such as couples making out in the hall. She felt embarrassed on these kids' behalf, like watching someone make a fool of themselves on reality TV.

In homeroom, the sight of male bodies splayed hugely across their desks was startling. Some smaller or more thoughtful boys sat normally. Most took up a crazy amount of space, with their hairy legs projecting into the aisles between the desks. The Man, with whom Elena shared a homeroom, somehow took up three whole desks.

Her old school required uniforms, so the range of fashion at Belvedere was intriguing. Many girls dressed like she did, in the unremarkable style that took careful planning to pull off: denim shorts and a fitted, but not too fitted, top. Others wore athletic shorts and T-shirts, stylish outfits with cute shoes, or hoodies and pajama bottoms. Nothing too terribly startling. Just, different.

Once Elena determined that Belvedere's students were more or less human, she moved on to worrying about her classes. Her junior year schedule was rigorous. She registered for all the Advanced Placement courses offered: calculus, English, history, and chemistry. When she walked into her first actual class after homeroom, calculus, she started to feel at home. Elena recognized the textbooks as those they began to use last year at her old school.

The windowless room was populated by only 13 students, which was fine with her; it meant less competition. There were only four other girls in the class and Elena began analyzing them, pausing when the bell rang and the teacher came in. She was a middle-aged woman with smeared coral lipstick and a belt featuring a bejeweled butterfly. She looked decidedly batty and introduced herself as Mrs. Vickers.

"Good morning, everyone." She eyed the class over her turquoise reading glasses tethered with a beaded chain. "Ladies, I see we're outnumbered once again this year. But we won't let that discourage us now, will we?"

Elena quickly figured her out. Mrs. Vickers longed for a smart, driven female to dominate the class. Elena could play that part in her sleep. She sat in the front row, volunteered several answers, and had Mrs. Vickers calling her by name without using a seating chart within the first 15 minutes.

Later that morning, chemistry included all the kids from calculus, plus a few more. The teacher assigned lab partners by lottery, instructing the students to check their lab equipment into the wooden drawers. Elena was paired with a vanishingly pale girl named Kayla who she recognized from other classes.

"Hi, I'm Elena," she said. "Sorry if I break something, but I'm kind of freaking out because I'm new."

"Kayla," the girl replied with a surprisingly huge smile. "I already noticed you. Most of the rest of us have been together since preschool. Where did you come from?"

"My family moved from Milwaukee this summer," said Elena.

"That's a big change."

"You're telling me," Elena replied.

Elena and Kayla talked through the last few minutes of class. Elena was acutely aware that lunch, the most worrisome item on the list, followed chemistry. She wasn't sure whether hot lunch or bagged lunch was the way to go at Belvedere, so she both packed a lunch and brought money for hot lunch. In addition to eating the wrong thing, there were all the other pitfalls: sitting in the wrong place, spilling food, sitting alone.

Eating alone was the worst-case scenario; once someone was branded a lunchtime loner, it was difficult to salvage their reputation. Elena walked out of chemistry with Kayla, hoping to barnacle along to her table. Luckily, Kayla didn't seem to mind. They grabbed lunches from their lockers, and Elena soon sat with three other girls in a lunch room that smelled of long-ago Taco Tuesdays.

"Guys, this is Elena, she's new," said Kayla. "Elena, this is the Herd."

"The Herd? I don't know anything about farm animals," Elena blurted. *What group did I accidentally attach myself to?*

"No," laughed a redhead. "We've been the Nerd Herd ever since middle school. It used to be some people's attempt at teasing us. I'm Addison." She waved her wax-paper wrapped sandwich.

The third girl was named Morgan. They asked a lot of questions, and Elena summarized her story: grew up on the East Side of Milwaukee, moved after her parents built their dream house in the country, blah blah blah. When they compared schedules, she found that she and the Herd shared a lot of classes.

"It's like we all have the same classes at the exact same times," Elena said. "What a weird coincidence."

"Not so weird when you live in a town where less than half the kids go to college," Morgan said.

The Herd had just enough time to finish scarfing their lunches before the bell ushered in the afternoon, which brought all sorts of other worries. All her non-advanced classes were in the afternoon, and the Nerd Herd's origin story did not comfort Elena. What would these other kids be like? She heard about how kids in small towns drank in cornfields and did meth out of sheer boredom.

In one of her easy classes, civics, she spotted the boy, Chris, whose locker was next to hers. He must have gotten the pack of pens open, because he kept flicking one around his finger. She slipped into to the seat behind him while she took the class's pulse. Junior US Civics seemed like some legislator's plan to create solid citizens in Wisconsin by academic force. For the students, it was a reunion of peers, following the inevitable tracking that separated them in middle school. The college prep kids mingled with the other kids with whom they once shared a carpet in kindergarten.

And the other kids freaked Elena out. They took up twelve bullet points on her list. The room was the most boisterous of the day and she felt the energy begin to rattle around her head. She waited for the teacher to calm the room, but no such luck. He was a youngish man who appeared just as unprepared as the students. He still had a tag attached to the back of his khaki dress pants, announcing his 30-inch waist. He held a single piece of paper and a pen.

"Quiet! Okay, let's take attendance," he said.

Elena assumed he was fresh out of college; St. Veronica's hosted student teachers, so she had seen this type before. She offered reassuring smiles, especially when he was startled by a loud belch from The Man. The exhausting hour was spent calling the roll, passing out textbooks, putting names in textbooks, logging textbooks, redirecting rowdy students, and reminding half of the class to take the textbooks with them when the bell rang.

Elena knew that she could probably teach this class as well as the assigned faculty and decided to surreptitiously mentor the poor guy with his still-tagged grownup pants. Her other non-advanced classes, Spanish and Choir, were similarly non-threatening and much better managed, with broken-in teachers in charge.

On the way to her last class, AP English, Elena found a single stall bathroom. Not being able to find a single-staller was on her list, a legitimate concern for someone who couldn't pee with anyone else in the room. After her much-needed bathroom detour, Elena took a seat in English near the wall, behind a girl with gorgeous black hair. Elena was jealous of any hair that could be described by the words "smooth," "lustrous," or "glossy." She was cursed with something between curls and waves that generally ended up in a messy bun on top of her head.

A mousy woman, barely five feet tall, interrupted Elena's hair reverie. "Hello. Hello! HELLO!" the teacher yelled, if the final "hello" could really be called a yell. She made a face like she was yelling, but her voice came out as an emphatic squeak. "I'm glad to see that you all are enjoying your time together already," she continued, weaving between the rows. "For those who don't know me, I'm Mrs. Stanton."

Appearances can be deceiving, Elena thought, as silence quickly fell over the room.

"Now," Mrs. Stanton continued, "I know this class has a reputation for being tough and that some of you, Kayla, are very concerned about your grades. Rest assured that there is no quiz today on the summer reading. And," she gently pushed Kayla's insistent hand down, "all the grading policies are in the syllabus for you to review." She gave Kayla a patient glance.

"I don't want you to think that this class is going to be awful. As long as we show some mutual respect, everyone will learn a lot from each other." She offered a small smile. "Enough kumbaya. Attendance." Mrs. Stanton pulled a pen out of her corduroy skirt and efficiently began, asking for preferred nicknames.

The girl with the glossy black hair raised her hand to the name, "Katherine," and asked to be called "Kat, please."

How could someone with such beautiful hair have such an exotic nickname too? Some things weren't fair.

Elena had enjoyed the class's summer reading assignment, *Middlemarch*. After a brief overview of the life of George Eliot and the era in which the book was written, Mrs. Stanton asked if there were any parts that they found interesting. A sandy-haired boy in a vintage R.E.M. T-shirt raised his hand.

"Yes, Stephen?" said Mrs. Stanton.

"First of all, this book was extremely dense," Stephen said, leaning back in his chair and flipping through the pages. "But I really liked this one quote I marked: 'And of course men know best about everything.'" He looked up at the teacher with a cocky grin.

"Oh, yes, a favorite. Did anyone else note that passage?"

"Um, yes!" Elena blurted without raising her hand. She had hoped to make it through the day without randomly shouting things out in class, but she couldn't help it. It was the end of the day and her defenses were worn thin. She had dog-eared that page too, and found it as soon as the boy started talking. "The quote's not quite so good without the ending. 'And, of course men know best about everything, except what women know better.'"

Elena blushed. She didn't want to be a know-it-all just yet. She bit her lip and glanced at Stephen who shrugged as a few people laughed.

"Good one, Elena," murmured Kayla. Her words were like a cool compress on Elena's burning face. Stephen's cocky grin returned, and he nodded at Elena as if to say, "It's on."

Maybe they brainwashed me at St. Veronica's, Elena thought. Her old school preached the gospel of girls-only classrooms being superior, but Stephen didn't seem so bad.

Mrs. Stanton assigned homework and the bell rang. As Elena joined the traffic in the hallway, she realized that none of her worst-case scenarios had happened, except for that minor outburst in English and tripping on the way in, which wasn't even on the list to begin with. She walked quickly back to her locker and waved to Kayla a few doors down. They fell into step on the way out.

"Looks like you survived your first day," said Kayla.

"Yup," Elena replied, a bit surprised that Kayla understood that she'd been on the defensive all day.

"How do you get home? I walk," said Kayla.

"Drive," said Elena. "Do you want a ride?" she offered, immediately regretting it. She couldn't wait to be alone, to be honest.

"No, thanks, I live close," Kayla answered. "Well, bye!" She turned away from Elena and joined the crowd of walkers.

It was nice to walk out of the school with someone. It was even better to finally be alone. Elena didn't fully exhale until she returned to the Civic, where she automatically began to worry about the next day, and the next.

CHAPTER 2
KAT

Kat: 1st day of school ugh how many days til summer
Val: too many :(how's wisco?
Kat: mid. how's iowa
Val: dreamy

Kat sat in her boyfriend's car and concentrated on sucking in her stomach. She probably should have been listening, but Ty was talking about football. He was boring when he started rambling on about the defensive line, but it could be worse. She could be single.

Last spring, everybody paired off all of a sudden, and she was the only one without a boyfriend. So, when he put his arm around her on the couch in her friend's basement, she went with it. Luckily, he was popular and nice enough. And he did have a cute butt, especially in his uniform. It was good to have a boyfriend to do things with on the weekends, to blend in with. She sucked her stomach in deeper and turned to offer him a dazzling smile.

"How was your day, babe?" she asked, using his preferred nickname. "I missed you. No classes together," she pouted.

He reached over and took her hand. "Right? I can't believe Coach made my schedule for me. I should say something, right?" He glanced over at her.

"Well, you *do* have to keep a 2.0 to play, so it'd probably be best to do what he says."

"Yeah, I guess," he replied. "Friday's gonna be rough. Springfield's quarterback is freaking amazing."

Kat sighed and relaxed back into her seat. She wouldn't see him after practice tonight. She had too much work to do. She was taking more honors classes than any of her friends, which meant she had to pull it off effortlessly. She wanted to do well in school, plus she needed the safety of her group. Paradoxically, the safety of the group required being disinterested in anything as basic as grades.

Ty pulled into her driveway and leaned over to kiss her. "Babe, I like your hair down," he said, breaking off the kiss and pulling the hair tie out of her thick hair.

Kat smiled and took the loop from his hand. "Call me later?"

"Yup," he said, backing out as she slammed the door.

Kat walked into her house, relaxed her stomach, and returned her hair to a ponytail. She flopped into her dad's chair with *Middlemarch* and her favorite comfort food: cereal. She went back and forth, evening out the cereal and milk, until the box was empty. She got up to put away the evidence and heard the garage door open. Kat's mom came into the kitchen, returning home from her job at the senior center.

"Hi, honey, how was the first day? Rough transition back?" Mom asked, unwinding herself from several scarves.

"I managed," Kat answered.

Managed was about it. Re-acclimating to high school was exhausting. She preferred the normalcy of summer camp and not having to fake it. Speaking of faking it . . . "There was a new girl in a couple of my classes. Do we know anyone named Tannin?" Kat asked.

"Don't think so," Mom replied. She glanced back at Kat. "Why?"

Kat shrugged and her mom did the same. Kat didn't feel like telling her mom about the fact that she somehow knew that girl sat down behind her without turning around or hearing her above the din. That she somehow guessed her name before Mrs. Stanton took attendance. Elena Tannin probably seemed familiar for some random reason. It was impossible that they were connected any other way.

CHAPTER 3
ELENA

Elena's tires kicked up a cloud of gravel, announcing her arrival home. She was greeted by a riot of colored chalk laid out like a red carpet on the concrete in front of the garage. Her younger siblings, Ava and Jacob, were similarly bedecked.

"Hi, guys," she greeted them.

"Lay-lay! Lay-lay! See my picture! I made it for you!" The twins harmonized in the sing-song "Lay-lay," their baby name for her. They were three now and could pronounce "Elena," but the nickname stuck.

"Hey, honey. How was it?" her dad asked, walking toward the car. He shooed the filthy kids from Elena and reached into the backseat to grab her bag.

"It was okay."

When the twins were born, her dad quit his job as an accountant to stay home full time. He still did some contract work remotely, but mostly, he was a homemaker. He might not have been the tidiest stay-at-home parent, but he made up for it in other ways.

"I'm worried—oof—that they're not going to give you enough homework," he said as he hoisted her stuffed backpack.

"It's not all homework," Elena replied. "I brought home all the syllabuses to put in my calendar."

Her dad smiled knowingly. "I made you a smoothie, it's on the counter. You two filthy animals, directly to the bathroom."

He dropped Elena's backpack inside the door, grabbed the twins' collars, and herded them into the bathroom. Elena skirted the grime and went into the kitchen. As ambivalent as she was about moving to the country, she had to admit that the view was beautiful. Their driveway traced through several acres of woodland that, thanks to some previous owner's whims, was not cleared to fields. The ancient oaks provided privacy and dropped limbs with every rainstorm. The back of the house looked out over miles of farmland.

Elena grabbed the smoothie and went out the back door to sit on the deck. The warm September sun beat down, and she peeled off her socks, revealing what she felt were the ugliest toes ever created. She extended her long legs to rest her feet on the deck railing and leaned back. If this couldn't calm her down, nothing would. This is my life now, she thought. No more easy walks to the coffee shop. No more hearing the neighbors when the windows are open. Instead, the only sounds were the fall death-rattle of drying leaves, the distant squeal of preschool voices, and her own buzzing thoughts.

The smoothie was thick and cool and strawberry. She felt it slowly make its way down her esophagus into her stomach, the route as familiar to her as if it were visible. She had studied her mom's anatomy textbooks since she was the twins' age. She tried to feel the cool outline of her digestive system, instead of the anxious knots forming in anticipation of tomorrow.

Autumn was different out here in the country. It wasn't just blazing colors and artificial pumpkin spice. The wide-open spaces stretched across miles and the only interruptions to the corn stubble were occasional huddles of farm buildings. The openness permitted passing breezes to follow an unrestricted course. The wind wasn't funneled into a Bernoulli-like vortex as it was in the city. Fall was much more auditory here. Auditory made more sense to Elena. She tried to listen to the rattling asters and not her internal critic rehashing the day.

It kind of worked, at least for a few seconds. For a moment, she almost forgot that she'd have to go back to school tomorrow. Almost.

"Okay, guys, here's your snack. One for each of you, so no fighting," her dad said from inside. "Keep the food on the table and your hands to yourself. I'm going outside by Lay-Lay."

The door slid open, and Elena's dad folded his lanky body praying-mantis like into the chair next to hers. "So, what was it like, really?"

"It was fine," Elena answered. "It was school. There were boys, so the place smelled worse, but overall, it was just . . . fine."

"How were things on the friend front?"

"I think I found a possible friend group," Elena said. "I sat with them at lunch. So, I won't spend my lunch eating alone or with the janitor." Joking worked with Dad.

"You must be relieved," he said. "I know you were worried about the janitor lunch date."

"*You* were worried about me not making friends," Elena insisted. "I was more worried about the work and the teachers."

"Okay, how were the work and teachers?" he asked.

"Easy," Elena said. "I think English will be challenging, also calculus because it's calculus, but it's the same book we were starting last spring, so I'm ahead already."

"Why do you think English will be hard?"

"It's the teacher. You know how I can kind of wrap teachers around my finger?"

He nodded. "Yeah. I noticed."

"Well, Mrs. Stanton, she's trickier. I think I'll have to do more than just be a good student and behave in class, you know?" Elena explained, trying to convey Mrs. Stanton-ness. "She wore a corduroy skirt and Doc Martens."

"Shocking," he replied, sipping his Spotted Cow beer.

"I'm pretty sure I'll be one of the best students. Not to brag, but I just didn't see much competition."

"No one wearing a pocket protector and horn-rimmed glasses?" he asked.

"Dad, no. I mean, no one really struck me, that's all."

"You can't always judge a book by its cover. Besides, not all the top students may be in your classes. They could be hiding out in shop class. You know, Einstein was a patent clerk when he wrote his First Theory of Relativity?"

Elena considered arguing, but didn't bother. When her mom got home, she'd have to review the day all over again in greater detail. Better save her strength.

•   •   •

By 5 o'clock, the sky was stained pinkish purple. Elena played the piano for a while—relaxing Broadway scores, no exercises or Bach. Dad made supper and the twins played in the family room. After a bit, she moved to work in the kitchen. In the old house, Elena did homework at the kitchen table. Now, she had a dedicated upholstered chair off to the side of the counters.

At a few minutes past six, the door clicked open. Jacob and Ava rushed to fling themselves at their mom who worked at a large hospital in Milwaukee. The commute took around an hour in good weather, and she often left in the morning before the twins were up. Mom gave them big squeezes before gently detaching them. She kissed Elena's forehead, reachable only because Elena was sitting.

"I want to hear everything," she said, shedding her shoes, badges, and bags. "Any trouble parking? Did you find anyone to sit with at lunch? Were classes okay?"

"No, yes, yes," Elena answered.

Mom looked up and gave her a look that said, 'Not good enough.'

Elena sighed. "Yes, I found everything. I sat with some girls from my classes. One was named Kayla, another was named Addison, there was a Morgan. I asked them to submit paperwork for background checks." Elena knew she was being obnoxious.

"That's nice," her mom said, oblivious to Elena's sarcasm. "Did you get a chance to talk with your counselor? If not, try to before the end of the week. You should get to know your counselor sooner rather than later." She finished sorting and looked up, smiling.

Did her mom not know how hard it was for her to simply keep it together that day? "Geez, Mom, give me a break. It was the first freaking day," Elena said bitterly.

That got her attention, and she reached down to hug Elena. "Honey, I just want to see how you're doing. You know I love you, and I—"

"Can we not talk about it?" Elena interrupted, inexplicably irritated with Mom's attempted affection.

Her mom stiffened then, broke the hug first, patting Elena on the back.

Elena sniffed, picked up her backpack, and strode out of the kitchen past the twins. They were no longer interested in *Paw Patrol*, instead focusing on the enthralling drama: Teenage Sister and Mom.

Pros of moving to Belvedere	*Cons of moving to Belvedere*
Get to have own car	*Have to drive to get anywhere*
School will be easy (classes)	*School will be hard (everything else)*
No one knows me—fresh start	*No one knows me—need to start fresh*
	Food options limited. People options limited. Everything limited.

CHAPTER 4
MEGHAN

Meghan finished dictating her notes around 10:30 that night. Some colleagues finished before leaving the hospital, but she preferred to hurry home and complete her work after the kids were in bed. Pathology charting tended to be routine, so she long ago made the process more efficient by creating a catalog of templates for most of the common findings. Ruthless efficiency, that was Meghan Walsh's guiding principle which allowed her to keep her complex life running predictably.

The mini-spat with Elena was a snag in an otherwise well-oiled day. "Do you think Elena's still awake?" she asked. Anders read in bed while she worked next to him; years of exposure to medical jargon made him immune to the distraction.

"I think we should just leave her be. She's a little prickly," he said, invoking their code for teenage moodiness.

"Did something go wrong at school that you're not telling me?" she asked.

"Meghan. She started at a brand-new school today. Even if it went perfectly, which it really sounds like it did, that's a lot."

"I suppose." Years of new classrooms blurred in her memory. Meghan was always good at school, and years upon years of education gave her plenty of practice. No, first days were exciting! She must have missed something to explain Elena's surly attitude toward her. "Maybe I'll just go say good night."

"Let it lie, Megs. There's always tomorrow."

Meghan was not comfortable with Anders' suggestion, but followed the suggestion which she had asked for. When Elena was younger, parenting books prepared Meghan for every possible situation. A few years ago, she could have handled the tension perfectly. She knew that the ideal mother would have a heart-to-heart, followed by an understanding hug and tuck-in.

But that version of motherly perfection was no longer right for her nearly-adult daughter. And the parenting books didn't provide clear templates on how to deal with a teenager like Elena. Meghan wasn't sure what unattainable ideal to hold herself to these days. She split the difference, sneaking into the hall and cracking Elena's door, whispering, "I love you!" into the darkness.

CHAPTER 5
ELENA

As September sighed away the last bits of summer, Belvedere High School started to feel normal-ish. Elena knew all the potholes on her way to school, and the building's appearance on the horizon no longer surprised her. Outside of the Herd, most of the kids remained mysteries. The noise and drama levels were overwhelming; being around Belvedere kids was exhausting. Elena began taking ibuprofen every morning to prevent pounding afternoon headaches. Was this school really that different, or had something changed with her?

Elena's schoolwork was manageable in terms of its difficulty, but there was a lot of it. She joined a couple of service clubs and Model UN to keep her college applications solid. Between that, practicing piano, and hanging out with the Herd, Elena was super busy.

Calculus was her hardest subject. She began calling the super-blonde girl, Kayla, at night for help. Kayla was her closest friend in the Herd, and her chief academic rival. One morning, Elena rushed into math, clutching her homework; she needed to check her answers.

"Kayla, what did you get for number four?" she whispered.

"Number four? Let's see...(f) is increasing at point A, decreasing at C, and has a maximum at B," replied Kayla, folding open her notebook to show Elena.

"Oh, good, that's what I had too," Elena replied, flashing Kayla a smile. Kayla briefly smiled back before turning away. She and Elena talked nearly every night, but she was still so shy.

"Good morning," announced Mrs. Vickers, striding into the room in bright green alligator pumps and a turquoise pendant. "Let's go over the homework. Any questions? No? I think that number four was the hardest, so let's work through it as a group." She wove between students' desks, leaving a trail of heavy perfume in her wake, glancing over their shoulders at their work. "Hmm, Addison, you had some problems, I see?"

Addison was not a fan of calculus in general or Mrs. Vickers specifically. She dramatically rolled her eyes at Elena and Kayla after the teacher passed.

"Who'd like to come up and solve number four?" She uncapped a dry erase marker and brandished it.

Elena raised her hand with a smile. As she determined on the first day, this teacher loved a confident girl.

"Okay, Elena, come on up." Elena took the marker and neatly outlined the problem. As she worked, Mrs. Vickers made comments and quizzed the class. I might not be the smartest one at calculus, Elena thought, but as far as Mrs. Vickers is concerned, I am.

Later, as class was wrapping up, the teacher looked up from her podium. "Elena? Kayla? Could I see you after class?"

Elena's stomach dropped, thinking that she was going to be called out for copying Kayla's work on number four. Instead, the teacher said, "Ladies, every year, I nominate two juniors to attend a summer engineering course at the University. This is extremely competitive, only 50 students are selected from across the state. This year, I chose you."

Elena's heart quickened with the thrill of the chase.

"In my years, I've had three students accepted, and you each have a good shot," Mrs. Vickers continued. "Needless to say, I'm counting on you," she said, peering over her bedazzled half-spectacles.

"When is the application due?" Kayla asked.

"When does the course run?" Elena asked at the same time.

"December 15, mid-June to mid-August," Mrs. Vickers answered. "Most questions can be answered on their website. I emailed links to you and your parents." Mrs. Vickers rose, signaling that the conversation was over.

Basically all summer. Ever since Elena could remember, her family spent two weeks every August in northern Wisconsin. They stayed at The Cottage, which was more of a small house, nestled on land owned by her dad's family. In the olden days, some of his relatives also started a camp on the property. The camp took up most of the south end, while the Cottage stood at the north edge, its residence shared among various relatives according to some obscure formula.

Elena's family always had the first two weeks of August. The old building along the rocky Lake Michigan shoreline was Elena's happiest place. The camp ran its business nearly a quarter mile away and the Tannins might as well have been there all by themselves, so complete was the wooded separation from Camp Zedernwald.

And now this prestigious engineering competition threatened to complicate things. Elena briefly considered not applying, but two things prevented that. One: she couldn't resist competing for things. Two: Mrs. Vickers already emailed her parents.

As the girls walked together toward their next classes, Kayla enthused. It was weird to see her having any emotion, let alone giddy excitement. "Wow, this is amazing! I hope that if I'm accepted, my parents will let me go," she said. "The last girl from Belvedere that got in ended up going to Harvard. It's such an awesome opportunity." She turned her glowingly pale eyes toward Elena.

"Yeah," said Elena, trying lamely to match Kayla's enthusiasm. "It sounds like a huge honor, and super competitive." She knew without looking that Kayla's excitement was dampened. She didn't seem to have a competitive bone in her body, and never once complained when Elena took credit for work that she helped her on. Elena swallowed a lump of guilt. "Thanks again for helping me with the homework last night," Elena said.

"That's okay. It's nice to have someone to talk to. My parents were starting to bug me that maybe I didn't need my own phone after all, because I wasn't using many minutes. So, thanks for helping me use my minutes, I guess." Kayla laughed awkwardly. "Well, see ya at chem." And she abruptly turned into the nearest bathroom.

Elena sighed. There were moments when she felt Kayla becoming a real friend, but those moments usually guillotined off abruptly.

•   •   •

If calculus was the bane of her existence, choir was her most relaxing class. Elena enjoyed singing, but she was much better at playing piano. She studied since kindergarten and was pretty good. At St. Veronica's, she accompanied the advanced choir, easily playing whatever pieces she was given.

In contrast, the student pianist at Belvedere was a disaster. The girl was painfully thin, with huge eyes and stereotypically blonde hair. Her real name was Bailey, but Elena mentally called her The Waif. At Belvedere, the smaller number of kids meant that students often doubled up on stereotypical roles. Addison, for example, was secretary of the Junior Class, a varsity golfer, and a member of the Nerd Herd. The Waif held the roles of head music girl and head popular girl. At Elena's larger old school with its more extensive cast, those roles were all played by different actors.

The Waif was the universally acknowledged alpha of The Beautiful People. Morgan explained that, back in eighth grade, they started calling themselves that. Inexplicably, the rest of the school followed suit. So, the Waif presided over both choir and the social hierarchy. She and her page turner sat in the front of the music room and whenever the director turned his back, they whispered furiously. Elena was certain that they were gossiping about the rest of the choir, arrayed neatly in front of them, easily dissectible.

The Waif's page turner was Kat, she of the glossy black hair, effortlessly chic nickname, and placid face. Elena reassured herself that the two Beautiful People probably never noticed her and her blurts. Elena tried to ignore their critical stares and whispers, but they got to her. She imagined criticisms so clearly, it was like she could hear them:

"She's so awkward...she's always showing off... look at that frizzy mess...I hear she got kicked out of her old school…"

Elena should have known better than to draw their actual attention, since the imagined hostility was unnerving enough. Nonetheless, one day, as the director took attendance, he noticed that both The Waif and Kat were absent.

"Probably skipping," whispered Morgan.

"Since we have no pianist, we'll just work *a cappella*," announced the director from his stand.

"I can play!" Elena blurted before she had a chance to weigh the pros and cons. She was quickly whisked to the bench as Morgan looked alarmed. Why do I always announce what's going on in my head? Elena scolded herself.

The director suggested that they warm up with the easiest piece, which she sight-read perfectly. She truly tried not to, but Elena couldn't fake mistakes. She played the notes more faithfully on her first reading than The Waif ever had.

The Waif was gone the entire week ("Mono," whispered Morgan), and the director had Elena keep playing. Kat did not appear pleased from the back row of the soprano section, but her laser beam eyes weren't as glinty without her leader.

After a week, The Waif returned. As soon as she entered the room, even before Elena saw her, she knew something was up. Elena felt Kat's boring eyes, fueled by the tearstained sniffs of The Waif from the soprano section. Apparently, the choir director elected to make the change permanent without asking her first. Elena saw her own folder waiting on the piano's music rack, to which the director motioned her.

"That's okay, I don't want to keep playing if she's back!" Elena insisted.

"I already discussed the change with Bailey and she's fine with it," the director announced.

When Morgan told the rest of the Herd at lunch, they shook their heads at Elena in pity. That ill-informed decision branded Elena an official enemy of the Beautiful People, with all attendant rights and responsibilities.

People to figure out
- *Locker Guy*
- *Hair Girl*
- *The Waif*
- *Kayla*

CHAPTER 6
KAT

From Kat: srsly tho you dont know an elena tannin
From Val: srsly tho no…obsess much
From Kat: tbh yeah

"And, it's not like I actually care, but I am still so pissed." Bailey droned on, obsessed about Elena Tannin at the piano. Kat would never admit it, but she played much better than Bailey. Maybe it was cuz she had really, really short nails. She didn't even need a page turner.

Kat knew she made Elena nervous. Normally, Kat didn't worry too much about the collateral damage that the BP's relentless toxicity leveled on the other students. But for some reason, with this new girl, she was uncomfortably aware of just how bitchy they all were. Obviously, she would feel worse if she pissed off Bailey, though. Being a bitch was required for the safety of membership in the BP, and her friends were how Kat coped. The BP's coldness normalized her own internal icy barrier. She hid in plain sight.

Ice fortress wasn't the recommended technique for managing the pounding waves of incoming human emotion, but it was the one Kat stuck with. For the past several summers at camp, they encouraged her to try more advanced techniques, but she was too scared. She wasn't interested in picking apart her own psyche and all its walled-off issues.

Even more important, the Beautiful People protected her from the other awful thing. More than anything, Kat feared people realizing she was fat. The rest of the BP's conventional beauty was camouflage. And both the camouflage and the iciness worked just fine, thank you very much. So, Kat fixed her glare and sent a wave of judgment to disruptive Elena Tannin, playing perfectly at the front of the choir.

"Totally," Kat finally replied. "What a hag." Her heart wasn't in it, though. As she did every day, Kat thought wistfully of her best friend from summer camp, Val. Kat missed her, and she really needed her opinion on this Elena Tannin situation.

CHAPTER 7
ELENA

Elena pulled her car into its usual place and exited to a leaf-clearing breeze. Inside school, the energy level hit her like a ton of bricks. It was fueled by a combination of the crisp weather, a home football game, and Friday-ness. Many of the Beautiful People wore their boyfriends' football jerseys, and cheerleaders wore their uniforms; a few girls had a combination of the two, the Waif included. It's like she's collecting powers, Elena thought.

All of Belvedere would have trouble focusing that day. People would make plans to meet up later, either in the bleachers or under them, depending on their interests. Adults would rush home from work, grab a bite somewhere serving fish fry, and head to the game. Elena would go with her family, sit with them for the first quarter, and then wander off to find the Herd in the stands by the pep band. Addison would play flute in the halftime field show, and then join Kayla, Morgan, Elena, and whoever else drifted their way. They'd go out for pizza afterward, their group melding with others. Elena didn't have a curfew, but she was usually home by midnight.

So, yeah, it seemed like a normal Friday. In chemistry, the teacher explained the experiment for the day and then turned the students loose to their lab stations.

"Hey, Kayla," Elena greeted her friend as she pulled equipment out of the drawers. "How are you?"

"Oh...fine," Kayla said distractedly, shuffling through papers. Her pale skin was smudged dark under her eyes.

No sleep and distracted, thought Elena. "Everything okay? You look tired."

"What? Oh, sorry, yeah, I'm just a little tired," Kayla answered, offering a weak smile. "Let's get started."

The experiment was on chemo luminescence, the production of light from a chemical reaction. After the class set up, then the teacher would require all electronics to be powered off to allow accurate measurement of the lumens produced. She promised "an amazing spectacle!"

The girls moved efficiently to set up the experiment. They were a great team, but Elena still wasn't sure where she stood with Kayla. Sure, they talked most nights, but it never seemed to stray much from calculus and the Herd. Elena figured out that Kayla was an only child, that her mom stayed home, her dad was an engineer, and she had three cats.

Elena used the downtime in chemistry to try and figure out the girl who was her biggest academic competition and potential best friend. "Did you have trouble sleeping last night?" she asked.

"I must have had some caffeine or something," replied Kayla. "Okay, so all we have to do is combine the reagents. Our light meter is ready. Should we double check our calculations?"

Before Elena had a chance to probe further, the teacher's voice cut through the chatter. "Is everyone set? Turn off your phones. One of you be ready to combine the reagents, and the other have the light meter going."

The class responded to her directions, automatically lowering their collective voices as the room was plunged into darkness.

"All right, ready?" said the teacher. "And . . . begin!"

Kayla held the light meter next to their beaker and Elena prepared to pour the chemicals together. The darkness was disconcerting. Elena steadied the beaker and lightly grabbed Kayla's arm to steady herself as she poured. A faint, bluish glow began to emanate from the glass vial, and identical orbs glowed around the rest of the room. Whispered

"Aww! Wow!" could be heard, warm blue light cast magical shadows on the faces of the students huddled around the lab stations.

Elena started to say something to Kayla, but she was interrupted by Kayla's sharp voice. 'Jesus, Elena, just mind your own business. You have no idea what I'm dealing with, and I'd like to keep it that way. Back off,' Kayla hissed.

"Jesus, Kayla!" Elena blurted. She abruptly withdrew her arm. "If you're so pissed at me, then why don't you finish this by yourself?" Her eyes stinging with tears, Elena set the beaker down, hard, on the lab bench. So much for a potential best friend.

"Elena?" Kayla said frantically, in her normal voice, "What's wrong?"

The teacher, who stood behind the girls, clearly wasn't sure who to calm down first, the fuming Elena or the panicked Kayla. She chose Elena. "Elena, calm down!" the teacher whispered, trying to keep the contagion of teen drama from spreading through the room. "What is this all about?"

"Honestly, I have no idea," Elena said. "We were starting the experiment and Kayla went off on me for no reason." She glared at the shadowy, panicky Kayla. How could she chew me out one second and then act like a cornered animal the next?

"But I didn't say anything!" insisted Kayla. "Elena, please don't be mad!"

"I don't like being attacked out of nowhere," whispered Elena, "and I really don't like liars."

The teacher cut in as Kayla gasped. "Elena, I have to agree with Kayla. I was right behind you girls, and the first thing I heard was you snapping at Kayla. Maybe you imagined her saying something?" she suggested.

The rest of the class grew silent, infected with the drama virus. Experiments were abandoned, and someone turned the lights back on. In the harsh light of the lab, the glowing orbs faded, and Elena doubted herself. Could I have imagined it? After all, why would a teacher lie? Elena's indignation melted into mind-racing mortification. She needed to get out of there as quickly as possible. "I'm sorry, Kayla," she mumbled, and hurriedly gathered her things together. "Can I go to the bathroom?" Not waiting for a response, she rushed out of the room, past a sea of drama-drunk teenage faces

Elena ran to her single-stall bathroom and locked herself in the redundant cubicle. She rested her head against the door and forced herself to take deep breaths. She imagined each breath squeezing Kayla's echoing voice out of her head. After a minute or two, she slowly opened her eyes. She focused on the chipped blue paint of the stall door, a rusted etching proclaiming: "Heather is a BITCH." She was dragged back to reality. She stood up, rested her hands against the cool tangibility of the door, and swung it open. Back to reality, brain quiet, armor intact.

•　•　•

Elena skipped lunch. Instead, she sat in the library, thinking. Kayla's attack was not typical of her cheerful character. She seemed genuinely confused after Elena shut her down. Reluctantly, Elena forced herself to mostly believe that she *must* have imagined Kayla's scathing comments. It was the only logical explanation.

Except that it *was* Kayla's voice that she heard, for real!

No. Stop it, Elena, she scolded herself. You imagined it and you need to make things right with Kayla. To make everything better, she had to be wrong. So, she'd be wrong.

When the bell rang at the end of lunch, Elena waited outside the cafeteria door for the Herd. She did her best to ignore the judgey stares of the BP, and the leering looks from some chemistry kids. The Herd walked out next to Kayla, as though protecting a baby bird. She looked even worse than in chemistry.

Elena felt awful. Without saying a word, she cracked through the people-shell of protection and hugged Kayla. "I'm so, so sorry I blew up at you. I must have been hearing things. It's all on me," Elena said, loud enough for the rest of the Herd to hear. After all, she was repairing the breach with the group, not just Kayla.

"Oh, Elena, I'm sorry too. I was acting so weird in chemistry, I can see why you were confused," Kayla said with a look of relief. The group relaxed as a unit. Kayla offered Elena a weak smile, and Elena flashed one back. Sometimes being friends was better than being right, even though Elena still knew she was right somehow.

Unmentionable Weirdness
- *Kayla in chem. Liar vs. voice-thrower?*

CHAPTER 8
MEGHAN

Meghan waited for Elena's light to click off before going to sleep herself. Elena was up past 11 most school nights, but Meghan was happy to stay awake and silently keep her company, even if they weren't in the same room.

Meghan had finished her own work and moved on to a favorite relaxation activity: emptying her email inbox. Her colleagues couldn't understand how an empty inbox was even possible; their unread messages numbered in the thousands. Meghan did it through a system of nested files and ruthless efficiency. She sat next to a gently snoring Anders and sorted.

She flagged an email from Elena's math teacher, regarding a prestigious summer engineering institute. If Elena didn't mention it by the end of the week, she would bring it up. She opened the Elena folder, revealing a number of subcategories: "Health, Extracurriculars, Elementary, Middle School, St. Veronica's, Belvedere HS." Automatically, she clicked open the St. Veronica's folder and saw the ugly subfolder: "St. Veronica's Debacle."

Was it only a year ago that things went south at Elena's old school, and they accelerated their move-in date for the Belvedere house? A group of Elena's friends started flirting with guys they met online and Elena was purposely left in the dark. By the time she was included in the secret-sharing, the girls planned to skip school and meet the random internet weirdos at the mall.

Upon learning the secret, Elena's self-destroying first move was to contact the girls' parents; not surprisingly, this didn't go over well. Elena became an outcast, and no number of restorative justice circles mended the damage. Elena spent the end of her sophomore year being completely ignored, which was worse than being bullied.

Why didn't she tell me first? Meghan still wondered. I would have advised her how to handle things more delicately. Meghan sighed in resignation: she was not an easy mom. Just today, before even saying hello, she greeted Elena with a reminder to not leave dirty socks all over the floor. She met Elena's recitation of her homework with an eyebrow crinkle, signaling "how did you let things build up so much?"

Meghan's judgmental responses were irritatingly automatic, but she couldn't help it. Her world came down to black and white distinctions. Were the cells cancerous or not? Were the margins clean or not? The pathologic judgments that she rendered were the linchpins on which entire lives revolved. There wasn't room for indecision or shades of gray.

Perhaps Elena's social self-destruction stemmed from the same underlying pathology. When Elena was younger, Meghan laughed about the fact that her daughter was a goody-two-shoes. She was amused by Elena's judgmental attitude toward girl drama. But when this intolerant perspective erupted all over the girls in her class, things changed. It wasn't endearing anymore.

The Tannins surgically removed themselves from that cancerous old life, with seemingly clean margins. She didn't think Elena talked to any of her former friends anymore. Meghan moved "Elena: School: St. Veronica's Debacle" into "Elena: Resolved" and promised to avoid reliving the incident again.

Down the hall, the crack of light under Elena's door disappeared. Meghan firmly closed the computer, the world set somewhat right by the "all done!" message left behind in her now gleamingly empty inbox, the day's problems tucked away in folders.

CHAPTER 9
ELENA

Elena was exhausted. She had so many school and extracurricular obligations, plus her headaches were getting worse. By the end of every day, she was drained by all this, plus the struggle to stay in control and not blurt the wrong thing. Sometimes, the only way she could stop herself was to bite her tongue. Whoever said that these were the best years of your life was clearly not paying attention.

As she walked to English, Elena practiced clamping down as a reminder to avoid blurting. She liked to be especially collected in English. Her mood was lifted by the sight of Stephen across the room.

The Herd asked her daily whether she liked Stephen, but she dodged the question. Is that tingly feeling that his grin gives me the beginning of 'like'? she wondered. St. Veronica's did nothing to prepare her for the day-to-day reality of mysterious boys. She decided that aloof control was better than unnerving flirtation. Nevertheless, she reflexively returned his grin when she walked past his desk.

Elena had a reputation in English, separate from the one she cultivated with Mrs. Stanton. Her work obviously endeared her to the teacher, but, to her classmates, she was a source of entertainment. Class was at the at end of the day, and her defenses were worn thin, so she blurted despite her best efforts.

She especially liked to argue with Stephen. Ever since their banter about *Middlemarch*, he seemed to do his homework with her in mind. During discussions, he made provocative statements, set a crooked smile, and looked at Elena. Inevitably, she took the bait. Then, the rest of the class fell silent and sat back appreciatively, their heads swiveling back and forth as the two did battle.

Everyone was amused, that is, except for Kat. Elena concluded that Kat was smart; a couple times, she saw Kat's papers returned with A's. She was prepared with answers if called on, but she never laughed or spoke up voluntarily. Elena supposed she was too cool to associate with The Herd, even in a class.

That day, the class discussed *Sense and Sensibility.* "What do you think about the ending?" Mrs. Stanton asked. "Did Sense prevail over Sensibility?"

"I think that Marianne completely *settled* when she married the Colonel," Addison annouced. "Sure, he saved her when she was sick, but give me a break. He's old enough to be her father!"

"All right," Mrs. Stanton said, "has emotional, so-called sensible Marianne settled by becoming more like her logical sister, Elinor? What did the author want us to think?"

The essay on Elena's desk answered that very question. Elena argued that Jane Austen viewed reason as superior to sentiment; therefore, Marianne leaving behind childish romance and marrying the Colonel was a good thing.

As she raised her hand to counter Addison's point, Stephen jumped in. "I'm pretty sure that Jane Austen saw the Colonel as a good husband for Marianne," he said. "Money? Yes. Decent guy? Yes. A little older? Sure, but I don't think she saw that as a big deal. And maybe he wasn't quite so handsome, but we can't all be dreamy," Stephen finished.

Addison shrugged in acknowledgement.

"And I agree," he continued. "Logic is best. That's why we have the scientific method, because humans' instincts are bad," he finished.

"Stephen, you gave us a lot to think about," Mrs. Stanton said. "Would anyone care to respond? Does the book present the position that emotion and intuition are entirely bad?"

Since Stephen presented the argument that *she* planned to make, Elena had to quickly pivot to the opposite viewpoint. "I think that Stephen's reading of the novel is a stereotypically masculine response," she said, warming up. "That there's only one right way to know something. But I don't think Austen presented an all-or-nothing position. And—" she added, before Stephen could interject, "we don't have any idea how good-looking the Colonel was."

"The title of the thing says it all: Sense and Sensibility," Stephen countered. "Two choices, two main characters. The only one who changes is Marianne, and she becomes more like Elinor, which was a good thing since her other boyfriend was a jerk! Why women always seem to want to go for the bad boy, I'll never know."

What to say? Elena thought desperately and, as if by magic, the right words simply came to her. "Why can't the two coexist? After all, Austen herself says that in addition to Elinor being logical, she is affectionate and has strong feelings; and even though Marianne is sentimental, she's also 'sensible and clever,' and has abilities that are 'in many respects quite equal to Elinor's.'" Elena wasn't sure where the words came from, but they were perfect. It was like an inspired blurt.

"Geez, Elena! Where do you come up with this stuff??" exclaimed Addison. "You're on fire."

Elena's cheeks burned in embarrassed pleasure. She glanced at Mrs. Stanton, but the teacher was laughing.

The bell rang and everyone jumped to their feet, turning in essays as they rushed for the door, eager for the weekend to begin. Elena worried about Stephen as students swirled around her. Did she come on too strong and embarrass him?

Stephen's head was down, rummaging in his backpack. He stood up, flashed Elena a grin, and tossed something small in her direction. Reflexively, she reached up and, by some divine miracle, caught it. The cellophane crinkled. It was an Atomic Fireball candy.

"See you tonight at the game?" Stephen asked over his shoulder as he trailed his friends out of the room.

Elena nodded as she popped the candy into her mouth and felt warm and tingly all over.

• • •

Elena's warm feelings buoyed her all the way home. She played chalk with Jacob and Ava in the driveway. She helped her dad start dinner, tuna noodle casserole. And she even managed to remain calm when her mom arrived home from work, full of disruptive energy and questions.

"Hi, gang," she said. "Oof, what a long day." She slipped out of her work shoes, deposited her bag, dropped the mail onto the counter, and swept her dark hair into a ponytail. Elena's dad walked over, gave her a kiss and a glass of wine, and moved out of her way.

"I really need to do something to cancel all these catalogs," she continued, sipping her wine and sorting through the mail. "I don't know how we keep getting so many, it's like they breed or something— Oh!" She paused and picked up a letter, her eyes gleaming, "I think this is about that summer engineering institute you're applying for!" she exclaimed, passing the letter to Elena.

Elena wiped her hands on her jeans and picked up the thick envelope. Inside was a brochure, showing a group of students laughing on a perfect collegiate quad. Elena flipped through it, avoiding eye contact.

"You don't seem very excited, didn't even say something 'til I mentioned it," her mom said, leaning over her shoulder to read. "This is a big deal to be nominated. I'm proud of you!" She gave her a hug. "When is it?"

"Pretty much all summer. Mid-June to mid-August," Elena replied.

"That will still give you a few weeks free to hang out with your friends."

"What about the Cottage?" Elena asked. Before the words left her mouth, she knew that she opened up a can of worms. The invisible worms slithered across the floor and changed everyone's moods.

"We're the same time as always," her dad said pointedly. "First two weeks of August."

Mom sighed. "Well, it was bound to happen eventually. There was no way that we could maintain the tradition forever. We can swing by and pick you up on the way home, I suppose, assuming the four of us still go."

I can't believe she's suggesting I just skip the Cottage, like it means nothing! Elena thought. It was as close to sacred as things got in her family's CEO (Christmas and Easter only) version of Catholicism. Elena sensed that her dad wasn't keen on the idea either. But, unlike Elena, he knew how to time arguments with her mom.

"I can't believe you think it's no big deal to skip the Cottage!" Elena exclaimed. "It's kind of what I look forward to all year. And this is more or less my last summer at home, since next year's my senior year, and who knows what'll happen after that, and—"

"Whoa there, Pistol," Dad said, standing between them. "This isn't something we need to decide right now, and no one's giving up our piece of Zedernwald. When's the application due, December? We have time to figure stuff out. Okay, girls?"

Elena watched her mom take a deep breath as if preparing to say something, make eye contact with her dad, and sigh in resignation.

"You're right," she said. She took a gulp of wine, and walked over to the twins and their easier, three-year old problems. Elena leaned her head against her father's chest, he rubbed her back a few times. Growing up sucked.

"This culinary masterpiece isn't going to get itself on the table," he said. Elena reluctantly stood up and moved toward the plates and the comforting promise of tuna noodle casserole with chips on top.

•   •   •

Annoyingly, Elena wasn't able to fully appreciate sitting behind Stephen at the game or next to him at pizza. Instead, she spent most of the time being mad at her mom. After she went to bed, she realized that she left her laptop downstairs and quietly slipped past the twins' room to retrieve it. She was halfway down the carpeted steps when she froze, hearing her mom say her name.

"I'm worried about Elena," she said. "I got an email from her chemistry teacher today about some sort of an incident in class. Elena lashed out at her friend, Kayla, out of nowhere. The teacher wasn't going to say anything, but there's a policy on threatening speech."

"How big of an argument was it?" Elena's father asked.

"The room was apparently dead quiet, and all of a sudden, Elena started accusing Kayla of instigating an argument. But the teacher didn't hear Kayla say anything at all. Have you noticed anything strange?" she asked. "She seems normal to me. Except, of course, for her not even telling us about the Engineering nomination until I brought it up!"

"She's been a little more high strung, but I chalked that up to switching schools. Other than that, same good grades, same with the twins, making some new friends. I'd say don't worry about it. Except…" A note of concern crept into his voice.

"Yup. Except."

"Nell," her parents said in unrehearsed unison.

From her perch on the stairs, Elena realized she was holding her breath. When she heard her dead aunt's name, her lips parted and she exhaled slowly and decided she didn't want to hear any more. She tiptoed back to bed and slipped between the covers. She stared out the window at the starry sky, visible between naked tree branches, reviewing what she knew of Aunt Nell.

This wasn't the first time that they were mentioned in the same breath. Nell died when Elena was a baby. She wasn't sure how she died, but Elena knew that there was tragedy wrapped up in it. Since then, Nell existed as a series of snapshots in albums. Elena learned not to ask questions about her, for fear of the worried crease appearing between her mom's eyebrows, or the droop in her dad's bony shoulders. Elena, the girl who knew everything, knew next to nothing about her aunt.

She assembled what little she knew from the bits of Nell's life left scattered around. The framed graduation photo of her, beautiful in a 1980's way. Her name, "Nell Tannin," written in pencil in the inside covers of old piano books. The random newspaper clipping describing Nell's graduation at the head of her own high school class.

Elena concluded that Aunt Nellie's shooting star burned out quickly and, somehow, sadly. More worrisome were the overheard comments comparing her with her aunt. Elena hated those comparisons and felt creepy every time she saw Nell's cursive script in those piano books. *So what if we're both good at school and the piano?* Elena tried to reassure herself.

It was strange that Elena accepted this incomplete reality since she was so blurtingly inquisitive about everything else. Whenever she was compared to Nell, she longed to ask questions. But she let emotion win out over logic and chose the peaceful status quo over unsettling information gathering.

Elena sometimes rehearsed how she would initiate such a conversation, were she ever feeling daring. "Do I need to ask you to explain things, or will you ever get around to it by yourselves? What exactly happened to Aunt Nell?"

"She died of a disease," they'd repeat.

Elena would boldly ask, "Did she kill herself?" But Elena never felt brave enough. Instead, the question hovered around the edges as she fell asleep, seeding all sorts of weird dreams as the October wind unquietly slipped around the house.

When it's OK to blurt
- *With parents if they aren't annoying.*
- *With friends if v. tired*
- *Never in school*
- *With Stephen, maybe, someday????*

Chapter 10
Kat

Kat: is there a list of us
Val: dont think so
Kat: dumb
Val: not sposed to write things down

Kat sat in the stands, admiring Ty's uniform pants. She wore his practice jersey over leggings, with a scarf and her hair in a ponytail. She'd take her hair down before meeting him after the game. They were up by 13 at the beginning of the fourth quarter.

She cheered when everyone else cheered, she clapped when everyone else clapped, and she looked at her phone when everyone else looked at their phones. But she wasn't thinking about the game, where they'd go after, or even Ty. Annoyingly, she couldn't stop thinking about that new girl, Elena Tannin. She was aware of her in a way that she wasn't of other students. It felt like this Elena saw through her icy shield of Beautiful invulnerability, a shield which easily kept out everyone else.

She kept going back to the obvious conclusion that Elena must have Talent. But Val was right; if Elena was one of them, she would have been to camp at least once, not showing up randomly in Belvedere. Maybe if she found out Elena's mom's unmarried name, she could see if the mom was ever at the camp and figure it out that way . . .

Because that wouldn't be awkward. "Elena, what's your mother's maiden name?" she'd ask. And then she'd be suspended for attempting to commit identity theft. No, Kat needed to fly low under the radar for two more years at Belvedere; she needed to survive.

But, annoyingly, Elena kept disrupting Kat's situation. Like the other day in English class, when Elena was arguing, a.k.a., flirting, with Stephen Callaghan. Kat could tell that Elena didn't know what to say next. Kat scanned her own essay, which contained the perfect comeback to the boy's taunting assertion. As Kat silently read her written words, Elena simultaneously said them out loud. The most likely explanation was that they both copied the idea from somewhere else, maybe read it online or something. The problem with that explanation, though, was that Kat wrote that paper with no help, no online suggestions, nothing!

It was like Elena was connected to her, *Communing* with her. It was like she was summertime Kat, and Elena was another camper. But summertime Kat had no place at Belvedere High School. She would ruin everything.

CHAPTER 11
ELENA

Elena drove past harvested fields edged by frost-tipped weeds gone brown and listened to *Morning Edition*. She pulled into her usual parking place, flipped to her decoy station, turned the car off, and made the now-routine walk into school. She was so lost in thought that she almost bumped into Mrs. Stanton, her English teacher.

"Hi!" said Elena.

"Good morning, Elena," replied Mrs. Stanton. Her eyes were serious behind her round glasses. "Can you come with me for a sec?"

"Sure," replied Elena. Something was wrong. She followed Mrs. Stanton into her room and was surprised to see Kat in the front row, carefully avoiding eye contact.

"Girls, I was very intrigued by the argument that Elena shared in class Friday. It was well-reasoned and quite articulate…"

For a second, Elena thought she might have misinterpreted Mrs. Stanton's mood.

"…and it was identical to something I read over the weekend in Katherine's paper." She passed Elena Kat's essay.

The relevant passage was underlined lightly in pencil. "After all, Austen says that in addition to Elinor's 'strength of understanding and coolness of judgment,' she has an affectionate disposition and strong feelings; and Marianne, though described as emotional and eager, is 'sensible and clever,' and has, according to Austen, abilities that are 'in many respects quite equal to Elinor's.'"

Elena was stunned silent-a rare occurence. She never saw Kat's paper before, but those were the same words that she used to counter Stephen. She scrambled, mortified, for an explanation for how Kat's words burbled out of her own mouth.

Meanwhile, Kat sat with apparent calm, giving Mrs. Stanton the briefest nod of understanding. She must have realized what happened last week, but didn't say anything.

"Please be careful," cautioned Mrs. Stanton. "I'm thrilled that you are becoming study partners. But try to avoid over-sharing each other's work." The teacher smiled at Elena's panicked face. "I just want to provide a word to the wise, which should be sufficient." She patted Elena's arm and stood to leave. "Now, stop worrying and move on with your days."

Elena slowly got up, hoping that Mrs. Stanton wouldn't contact her parents. Kat walked out of the room ahead of her, somehow already in control of the situation. Oh, God, why did it have to be Kat? What new kind of BP negativity would this screw-up bring?

But shockingly, there were no fireworks, no additional glares. When Elena glanced up during choir, the Waif studied her phone and Kat shot no daggers. Instead, she flicked Elena a look of something close to curiosity. How could Kat be livid about a slight to the Waif, but nonchalant when Elena crossed her personally?

Her attitude was the same in English. Kat's flannel-covered back and glossy hair greeted Elena with complacency. She really had amazing hair. It seemed almost friendly. Weird.

Unmentionable Weirdness
- *Kayla in chem, no one heard. Liar vs. voice- thrower?*
- *Kat in English. Shared research vs. Kat a ventriloquist and I'm her dummy?*

CHAPTER 12
MEGHAN

It was one of those nights where Meghan looked at Anders and realized that you can never totally know a person. Sure, they'd been together longer than they were apart, they long ago stopped shutting the bathroom door, and she knew him better than anyone else. But, in some ways, she didn't know him at all, especially those bits of him that had to do with his family.

"Anders," she said, rolling to face him, "what was Nell like before she got sick?"

Anders took off his glasses and laid his book aside. "Well, she was the golden child. She was funny and smart and good at everything."

"But you must have seen signs before her first hospitalization, right?"

"I was in college when she started getting bad," he said, eyebrows crinkling. "But Mom and Dad knew something was wrong. They just couldn't agree on what to do about it, or even what it was."

"What exactly was she doing? At first, I mean."

"I think it was the usual stuff. Losing interest in her activities, pulling away from friends, behaving erratically. She always kept her grades up, though."

Meghan sighed. "I keep trying to reassure myself that Elena isn't going down the same path. You're sure that you don't know of any other cases of schizophrenia in your family?"

"Nope. Just a lot of regular weirdos," Anders replied, returning to his book.

"I guess all we can do is keep an eye on her."

Anders rubbed Meghan's back after she rolled away from him. She turned things over in her mind, trying and failing to fall asleep.

Anders' family was so different from hers. Meghan grew up in a suburb of Minneapolis, where Sunday dinners were served on the good china and weeknight meals always included a vegetable. She saw her grandparents, aunts, uncles and cousins on the holidays. They politely exchanged gifts and pleasantries, then returned to their normal lives. Extended family was a decorative addition to real life, not a central feature of it.

In contrast, Anders' family was a confusing jumble of relatives enmeshed in each other's daily business. Keeping track of the relationships was tricky; his abrupt estrangement made things neater, but no less confusing. The only tie that they maintained with his mom's family was the massive property up north, Zedernwald.

Anders' great-great grandfather was a moderately successful Chicago businessman and had the foresight to buy a nearly half-mile stretch of land along Lake Michigan, before it became a popular vacation spot. Over time, the man built a big house, "The Lodge," and a separate tiny house, "The Cottage," on the property. His family stayed there during the summer, back when being a moderately successful businessman meant having enough money to suspend one's life for three months and "summer" elsewhere.

While the land around it became a tourist destination, Zedernwald remained an unspoiled bit of heaven. As the generations multiplied and the family grew, so did the Lodge. Additions sprung up and it eventually gained plumbing and electricity.

In the 1920's, the family's women convinced their spouses to let them turn the Lodge into a girls' summer camp; something about a tax write-off and the Nineteenth Amendment. At first, it was mostly the extended family's girls that attended. Over time, girls from all over the Midwest came to stay at Zedernwald for the summer, from after Memorial Day to just before Labor Day. During Labor Day weekend, the extended family convened at The Lodge for a massive reunion. The relatives divided up profits (if any) from the camp and developed a system of shared time at The Cottage.

Meghan learned these details from Anders' mom and her sisters before the great rift occurred. Interestingly, the property passed through a maternal line. The original man left it to his two daughters, and somehow, the practice continued, defying convention. Because of this, it didn't bear a primogeniture family name, as the family name kept changing as these daughters married. Rather, it was called Zedernwald, or Birch Forest, in the family's native German.

Anders recalled Labor Days spent there with random cousins and elderly relatives, all known by appearance, if not by name. The old people slept in The Lodge, filling every inch of the Habitrail-style additions. The younger people stayed in pop-up campers and tents. According to Anders, it was magical. To Meghan, it sounded weird. Her family took one neat, tidy vacation per summer, involving a national park or a museum.

When he was in middle school, Anders' mom, Helen, took over the camp, along with her two sisters, Mary and Sylvie. Around the same time, Nellie became a camper. He and his dad spent "bachelor summers" alone, and his mom and Nellie summered at Camp Zedernwald. It was the perfect arrangement for his family. His dad was happiest while working, and Anders was a three-season athlete; neither wanted to be far from home for any length of time.

The Zedernwald magic ended when Nellie died. She got sick in her twenties and died a few years later. Mary and Sylvie took a lot of interest in how Nellie was being cared for leading up to her death. His dad wanted to take every suggestion offered by the doctors, from involuntary hospitalizations to drugs. His mother did not. She and her sisters wanted to care for Nellie at Zedernwald. Something about nature being good for the soul or some such nonsense.

Meghan and Anders were only married for a short time when Nellie died. The only version of her that Meghan knew was either stably catatonic on meds or unbalanced off them. When she died, Anders' mom disintegrated and died several months after. Her sisters, Mary and

Sylvie, blamed Anders' dad for both Nellie's and Helen's deaths. They did so publicly at Helen's funeral luncheon. It was ugly stuff. Of course, Anders defended his dad, who promptly drank himself to death within two years. Neither Mary nor Sylvie attended his funeral, and the schism was complete.

After all this, it amazed Meghan that Anders wanted anything to do with Zedernwald. He took over Nellie's shares, which worked out to two weeks at the Cottage and an occasional check from the camp at the end of the year. In the early days, when money was tight, this counted for a lot.

When the Tannins took their two-week stay at the Cottage every summer, Meghan knew that the old women, Mary and Sylvie, were at the Lodge with a camp full of girls. There was smoke from the fireplace, and their cars frequented the main driveway. If the wind was right, she heard girlish laughter. But everyone studiously ignored each other, even if they brushed shoulders in the tiny grocery store in the nearby town. It was all so melodramatic and senseless, so un-Minnesotan.

Meghan hoped that if Elena was accepted to the engineering institute and they missed their two weeks this summer, they could just sell their share and be done with it. But Anders' and Elena's responses to her suggestion about missing Zedernwald made it abundantly clear that she was alone in this view. Oh, well. At least Anders' family drama came with a lake view.

CHAPTER 13
ELENA

Elena continued to ignore the list of weirdness as best she could and, by Halloween, all was normal-ish. She and Kayla were tied at the top of the junior class, to Kayla's delight and Elena's annoyance disguised as amusement. Kayla quickly submitted her application for the engineering institute, and she harassed Elena to finish hers. Instead, Elena started working ahead in classes, her headaches worsened, and she took ibuprofen twice a day.

Once football season ended, The Herd got together on Fridays to play board games, usually at Addison's or Morgan's, but once or twice at Elena's. Eventually, after she finally started to believe she could trust them, she dared to disclose her "possible" crush on Stephen. No one laughed, except for Addison because she couldn't help but make a joke about everything. They confirmed that Stephen hadn't had a girlfriend since a brief interlude with a soccer player freshman year.

It felt good to finally be able to trust friends again. It made Elena feel bold. So, on the phone one night, in a burst of nascent best-friendship, Elena told Kayla about the stuff that happened at her old school.

"Did I ever tell you about my friends at St. Veronica's?" Elena asked.

"Nope. I assumed maybe you were testing us out before introducing us to them."

"Nope," Elena said flatly. "I don't have any."

"Didn't you go to school there for, like, eight years?" Kayla asked. "You're too friendly to not have friends."

"Oh, I *had* friends," Elena said. "But not after fall of sophomore year." She told the story of how she tried to intervene to protect her friends from online predators, and how they just froze her out after that. About the lunches with the secretary in the office. About always being stuck with some rando for group assignments. Or, worse, not having any partner at all.

Kayla listened with the saddest look on her face.

"So," Elena finished, "my parents decided to move to Belvedere two years earlier than they planned. Luckily, the house was already started and we were able to move last summer. I don't talk to anyone from my old school at all."

"It must have been pretty bad for you to have to move. Good thing your parents have money. Imagine if you would have been stuck there," Kayla said.

"Yeah, it was bad," Elena said, uncomfortable over the money comment.

"People can freak out over the tiniest things, so I'm not surprised that they ghosted you over ratting them out. Even though," Kayla quickly added, "it was the responsible thing to do."

Elena nodded. "I don't like to talk about it much, but I wanted you to know."

"Thanks for trusting me," Kayla said.

Kayla didn't offer any reciprocal secrets that day, or any day. She remained frustratingly closed off about anything personal. Sometimes, Elena wondered if she only imagined that they were friends. Realistically, Elena assured herself, she probably overwhelmed the quieter girl into forced silence. Whenever she hung up with Kayla, Elena berated herself for not shutting up and giving Kayla a chance to talk.

•   •   •

Elena's 17th birthday was October 30, a Wednesday. Her mom woke her before leaving for work, to sing happy birthday and give her pancakes. In their footie pajamas and bed heads, the twins sang, "Happy Birfday to Lay-lay."

At school, the Herd decorated her locker. Kayla and Addison looked up expectantly as she walked into calculus. "Thanks, guys," Elena said, giving them each a hug. She received wishes throughout the day and anticipated what Stephen might say during last hour. He offered a disappointingly basic "Happy birthday," accompanied by a crooked grin that made up for it. But the real treat was when she found an Atomic Fireball candy tucked under the door handle of her Civic that afternoon, and every afternoon after that.

Her family always carved jack o' lanterns on Elena's birthday. Since overhearing her parents comparing her to Nell, she knew they watched her like a hawk for signs of anything being off. So, she stayed home and followed the tradition to the letter, even though the Herd was getting together that night to make costumes. Since she would miss out on making a group costume anyway, she offered to take the twins Trick or Treating the next day. She didn't mind. It wasn't like the Herd was going anywhere in their costumes, just taking selfies and handing out candy.

As they carved pumpkins on the kitchen floor covered in yesterday's newspaper, Elena talked the three-year olds through the Halloween plans. "I'll take you to McDonald's for dinner."

"Can we have fries?" Ava asked, looking up with a handful of pumpkin guts squishing between her chubby fingers.

"Yes, we'll have fries," Elena continued, scraping out her pumpkin. She liked it perfectly clean before carving. "And then we'll Trick or Treat."

"We will have our costumes on at McDonald's?" asked Jacob, his nose wrinkled in inquiry. He used a marker to draw a face onto his gut-smeared pumpkin, which Dad would eventually carve for him. Jacob avoided cleaning the inside of his pumpkin. He didn't like slimy things.

"Yup," said Elena. "You'll have on Transformers and Ava will have on her cowboy princess costume—"

"Cowboy princess *detective!*" corrected Ava, who added accessories daily.

Her mom laughed from the sink, where she washed pumpkin seeds free of slime. She insisted on making roasted pumpkin seeds every year, even though no one really liked them.

The next day, Elena came home from school to find Ava and Jacob already costumed and full of energy: store-bought red Transformer for Jacob and a fancy dress, cowboy hat, cowboy boots, magnifying glass and notebook for Ava. Leave 'em guessing, kid, thought Elena. She put on her non-costume costume, Smarties candy taped to her pants.

"Smartie pants, get it?" she told the confused preschoolers. After Mom took pictures, they climbed into Elena's car and made the short drive into "downtown" Belvedere, since Trick or Treating along their county road was a bad idea for any number of reasons.

After Jacob and Ava ate Happy Meals, they began a loop of some Belvedere neighborhoods. She didn't think the twins would last more than an hour, despite the optimistically oversized candy bags they carried. Elena planned to stop at Addison's house so that she could show her cute siblings to the Herd. She knew that Stephen lived somewhere near Addison, too.

Elena stood back from the porches, allowing the kids to climb up the steps, shriek their "Trick or Treats!" and dutifully chime, "Thank you!" She saw some familiar faces from school. The older librarian sat in a matched easy chair next to her husband, watching *Wheel of Fortune*. A girl from Spanish answered the door and waved to Elena. She carefully avoided the Waif's house, which was easy to identify, with all the cars parked out front and the sea of dimly lit teenage heads swirling in the tiny basement window.

"Why are we skipping this one?" Jacob asked, as Elena ushered them past.

"They're giving out apples," Elena lied.

At Addison's, her friends gushed over the kids. No one else had siblings that young, so they were a novelty. The Herd looked good in their crayon costumes: leggings, tutus, and crayon T-shirts in different colors.

Before they left, Morgan whispered, "Um, you'll want to stop there." She pointed to a brown house down the block and grinned.

Elena blushed and mumbled, "Thanks."

When they got to that house, she saw Stephen through a living room window. She felt giddy and barely heard the twins shriek, "Trick or Treat!"

Stephen came to the door and smiled at her over the candy bowl. "Hey, Elena. Why aren't you wearing a costume?"

"I am," she said, motioning to the candies on her pants. "Smartie pants?"

"Nice. Aren't you going to ask about mine?"

"Okay, where's your costume?"

He opened his hoodie to reveal a T-shirt with a message drawn in Sharpie. It was in the style of a computer code and said, "Error: Halloween costume still loading."

"I guess neither of us are into dressing up," Elena said. "This is my little brother and sister. Jacob? Ava?" The kids reluctantly looked up from their candy bags. "Say hi to Stephen."

"Hi, Stephen," they said in twin unison.

"Hi, guys," he said, crouching down expertly in front of them. "I like your costumes. Red Transformer and princess ...cowboy...detective?" he guessed, pointing out Ava's costume components.

"You were the first one to guess right," Elena said.

It was getting late, and the kids began to yawn dramatically. "Well, I guess we better get going," said Elena.

"Here," said Stephen, reaching for the candy bowl. "I think you need some extra, don't you?"

The twins stared as Stephen dropped handfuls of candy into their bags. Elena knew her mom would make most of it disappear, but she liked that Stephen wanted to keep them on the porch longer.

"I have something for you, too," he said to Elena.

She was caught off guard and just stood there.

"What do you say?" Stephen prompted.

"Please?" Elena guessed

"No, Lay-lay!" hollered Ava in horror. "You say 'Trick or Treat!'"

"Okay, Trick or Treat?" she said.

"That's better." Stephen smiled. He reached into his hoodie pocket and pressed a few Atomic Fireballs into her outstretched palm. His hands were warm and dry.

When Elena buckled the kids into their car seats, they were a mix of candy-fueled hyperactivity and exhaustion. She drove home in a daydream, built upon the warmth of Stephen's hand against hers.

Does Stephen like me?

　　Pros:

- *Facial expressions*
- *Messages me daily*
- *Doesn't have a girlfriend*
- *Atomic Fireballs*

　　Cons:

- *How could he like me, totally immature, never say the right thing, slowly going unmentionably insane.*

CHAPTER 14
KAT

Kat sat in Bailey's basement bathroom, crying. Outside, her friends' voices competed with booming music. She glanced up and made eye contact with her bleary face in the mirror. She looked ridiculous in her sexy Snow White costume. Was it just a few hours ago that she examined herself with approval?

Ty just destroyed her mood with a single comment. He picked her up and deemed her ensemble "hot," so that the night started okay. The rest of the Beautiful girls were dressed as different sexy Disney princesses too. They took selfies and drank hard seltzers; it was a typical party. Kat discovered a full-sized Almond Joy, her favorite, in the candy bowl. She shouted something about her luck! Ty loudly joked that she should leave it there, cuz Bailey definitely needed it more than her. He laughed, a couple of the guys around him laughed, and then he slapped the side of her butt, right in the middle of her grossest fat.

Her defense mechanism, cold bitchiness, crumbled under the weight of his criticism. Once the barrier melted, unspoken feelings and judgments poured in and began to overwhelm her. She hated the way she looked. She knew everyone else did, too.

Kat studied her face in the mirror and nearly gagged. Her swollen eyes made her cheeks look even rounder. And her hair, usually her best feature, was a ratty mess.

Eventually, Bailey came to the door. "Is everything all right?" she asked tipsily.

Kat cracked the door.

"Kat, your makeup is all streaky!" Bailey said, squeezing in and giving her a hug.

Kat glanced over her friend's bony shoulder and saw Bailey's bare back reflected in the mirror, clearly visible in her sexy Ariel costume. Her ribs were enviably visible, along with two clear dimples on either side of her lower back. Kat wiped her face carefully. When she finished, Bailey grabbed her hand and pulled her out of the bathroom.

Kat's mind filled with all sorts of details of Bailey's life, and it made the out-of-control feeling even worse. She jerked her hand away, reassuring Bailey that she'd catch up with her later. Kat quickly walked to the basement bedroom. She dug her coat from the pile and briefly considered asking Ty to drive her home. Instead, she decided to just walk. She'd text Ty, Bailey and the rest of them after she'd gone.

It only took half a block for her legs, in thin white thigh high tights, to become uncomfortably cold. Her feet ached in the Mary Jane platform heels. Whose stupid idea was it to dress like this, anyway? She wanted to go as Winnie the Pooh characters in fuzzy onesies. Of course, she kept that lame idea to herself.

Her breath burst forth in gasps, visible in the chilly October air. A few stray fall leaves rattled in the gutter. Her heels clomped, her heart raced. Kat was taking forever to reset; she wouldn't be able to do it on her own. As usual, she called Val for help, and, as usual, Val answered on the second ring.

"Hey," she said. "Where are you?"

"I'm walking home," Kat replied.

"What about the party? Your costume was so cute."

"I had to leave. I Spiraled at the party."

"Oh, no," Val said. "How are you feeling now?"

"Not great. I can't reset."

"Text your mom. If she's not around, I'll talk you down when you get home. In the meantime, I'm staying on the phone, since it's eleven o'clock and your town doesn't seem to believe in streetlights."

Kat could always rely on Val and her mom to help her. Val stayed on the phone while Kat shivered along the sidewalk, until her mom pulled up mere minutes after Kat sent the text. At home, her mom traced gentle circles on Kat's back to drive the echoes out and allow her to reset. If she were a normal mom, there would have been all sorts of questions about what happened. But she was the mom of a poorly-controlled daughter, and the answer "Spiral" sufficed.

Kat could also rely on Val and her mom to lecture her after the Spiral passed. She heard the lecture before: she needed to learn better Tempering methods. She never progressed to more advanced Tempering since she couldn't master the necessary first step: comfort with one's inner voice. There was no one that she reviled more than herself.

And, right about now, maybe Ty, and his dumbass need to constantly remind her that she was lucky that he was a guy who "didn't mind curvy girls."

CHAPTER 15
ELENA

The bright red sumacs writhed in a fierce November wind, a last gasp of fall color in Elena's headlights on the drive to school. The sky was dark, thanks to an approaching storm. The wind was especially strong, and soon, the trees would be naked. Where did all the dead leaves go? Did they just keep blowing and blowing forever? There must be a huge pile somewhere, at the end of the wind.

She found the Herd in the commons, merging with a larger group of students that Elena thought of as school friends: people she talked to during the day and hung out with sometimes, but not Herd-level. They discussed the newest season of *Schitt's Creek*. She laughed over something Moira said, when an especially loud burst of thunder cracked overhead.

The school's background hum went silent and the lights flickered out. The wind must have taken out a power line. A few girls shrieked, everyone else grew louder to make up for the unsettling lack of mechanical noise.

"I hope they don't cancel school," said Kayla. "Sometimes it takes hours for them to get the power back on."

"Don't jinx it for the rest of us, Kayla!" Addison exclaimed. "Hey, what's wrong with Elena?"

Elena heard Kayla and Addison as though from a distance, but she couldn't respond. She couldn't move her hands, or her mouth, or her eyelids. She couldn't see anyone.

Later, Elena imagined how she must have looked to everyone gathered around that windy November morning, in the sudden darkness. One second, she was talking to Addison and Kayla. The next, she was lying on the floor with random people hovering over her. Her senses started to go offline, her body went numb, her vision faded to black.

But her hearing remained intact, like hundreds of speakers all set on a low buzz. She drowned in a pit of auditory chaos from which she couldn't escape, an echo chamber of random voices, ricocheting through the blackness. She was oblivious to any sensations from the real world of Belvedere High. It was like someone pureed up every emotion in the school and poured the slurry into her overcrowded brain instead.

And then, the voices reaching an unbearable crescendo, she sort of traveled through the mosh pit of sound and feeling. It was like at the beginning of a movie about New York, when the camera starts with a wide view of the city from above and slowly zooms in to focus on one window. Elena zoomed into a window that peered straight into Kayla. It was like an auditory memory box.

She listened to Kayla's refrains. She recognized a few voices, such as Kayla's mom saying, "Just try to be pleasant!" and her dad saying, "That's my little princess!" Kayla's own voice repeated catch phrases and a smorgasbord of Kayla-ish data, and something about "The Issue." Plus, the slightly off version of Kayla's angry voice from chemistry that day. Elena didn't like it, and she needed to get out of the drowning, pounding surf of Kayla.

One time, when Elena was nine or ten, she passed out. She had a high fever, got up from bed to use the bathroom, and fainted. It was the strangest feeling. It didn't happen all at once, but rather bit by bit. First, her arms and legs lost sensation, like they were falling asleep, then her vision started to go. Starting from the edges, a field of blackness crept in. Then noises became muffled, and then it was done. She didn't know how much time passed before her senses started coming online. Eventually, she felt the coolness of the tile floor against her sweaty cheek, and the caulk line along the base of the toilet came into focus, and she was back.

What happened that morning in the commons sort of felt like that. Sort of.

When she passed out as a child, the feeling of the cool bathroom tile dragged Elena back to reality. This time, the first real thing she noticed was the smell of yesterday's Salisbury steak. She concentrated on that real, actual thing over the auditory nonsense. Her sense of time and place slowly returned, through the miracle of Salisbury steak.

Morgan, surprisingly, had taken charge. "Stephen, prop her legs up on something," she instructed. Elena felt something soft under her calves. When she opened her eyes, she saw the Herd: Morgan fanning her with a notebook, Kayla holding her hand and looking concerned, and Addison leading the principal over.

The power must have come back on. A secretary came over the P.A. and told everyone to report to class. At the principal's insistence, Elena remained lying on the floor, much to her growing embarrassment. Her legs stretched across Stephen's lap and several coats. At least she had a medical excuse for blushing.

"Are you okay if I go?" Stephen asked.

"Yes," she croaked, her mouth not yet under control. She cleared her throat. "Yes."

He smiled, squeezed her ankle, and gently slid himself out from underneath her. "I heard them say that they called your parents and an ambulance."

Groan.

"Let me know how you're doing later," he said.

"I will. I'm okay now, just go!" she said, anxious for him to avoid whichever parent showed up.

"Yes," she heard Morgan say. "I've got everything under control." Morgan was in her years-of-scouts element, and the nervous principal didn't seem to mind. A secretary appeared with a cup of juice. Now fully returned to herself, Elena sighed, accepting the ministrations of her friend and the school staff.

She pulled herself upright and sipped. There were a few students still in the commons, including Kat, who sat on a chair across the room, her head in her hands. Elena watched her slowly get up. Her face was shockingly pale against her dark hair. One of her friends gave her a water bottle and she appeared to say, "Thank you."

I guess I'm not the only person who doesn't feel well this morning, she thought.

Soon, her dad arrived. She imagined Mom pacing worriedly as she awaited them at the hospital, flipping through medical worst-case scenarios. What would she be most worried about? Seizure? Brain tumor? Turning into Auntie Nell??

The commons was empty now. It was just her, Dad, the twins, the principal, two EMTs, and Morgan, who reluctantly handed off Elena's care and offered to go and sit with Jacob and Ava. Her dad must have dropped everything and rushed to the school. They would remember Morgan from Trick or Treating, Elena reassured, and would be fine.

The EMTs took her vitals and asked questions about the vice president and what year it was. Once they determined that she wasn't dying, they agreed that it was safe for Elena's dad to drive her to the hospital. Elena died a little inside as the EMTs helped her into a wheelchair. She sat awkwardly while they wheeled her out of the front doors of the school to the van, Dad, Morgan, and her siblings in tow.

Once Elena was settled, Dad buckled Ava and Jacob and drove more quickly than usual.

"Feeing better?" he asked.

Elena knew that Dad wouldn't dig too deeply, since Ava and Jacob were listening.

"I feel totally normal now. Sorry for the drama."

"No apology needed," he said, and they completed the speedy drive in silence.

Elena's reassurance was true; she felt completely back to normal, except for small bandage on her finger where the EMTs took a pinprick of blood. At the same time, everything was totally different. What the heck happened back there?

<u>*Unmentionable Weirdness*</u>

- *Kayla in chem, no one heard. Liar vs. voice- thrower?*
- *Kat in English. Shared research vs. Kat a ventriloquist and I'm her dummy?*
- *Commons incident. WTAF.*

Chapter 16
MEGHAN

Differential diagnosis for loss of consciousness. Mnemonic: CAMP-SS
  Coronary artery disease
  Arrythmias / Aortic stenosis
  Migraine / Medications
  Psychiatric
  Syncope
  Seizures / Strokes

Meghan knew the differential diagnosis list for "loss of consciousness" like the back of her hand. She ran through the list repeatedly that morning, mentally caressing the bulleted items like beads on a rosary. She spent the entire morning into the early afternoon in the emergency room with Elena, arriving before Anders. Meghan normally carefully separated her work-self from her mom-self, but as she sat with her daughter in the emergency department after the frustratingly ill-defined event, the collision between the two versions was unavoidable.

A nurse efficiently settled Elena in, gave her a gown to change into, and collected basic information. Anders and the twins went home, securing a promise for frequent updates and some stickers for the bored preschoolers.

Elena looked fine, a little pale, perhaps. The school's description of the event indicated a simple syncopal event, a.k.a., a fainting spell, which was reassuring. Meghan remained calm until she heard Elena's recounting of events to the resident doctor.

"Hi, Elena," the shockingly young resident said. "I'm Dr. Laird. What brings you in today?"

It was such a ridiculous question, and asking it was the mark of a young doctor, still doing things completely by the book. Elena's chief complaint, "loss of consciousness," was printed on her paperwork and written on the whiteboard on the wall. Meghan sighed and bit her tongue to prevent herself from interrupting what promised to be a long interview.

Elena must have found the question ridiculous, too. Meghan recognized an eye-rolling tone in her answer, "I had a 'loss of consciousness.'"

Dr. Laird glanced up. "Can you start at the beginning? What were you doing before you started to feel poorly? Start with this morning."

Elena recounted the day's events, going all the way back to what she had for breakfast. She answered questions about her periods, which the resident explained that they "asked everyone." Elena was on her period, and it was heavy as usual. She blushed and put her hand over her eyes while admitting that. Fortunately, Dr. Laird wasn't particularly attractive, or Elena's mortification would have been unmanageable.

The doctor didn't interject much, until Elena got to the part about what actually happened. "I was talking to my friend," Elena said, "and then all of a sudden, it was like I couldn't see or feel anything anymore, and I couldn't hear most of what was going on around me."

Textbook description of fainting. So far, so good.

"But then I started just hearing weird stuff too," Elena continued.

"What stuff?" the young man asked.

"Random voices saying things," Elena said. Meghan's mouth went dry and her heart pounded in her ears.

"Were you hearing people in the room, talking?" Dr. Laird asked, pausing his writing to study Elena.

"Umm, yeah, maybe. It sounded like they were next to me," Elena said, glancing at her mom.

She somehow knows her description made me worried, Meghan thought, and ironed out her forehead, desperately trying to keep from interrupting. But this line of questioning was too vital and delicate to be left to the hopelessly green Dr. Laird. "Did the voices tell you to do anything? To yourself? Or anyone else?" Meghan blurted, effectively taking over the interview as she asked questions about psychosis.

"No. I don't remember. I was confused," Elena said, glancing with keen observation between the two doctors. "I just blacked out. I don't know how long. Then I woke up and was laying on the floor, and my friends were taking care of me," she quickly finished.

The resident was focused on his stack of paperwork, visibly preparing to move on to a new line of questioning. "Any loss of bowel or bladder control? I wonder if it was a seizure," he explained, glancing at Meghan for approval.

Meghan offered a tight-lipped smile. Me and my big mouth, she chastised herself. I shut Elena's honesty down, and I threw the poor guy off his game. He won't help me figure out if she's turning into Nell.

"No. Ugh," Elena replied.

The resident asked a few more questions that, unfortunately, didn't touch further on psychiatric symptoms. Elena's exam was normal, save for a slightly elevated heart rate. The resident returned a couple of more times to give updates on her head CT (normal), and bloodwork (mild anemia, probably heavy periods). Elena was connected to an IV and lay back, engaged with her phone.

Eventually, Dr. Laird settled on a benign diagnosis: vasovagal syncope with mild anemia and dehydration. He recommended iron supplements and consideration of birth control pills to help regulate Elena's periods. Meghan couldn't fault the young doctor's management, given what he knew. But, Meghan was hiding something, and she now knew Elena was hiding something too. Meghan wasn't at all reassured by the benign conclusion to the visit.

She worried the entire time about how best to approach the bit of the family history that neither she nor Elena shared with Dr. Laird.

Elena failed to mention the family history because she didn't yet know, and Meghan didn't mention it for the same reason.

Because naked under a hospital gown, surrounded by strangers, was not the ideal manner in which to learn that Nell's schizophrenia-fueled voices eventually convinced her to kill herself before she saw 30.

·   ·   ·

That evening, after Elena and the twins were tucked into bed, Meghan updated Anders and made an unusual ultimatum. "We need to get Elena in to see someone to check for psych stuff. We can't just cross our fingers and hope that nothing's going on. And she deserves to know about your family history. It's why we're so worried, after all."

Anders took a pull of his beer and gazed at her across the table. "I know," he said softy. "Maybe we can tell her after she sees the doctor? After we know what's going on?"

"I know it never felt like the right time to tell her before, but we need to share Nell's history with her. Before she sees someone, so it's not a surprise. She needs to be armed with the facts," Meghan said.

Anders' nods grew more vigorous with Meghan's demand-studded pep talk. "We'll tell her over winter break, no backing down," he said with uncharacteristic intensity.

"And you agree that she should see a therapist?" she asked.

"Nell always saw psychiatrists," he said, making the statement a question.

"Nowadays, psychiatrists mostly deal with managing medications," she explained, hoping against hope that there wouldn't be a need. "I'll find out who's a good mental health person, and if they feel that she needs meds, then we'll go that route."

"Okay," Anders said. "I'm glad you know what's going on."

Meghan silently agreed. How non-professionals managed to navigate the medical system always astonished her. "Then we have a plan," she said, relieved.

"Okay," he said, draining his beer. "Do you really think her symptoms could be what Nellie had?"

"I'm not sure," she said. "I hoped that she'd be honest with the resident in the E.D., but Elena started to backtrack as soon as she saw our reactions to the word 'voices.' And then I went and opened my big mouth, and she clammed up entirely."

"She's too smart for her own good. Wonder where she gets it?"

"She's a hundred times smarter than I ever was. I just work hard. Jesus, I hope she's okay."

"She is, Megs. She has to be," Anders said, getting up. "This is a three-beer night. Can I grab you one?"

"For sure."

CHAPTER 17
ELENA

Elena spent the weekend in bed. It felt unnecessary, but it was nice to sleep without any homework, since her schoolbooks were locked away at school. Mom instructed her to stay off electronics for 'brain rest.' She considered arguing, but didn't. She didn't want to confront the version of her story on social media. She posted a "doing OK, going to rest this weekend" update and gladly surrendered her phone.

Even though Mom had no idea what really happened, she was right: Elena needed to rest. Elena was tired to the core. In between naps, she lay in bed and replayed what happened in the commons. She searched for a pattern, a logical explanation, or a scrap of reassurance.

When the power went out, she was bombarded by the general teenage angst around her. She was used to this everyday onslaught, relying on ibuprofen to quell the headaches and earbuds to tune out the emotional hum of the school. Whatever happened that morning was an overdose of the fatigue-inducing flood of pheromonal nonsense.

The Pandora's Box of Kayla that erupted in her ears was something different, though. Her brain quickly filled up with Kayla's *stuff*, like an audio book read at 300x speed. The theme of the story? Kayla's role in life was to please everyone by always being perfect and earning good grades, and shameful avoidance of The Issue, whatever that was.

After seeing the look on her mom's face in the ER when she mentioned the voices, Elena knew she had to keep it all a secret. Just like Kayla, she now had an absolutely unshareable Issue. Her mom used to know everything about her. Elena felt unmoored. All the more reason to nap.

• • •

Elena walked into school on Monday, feeling exposed. She knew that news of her episode spread through school with contagious speed. Kids that she never spoke to smiled and said generically nice things. Some asked about her hour-long seizure, others about the huge gash she sustained when falling. Apparently, the story had been embellished.

Her locker was decorated again. Her friends plastered it with paper flowers and "get well soon" signs. She smiled, and then looked up at Stephen coming toward her. This isn't his locker hallway, Elena thought. And he's carrying…

"Hey," he said. "These are for you." He pushed a plastic-wrapped bouquet toward her. "I'm glad you're okay." His neck was red over the collar of his shirt.

"Thanks. Probably just too much stress," Elena replied. "Thanks for the flowers, that's really—nice."

"Yeah, I'm glad you're fine!" He gulped and started to back away. "Let me know what you think of the card," he said, and tossed a grin over his shoulder before jogging away.

Elena smiled as she fumbled with her jacket, bag, and the riot of flowers. Wow, she thought. I guess I wasn't imagining it. He must like me a little bit to act so awkward.

She managed to get her things put away and asked the home ec teacher across the hall if she could keep her flowers there during the day. She nestled the purple blossoms in water and walked on air to her first class. It wasn't until the end of the day, after she collected the bouquet and returned to her car, that she remembered Stephen's parting comment: "Let me know what you think of the card!"

Oh my God. No wonder he looked so questioning all day! She quickly got in and shut the door. Her hands sweat as she worked the tiny pink envelope free of the plastic holder. Her ragged thumbnail caught on the flap and she paused briefly to nurse the blooming paper cut. She took a deep breath and managed to pull out the cardboard rectangle. There was a standard "Feel better" sentiment with a spray of flowers. Below, in masculine printing that was familiar, yet strange, was the phrase, "Will you be my date for Snowball?"

The winter dance. Elena gulped. No wonder he was so unusually quiet in English!

She never had an official date before, one where the guy asked her out and it was planned. Not many boys her age felt confident enough to attempt piercing Elena's carefully constructed armor.

Despite all her blurting and showing off in class, Stephen liked her. He really did, it wasn't her imagination. And now she was actually being asked to a dance. She'd get to buy a dress and pick out a boutonniere, and...and ...*and.*

Elena considered texting Stephen that evening to say yes. In the end, she decided to wait and tell him face to face. She wanted to see his grin when she said yes. Plus, she couldn't come up with a text that struck a balance between carefree, yet appreciative, yet suggestive. After two hours of false starts, she gave up and went to bed with *Anne of Green Gables,* imagining Stephen in the role of Gilbert Blythe.

•　　•　　•

The next day, Elena walked deliberately into school, not wanting to betray the development in her personal storyline. She greeted Chris calmly at their lockers, deposited her things, and proceeded around the corner to the commons. She immediately spotted Stephen and kept an eye on him as she greeted the Herd. As he finished his conversation, with overwhelming calmness, Elena stood up and walked toward the drinking fountain, directly past Stephen. And, as though summoned, he followed her, stopping at the soda machine.

She gulped some water and choked on it, spraying the front of her shirt. *Typical.* She caught his eye and he started laughing, so she decided to laugh too, wiping her mouth with the cuff of her sweatshirt.

"Hey," she said, "I didn't get a chance to thank you again for the flowers yesterday." He looked as though he wanted to say something, but Elena needed to rush through her speech, before she lost her nerve. "That was so kind of you, and it meant a lot. And, of course, I want to go to the Snowball with you. That would be really fun." Whew.

"Great!" Stephen said, rocking a little up and down on the balls of his feet. "I was worried when I didn't hear from you that maybe you were looking for a way to let me down easy."

"No, nothing like that," Elena said. "I didn't see the note 'til after school. And then I just wanted to tell you face to face. To see your face, I mean dimples, I mean reaction," she blurted.

Stephen snorted his Dr. Pepper, laughed, and wiped his own mouth with a cuff. "Dimples, huh? I never knew you noticed."

"Yeah, well, they're pretty obvious," she replied, struggling to regain composure, tucking her curls behind her ears. "Anyway, we both seem to have a drinking problem, so we better pick someplace with lots of napkins for dinner."

"Don't worry, I'll take care of you," he said, and shockingly pulled her into a little hug, right there in the middle of everyone. Elena briefly closed her eyes and smelled him, a combination of masculine deodorant and boy, filtered through fabric softener on his flannel shirt. She opened her eyes and was relieved to see that the eddying swirls of Belvedere students continued to flow unimpeded around their moment of intimacy. The only ones who seemed to notice were a grinning Kayla and Addison.

Elena was out of words, blurty or otherwise, so she turned and slipped away from Stephen, mumbling about her locker. She never wanted to be one of those girls paired up with someone in the hallway, wrapped like a snake for everyone to see. She hurried away, her stomach actually fluttering, instead of knotted up like usual. She opened her locker door and pretended to look for a book, but really just took deep breaths.

"So, I guess that's where those flowers came from, huh?" said Chris, leaning on his closed locker and looking down at her. "I used to hang out with Stevie when we were kids. Rode bikes and stuff."

"What? Oh, yeah. He felt bad that I fainted the other day, and I guess we're going to the winter dance together. That's all. It's not like we're a thing or something,"

"Okay," said Chris, raising his eyebrows and walking away.

•   •   •

At lunch, Addison was ready to talk. "So, is anyone else looking forward to Snowball?" she asked innocently, turning to face Elena. Kayla wiggled her transparent eyebrows and gently elbowed her. Elena turned crimson and buried her face in her hands.

"Oh my God, I really don't know why I'm so embarrassed! Clearly, you guys know that I'm going with Stephen!"

"It's been pretty obvious that you guys are into each other," said Kayla, smiling smugly.

"We've been saying so for weeks," interjected Morgan.

"We??" asked Elena.

"Obviously," said Addison. "I'm so happy you're going! You wanna go as a group with Jackson and me?" she asked, mentioning her current boyfriend.

"Well, sure, I mean, I have to check with Stephen…"

"Yes. It'll be great. We always go to the Prime Quarter. The guys cook our food and we check out their butts in dress pants while they're cooking," said Addison.

"Okay…"

"Morgan and Isaac will come too, and I'm sure a couple of Stephen's other friends will bring their dates…"

"Do you wanna come this time Kayla?" Morgan asked.

"Hell no," Kayla said, laughing, "as usual."

"I know you don't like dances, but if you ever change your mind, we've gotcha," Elena said. She felt extra protective of Kayla ever since the commons incident.

"Thanks, but I'm good," said Kayla. "Besides, we always do the end of the year dance as a huge group, so I get to dress up then."

"All right, but I want you to go dress shopping with me. Okay?"

"Okay," said Kayla.

•   •   •

Elena and Stephen started sitting together before school. They weren't officially dating, just hanging out. He teased her and whispered jokes in her ear. She laughed at all of them. Their classroom arguments continued, but even Mrs. Stanton seemed to notice a new intensity between them.

They didn't have an actual date before the Snowball, which happened just before winter break. They hung out in groups a few times, but nothing alone, which was okay with Elena. The dance would be their first official date.

The other reason Elena looked forward to the dance was that it marked the beginning of a couple weeks off. School was starting to literally make her sick. She ended each day exhausted and headachy from combating the emotional racket. The worst was when a classroom was silent and the internal monologues took over. The only way she found to block out the unwanted onslaught was nonstop noise. If a space was quiet, she tried to have earbuds in. Anything to avoid the head-pounding, cacophonous silence of a quiet classroom.

The only time she trusted quiet was when she was alone. She started spending most of her time at home holed up in the glorious silence of her room. She knew this worried her parents, so she kept the door open in an attempt to reassure them. At night, when Elena's tight rein on her thoughts loosened, she wondered. She wondered whether the auditory intrusions were a creation of her tightly-wound personality or worse, or whether something antenna-like was actually going on. She remembered reading about people who picked up radio transmissions through their dental fillings. Was it something like that?

Or was it something like Aunt Nell?

Elena tried to find answers online. She Googled "why am I hearing voices," the most popular suggestion for "why am I hearing…", followed by "why am I hearing sirens," and "why am I hearing birds at night." Her nebulous fears were confirmed when she read that voices, or auditory hallucinations, are the most common type of hallucination in people with schizophrenia. Shit. She carefully deleted her browser history and battled the words "schizophrenia" and "psychosis" our of her consciousness.

Whenever her thoughts started to veer into the "I'm going crazy" lane, she shoved them back in the "Grades! Snowball Dance! Piano!" lane with stubborn, exhausting determination. *If I don't acknowledge it, it's not there. Plus, wouldn't I* know *if I was going crazy? Or is* not *knowing you're crazy part of being crazy?*

She stayed in her safe mental lane easily with Stephen. With him, there were neither silences nor intrusions. He had opinions on everything and happily shared them. The old, clear-headed Elena might have been annoyed by his nonstop chatter, but the Elena who feared silence loved it. No one could occupy her brain like Stephen.

Stephen's Random & Gloriously Distracting Opinions
- *Green should taste like lime not apple*
- *Fall as the best season, followed in order by spring, summer, and winter*
- *Taco Bell will never be challenged as the superior fast-food option*

Chapter 18
Kat

Val: Get ur dress yet?
Kat: No

Ty drove her home from school and Kat mentally reviewed her day. Apple 95 calories, two rice cakes 70 calories, diet soda for lunch equals 165 calories. Four Jolly Ranchers to survive the afternoon, 95 calories. That left 540 calories. 360 calorie Lean Cuisine for dinner, can have one bowl of Cheerios plus skim milk, 150 calories. 30 calories left, carrot to chew slowly all evening. Total, exactly 800.

They pulled into her driveway and Kat unbuckled her seatbelt and grabbed Ty's neck, pulling him in for a kiss. He slid his hand under her shirt. She glanced around and, seeing no one around, let him. Her boobs were her secret weapon—the one thing that benefited from fat. As long as she kept him focused there, he wouldn't notice the problem areas. His hand grazed her stomach. Kat flinched and pulled away.

"What's your problem?" Ty complained.

"Sorry, you know I don't like you touching my stomach."

"Well, you better get over it, cuz I'm gonna be touching a lot more than that soon."

Kat tried to giggle, but she was petrified. She wanted to sleep with Ty in theory, but once they established a time frame, she wasn't so sure. She finally yielded and promised that the time would be after the dance, at the after-party, cliché but true.

She needed to lose weight first, deciding to lose 15 pounds in the month before the dance. She bought the time by explaining that she needed the month to get on the pill. Actually, she'd been on it for two years. She really needed time to get to a weight that would get her into a single digit dress size. One that would make her acceptable.

And her diet was working, just like every other time. She knew for years that one pound equaled 3500 calories. If she only ate 800 calories per day, and burned 500 on the elliptical, she should drop 3.5 pounds per week. So, 15 pounds in the month before the dance was totally doable! She already lost 13, only 2 to go with a week left. No problem. She felt exhilarated.

CHAPTER 19
ELENA

The weekend before the dance, the Herd went dress shopping. They left their coats in the car and dashed through the bitter December air into the Cinnabon-scented mall. The girls started at a boutique that specialized in high school dance dresses. A saleswoman explained that they kept a list of all the dresses that they sold, to be sure that no two girls attending the same dance bought the same dress.

Elena was nervous. She usually shopped with her mom or online, and she never shopped for a formal dress before. She had no idea how to find something alluring and grown-up. She despised her flat chest and lack of hips. As they started clicking through racks, she anticipated a disaster.

However, she quickly discovered that her real problem had been shopping with her mom, not her body. Neither she nor her mother had an eye for what looked good on her "androgynous" figure, as Morgan described with a sigh. Addison said that Elena could wear anything, since she didn't need a bra.

In the end, all three found tons of dresses to try on, while Kayla grabbed sizes and provided moral support. After all, Elena thought, Kayla's role is to make others happy. Elena looked good in several, and felt so unexpectedly relaxed that she managed to laugh. Morgan quickly chose a dress with more ruffles than Elena would have considered. Addison settled on one with a deep V-neck. They paid and carried their wrapped dresses back to the dressing room where Elena still couldn't decide. She tried on over 20 dresses that all looked good, but none were just right. All that was left was a black strapless sheath that looked like next to nothing on the hanger. Kayla picked it for her.

Eventually, her friends told her closed fitting room door that they were going to the bathroom and would be right back. Elena stared suspiciously at the final dress. Eventually, she slipped it from the hanger and stepped in, contorting to zip it up. The strapless neckline clung to what little chest she had, and it gently curved in at the waist, with a simple bit of shimmer that graced the short, short hemline and faded upward with an ombre effect. Even standing there in her ugly bare feet and unshaved legs, she had to admit that she looked *good*.

She turned slowly to the side and raised her eyebrows. Her legs looked so long. So did her arms. She looked…pretty. Stephen would die. Her dad might die too. Elena cautiously stepped out of the dressing room into the viewing area and approached a three-way mirror, staring at the floor.

As she worked up her courage to look, she heard a familiar voice angrily muttering, *"Gross, I look like a whale. At least it's a single-digit size."* Elena froze and listened as the hate-filled voice continued. *"Jesus Christ, and look at her. She's so freaking skinny. Oh shit, it's Elena Tannin."*

Elena dared a glance toward the angry voice. Kat. Kat was facing the other direction at a different mirror, wearing a pink halter dress that emphasized her amazing figure. Elena quickly glanced away, hoping that Kat hadn't seen her look. *She looks like a model!* Elena thought. *She looks amazing!*

After Elena thought this, she heard Kat chide, *"No one will be able to take their eyes off you, you look like the fricking supermodel. Supermodels don't wear a size 8."*

Are you kidding? Elena thought-blurted. *You look like an adult!*

"Is that supposed to be a compliment?" Kat spat out loud.

Elena and Kat made eye contact in the mirrors and froze. Elena's mind skidded all over the highway. It'd been her *voice*—Kat's voice. But she hadn't actually said any of it out loud. Just the last bit. *Jesus Christ.*

What the hell is going on? Elena frantically thought. *How did I not notice that I was just having an entire conversation in my fricking mind?*

"I have no idea," Kat said flatly, her voice floating through the empty dressing room.

Both girls' eyes widened as they took in each other's multiplying reflections. Kat's olive complexion played off the hot pink dress. She looked sad. Elena's pallor complemented the black dress, her face simultaneously confused and calculating.

Like a record being scratched, the moment shattered. The Waif's voice cut through the store. Elena panicked and glanced at Kat for guidance. Kat composed her usual look of disdain and jerked her head toward the open curtain. Elena awkwardly jumped back into her changing room and whooshed the curtain shut, narrowly avoiding the Beautiful People.

She heard one of them say, "Kat, oh my God, you look amazing. You'll have to wear a convertible bra, though."

"Did you try on the black one with the ombre sparkles?" someone else asked

"No," Kat replied. "It's already taken by someone at our school. I'm going with this one."

"It looks good. Do you want to take a picture for your mom? Or Ty?"

Please leave, please leave, please leave, Elena silently begged. Before the Herd comes back.

"I'm good. I already showed it to someone and I think it'll work," said Kat.

"Who, the worker? Of course she said it looked good. Are you sure?"

"Yes, let's get out of here," said Kat. "I'll pay for this and meet you at Starbucks."

Elena sat down on the narrow bench in the dressing room and drew her knees up to her chin to avoid being noticed by the Beautiful People. Her position sent the short dress awkwardly up to her waist, and she turned sideways on the bench to avoid flashing herself in the room's small mirror. She heard the group walk away, and Kat exited soon after.

People joked that hearing voices in your head wasn't necessarily bad, unless you started answering them. Well, what about if you answered them and then they answered you back? Out loud. Coming from another actual person. What exactly was that, huh? Elena had a sneaky feeling that neither Google nor her mom's DSM IV manual of psychiatry would have an answer.

Her thoughts were interrupted by her friends returning. "Sorry we took so long, but the bathrooms were being cleaned," she heard Morgan say. The Herd entered, narrowly avoiding the exiting Beautiful People by a minute or so.

"Did you pick one?" asked Addison.

"Umm, yes," said Elena forcing her mind back into the normal lane. "I chose this one," she announced, pulling back the curtain with a dramatic swish. Her friends looked at her and didn't say anything immediately, so she started to panic. "Unless, do you think it's too short? Too tight? I'm not sure after all…"

"God, Elena, calm down!" said Addison. "You look amazing. Seriously, gorgeous."

"Yeah, I couldn't find the words fast enough!" said Morgan. "I mean, we all know you're pretty, but you look, like, really hot!"

Elena blushed and felt better. "I wasn't begging for a compliment. But I think I'll get this one, right?" she asked, glancing at Kayla.

Kayla was grinning from ear to ear. "I knew this dress would look good on you!"

She was so lucky. None of them even suggested she take a picture for Stephen's approval.

•   •   •

After the Herd went out for Chinese, Elena came home and modeled her dress for her parents, whose smiles of approval didn't extend all the way to their eyes. Later, Elena lay in her bed, fighting to keep her mind from drifting back into the "going crazy" lane.

She tried to Google what happened to her. "Hearing someone else's thought." "Shared dressing room conversation without words." "Frenemy telepathy." Google kept steering her to sites talking about mental illness, or wishy-washy sites about empaths. Clearly neither of those applied...right?

She snuck into her mom's office and found the DSM IV psychiatry textbook. It was already out on the desk, opened to the section on "schizophrenia." That was worrisome enough. Even worse were the words on the page. Elena's eyes swooped to a passage stating that "only one symptom is required if delusions are bizarre or hallucinations consist of a voice keeping up a running commentary on the person's behavior or thoughts, or two or more voices conversing with each other." How bizarre was bizarre? Did complimenting her enemy's outfit and being complimented back count? How running was running? Did any time it was quiet count? And what if you recognized the voice, and it belonged to the person standing right next to you?

I'm Elena Tannin. I'm precocious and smart and untouchable. I'm not crazy. If I'm psychotic, that would cancel out everything else about me, and I'm still me. Right?

Unmentionable Weirdness
- *Kayla in chem, no one heard. Liar vs. voice- thrower?*
- *Kat in English. Shared research vs. Kat a ventriloquist and I'm her dummy?*
- *Commons incident. WTAF.*
- *Fitting room. WTAF????*

Chapter 20
Meghan

Dear Dr. Johnston,

Thanks again for agreeing to fit my daughter, Elena, into your busy clinic schedule. You come highly recommended. Given my husband's family history, you understand my concern. Attached, please find the patient and family history form. I look forward to meeting you on December 27.

Best,

Meghan Walker, MD, ASCP

Associate Professor, Department of Pathology

Meghan always ate at her desk. She needed to get things done during her brief lunch break, and she didn't care for the People magazine-style chatter that dominated the pathology department break room. She crossed a few tasks off her to-do list that day.

First, she made Elena's appointment with an adolescent therapist recommended by a colleague. She called Dr. Johnston's nurse directly to see if Elena could get an early appointment, as a professional courtesy. Meghan didn't like to play the "doctor" card, but this time was different. She got an appointment during winter break, so all she needed to do was keep Elena safe 'til then. And tell her about the appointment without a dramatic blow-up.

And tell her about Nell. Perhaps she and Anders made a mistake, not telling Elena everything sooner. Oh, well. Too late to second guess now. But that was going to be one hell of a conversation with Elena…

As part of the clinic's intake paperwork, Meghan completed an extensive medical and family history questionnaire on Elena's behalf. It covered the usual things, such as cancer and heart disease, while also delving into things unique to a mental health practice: family history of eating disorders, postpartum depression, and, of course, suicide. Check.

Meghan didn't have a medical grasp on her late sister-in-law's situation. Most of what she knew about Nell were layperson-style facts involving vague phrases like "mental breakdown" and "risky behavior." She knew that Nell died of an overdose, but had no idea of what, or what diagnoses appeared on some long-since-shredded medical record.

It was uncharacteristic that Meghan never dissected Nell's case with her usual attention to detail, but being a doctor for one's own family was tricky business, let alone one's married-into family. It was a weird combination of knowing too much from all her studies, and knowing too little from all the secrets. Plus, the Tannins were a foreign tribe, so, she didn't ask.

Until the question of what happened to Nell began to relate to Elena. As Meghan probed for answers, she quickly realized that Anders didn't know many details himself, and both of his parents were dead. On a whim, she typed, "Nell Tannin" into her search engine. The results included links to newspaper clippings about Nell's academic achievements: valedictorian in her high school class, summa cum laude from college, announcements about her beginning an MBA program. Plus, the obituaries.

Meghan clicked over to the "image" results and saw Nell's face, a feminine version of Anders, in a couple of graduation photos. She had the same long nose and neck, the same honey blonde hair. A little way down, there was a snapshot of people in front of a lake. Curious, Meghan clicked on it. She ended up on someone's social media page, where Nellie was labeled, along with a bunch of other women. The photo captured about 30 girls, mostly preteens to teenagers, with the big hair and popped collars of the late 80's. The laughing, tanned girls posed along the familiar Lake Michigan shoreline of Zedernwald. Next to the girls stood three women. Meghan zoomed in and recognized Anders' mother and her two sisters, Mary and Sylvie, happily draped on each other. Meghan hovered over the girls' faces, watching unfamiliar names pop up. If anyone knew of the details of Nellie's precipitous mental collapse, it would be these girls. At that age, only your peers are privy to your innermost thoughts.

Maybe I should try to get to know Elena's friends better, Meghan mused. If she's not talking to me about what's going on anymore, maybe she tells them. She recalled her own childhood house phone, the 12-foot cord's coils stretched out the kitchen door and into the laundry room. Meghan spent hours on that phone, talking to her friends about everything and nothing. Maybe Snapchat and Facetime were the new version of phones in the laundry room?

Who am I to be filling out any medical forms for her? Meghan thought. There are days I barely know her! And that dress! She hadn't realized just how stunning Elena became over the past couple of years. She didn't usually dress to highlight her body, preferring leggings and sweatshirts. Somewhere along the line, Elena developed a waistline to complement her long legs. She looked like she could walk into a bar in that dress. She looked like she could get into a lot of trouble in a bar in that dress.

There's no way I would have let her get it, Meghan thought, but the horse is out of the barn now. On the other hand, I wish I would have dressed that confidently when I still had the body. Clearly, she wants to impress this boy, Stephen. It was good that Elena was doing all these normal things, in addition to being an excellent student. It spoke to her balance and sanity. Right?

Meghan shuddered and closed the tab, eager to change her mental subject. The next item on the to-do list, register the twins for swimming lessons, was a welcome distraction.

CHAPTER 21
ELENA

Somehow, Elena survived the last weeks of school before the dance. As she left the final day before break, the sky grayed with the season's first real snowstorm. She eventually made it to the two-lane country road home, which hadn't yet been plowed. Her wheels briefly skidded off the invisible side of the road, slipping over the edge of the asphalt onto the gravel shoulder. She corrected her course, just as Dad taught her. Don't skate along the edge of the asphalt if you go off the road, or it'll grab your tires and pull you off completely. You have to cross back onto the road at an aggressive angle to avoid being sucked off into the ditch.

That was her approach to her brain, too. She course-corrected her thoughts from being sucked into dangerous territory by slippery voices and the Kat situation. She white-knuckled her mental steering wheel all day long. Her headaches pounded nonstop and she was more exhausted than she ever imagined possible. She actually fell asleep on her homework one night and showed up to school the next morning with incomplete assignments, sloppily finished in the commons with Kayla's help.

While clearing her mind of voices and worrisome thoughts was difficult, avoiding Kat was easy. Elena changed seats in English, didn't look at her, didn't listen to her voice, didn't smell her hair products, none of it. And if she caught herself starting to think about Kat and her infinite reflections in that fitting room mirror, Elena aggressively steered her brain back into its appropriate lane.

That final Friday afternoon, when she pulled into the garage and stamped off her snow-crusted boots, she felt close to making it. She just had to get through that night and the next day's dance. And then….she'd be okay. She had to be. Everything would somehow reset over winter break.

Elena stayed up and watched a movie with her parents, took a Benadryl to fall asleep, and got up the next morning with plans to meet at Addison's to get ready. There was just the empty morning to fill up. She lay on her back and glanced over at her dress, barely discernible in the December pre-dawn light. It hung on her closet doorknob and just touched the floor, it was that short. She briefly allowed her mind to wander to imaginings of a successful dance.

That morning, her parents circled her in a tentative way that had something to do with her behavior, her first official date with a boy, and the length of that dress. She left at noon, reminding them of the plan. She'd get ready at Addison's, the guys would meet them there, then they'd come to the Tannins' for pictures. Her parents insisted on meeting Stephen, and Addison thought that the Tannins' windows looking south would make for the best pictures. Addison curated her social media like it was her job.

By 4:00, the girls were ready. Addison curled her stick straight hair, Elena straightened her wild curls, and Morgan created a complicated updo with tendrils and braids. They shared a pile of makeup and periodically checked their phones to assess others' progress.

The last step was to slip into their dresses, and Elena couldn't decide what to do with her legs. She brought tights, but in the end, went bare-legged. Addison instructed that bare legs were required, no matter that they lived in Wisconsin in December. Elena looked at herself in the mirror and realized that she was wearing only her underpants, a strapless bra (which her mother insisted on), and a dress that could be folded down to fit into a Ziploc bag. Go big or go home, as Addison liked to say.

Eventually the doorbell rang, and they heard a rumble of male voices mixed with the higher pitch of Addison's mom.

"Okay, time for our entrance," announced Morgan. The three teetered down the carpeted stairs in their strappy heels, crowding into the small foyer. Elena unsteadily squeezed through the group to find Stephen, whose eyes widened as he did a stereotypical once-over. He paused at the hemline of her dress, and quickly shifted up. He gulped and then his dimples appeared.

"You look amazing. Seriously, wow."

"Thanks," said Elena. "You look good too."

Stephen wore a sport coat and a blue checked shirt, open at the collar. When he pulled her in for a hug, she smelled his usual smell, along with cologne. She wasn't the only one putting in effort, she realized. He grabbed her hand and held it tight as they moved through a series of introductions and photos. Elena didn't hear much as she smiled and posed. Instead, she paid attention to the exact location of each of Stephen's fingers laced through her own.

They finally finished, and he led her out to his Toyota, reluctantly removing his hand to open the passenger door. She smiled up at him and ducked into the bucket seat, her sparkly dress sending light beams incongruously across the faded upholstery. She felt giddy during the brief drive to her house, where all her worlds collided in the living room. The Herd. The twins. Her parents. Stephen. Her legs.

More parents arrived to see their children playing at being grown-up. Her dad took on the role of host, slipping beers and wine into parents' hands. With the addition of some of Stephen's friends and their dates, ten couples cycled through a series of poses, the muted pinkish twilight sky through the window in the background. When Elena and Stephen posed for their individual shot, she felt her parents' eyes on her, and started to feel sentimental and weird. Then she felt Stephen's hand settle firmly on her lower back, and all sepia tones were erased in a burst of adolescence. She knew that Stephen felt it too. She couldn't wait to get back to the privacy of his car.

Unfortunately, one of the other guy's car wouldn't start. Dead battery. Being Wisconsinites, everyone had jumper cables, but they didn't have the time, since they were already late for their reservation at the Prime Quarter. The guy's dad offered to stay back and jump the car, and Stephen offered his buddy and his date a ride to the restaurant. He gave Elena an apologetic look and, before she knew it, another couple was tucked in the backseat as they hurried to make their reservation.

The cook-your-own steak restaurant, popular in the 90's, remained a fixture in Belvedere. That night, it was full of dressed-up teenagers; a patient waitress dealt with separate tabs for their group. When the boys left to cook the steaks, Addison made sure that they photographed the line of butts at the communal grill. Stephen was the second tallest in the group. Elena couldn't really make out his behind under the sport coat, but she appreciated the height that made him a valuable volleyball player.

"I hope it's okay," he said when he returned to the table with their steaks. "My dad tried to give me some tips, but I've never really grilled steaks before."

He watched expectantly as she took a bite. She raised her eyebrows and nodded as she chewed the well-done steak. Stephen looked relieved and cut into his. As he chewed, his expression grew concerned. He glanced back at Elena with a questioning look. She shrugged and continued to gnaw on her woefully overcooked steak. Stephen snorted and then laughed outright, taking a big gulp of water to get his steak down. Elena did the same. They mostly ate the potatoes and salad after that. The restaurant was wonderfully noisy, and her head remained clear. She mostly focused on Stephen's hand, which took up residence on her bare leg, not moving an inch from its distracting landing point.

As they left, she saw the other boy's freshly-jumped car waiting in the parking lot, so she and Stephen would be alone! Stephen walked her to the passenger door and, once she sat down, tucked his jacket over her goose-bumped legs.

"You look cold," he said, letting his hands rest on his jacket on top of her legs, looking at her questioningly. For once, Elena was at a loss for words. Stephen leaned in and brushed his lips ever so gently across hers. She didn't know what to think. Her mind was gorgeously blank.

She smiled against his lips, and he pulled away just enough to look at her.

"Hi," he said.

"Hi," Elena choke-whispered back.

How could he be so perfect, with the crisp night sky sparkling behind him through the door of the car?

"You're perfect," he said. "Let's go to the dance."

•   •   •

The Snowball was complete with balloons and streamers incongruously taped over the day-to-day reality of the cafeteria, and a DJ swirling lights and playing popular music. Most kids danced in the middle of the gym floor, some stood outside the foul line and watched or checked their phones. The Beautiful People, including Kat in her amazing dress, hung around the edges and disappeared frequently through the door to the cafeteria loading docks, most likely drinking whatever cheap booze one of their older brothers scored for them.

For the first time in two weeks, Elena didn't particularly care what Kat was doing. The music pulsed, her friends grinned and swirled, and Stephen pulled her in for a slow dance whenever the music cooperated. She became acquainted with the hollow of his back and the feeling of his heart thrumming under her cheek. It was all going according to plan, until she heard the voice.

Elena was in the bathroom. A group of girls filtered out as she entered, leaving behind a vacuum of silence. She entered a stall, and the girl in the adjacent stall began crying almost as soon as the previous group left. Oh dear. The poor thing was so sad, proclaiming her own self-loathing, and cursing a boy, Ty, who forced himself on her, after calling her all sorts of awful things.

Elena stood frozen, focused on the despair pounding on the stall divider. She leaned against the cool metal, drawn as if by a strong magnet. She held her breath, inches away from this pathetic, self-loathing girl, whose words echoed through the room. Elena gasped, remembering to breathe when she recognized the voice.

It was Kat. And the awful Ty was The Man, her boyfriend. As the bathroom door creaked open and someone new entered, Kat's voice continued to choke through her tears, but the new girl simply went about her business and left. A dawning realization washed over Elena. Kat's not talking out loud. I'm the only one hearing this. It's happening again, and I'm the only one who can help her.

Elena didn't bother to panic or question her sanity. She was too filled with rage. Rage for whatever Ty did to Kat. Rage for the insulting words he used to describe her beautiful frenemy. Rage at the stupid, dumbass Man ruining her perfect night. "That's it," Elena muttered. "Enough is enough." She waited for the new girl to leave the bathroom. Then, Elena took a deep breath, walked to Kat's stall, and knocked on the door. "Kat? I know it's you. Get out here, " Elena commanded.

Kat cracked the stall door open and whispered, "What the hell, Elena? What do you think you're doing?" Half-crying, half-growling, she shoved her black hair back from where it stuck to the tear-tracks on her cheeks.

"Doing? Well, I thought that it was about time that someone stood up for you," Elena blurted, quickly locking the main bathroom door. "None of your so-called friends seem to care that you are having a breakdown in the bathroom—"

"Because I didn't say anything, Elena," Kat yell-whispered. "No one heard anything except you, okay? As far as they're concerned, I'm fine. And I'd like to keep it that way."

"Bullshit," Elena declared numbly. The secret was spoken, that she could hear Kat's thoughts, and Kat didn't seem particularly surprised by it. Instead of dealing with that little bit of unreality, Elena focused on the other bit of bullshit. "There's no way that they can assume you are fine. You are anything but fine."

"Don't you get it, Elena? No one knows but you, because what I was saying was all in my head—and your head, somehow," Kat explained, desperately glancing at the bathroom door. "No one knows about you, and yet this is happening. And it can't be happening, because you'll ruin everything."

Elena shook her head, trying to loosen the cobwebs of confusion. Her bravado started to slip as Kat wrested control of the situation.

"Look, you're out of control," Kat said, grabbing her shoulders and pulling her into the stall with her. "Do you get that? Do you have any clue what is happening?"

Elena creased her eyebrows and stared at Kat's mouth. Words were coming out, but she couldn't arrange them into logical statements.

"Where the hell did you really come from?" Kat demanded.

Elena stared at her blankly.

"Whatever. You've got to go. Now."

Elena finally found her voice. "No. I might not understand what you're saying, but I understand that whatever happened tonight with your so-called boyfriend is not fine. You can't just go back out there and pretend everything is normal. You need to leave."

"Oh my God, no. You leave!" Kat demanded, shoving Elena out of the stall.

Elena wasn't sure how she expected Kat to respond, maybe a thank you or some grateful weeping, but definitely not an attack.

"What's going on with you, Kat? One second, you're a snob, the next minute, you're crying, and now you're mad? At me?" Elena demanded. "I'm not the one who needs help. You need help. Or maybe I really am crazy after all," Elena said, tears filling her eyes.

"No," Kat said, pointing at Elena. "You. Aren't. Crazy. And we will take care of this, all of this, ourselves." She narrowed her eyes and examined the specimen that was Elena. "Be honest. Are you hearing voices?"

Elena blanched, and she knew that Kat knew it was true.

"Jesus Christ. I've got to get you help."

Suddenly, Elena felt knocked over by a wave of exhaustion. Her mask of normalcy wasn't just ripped off by this exchange, it was trampled to death. All the previous weeks' frantic holding it together caught up to her in one awful, overwhelming wave. She was absolutely, completely done. Theoretically, she wanted to go back to Stephen and the dance. But in her heart and muscles, she knew it was impossible. She needed help. And, somehow, Kat wanted to help her.

"All right," Elena said, closing her eyes.

"All right, what?" said Kat, walking over the bathroom door and checking the lock.

"You're right. I'm hearing voices, no one has a clue what's going on, I need help. But—" she said, suddenly rallying and opening her eyes. "If I'm going to leave and take care of my situation, then you have to leave, too."

Kat's eyes narrowed, but she didn't look away.

Elena continued, "You have to go home, not to whatever party your friends have planned. And definitely not anywhere with The Man, I mean, Ty."

Kat paused, apparently considering Elena's words.

Elena worried that Kat would change her mind, so she continued, "Otherwise, we both go to the E.R. I can have a psychiatric evaluation, and you can have a rape kit done."

Kat grimaced. "Ty's my boyfriend, Elena, don't you know that?"

"Well, that doesn't mean he gets to have sex with you whenever he wants," Elena said.

Kat laughed wryly. "He doesn't get to have sex with me at all. And that's why he acted the way he did."

"But you said he hurt you?" Elena said, remembering what she heard across the stall.

"Yes, but I don't need a rape kit. I do need a sandwich."

"So, no ER, but will you go home? And not back to that toxic relationship?" Elena asked.

"Fine," Kat said, glancing at the door. "We both get out of here."

"As long as Ty doesn't drive you home," Elena said. As if she had the energy to stop her anyways.

"Okay," Kat agreed. "I'll get a ride home and deal with my 'toxic relationship.' But you need to leave too, and you need to talk to someone."

"Who? A psychiatrist?"

"No," Kat interrupted, grabbing Elena's bare arm and staring at her intensely. "You aren't crazy. I know that you have absolutely no reason to, but you have to trust me."

"I'm not a big truster," said Elena. "I like explanations."

"How about this?" Kat said, "I promise that, by this time tomorrow, you will have answers."

"From who?" Elena asked, pulling her arm away. "You?"

"No, not me. Someone will contact you, I promise," Kat said, pulling out her phone to exchange numbers. "But for now, you need to leave and go someplace away from people. Do you share a room?"

"No…"

"Great. You need to get home and just go to bed, be alone. Do you think you can get a ride home?" Kat asked.

"Yeah, I'll tell Stephen I'm sick," Elena said.

"That won't be too much of a stretch, you look like hell."

"Same."

The girls glanced at themselves in the cracked bathroom mirror. Kat's hair was a tangle, gone from beachy waves to shoreline debris. Her face was flushed, and there was a stain on her pink dress. Elena looked like an accidental goth, unnaturally pale in the black dress, with blooming dark circles around her eyes. Her sweaty forehead encouraged errant curls to re-form around her hairline. Both girls turned away in distaste.

"Ready?" Kat asked.

Elena nodded, walking toward the door. She felt more relieved than she had in weeks. "I don't know why I'm trusting you, Kat. You've never said one nice thing to me before."

"A girl's gotta do what a girl's gotta do," said Kat, composing her usual look of disdain. "You leave first, I'll follow."

Kat was right. When Elena walked out of the bathroom, Stephen didn't need to be convinced to take her home. He glanced up, saw her across the gym, and ran to her side. He put his jacket and arm over her shoulders and walked her out of the dance like a bodyguard. If she had more energy, Elena would have been thrilled with the valor. Addison and Morgan hugged her goodbye, promising to call in the morning. As they left, Elena glanced back through the closing gym doors and saw three concerned faces tracking her exit: Addison, Morgan, and Kat. She better hold up her end of the deal, Elena grimly thought.

"I hope it wasn't the steak," Stephen said as he started the car.

Elena smiled and, without thinking, flopped her head on his shoulder. She must have fallen asleep on the ride back to her house. The next thing she knew, the dome light came on and he was saying her name and gently shaking her awake.

"I'm so sorry I ruined the night," Elena apologized, sitting up and weakly removing the jacket from her shoulders.

"Are you kidding?" said Stephen. "Even though my cooking made my date sick, this was still an excellent night. First of many, I hope?"

Elena smiled and nodded. He leaned over and kissed her forehead before escorting her to the door. He insisted on handing her off directly to her parents. At first, they were confused to see her home well before her 1:00 curfew, looking so awful. Once they understood that she was feeling sick rather than drunk or drugged, they thanked Stephen profusely. Her dad even shook his hand.

"It's just a bad headache," Elena said.

Her mom helped her into bed with a glass of water, ibuprofen, and an extremely concerned backward glance. Elena promised to call if she needed anything, but, of course, she didn't.

New Reality

- *Unmentionable secret weirdness=> I am psychotic.*
- *My parents know almost everything.*
- *I have some sort of weird connection with Kat*
- *I might have my first boyfriend.*

Chapter 22
Kat

Kat: call asap spiral 911
Val: in a sec

Kat texted her camp friend, Val, on the way home for advice, while riding silently in the neighbor boy's car. Luckily, he was at the dance and agreed to drive her home when she asked. Typical Val, she didn't have to wait long for the phone to buzz. "Hey," Kat answered, slamming the door shut on Chris's car and waving her thanks.

"Hey," Val said, with a concerned look. "What'd he do this time?"

Kat sighed. Val was not a Ty fan. As much as she trusted her best friend, she wasn't ready to share the details of what happened. Besides, there was a different crisis to manage. "Ty later. You know that girl, Elena, I mentioned?"

"Yeah…"

"Now I'm positive she's one of us. We accidentally Communed again tonight, and she said she's hearing voices," Kat said, widening her eyes to convey the craziness of it all.

"Wow. Is that why you're Spiraling?" Val asked.

"No, not me! Her! She looked drained. I have a feeling she's been active for awhile and totally out of control."

"Doesn't she have a mom? Or some aunts, or a grandma?" Val asked.

"Yeah, her mom's a doctor, I looked her up. My mom swears that she's never met her before! Something doesn't add up, cuz Mom knows everybody in our area."

"That makes no sense. What are you going to do?" Val asked.

"I think I have to tell Mary," Kat said with more assurance than she felt.

"Shouldn't you tell your mom first?"

"You know how she is. She can't make a decision to save her life, and Elena is in big trouble right this second."

"Then, yeah, Mary's the best choice. Call her in the morning."

"That's just it," Kat said. "I don't think this can wait until morning."

"Whoa."

"I know."

The girls stared at each other before Val broke the silence. "Well, call me after and let me know how it goes. And to tell me what happened with Ty. Good luck."

"Yeah, thanks," said Kat, with a shuddering sigh, remembering what happened in Ty's car. "Bye."

"Bye."

Kat took a deep breath, pulled up Mary's info, and stared at the green icon. She imagined Mary hearing her flip phone ring on her old lady bedside table, scrambling for her glasses. It would be hilarious if it weren't petrifying.

Kat finally touched the call button and listened as it rang once. Twice. Three. Four times. Maybe it would go to voicemail?

"Hello," cough, "hello?"

Gulp. "Um, hi, it's Kat Kowalski. From camp? I have a Spuren emergency," she said.

"Who's in trouble?" the woman asked, audibly snapping awake.

"You don't know her, her name's Elena Tannin," Kat said. How in the world was she going to explain this whole thing? "She lives here in Belvedere," she began.

"I know where to find her," the older woman said.

Weird, Kat thought.

"I'll call you back in a second for details. Gotta find my glasses."

Before Kat could respond, the call ended. She tiptoed to her parents' room and knelt down on her mom's side. "Mom," she whispered over the roar of her dad's CPAP machine. "You'll never believe what happened."

CHAPTER 23
ELENA

920-123-4567: Dear Elena. Katherine Told Me You Need Help. Please Meet Me At The Star Bucks At 11.30. Sincerely. Mary Schultz.

The morning after the dance, Elena slept until 10:30. She awoke to missed messages from the Herd, Stephen, and a random 920 area code number. Elena usually ignored random phone numbers, but the generically-named Mary Schultz must be the person that Kat promised would give her answers. It felt insane to go along with the suggested coffee shop meetup with a stranger, but what other choice did she have?

She had 45 minutes to get ready. As she scrunched her curly hair into a bun, Elena thought about how to get by her parents; lying to them was becoming remarkably unremarkable. She looked better than she did the night before, but she still put on under eye concealer and blush. If she looked anything less than 100%, Mom wouldn't let her leave.

"Morning!" she said brightly, entering the kitchen where her parents sat with the newspaper. "Can I go to Starbucks to meet the Herd?"

Her mom jerked to attention and scanned Elena. "Are you sure you feel up to it, honey?"

"Yeah, I'm much better. I think I ate something bad last night," she said in her cheeriest tone.

"I've never been a fan of those cook your own food places," Mom said. She glanced at Elena's dad.

"Fine with me," he said.

Her mom nodded. "Can you be back before evening? We need to talk about some stuff."

Ugh, Elena thought. But, instead of complaining, she said, "Okay, love you, bye!"

The car was chill-your-bones freezing, the heater just beginning to sigh bits of warmth as she pulled up to the coffee shop, but Elena was too preoccupied with the events of last night and this morning to mind the cold. She couldn't decide whether she hoped that this Mary person was waiting for her, or that no one waited at all. Either option was scarily unpredictable.

Like most businesses in Wisconsin, Starbucks had two sequential entry doors, creating an airlock to keep the winter out. As Elena neared the entrance, she saw a tall, solid woman standing in the vestibule between the doors. She wore a practical blue coat and stocking cap and looked vaguely familiar. To be honest, though, every old lady in a puffy coat and stocking cap looked the same. Elena opened the outer door and caught a whiff of the woman's heavy floral perfume.

"Elena Tannin," the woman said without interrogative inflection, indicating she already knew the answer.

So, this was Mary and this was really happening. "Yes?" Elena answered, and reflexively held her hand out to shake the one extended by the solid woman.

"Nice to meet you. I'm your great Aunt Mary." Before breaking the handshake, she added, *You look a lot like your dad. And your hands are cold. Where are your gloves?*

"Sorry," Elena said aloud before registering the fact that Aunt Mary, for that's apparently who she was, thought-talked to her just like Kat did. Elena jerked her frigid hand away and pulled the inner door open for Mary, who limped into the coffee shop like this was a regular ol' meetup, rather than one involving telepathic communication.

She lumbered to the counter and studied the menu board, dramatically squinting as she adjusted her glasses. "I always get a black coffee, but I can never remember what they call the damn things," she said to Elena who hovered numbly in her wake. "Tall...plain old coffee.

And put two of those cardboard things on it so I don't burn my hands," she instructed the barista. She looked over her shoulder expectantly at Elena.

"Tall nonfat chai with a shot of espresso," Elena mumbled automatically. Mary paid for both drinks with exact change, and the pair waited in heavy silence. When her drink arrived, Elena gripped the familiar bumps of the cup, reassuring herself that this was, in fact, the Belvedere Starbucks and that she was, in fact, not dreaming.

Mary led the way to a table at the back of the cafe, which was empty except for a frazzled mother with three kids near the front. Mary settled in and her bosom overlapped onto the cafe table, bisecting the cardinal embroidery on her sweatshirt. She spread her hands on the surface next to her coffee, from which she occasionally took a generous slurp. "I imagine you have a little bit of an idea why I'm here, *right?*" she mentally added, briefly touching Elena's hand.

Elena felt her eyes widen in response to the casual thought-talking, and she nodded.

"I'm awful sorry that I pulled that on you." Mary glanced at her hand as she spoke, "but I had to make sure it was true. From what Katherine said, I was pretty darn sure that you had it, but I needed to confirm."

"What's it? Will someone just tell me!" Elena said.

Aunt Mary smiled gently, quelling Elena's angsty energy in an instant. "Elena. I'm pleased to tell you that you have a special gift shared by mothers and daughters in our family. A precious gift that grants you admittance to a group that you're lucky to belong to."

Jesus, Aunt Mary sounded like her mom when Elena got her first period.

"I've never had to just tell someone all at once, so I'm winging it, but here goes. Honey, you have the Talent. You can read people's emotional energy in a very powerful way. And in some instances," she patted Elena's hand again, "*you can send and receive that information directly.*"

Aunt Mary's thick nails were clipped to a practical length, she wore a wedding band and no other jewelry. Maybe it was the mundane practicality of those hands. Or maybe it was that Mary's words, while foreign, explained concepts that were unnervingly familiar. Either way, Elena ignored every skeptical alarm bell and chose to believe her.

"How?" Elena asked, not entirely sure which bit the 'how' was meant for.

"We're not entirely sure. Never bothered to run a bunch of lab tests," Mary said, abandoning sentiment for practicality. "But, you know how your cell phone picks up on a signal, even though you can't see that signal in the air? It's the same with the Talent. Women with the Talent, Spuren women, we're called, have a special receptor that's tuned into people's energy. Their emotional energy." Aunt Mary gestured broadly while she tried to convey the nebulous concept. "I guess that this kind of makes sense to you, right?" she asked hopefully.

Elena shrugged. It did make sense, in an entirely irrational way. Elena felt simultaneously vindicated and appalled. She always joked that her 'magic talent' was reading people, especially adults. Vindicated. But, this talent, er, Talent, wasn't unique to her. Apparently, there was a whole gang of people like her out there, rendering her not that special. Appalled. What were these copycats called again?

"What was that S-word again?" Elena asked.

"Spuren. I'm not pronouncing it right, and we definitely don't use it right anymore, but it's German. Way back when, there was a German lady came to America, and she had the Talent, passed it on to her daughters, yada yada, lots of Spuren ladies today." She wiped her nose and tucked the tissue up her sleeve. "Spuren means something about sensing, so that's what we call ourselves. Luckily, the rest of the German words dropped out long ago. All I know how to say is 'gimme another beer' and 'where's the toilet.'"

Etymology and history nudged Elena back into her comfort zone, and her mental wheels resumed turning. "I have soooo many questions."

"You must be overwhelmed," Aunt Mary said. "We're all confused at times, but most of us have entire childhoods getting prepared by our mothers!" Mary unzipped her voluminous black purse and rummaged out a notepad decorated with bowling pins. She pushed that and a pen across the table. "You better start taking notes, writing down questions."

Elena began to scribble furiously, taking bulleted notes in her usual style. As she wrote, the scariest question slipped out. "Are you saying that the voices I've been hearing are my, um, Talent? Not that I'm going crazy?"

Great Aunt Mary choked on her coffee dramatically, dabbing at her eyes with brown napkins.

Oh, no, Elena scolded herself. I should've kept the voices secret! She's freaked out and will probably drive me directly to the psych ward!

Aunt Mary finally caught her breath and gave Elena an intense stare. "You're. Not. Crazy. You've just got the volume on your Talent receiver turned up to 11! Those voices aren't made up in your head. They're what's going on in everyone else's heads!" She leaned back and smiled. "Did you get that reference? *Spinal Tap*? Last movie I saw in the theater."

For the first time in weeks, Elena relaxed a notch, allowing herself a small smile at Aunt Mary's joke. "Not to be rude, but what if I don't want this Talent? Is there a cure?"

"You can't get rid of the Talent, even if you wanted to," Aunt Mary said. "That's why I'm here. To get you started learning to live with your Talent before the summer, since you're a special case."

Elena looked up, mid-bullet point. "What do you mean, 'special case?'"

Mary leaned in dramatically. "There's a lot we don't know about the Talent. But one thing we know for sure is that it passes from mothers to daughters. Only. But honey, your mom isn't even a little bit Spuren!"

"No kidding," muttered Elena.

The old lady cracked a smile. "So, you must've got the Talent from our side of the family, through your dad somehow. Maybe that's a good thing; you could continue the Schultz family line!"

That's where Elena recognized the name Schultz. It was her grandma's maiden name.

"Maybe the Schultz Spuren line won't die with me and Sylvie. That's a wonderful thing plus it proves I was right all along! For years, I suspected that something was up over at the Cottage. Whenever you and your family came to stay in the summer, I swore up and down that there was a Spuren over there," she said. "Sylvie never noticed, but I've always been the more sensitive one," she said conspiratorially.

And that's where she recognized Aunt Mary's face from! When she was little, Elena used to sneak along the lakeshore path from the Cottage to the Lodge, to spy on the campers and counselors, including Mary. When she was around 10, her dad caught her and got so mad that she never sneaked over again.

"I've got about half an hour before I have to head back home," Mary said, "so what questions do you have?" Elena must have appeared disappointed, because she added, "I can't stay longer, I have to get back for a senior women's bowling tournament."

Elena tried and failed to imagine Great Aunt Mary bowling, with her limp and wide hips. "How come it—the Talent—comes and goes? The voices and feelings aren't constant."

"Jumping right to the advanced questions, I see," Aunt Mary said with a look of pride. "The Talent is always there, but a lot of times, it's blocked out. Like when you get bad reception with your TV antenna."

Elena looked at her quizzically.

"It was always so much easier to explain when people still used rabbit ears. Like bars on your cell phone, I guess."

"So, I can control it? Block it out?" asked Elena excitedly. "Or find the spots that have better signal?"

"Yes and yes, but it takes practice. You have to do some catch-up work first."

Elena felt panicky. She never did anything remedial in her life.

"Don't worry, we don't give out grades," responded Mary. "You just have to learn a few things before camp this summer."

"So, is Zedernwald some kind of secret Spuren training camp?" Elena asked, connecting the dots.

Aunt Mary laughed. "Far from it. It's just summer camp, with some extra time learning to be Spuren. The most secretive thing about Zedernwald is Sylvie's recipe for tater tot casserole. And the fact that none of the men have any clue."

"So, does my dad know about all this?"

"No, not at all," Mary replied. "And I hate to ask you to lie, but you *cannot* mention this to your folks. Or anyone else, not that they'd believe you. If you tried to explain, people'd figure you were one of those so-called empaths. We'll have to figure out how to manage your family situation. For now, can you be a dutiful daughter and try not to ruffle any feathers at home?"

"I've been doing that my whole life," Elena replied.

"Good girl."

"How far behind am I? Are there books I can read?" Elena asked.

"Most girls start coming to camp when they're around 12 or 13. Whenever their Talent turns on. As for books—honey, none of this is written down. No books. Strictly oral tradition."

"How am I supposed to do remedial coursework then? Are you going to keep driving down to tutor me?" Elena hoped so. Great Aunt Mary was so calming and solid, like a heavy quilt.

"No, I don't drive on the highway if I can help it. It was real touch and go this morning. I stayed in the right lane the whole time, cruise control at 50," Mary said, wiping invisible crumbs off the table. "But I needed to make sure you'd be safe for the next little bit, which I think you will with a few tips. I asked Linda Kowalski to work with you."

"Wait, Kowalski, as in Kat Kowalski?" Somehow, Elena managed to forget that Kat was tied up in this whole thing. But if Talent was passed from mothers to daughters…

"Sure, Linda is Katherine's mom," said Mary. "I thought you would've figured it out by now. Katherine Kowalski is Spuren, so's her ma. Katherine's the one that called me last night and got me down here, let me know your Talent was running amok. You were lucky she was there, looking out for you. I talked to Linda this morning, and she'll start working with you in a week or so. I asked her to pop by here just to get things squared away. I'm not sure why she's not here yet. Can you excuse me while I run to the ladies?" Aunt Mary loudly got up and walked away, not bothering to wait for an answer.

At that point, all Elena could do was nod.

And think about starting a new notebook for the list of questions. If they only had a half hour, they'd barely make a dent when Mary returned from the ladies. She flipped the piece of paper and started writing on the back, through which the shadow of bowling pins peered incongruously.

She looked up when the café door chimed and a woman walked in. She looked like Kat, except softer, curlier, and actually smiling. So much for a normal winter break.

<u>"Spuren" (sp?) Questions</u>
- *~~What makes the Talent work?~~ No one knows. Genetic?*
- *~~Can we turn it off?~~ Nope. Rabbit ears???*
- *How do we keep secrets from each other?*
- *How come I've never heard my parents' voices?*
- *Am I related to Kat?*
- *How do people <u>use</u> their Talent?*
- *How can you sense me from all the way across the camp? Will I be able to do that someday?*
- *Can people tell that I have it?*
- *What did Kat tell you about me? Does she talk to you all the time?*
- *Did Aunt Nell go to camp? What happened to her? Will the same thing happen to me?*

CHAPTER 24
MEGHAN

After Elena left the house that morning, Meghan decided that Starbucks sounded good. And checking on Elena wasn't the worst idea either. As she sat at the drive-through window and waited for her drinks, she glanced into the shop past the hissing espresso machine and recognized Elena's hair. Weirdly, she wasn't sitting with a bunch of teenage girls, but rather, a solid person with a cap of steel gray curls. Who was that? Meghan craned her neck and tried to make sense of the scene on the other side of the flavored syrups. As the mystery person shifted in their seat, it hit her. It was the squarer, more masculine version of her late mother-in-law. It was Anders' Aunt Mary.

What the hell? Elena was meeting up with someone on Anders' very short 'people I don't care for' list? And lying about it?

Meghan's first instinct was to slam the minivan into drive, zip into a parking spot, and storm into the store. The car ahead of her in line forced her to pause and consider. If she barged in, what would happen? She'd be rude to a woman who she barely knew, alienate Elena in the process, and learn nothing. So, Meghan didn't barge in and continued to observe instead.

Aunt Mary, her sweatshirt printed with, what was that? A cardinal? looked completely unremarkable. Clearly Anders' version of his family must be unreliable. Maybe she, with her medical approach, could judge the woman more accurately.

"Sorry about the wait," the drive through barista said, intruding on Meghan's thoughts.

She distractedly paid for her drinks and left, officially abandoning Plan A, bursting in and confronting them. During the ten-minute drive home, she developed a Plan B. When she pulled into the garage, one question remained: should she tell Anders what she saw? No, surely, not telling him was best; it would needlessly upset him and add an unnecessary wrinkle to Plan B.

Meghan needed Plan B to work in order to douse her maternal worry fire, a metaphor that Meghan used to explain the constant low-grade worry that she kept simmering since the moment of Elena's birth. She suspected that all mothers maintained such a worry list, like the heaped-up embers of a fire just waiting to be quickly rekindled into a roaring blaze. Lately, Meghan's was less pile of embers and more barely-contained bonfire.

She knew too much to quell the flames. As a doctor, she knew too much about psychiatry and genetics to chalk Elena's behavior and exhaustion up to teenage dramatics. She knew about scary places littered with behavioral plans and drugs with horrendous side effects.

As Anders' wife, she knew too much about his messy family history. About the old ladies in the family interfering with Nell's treatment, and all the blame and bitterness that grew up around it. She knew that toxic presences sometimes showed up in old-lady outfits and permed hair.

As a former teenage girl, she knew too much about the roiling undercurrent of it all. Of violently hating one's mother and simultaneously loving her so fiercely that she never wanted to leave home; of being supremely confident and hopelessly petrified; of both longing for and fearing adulthood.

She knew that her tie to Elena was a gossamer thread, straining daily under the pull of school and friends and boys and hormones and insidious ideas and crazy short dresses. Meghan once knew every crevice of Elena's body, gently scrubbing the baby fuzz and drool away in a nightly bath time ritual. Now she had no idea what was going on in that slender frame, that scary brain.

The psychiatric evaluation couldn't come soon enough. She couldn't wait to get a diagnosis and plan to put Elena back to normal, whatever that meant. She couldn't wait to figure out what on earth was going on with Elena.

And she couldn't wait to figure out what the hell Mary Schultz was doing lurking around her daughter. When she got home, Meghan gave Anders his coffee and made up a work excuse. She shut herself in the office, found Mary's address in her files, and wrote a letter, kicking off Plan B.

Dear Mary,

We haven't been in contact for many years, and I hope this letter finds you well. Let me cut to the chase. I know that you have been in touch with Elena, and I hope that we might chat and clear the air. I have not told Anders or Elena that I am writing you, nor does Anders know that you have been in touch with Elena. I hope to hear from you within the month. If not, I can see no other recourse than to involve Anders, who still holds a great deal of hostility toward you and your sister. I hope that you still live year-round at Zedernwald and that this letter reaches you.

Sincerely,

Meghan Walker (Anders' wife)

She slipped the letter inside her work bag. She'd mail it on Monday and hopefully hear back from the old lady. She needed to be careful not to let her accidental Starbucks spying slip, completely losing the bits of Elena's trust she maintained in the process.

CHAPTER 25
ELENA

Elena was antsy driving home, reviewing the rules that Mary and Linda gave her. Protect herself from too much sensory overload. Try to spend time alone to avoid getting run down by too much sensory input. Show up at the Kowalskis' the day after Christmas at 3:00. Keep an enormous secret from her parents and act totally normal.

She walked into the house, aware of the feel of the doorknob, as though entering for the first time. Everything looked different in light of her new reality. Her mom and dad still sat at the kitchen table. *Daniel Tiger* echoed from the family room, keeping the twins at bay. And she was a Spuren.

"Elena, sit down," said her father. "Mom and I want to talk to you about something. We've noticed some changes in your behavior lately that are concerning to us for a number of reasons."

"What changes? I haven't seen any changes," Elena bluffed, sliding into a chair.

"Elena, we can't help but worry about you," her mom said, ignoring her comment. "I see so much bad stuff at work that I don't want anything bad to ever happen to you."

"But Mom," Elena interrupted, "nothing bad is happen—"

"Please, honey," her mom said, raising a hand. "Please just let us finish what we have to say."

Elena considered rolling her eyes, but she remembered the rules. Besides that, her mom was more freaked out than usual.

"Your behavior lately has been so out of the ordinary," she continued. "And it seemed to change abruptly. The chemistry lab incident, the trip to the hospital, your reaction to the engineering scholarship, the headaches—yes, I noticed the ibuprofen disappearing,—the exhaustion, spending so much time holed up in your room. For a while, I worried about drugs, but I don't think that's it. I'm right, right?" she asked.

Elena nodded. She barely had time to watch TV or go to a movie, let alone nurse a secret drug habit.

"So then, we start to worry about mental health. How do *you* think that your mood has been lately, Elena?"

Freaked out. Barely holding it together. Not sure who she was anymore. "Fine," she said. "I've just been super tired."

Her mom nodded. "You know that if you did ever start to feel really, really sad, you can come to us, right?"

Elena couldn't help it. She rolled her eyes and flopped back in her chair. Mom was being so dramatic.

Mom gave her a frustrated look and flopped back in her own chair.

"Elena, now that you're older, you need to know something," continued her father, patting her mom's leg under the table. "Mental illness runs in my family. Your Auntie Nell had severe depression and schizophrenia."

Elena glanced up, surprised, but not surprised.

"And her disease eventually killed her. She—-she died by suicide."

Elena felt tears well up in her eyes, seeing her dad struggle through the telling. She always knew this somehow, but now, it was official, another weird new reality to integrate.

He took a deep breath, glanced at her mom, and continued. "So, mental health is something that our family needs to be aware of, including you. If you *are* having problems, that's okay, we'll get through it. We just want to catch any issues early," he concluded.

"That's why Dad and I want you to see a mental health professional, just for a check-up," her mom said. "We want to make sure everything is functioning normally with your mood and thinking. Would you be willing to do that?"

For once, her dad was being honest about his family, and her mom was actually asking her opinion. This was progress! She longed to tell them that she wasn't mentally ill, rather mentally gifted. That not being an option, Elena developed a plan as she spoke, carefully choosing her words.

"Thanks for telling me about Aunt Nell," she said. "I always knew that something bad happened to her, but I was too afraid to ask what."

Her dad gave a sad smile of apology.

"But I don't think there's anything wrong with me. I'm not on drugs, I haven't joined a cult. I'm just super tired and glad for winter break. I don't think that a psychologist would find much wrong with me, so could I not?" Good speech.

"I appreciate your perspective, Elena," her mom said. "But sometimes when people are in the midst of a mood disorder, their symptoms can fool even them. That's what makes it so tricky."

"So, I don't really have a choice then?" Elena said sarcastically.

"It's just a single, hour-long appointment," her mom pleaded. "The therapist keeps everything you say confidential. You can speak freely to her about things going on in your life, things that maybe you can't speak to me or Dad about. Like boys, or friends, or…other people."

Elena was getting really worrisome vibes from her mom. "Okay, fine, whatever," she said, shrugging to signal that it was not really fine at all.

Her parents exchanged relieved glances. "Excellent," her mom said. "I managed to get you in with an adolescent psychologist on the 27th."

Elena was tempted to say something obnoxious about asking her permission, but again, she heeded Mary's advice. If she wanted to keep the appointment that really mattered, with Linda Kowalski, then she needed to remain perfect, compliant Elena.

"Sounds fine," she said, smiling through clenched teeth. "If you think it's best."

"Oh, honey. I do," Mom said. "Now come give us a hug."

Elena got up from her chair and joined in a familiar three-person hug. She felt guilty, though, because as she was hugging them, she was congratulating herself on another successful lie. She broke the hug first.

. . .

During the days before Christmas, the Tannins pretended like everything was normal. In between the rituals of baking, wrapping presents, and watching Christmas specials, Elena spent a lot of time in her room. Mary was right. Being alone helped, even more than ibuprofen. Now she understood that, by being alone in her room, she wasn't inadvertently picking up anyone's exhausting emotional energy.

To further assure her parents that all was well, Elena finally completed the application for the summer engineering institute. Even though there was no way she could do both that and Zedernwald, she still wanted to win it. She gave the lengthy application her best effort, writing a superb and overinflated essay.

Then she turned her academic focus on Spuren-ness. She quickly learned that the hardest thing about Aunt Mary's revelation was the lack of supporting documentation. Despite this, she remained tentatively convinced that being Spuren was better than being psychotic. When Elena thought she was having a mental breakdown, there were tons of alarming websites to read. In contrast, the word "Spuren" didn't appear in any of the medical texts that she smuggled upstairs. Numerous Google searches brought up only German to English dictionary translations of the word itself. If Aunt Mary was telling the truth, she was telling the whole truth: Spuren women communicated strictly through oral tradition, hiding in plain sight. It was all so magical, non-factual, and un-Elena-ish. If it was true, could she still be the same Elena?

. . .

The day before Christmas Eve, Elena waited by the door for Stephen's car. They were finally going on a date, just the two of them. She ran through conversation topics in her head: volleyball, the weather, next semester classes. She smiled, thinking of his dimples, when headlights cut through the darkness of five p.m. in wintertime Wisconsin.

"Bye! I'll be home by eleven-ish!" she yelled. Before Stephen had a chance to be polite and come to the door, she crunched to the passenger side and quickly got in. "Hi," she said, in a voice that felt loud in the small space.

"Hey," he said, producing a real-life dimple, and then he leaned over and gave her a kiss.

So, this was how it was going to be.

Stephen's car was a manual, and Elena babbled, "I never learned how to drive stick. I couldn't figure out what was going on with the clutch. Like, what is it actually doing?" Oh my god, how lame can I be?

"Have you ever tried to just listen to the car, rather than thinking so hard? Oh wait," he interrupted himself, "I forgot who I'm talking to!"

"Shut up!" Elena said, punching his arm, the physical form of blurting.

"Whoa, whoa!" Stephen laughed, grabbing her hand. "I have to be a safe winter driver, Elena!" He didn't let go, instead trapping her hand between his own and the gearshift. "Here, just listen to the car and feel when we need to shift, and we'll do it together. Okay?"

"Okay," said Elena. Her mind was blank. She was just a ball of feelings, focused on her left hand and his right hand.

They drove to the theater to see a Marvel movie. She wasn't a huge fan of action movies, but the only other choice was a teen romantic drama involving werewolves. Elena insisted on paying for the concessions after Stephen bought the tickets. She followed him into the theater, and he paused at the far-back row. She started to worry about the opinions of everyone else in the theater. "Oh my God, could we be more obvious?" she whispered to Stephen with raised eyebrows as they walked into the aisle.

"Nope." He grabbed her hand and pulled her into the darkest spot.

Elena took off her coat and settled the popcorn between their adjacent legs while the previews started. As soon as the lights went down, she felt the popcorn move.

Stephen set it on the floor. "I'm sorry," he whispered, "but I hope you don't mind waiting to eat. If I don't kiss you soon, I think I might go insane. Do you mind?"

Elena's eyes widened and, instead of answering, she reached behind his neck and pulled him down toward her. She must have moved too quickly, because their teeth clunked together. She started to say, "Sorry!", but Stephen sighed and gently brushed his lips against hers.

Gentle lasted a hot minute.

When they finally came up for air, it was the middle of a battle scene. Elena's lips were tingling and she learned a great deal about the intricacies of Stephen's mouth. She lifted his arm and ducked under it, tucking her feet under herself. They nested together nicely, with his height and her long legs.

"Listen," he whispered, tucking her curls behind her ear. "I'd really like to keep kissing you, but I'm also interested in the movie. Can we watch for awhile?"

"Yes," Elena said. "It kills me to see a movie, but not see a movie. Like when someone is talking or, well, whatever through the whole thing."

"Exactly," he replied, reaching down to retrieve the popcorn

"Fine," said Elena, feeling empowered. "But only if you promise to find somewhere quiet to park your car after."

"Oh, I've had it planned for days," he and his dimples replied.

Later, after parking in the empty lot behind Stephen's old elementary school, they pulled into Elena's driveway with ten minutes to spare. Their feet crunched in the super-frozen snow, and their breath clouds mingled in the air. She opened the outside door and Stephen followed her in. It was a little warmer inside the mudroom, and Stephen took the opportunity to take his hands out of his pockets and kiss her some more.

It felt wrong to be doing this next to the twins' snow boots. Elena couldn't completely enjoy herself, afraid that her parents waited on the other side of the door. But she still managed to enjoy it a little bit. Could kissing ever get boring?

"Hey," Stephen said, taking a step back. "I have a question. I'm wondering if you, uh, want to be my actual girlfriend? Not just hanging out? I know we've only gone out on, like, one and half dates, but-"

"Yes," said Elena, and jumped up to wrap her arms around his neck. The only thing in her mind at that moment was the sound of the wind howling outside and the smell of his neck. No voices. Blissful, joyous emptiness. She finally was joining the boyfriend club!

Inside, her mom slept on the couch, waiting for Elena. Some of her friends didn't even have to wake up their parents when they arrived home. Elena's mom waited downstairs and went from sound sleep to fully awake at the drop of a hat. She said that it was because of all those years wearing a pager as a resident.

"Hey, honey. How was the movie?" she asked. She folded the blanket and turned off lights, trailing Elena upstairs.

"Good," Elena said. How to tell her mom about this new reality? "So, Stephen and I are officially dating," she said.

"Like, you're an item?" her mom asked.

"Yeah, I guess. Weird, huh?"

"Not so weird. Probably just more of an adjustment for me than you," she said. "Night, honey. Love you." Her mom left her bedroom door open a familiar crack.

"Night, love you too," Elena said. Tucked in bed, she tingled reliving the events of the evening, whole simultaneously longing for a normalcy that was constantly shifting away under her feet.

New Reality
December 17—Amended December 23
- *Unmentionable Weirdnes →I am psychotic. → I am "Spuren"? (try to find out more about this.)*
- *My parents know almost everything. → My parents know absolutely nothing—I think.*
- *I have some sort of weird connection with Kat. → And it's that we both have a metaphysical gift. Fabulous.*
- *I might have my first boyfriend. → I definitely have my first boyfriend!!!!*

CHAPTER 26
KAT

Kat: Why am i being such a freak about this
Val: Cuz you hate change?
New people?
Getting out of your comfort zone?
Anything unpredictable?
Kat: K, thanks a lot so called BFF
Val: 🖤

Kat wandered between the rooms of her house. She couldn't remember the last time she was so nervous about someone coming over.

Okay, that was a lie; she could remember. The last time she was this nervous for people to come over was her fifth grade birthday party. That was before she became a Beautiful Person, back when Kayla was her best friend. Friend groups still eddied and swirled, not yet coalesced into the solid planets of the middle school universe. Mom made her invite all the girls in her class. She worried about what the girls would think of her house, her bedroom, and her non-store-bought birthday cake. That year, Mom flavored it with maple, which was weird, but not as bad as it could have been.

That was the first day that she noticed how her stomach pooched out in her bathing suit. It was a Slip and Slide party, and Mom took Polaroids of the girls posing. As newly eleven-year old Kat watched the row of squares come to life from their watery blackness, she noticed one girl's enviably knobby knees and another's prominent clavicles. Kat sucked in her tummy and didn't have any birthday cake. At least not then. She snuck some pieces off the end later.

Elena Tannin's long legs reminded her of the girls in the Polaroids. What would she think of, well, everything? Kat wandered to the kitchen and grabbed a sleeve of graham crackers to calm her nerves. She reminded her mom to make an organized list of things to tell Elena, to not overwhelm her. Kat learned about being Spuren slowly, over time, but Elena's education would be like drinking from a fire hose. But if anyone could handle a crash course, it was Elena Tannin.

Could Elena possibly be smart and pretty *and* nice? Her vibes were hard to read. She was friends with girls who were nice. Too nice. And then there was the way Elena went out on a limb during the dance to confront Kat about the way Ty treated her. That was nice.

"Seriously, Mom, this girl is smart," Kat said. "Do you know what you're going to talk about?"

Her mom stood at the counter with piece of paper, pulled a pencil out of her hair, and started writing. "Mary gave me some suggestions. I'll write them down, just to make you happy," she said. "Do you think I should frost the cake?" she asked, distracted.

Kat still marveled at the coincidence of Elena being not only Spuren, but related to Mary. Hopefully, Mary already gave Elena some guidance to supplement whatever Mom came up with. I wonder what she said? I wonder what Elena said?

She's gonna think we're crazy, thought Kat, crunching into another cracker with a milk chaser.

CHAPTER 27
ELENA

Worst case scenarios
1. *Kat realizes that I'm clueless about the whole Spuren thing*
2. *Kat thinks I'm a loser for even being interested*
3. *Kat has no idea what the Spuren actually are and I'm suffering from a very detailed delusion*
4. *The house is covered in candy and Kat's mom is an honest-to-goodness witch.*

"Okay if I go over to Kayla's house?" Elena asked, pulling on her coat. It was easier to lie about her destination than explain a new friend named Kat.

"Sure, have fun," her dad said.

Mom gulped her coffee and hastily added, "Don't be too long."

Whatever.

Once she was driving, Elena worried about the Kowalski meeting. She parked in front of the address Linda gave her, got out of the car, and tripped over the crumbling curb. She collected herself and made it to the doorbell intact. When Linda pulled it open, Elena automatically shifted into charm mode.

"Hi, Mrs. Kowalski. Nice to see you again," she said, flashing an adult-winning smile and reaching out her hand.

Linda smiled and stepped onto the porch, her purple palazzo pants ruffling in the brisk winter air. "Come it!" she said, pulling Elena into a hug.

Could a mother and daughter be less alike? "This whole thing has been a little weird, but I'm hoping that you and, um, Kat can help me figure it out," she said.

"What a surprise it was to find a Spuren hiding out in plain sight in our own town! It will be so good for Kat to have a friend close by," Mrs. Kowalski said. She led Elena inside and shut the door. "There's only so much that social media can do to keep her spirits up when she's away from Zedernwald."

Elena filed away the information. She smelled vanilla mixed with something that she couldn't pin down.

"I made a cake to celebrate," Mrs. Kowalski said, walking to the kitchen. "Why don't you two hang out for a bit while I finish cleaning up?"

Kat stood at the kitchen counter, half-smiling embarrassedly. "Hi, Elena," she said awkwardly. "Do you want some cake? We can eat it downstairs," she said.

She's as nervous as I am, Elena realized.

Kat glanced at a man in a recliner, watching football in the adjacent family room. "That's my dad, by the way. Just ignore him." She cut them both slices while she talked. "Come on." She handed Elena a fork and briefly made nervous eye contact.

"Thanks. Your house is nice," offered Elena, trying to break the ice.

"Do you really think so?" asked Kat. "This way. My room's in the basement. That way, Mom and I can each have our own space, if you know what I mean."

"Do you not get along?" asked Elena, following Kat down wood-paneled stairs into a similarly wood-paneled basement.

"We get along okay. It's just a bit too much Spuren-ish-ness in one house sometimes. I moved to the basement in eighth grade," said Kat.

"My mom drives me crazy and she isn't even, well, you know."

"But you still pick up on all her moods, though, right? I can always tell when the Packers lost. Dad's grumpiness is readable from the garage. At least we can't thought-read our families, though. That'd be a mess," Kat said drily.

"I was so afraid of that happening with my parents, I've been avoiding them. So, it won't happen? Thought-reading, I mean?" Elena asked, entering Kat's non wood-paneled bedroom.

"Nope. As long as you guys love each other, you somehow block out their inner voices. A relief, right?"

"I'm just relieved to kind of understand what's going on," Elena said, glancing around for somewhere to sit.

Kat arranged a beanbag chair with her feet. "I'm glad you could come over today, or I would have been dying of boredom." She plopped on her bed.

"Your mom seems nice. Her curly hair is pretty," said Elena, trying to copy Kat's apparent ease.

"I know, right? I've always been jealous. I have this stick-straight situation," she said, running a hand down what Elena considered hopelessly elegant black hair.

"Well, curly hair is dominant, so she must have been a non-curly carrier," Elena blurted.

"You are such a nerd!" laughed Kat. "I knew you were smart, but you're smart all the time, not just at school?"

Elena felt a flush of embarrassment creep up her neck.

"You're embarrassed to be smart? I never picked up on that from you. You shouldn't be, you know," said Kat. "Not that I'm one to talk about not being embarrassed." She took a big bite of cake.

Elena took her first bite and the two girls exchanged bewildered glances. The smell that Elena couldn't pin down declared itself: anise. They set aside the cake.

As they talked about kids at school, teachers, and TV shows, Elena realized that they actually had a lot in common. The biggest was their mutual love of Zedernwald. Kat explained about friends from camp and Elena described vacations spent with her family in the small Cottage. Elena greedily listened as Kat described being a Spuren camper at Zedernwald. Eventually, Elena said, "I feel like I'm learning so much about you all at once. It's almost overwhelming."

"This is what it's *always* like at Zedernwald. You can't be fake, not with everyone being Spuren," Kat explained. "I think that's why I was so bitchy to you at school. Before I knew you had the Talent, I could tell that you read me like a book. It scared me to death to not know why." Kat fiddled with the stitching on her bedspread.

"I still don't understand exactly what you're so scared of. I mean, you're smart, you have friends and boys who like you, you're pretty," Elena said.

Kat snorted. "Yeah, right. Well, why are you embarrassed about being so smart? Same thing."

It was Elena's turn to snort. She stretched out her legs and flopped backward, staring at the ceiling and a daddy longlegs in the corner. Kat copied her, and for a while, the room was filled with comfortable silence. The furnace in the adjacent room clunked to life, and the hum of forced air filled the silence.

"Hey," Elena eventually said. "How well do you know my Aunt Mary?"

"I've spent all summer at Zedernwald for the past four years, so I guess pretty well," she said, sitting up.

"Do they ever talk about family stuff?" Elena asked.

"Not really," Kat said. "They know our moms, and there's a mom and daughter week in July, but they don't really talk about their, er, your family. But we all know her and Sylvie pretty well."

Elena felt a surge of jealousy. "That kinda sucks," she said.

"Because you're her actual family, huh?" Kat correctly guessed.

"Yeah," said Elena. "Just because my dad doesn't like her, I had to miss out on this whole part my life. It's unfair."

"Yeah," said Kat, nodding. "But, Elena, I don't think you would've gone to Zedernwald, even if you *did* know Mary and Sylvie. Only daughters of Spuren moms go. Dads' families don't have anything to do with it."

"There's no other girls like me at camp?" asked Elena, already knowing the answer, but hoping nonetheless.

"Not that I know of."

"So, I'm a mutant."

"You seem about as normal Spuren as anyone I've met. If you can call us normal."

For some reason, this struck the girls as hilarious, and they burst out laughing.

"Girls?" Kat's mom called down the basement stairs, "I'm supposed to do some teaching, so why don't you come on up?"

Elena glanced nervously at Kat.

"Don't worry," Kat said. "She's so disorganized, there won't be a test. There probably won't even be a plan."

Mrs. Kowalski sat at the kitchen table with a piece of folded paper. Elena took a vinyl upholstered chair, and Kat sat between them like an interpreter. Elena glanced at the paper (she taught herself to read upside down long ago), and saw three things written in pencil: Electricity, Tempering, Milk.

"This isn't really my thing," Mrs. Kowalski began, "but, like Mary said, we just have to cover some basics, to keep you safe 'til summer. I wasn't sure what she meant by basics, so Kat gave me some ideas."

Kat and Elena exchanged smiles.

"Umm, okay, so, electricity," she continued. "I don't really know how electricity works, but I know the Talent has something to do with it. . ."

Elena shifted into helpful student mode. "Mrs. Kowalski? How about if I ask questions and you answer them," she suggested.

"Yes," she said. "Good. And, please, call me Linda." She took off her tortoiseshell reading glasses.

"So, the Talent is somehow connected to electricity?"

Kat and her mom both nodded.

"We can, um, 'pick up on' people's electricity?" Elena used air quotes; it sounded ridiculous.

"Yup," replied Mrs. Kowalski—Linda. "That's the best explanation we've got. How, exactly? Nobody knows. But we've figured out that electricity has something to do with it."

"I know this is killing you, Miss Top of the Class," Kat said.

"Tied for top," Elena corrected.

Kat glanced briefly at the ceiling. "Tied for top. But it's not totally ridiculous. I read somewhere that our brain produces enough electricity to run a light bulb."

Elena decided to address the "how" questions later. She wouldn't solve the mystery of her inheritance with Linda. Time to focus on the "how-tos." She recalled how her Talent roared uncontrollably to life in the commons during the power outage. "Is the Talent blocked by *actual* electricity," she asked, gesturing to the toaster.

Linda nodded. "Exactly. If electrical stuff is running, it kind of dulls the Talent. For example, around here, Kat's dad always has the TV on, there's computers, the appliances, so Kat and I don't have to do any significant Tempering at all. Our Talent is mostly muddled by electricity." She checked off an item on her list.

"Tempering. Is that how you sort of manage your Talent?"

"Yes. To get through certain situations, you have to Temper your Talent. And there's lots of ways to do it. Electricity is one that just sort of happens automatically," Kat said.

"Electrical interference can be a good thing, to help keep your mind clear without any effort," Linda continued, crossing off another item on her list. "But it can be a problem if you are trying to actually use your Talent. Does that make sense?"

"Kinda. The two times that the Talent overwhelmed me were in chem when we shut down the power for an experiment, and when a storm knocked out power to the building," Elena said, making connections out loud.

Kat nodded. "At school, the electricity everywhere makes us pretty normal. But that day when the power went out, my Talent overwhelmed me, too. I managed, cuz I know some Tempering," she said. "Also, everyone was so distracted by your drama that they didn't notice me freaking out in the corner."

"Happy to help," said Elena sarcastically. "I wonder if that's why I always feel so much better when I have my earbuds in, listening to music? I'm close to electricity, so my Talent is shut down?"

"Yes, definitely," said Linda. "Plus, a lot of us sense people's energy as voices and sounds."

"I hear voices too," Elena admitted nervously.

Kat nodded. "So, if you mostly *hear* your Talent, you can use other sounds to drown it out. That's Tempering. That and the yoga type stuff."

Her mom enthusiastically continued. "Yes, yoga. And, really, any mindfulness strategies work beautifully to Temper the Talent. Oh, it's just so much fun to learn about different practices that we can apply—"

"Mom. Seriously," Kat said, noticing Elena's eyes widen. "She just needs to know the basics today. 'Calm yourself, calm the Talent.'" She turned and made serious eye contact with Elena. "If it's getting to be too much, shut out the world the best you can, and just breathe," she said to Elena. "I keep everyone's emotions far away at all times, including my own. That's my best Tempering: freeze it all out constantly."

Elena looked at the friendly Kat sitting next to her and was uncomfortably reminded of the ice queen version that sauntered the halls of Belvedere High.

"A habit that we continue to discourage," her mom said, frowning.

Elena glanced away from the awkward disagreement and checked her phone.

Linda noticed and said, "So, let's just plan to meet on Sundays when we can. Starting after the break? And keep track of your questions to ask me. That's the way we all learn, by asking questions, although most of us just ask our moms." She started to stand up.

"Wait," Elena said. "Before I go, what about milk?"

"Milk?" Linda looked confused.

"Your list of things to talk to me about. Electricity, tempering, and milk," said Elena, pointing to the scrap of paper on the table.

"Oh, that! I was starting my grocery list. I'm not sure if you noticed, but I tend to be a little scatterbrained."

•   •   •

"Tell me more about that," the woman said. She sat in a comfortable chair in front of a bookcase filled with textbooks, diplomas, and family pictures. The version of the woman in the photos was about twenty years younger than the 60-something woman across from Elena. The same thin frame and dark bangs connected the therapist to the version of her in the pictures.

Elena carefully answered the therapist's questions. She fought an urge to drop her guard and blurt whatever came into her mind. Instead, she stayed focused and provided acceptable answers. Elena needed to both acknowledge a version of the truth without including any red flags. Her carefully rehearsed answers told a story that acknowledged her parents' concerns without admitting to anything really bad. She tried to sound neither psychotic nor Spuren, but somewhere in the angsty teenage middle. "More about the dance?" she countered. She already shared that she left with a headache, hoping it would be enough.

But Dr. Johnston clearly knew what she was doing. She sat back calmly in her chair, her long arms and legs folded like a probing sandhill crane. Occasionally, she jotted notes, but mostly, she nodded and prodded seductively. "Yes," Dr. Johnston agreed with a gentle smile, "and about how things are going with Stephen."

"He's my first boyfriend," Elena said. "It's just high school dating."

"What do your parents think of you dating?" she asked.

"I think that they're glad that I'm doing something normal," Elena said. Her answers described parents who were worried about her for no reason, other than Elena being a stressed-out teen. It was sort of true and sort of not, the best kind of lie.

"Mmm hmm…." Dr. Johnston nodded, taking off her glasses and focusing on Elena.

"They obviously don't want me spending every minute with him. I have to keep up with my work and activities and friends. And I suppose they're not super excited that I'm, um, getting closer to a guy."

"Yes, that can be difficult for parents. We run an adolescent health clinic out of these offices too, so keep that resource in mind. What do you think of your parents' concern that you are overwhelmed?"

Man, she's good, thought Elena. Not a "yes or no" question in sight. "I think they have a point," Elena said. "I was really tired and stressed out before break."

"How did your stress show itself?" she asked, resting her narrow face on her hand.

Be careful, thought Elena. Don't mention the voices. "I was really tired and getting headaches. And one time, I passed out at school because I was anemic. And I've been madder with my parents, especially my mom. But I managed to keep things under control, with school and stuff."

"How would you know that things have gotten out of control for you?" asked Dr. Johnston.

"I think I was pretty close to that point, to be honest," Elena said, sidestepping the question. "Luckily, my schedule next semester is a little easier. I need to be better about managing my time. And I probably need to find a better outlet for my stress than yelling at my mom."

"Do you have any outlets that work currently?"

"I play the piano, that helps. It's most relaxing to just be alone in my room. I know my parents get anxious when I spend too much time there."

"How do you tend to feel when you are around a large group of people? Does it energize you? Drain you?"

Not sure where she's going with this one, thought Elena. "I like to hang out with my friends, but some days, I'd rather just be alone with a book. My friends get it. My parents used to understand, but they've just gotten so hover-y lately!" Elena said.

"Why do you suppose that is?" she asked, rearranging her legs.

"They're probably afraid I'm on drugs or talking to a pedophile online or becoming a sexual deviant or going crazy or something," said Elena, rolling her eyes. "They watch too much *Dateline*."

"What do they say when you talk about these concerns?" asked Dr. Johnston.

"Well, they just recently told me about my dad's sister killing herself, so there's that."

Dr. Johnston nodded. "Yes, your mother included that information in your paperwork. What do you know about schizophrenia?"

Elena knew a lot, but she decided to fake ignorance. "Isn't that like split personalities?" she asked.

"Not exactly," Dr. Johnston said, temporarily replacing her glasses to lecture. "When poorly controlled, a person with schizophrenia has difficulty distinguishing reality from tricks being played by their mind. Sometimes these tricks take the form of seeing things or hearing things that aren't really there. So, to that end, I just want to ask a few questions that I ask of anyone who comes in with a family history such as yours," she finished, picking up her pencil.

Elena nodded, trying to keep her face neutral. Here it comes.

"Have you ever heard a voice speaking to you that no one else does? This is different from talking to yourself in your mind."

Oh man, have I ever. I've heard voices of my friends and voices from their own minds of people that I've never met. I have a whole antenna's worth of voices being picked up when I least expect it—"Nope, never."

"Does anything unusual seem to be happening, or have you thought that strange things are happening around you or to you?" asked the good doctor empathically.

Like learning that I'm part of a secret society of women with super mind powers? Or talking to my frenemy through some sort of ESP? Like that sort of unusual? –"Uh-uh, nope."

"And have you worried that something really bad might happen to you? Or that people are planning to turn against you in some way?" Dr. Johnston asked.

You mean, like the entire group of the Beautiful People? Or my parents? Or my teachers? Or myself? "I mostly worry about my grades, if that's what you mean," Elena answered. "And my parents getting in a car accident or something happening to my brother or sister. Stuff like that."

"Thank you, Elena. I know those questions can be a bit heavy," the doctor said, leaning back into her chair, replacing her glasses on the top of her head.

Whew, Elena thought. If I hadn't learned about being Spuren, I don't know what I might have said.

Toward the end of the appointment, Dr. Johnston brought in Elena's mom.

"Elena is a delightful young woman," Dr. Johnston began, "who is under an inordinate amount of stress. Given our society and her own expectations, much of this is something to be managed, rather than eliminated."

"Yes," her mom nodded, "I'm sure some of my drive has worn off on her."

"Interesting," said Dr. Johnston noncommittally. "I don't recommend any medications at this time, but I would like to see Elena back every two weeks or so. In the meantime, I've given her some papers to read and asked her to begin journaling. We can discuss any insights or themes that emerge at our next visit."

Mom looked pleased. We do love homework, thought Elena.

The two women confirmed the details of Elena's next appointment, and soon she was alone with her mom in the elevator.

"So, how'd it go?" her mom asked.

"Fine. I liked her," lied Elena. She didn't dislike the psychologist, exactly.

"I'm glad. It's sounds like she's not concerned about any issues like Aunt Nell had," her mom said.

"Yup," Elena replied. "Just normal teenage stress."

Her mom should have looked relieved, but she fiddled with the clasp of her bag and pursed her lips the way she did when she was worried. The atmosphere in the elevator was thick with tension. What more did she have to worry about?

•   •   •

Elena wasn't excited about Dr. Johnston's journaling assignment, but she always did her homework. She used her current list notebook, which was teal. Even though Dr. Johnston reassured her that she would never ask to see the notebook, she was careful to write neatly. Just like she was careful to write anything Spuren-related in a double-substitution code, thereby skirting the "don't write anything down" rule, she figured. Her journal alternated between indecipherable code, indecipherable train of thought lists, and now perfectly neat therapeutic insights.

Here goes, she thought. Let's see what amazing insights I've been keeping from myself.

Prompt #1: I wonder . . .

- *I wonder how Kat will act when we get back to school? Will we talk to each other sometimes? Or should I pretend that everything is the same as it was before?*
- *I wonder how Stephen will act when we get back to school? Will we make out by my locker? Will everyone be able to tell that we're dating? Will we be one of those couples?*
- *I wonder how the Herd will act, now that I have a boyfriend and Kat? Will they be able to tell that everything has changed? Or has everything really changed at all? I can't let Kayla feel left behind. I can't let them think that I am friends with Kat over them. I can't let Kat think that I'm friends with Kat over them...*
- *I wonder what I'm going to do about that Engineering Institute and Zedernwald? Maybe I won't even be accepted to the Engineering thing. I hope that the decision somehow gets made for me and that I can avoid disappointing anyone. Disappointing Mrs. V would not be the end of the world. Kayla really deserves to be her golden child, not me.*

Revelation: I hate math.

CHAPTER 28
MEGHAN

It was four o'clock and Meghan still had a few more slides to review before she could leave, followed by several hours' worth of charting after the kids went to bed. Luckily, the medical students were still on winter break, and she could complete her work without stopping to teach at the multi-headed microscope. It would still be dark and frigid when she left for the day, though.

She enjoyed teaching, but some days, she envied her colleagues in the non-academic world. They could quickly complete their work without finding teachable moments to bestow. As a rule, medical students were eager to learn and, perhaps more importantly, eager to prove their eagerness. Medical training was all about proving yourself to the person next-highest in the chain of command, in order to eventually become that next person.

Elena really would make an excellent medical student, Meghan thought, not for the first time. She's so good at convincing teachers of her interest in everything, whether she actually enjoys it or not. She instinctively knew how to butter up the right adults. Which was why the business with Aunt Mary didn't fit. Great Aunt Mary was only a footnote in the family tree, not an adult from whom Elena would derive any benefit. So why did she lie, and then stare at the old woman with such rapt attention, that morning in the Starbucks?

And what of Mary's response to her own warning letter? It was prompt, polite, written in Palmer-method script, on stationery decorated with bowling pins and the phrase, "Let the good times roll."

Dear Meghan,

So nice to hear from you after all these years. Yes, I had the pleasure of sharing a coffee with Elena the other day. We were recently re-introduced by a mutual friend. While I happened to be in the area, I thought it would be nice for Elena to learn something about our family history, since I know that there were a lot of bridges burned after my sister's passing. I do apologize for meeting with her without your knowledge; I should have confirmed that she told you. In the future, should we have occasion to meet again, I will insist that she let you know where she is going! Deceitfulness in adolescents is a bad habit not to be tolerated. That's what I always say to Sylvie at least once a summer at camp. All the best to Anders and the children,

"Aunt Mary"

Except for the unfortunate use of quotation marks around the signature, it was something that Meghan herself might write. But the letter raised as many questions as it answered. Mostly, who was this "mutual friend" that somehow crossed paths with both Elena and Mary? And why didn't Elena tell her and Anders where she was going? And how was she going to bring this up to Elena now, weeks after the fact?

The Aunt Mary situation was a snag in the otherwise nicely resolving Elena situation. The psychologist was reassuring in her lack of concern for depression or worse. Elena submitted her application for the engineering institute. Her moods were better, there were no more fainting or hearing things episodes, the medicine bottles remained full. All seemed mostly quiet on the Elena front.

Except for Aunt Mary and, of course, the boyfriend. Meghan tended an ember of smoldering concern about Stephen, sparked by a pamphlet that Dr. Johnston thrust in her hand, startlingly titled, "Adolescent Sexual Health: A Family Approach."

CHAPTER 29
KAT

It was depressingly dark by 4 p.m. the evening before school resumed, and Kat still had a lot of things to get straightened out. She had to polish up the icy attitude that kept her Talent in check. Emotional frigidity was the most basic Tempering method, one that most girls quickly moved past. Not Kat. To progress beyond freezing out one's emotions, one had to actually listen to their inner feelings, but Kat wasn't interested in learning to love herself.

After that, she had to address a whole list of Ty-related problems. The night of the dance, Kat simply disappeared without telling him. She got a ride home from a neighbor, talked to Val, called Mary, and shut off her phone. Ty sent texts all night, demanding to know where she was and what she was thinking. Kat awoke to 143 messages from him, each more unhinged than the last.

On Val's advice, she blocked his number and ignored his attempts to contact her through other apps. She changed the subject when any of her Beautiful friends tried to figure out what was going on with them. But she couldn't ignore Ty when he showed up at her house the week after Christmas, and her dad invited him in to watch football. She was furious that Dad made this decision without asking, but he and Ty watched Packer games together regularly, and she hadn't told her dad that anything was up with her boyfriend. Mom knew that something happened between them, of course, but not the details. No one knew the details.

Once Ty was inside, Kat tried to avoid him, but he moved through the house with confident free rein, eventually cornering her in the laundry room. "Babe, I'm so sorry, it was all a misunderstanding," he whispered, pulling her insistently to his muscled body. "I miss you. I love you so much. Please forgive me." He pulled a jewelry box out of his pocket.

Kat felt herself melting under the pressure of his affection and eventually leaned into him. She popped open the velvet box, revealing a pair of minuscule diamond earrings.

"Merry late Christmas," he whispered into her hair. "Jewels for my queen."

It was so corny, but Kat couldn't resist. He really did love her after all! It really was a misunderstanding. He really was going to be better from now on. "They're beautiful," she whispered.

"Not as beautiful as you, babe," he said and lifted her up onto the washing machine for an epic make-out session, their privacy assured by the ongoing play-by-play announcement from the family room. Dad never left his chair during a Packer game.

She eventually followed Ty downstairs, free from the "no boys in the bedroom" rule by virtue of her mom's absence and her dad's fervent fandom. She remained intoxicated by Ty and the promise of better days to come. It wasn't until her bra landed on the beanbag chair next to the bed that the spell was broken.

Annoyingly, she thought of Elena, who just days before, sat on that beanbag chair. She remembered the things Elena said to her in the bathroom that night of the dance. That even though she was his girlfriend, he didn't get to maul her whenever he wanted. That she, Kat, was actually pretty, and that Ty wasn't doing her some kind of favor by being her boyfriend.

Elena's insistent voice was joined by those of Val and her other Zedernwald friends, reminding her that she had to love herself first. And then came the echoes of the times Ty called her fat, ugly, stupid. All the voices rang with crystal, Spuren clarity.

Kat felt suddenly sickened by Ty's mouth on her. A fire rose in her chest, and she got brave. She stood up and grabbed for her sweatshirt. "Stop, Ty. It's not happening," she insisted, pulling it over her head, inside out.

"Jesus Christ, Kat, you've become a real tease," he said. He grew visibly angry as he ran his fingers through his hair.

"No, Ty, I'm just not interested in this anymore," she said, stumbling toward the door.

"But, babe, I love you," he purred, reaching for her, changing tack with the skill of an experienced sailor. "You're so gorgeous, I can't resist you."

"You can't pretend that all the awful things you've said and done to me just disappeared," she said, grabbing the doorknob like a life preserver.

"I told you I was sorry. You pushed me over the edge that night of the dance," he whined, walking toward her. "C'mon, babe, you gotta forgive me. We're a couple, this is what couples do. Fight and then make up," he said, stroking her cheek.

"No," Kat choked, struggling with the doorknob against her sweaty palms. "And to be clear, I don't want to be a couple anymore,"

"You were sure acting like it a minute ago," Ty said.

"Well, I'm taking it back," Kat said, finally getting the door open and walking toward the stairs, a shirtless Ty in her wake. "I'm finally in my right mind."

"Dammit, Kat, you can't keep leading me on like this," Ty said, raising his voice.

Kat felt her resolve slipping as Ty crushed her in an embrace against his gorgeous chest. She looked past him and caught sight of a bit of her artwork, framed on the basement wall. It was a collage of photos from camp, along with the cringy phrase, 'Girl Power!', spelled out in macaroni and glitter. The incongruity of it all was ridiculous, and Kat began to laugh wildly.

"No, you don't get it," Kat said, laughing and crying at the same time. "It's not happening tonight, it's not happening ever, because I'm ending things with you." In a sudden fit of strength, Kat shoved Ty toward the stairs. Her voice grew progressively louder. "Stop calling, stop messaging me, stop showing up at my house!"

The door at the top of the stairs opened, and her dad peered down from above, a fresh beer in his hand.

He only left his chair to replenish his Miller Lite.

"Everything all right?" he asked. His eyes widened as he took in the scene of a contraband, shirtless boy in the basement, with a furious, disheveled Kat shoving him away. She knew how it must have looked, and she couldn't have loved her dad more when he said, "Tyler, I think you need to leave. Now."

Powerless in the face of a more dominant man, Ty's shoulders drooped. He trudged, defeated and half-naked, up the stairs, grabbed his jacket and rushed out through the garage.

"Honey, I *never* want to see a scene like that again," her dad said, ignoring a touchdown from the next room. "Because I'm too old to go to prison, and I'd kill the asshole." He held her shoulders and forced awkward eye contact. This was as affectionate as he got.

"Don't worry, Dad. He won't be coming around here again," Kat said.

"You don't have to put up with crap like that from anyone. Ever," he said, pulling her into an Old Spice scented hug. Kat rested on his sweatshirt, and neither seemed in a hurry to break the embrace. She remembered falling asleep on his belly during countless Sunday afternoon football games during her younger years, before she deemed herself too big.

•   •   •

While Kat banished Ty from her house and phone, she would still have to see him at school. As she went back and forth about how this might play out, Bailey called. Automatically, Kat swiped across her friend's perfectly made-up face.

"Hey," Kat said.

"Hey. Soooooo I just was actually messaging Ty, and he mentioned that he broke up with you! I can't believe it, and why didn't you tell me?"

"He said he broke up with *me*? Not quite. I ended things with him a few days ago. Sorry I didn't say anything, I was still processing."

"Oh, he made it sound like it was pretty one-sided. That's what he's saying in the group chat…"

"Wait, which group chat?" Kat asked, growing concerned.

"Oh, this one with some random people he's on. Of course, since you aren't on it to stick up for yourself, I knew I needed to talk to you!"

"Um, thanks? It's true that we're not together anymore, I wasn't dumped, if that's what he's saying." Controlling the narrative was vital.

"Do you want me to say anything? Before people start spreading rumors?" Bailey asked, a delicate worry line forming between her perfectly arched brows.

"What kind of rumors, exactly?" Kat asked, her stomach sinking.

"Oh, hon, I totally don't believe it. None of us do. But he's saying that you cheated on him."

"What?"

"And that's the reason that you didn't leave the dance with him, cuz you left with some other guy."

"That's crazy. I mean, you saw me at the dance. I was a mess! I got a ride home with my neighbor, and that was it," Kat said.

"Totally. Totally. I know. I'll start spreading the truth."

Bailey continued to talk, and Kat made sounds like she was listening. In reality, her mind was racing. If people thought that Ty broke up with *her*, then they'd want to talk about her feelings. She kept her Talent Tempered by not *having* any feelings. Usually, the superficiality of the Beautiful girls was an adequate defense, but they swarmed to a breakup like vultures.

She had to do damage control with all the breakup voyeurs tonight, from the safety of home. Nobody needed to know about the real reasons that she broke up with Ty, but they should know that it wasn't his idea. They should definitely know that she didn't cheat with her neighbor,

Chris fricking Nolte, who she knew since they were toddlers. He was just the car freak next door, not exactly cheating material. She opened her phone and got to work. It was exhausting, and she briefly speculated on how impossible it would be to ever tell anyone what really happened with Ty that night at the dance. They barely believed that the breakup was mutual.

Kat was so busy running Ty damage control that she forgot to talk to one other key person: Elena Tannin. She remembered in the middle of the night when she woke up from an unnerving dream involving all her teeth falling out. Crap. I hope she doesn't plan to try and be friends at school.

CHAPTER 30
ELENA

<u>First day 2nd semester worst case scenarios</u>
1. *Spiraling*
2. *Stephen into PDA*
3. *Too many friends @ lunch*
4. *Nothing else! Everything fixed!*

Elena sat behind the wheel of the Civic and watched the clock on the console move toward 7:35, giddy with excitement. She idled the car to keep out the January wind. In the mostly empty parking lot, dry snow eddies swirled in the breeze like a troupe of skaters on freshly laid ice.

She reviewed her plan to Temper her Talent at school. Elena researched and practiced some of the mindfulness techniques that Mrs. Kowalski recommended. A few days ago, she went to the grocery store and tested herself. She imagined shoppers' emotional energies wafting past, like the trail of perfume left in someone's wake. And just like learning to inwardly hold her nose against noxious scents, she practiced blocking out these intrusive emotional clouds, using deep breaths, calm, and visualization.

She had another date that Sunday for more Learning with Linda, as Kat's mom wanted to call it. Elena didn't like to call adults by their first names, but things were more casual at the Kowalskis'. Was it like that with all Spuren women? Elena wouldn't know until summer. Mary sent her and Linda an email, saying that it would be best if she, Mary, stayed out of things for a while, something about not wanting to cause familial strife. Linda and Kat would be her only Spuren contacts for now.

Elena couldn't wait to see Stephen. Would her teachers notice that they were dating? She hoped that this wouldn't make them think that she was a less serious student. She liked that Stephen was serious about school too.

And what about Kat? Elena was pretty sure they were starting to be friends. They messaged every day, Kat always checking to make sure that Elena was doing okay with her Talent. Kat taught Elena to use the word "Spiral" for when the Talent drowned you with emotion. Too much Spiraling led to all sorts of problems, like headaches and exhaustion. She confirmed that Elena probably was in a low-level Spiral for a while before Christmas. When Kat Spiraled, she sometimes needed to be talked down, usually by her mom or her friend, Val.

Elena had an annoying twang of jealousy when Kat told her about Val, because she briefly hoped that she could be Kat's closest Spuren friend. Plus, Elena was simply jealous of all the Zedernwald girls. She envied their head starts, their camaraderie, and their mothers who knew what to do when they Spiraled, instead of taking them to psychiatrists.

Elena flipped the radio to Top 40, zipped her keys in her backpack, and exited. By starting her crunching walk just then, her entrance was perfectly timed. She would have enough time to stop at her locker and arrive in the commons just after Stephen did.

Chris was already there, with his usual bag of Kwik Trip food. His legs were a bloodless white, despite the warm building, since Chris was one of those guys who wore shorts year-round.

"Santa didn't bring you any pants for Christmas?" Elena asked.

"Nope," Chris said. "But he kicked in a few bucks and look what I bought." He showed her a picture of a massive old car without tires.

"Um, nice?" Elena said. "Is it drivable?"

"Hell no," he replied, putting his phone in his pocket. "But eventually, she'll look like that." He pointed to a second picture duct-taped to his locker. The sleek car bore a passing resemblance to the one on his phone.

"Are you going it fix it up by yourself?" Elena asked.

"Yup," Chris said.

"That's amazing. I can't imagine being able to do something like that," Elena said, genuinely awed.

Pride radiated off Chris.

"Good thing you still had your old car at the dance," Elena said. "Kat really needed a ride home that night."

"It was no big deal," said Chris.

Elena detected a hint of embarrassment wafting off of him and tuned in to that feeling while he spoke.

"I was just there, checking it out. And since I live next door to her, it wasn't out of my way or anything."

He downplayed himself, a shift from the pride of the previous moment. Interesting. "I know it helped her out," Elena said as she walked away.

Her heart thudded against her binder as she entered the commons, clueless about how to behave. She was playing the part of a girlfriend without a script, with nothing but the example of peers and TV to follow for cues. For a moment, she irrationally feared that Stephen would jump up, sweep her over his shoulder, and carry her away.

Of course, that didn't happen. Elena said hi to Kayla and sat between her and Stephen. She wanted to make it clear that, even though she was part of a couple, her friends were still a priority. She felt Stephen's hand on the small of her back, and suddenly understood why women of her mom's generation felt compelled to get tattoos there. Of course, I'm not in this alone, we're a team. A team who communicates through searing-hot touches.

Elena tried to catch Kat's eye all day, but Kat avoided her. Elena alternated between worrying that she did something to piss Kat off, and reassuring herself that Kat actually looked very preoccupied. Elena was anxious to corner her before English and was in her seat before Kat arrived. Kat breezed into the room with seconds to spare.

"Hey," Elena greeted in what she thought was a neutral voice.

Kat gave her a tight-lipped smile and widened her eyes as though trying to communicate something before turning to face the front. Elena squinted at Kat's black hair and encountered just as impenetrable a wall she had on the first day; she was totally blocked. Weird.

CHAPTER 31
KAT

Kat: call when able
E.T.: is something wrong?
E.T.: u were avoiding me all day
Kat: np call ltr

Kat walked the several blocks to and from school that day. Chris offered to drive her, but she didn't want to stir anything up. Her late-night social media marathon worked, and the Beautiful People abandoned the gossip that Ty dumped Kat because she cheated on him. Some of the BP offered her rides too, but she needed a break from their attepmpts to mine her breakup for emotional ore.

She guessed that Elena would have given her a ride, but Kat avoided her all day. Elena kept sending up psychic Spuren flares across the crowded school hallways, and Kat worked hard to dodge them. This was what she was afraid of.

She hadn't felt this emotionally drained since sixth grade, after her periods started and her Talent switched on practically simultaneously. She was too embarrassed to tell her mom about either thing, despite years of preparation. Kat spent months with headaches and exhaustion before Mom caught on and forced her to learn some basic Tempering. And showed her how to use tampons. In the meantime, her unbridled Talent led her to misread Kayla and drop her as a friend, fearing the emotions she read from Kayla.

She wasn't about to let Elena ruin her carefully balanced situation. To be fair, it wasn't Elena's fault; Kat forgot to warn her that nothing could change at school. Besides, she wasn't sure whether she wanted an actual friendship with Elena Tannin. Kat distrusted willowy people. Could someone possibly be skinny *and* smart *and* a good friend? It seemed unlikely. She didn't know where she stood with Elena Tannin, but she needed to set some ground rules about school. Elena needed to call her back ASAP.

She called while Kat was doing homework. Kat sighed, anticipating an awkward conversation.

"Hey," Kat said.

"Hey," Elena said. "I got your messages and decided it would be better if we talked in person. I'm outside."

Well then. "All right," Kat said, walking upstairs. "Hold on a sec." As she passed through the kitchen, she told her mom, "Elena Tannin's here."

"Invite her to dinner! We're having bulghur salad!"

"Hey, Elena," Kat said, opening the front door to a blast of cold air.

Elena stamped her feet and stepped in, removing her boots in the entryway. "It's so cold, my eyelashes are frozen," she said, laughing.

"I hate winter," Kat said flatly.

"Hi, Elena!" her mom called. "How was the rest of your break?"

"Fine, Mrs. Kowalski," Elena answered.

"It's Linda, remember?" her mom said.

"Linda, we're going downstairs," Kat said.

"Nice to see you again," Elena said as Kat practically pushed her down the carpeted stairs.

"Be careful," Kat said, "or you'll be forced to stay for dinner. It's bulghur salad night."

"I've never had that," Elena said, sitting in the beanbag chair that was somehow already her designated spot. "My dad does the cooking, and he is more of a 'three piles of food' kind of a guy."

"Three piles of food?" Kat asked, forgetting to be aloof.

"A meat pile, a veggie pile, and a carb pile."

Kat laughed. Dammit, she's funny too.

"So, what do you want to talk about?" Elena asked. "Are you mad at me?"

"No," Kat said, shifting awkwardly on her unmade bed. "How do I say this…I need you to keep everything the same at school."

Elena looked confused. "What, like, not talk to you?"

"Yes, I mean, kind of," Kat said, slammed by Elena's hurt feelings.

"Okaaaay," Elena said, blinking quickly. "I'm sorry if I threaten your reputation, I guess?"

"It's not that," Kat said. "It's just that—Elena, the only way I can *be* at school is to be that version of me."

"A Beautiful Person, you mean?" Elena asked, her voice dripping with sarcasm.

"Yes. A 'Beautiful' Person," Kat answered, making air quotes. "I know I'm not beautiful. And I know I'm not totally like Bailey and all of them. But I have to keep my emotional stuff locked up in boxes. I—I don't know how to Temper my Talent any other way."

"How is that possible? You've been learning for years," Elena said, morphing from sad to irritated.

"Learning the ideas, yeah, but—I just can't do it. It's hard to explain."

"Try me," Elena said, folding her arms. "Explain to me how someone with all your advantages gets a free pass when I'm over here, stumbling through. You're a lifelong Spuren, faking being a bitchy, popular girl. Maybe you just want the best of both worlds?"

"That's harsh, Elena," Kat said.

"Well, it hurts when you forbid me from speaking to you in public. Am I really that bad?"

"No. It's me. I'm the problem," Kat said. "Look, it was fun hanging out with you over break, and I know it'll be great hanging out over the summer, but I just can't at Belvedere."

"You make it sound like I'm your secret girlfriend," Elena said.

"That's a little dramatic, don't you think?" Kat said, accidentally quoting her mom. "We can still talk on the phone and stuff, and you'll still be over here for lessons with my mom…"

"But I should probably park a block away and come in through the back door."

"Elena, come on. I still want to be your friend. I'm just asking you to help me out at school. It's not you, it's me."

"This is the weirdest break-up ever," Elena said.

"I'm *not* breaking up with you as friends," Kat insisted. "I'm just asking you to keep it on the down low."

"Well, you have to at least try to Temper better," Elena said.

"Okay, I'll try," Kat said, raising her hands in surrender. If that's what it took to maintain some kind of pseudo friendship with Elena, she was willing to try.

"Fine. And, I guess, I'll pretend I don't know you. Maybe it would be easier if we didn't hang out, even when I'm here to meet with your mom. I wouldn't want to accidentally ruin your cover," Elena said.

"I guess I deserved that," Kat said, feeling about a millimeter tall.

"I have to get to a piano lesson. Bye, Kat," Elena said, leaving the room with a sad smile.

"Bye."

It's for the best, Kat thought. The BP would eat Elena alive, it's for her own good. Okay, fine, and my own good. She has no idea how hard it is for me. She acts like she enjoys being in her own head. She must actually like herself. Weird.

CHAPTER 32
ELENA

January smeared into February with halfhearted gray days punctuated by freak snowstorms. The snow was no longer charming. Instead, fresh layers built up on old piles darkened with grime. The whole breakup or whatever it was with Kat added to the grimy feeling.

Experimenting with her Talent was a welcome diversion. As Elena gradually learned to modulate her Tempering, manageable bits of Talent-derived information became welcome parts of her day-to-day reality. She began to differentiate the unique energies of some people from the general background thrum. Kayla was a pinging, blushing pink sensation; The Man was an eggplant drumbeat. She couldn't sense anything from her parents or the twins, but Linda explained that was normal within families.

The other bright spot was Stephen, whose mood never seemed to dip below buoyant. Now that volleyball was over, they could hang out most weekends. Because the weather was so gross, they mostly stayed in and streamed movies at his house, which was perfect.

Stephen was the youngest of three boys. Both of his older brothers were at college, and his parents seemed to be gone a lot, checking in on his oldest brother in Madison. When they were around, they were pretty hands-off. After exchanging a few pleasantries, they left Stephen and Elena alone. Her house was the opposite. Between the twins and her parents, someone was always popping a head into the family room.

His family lived in an older home that was gracious without being fussy. Even though only Stephen remained at home, the remnants of multiple teenage boys persisted. A TV sat across from a well-loved blue couch, in a room just off the side entry that everyone used instead of the front door. Once his parents were in for the night, Stephen and Elena were sure of having that room to themselves without interruptions. It was very nice.

Okay, nice was an understatement. Making out with Stephen was her new favorite hobby. Occasionally, Elena paused long enough on the blue couch to wonder about her Talent, or lack of Talent, actually. While she received plenty of other sensory input from him (his smell was especially nice), she never picked up anything from her Talent sense. And she should have been able to, since there were no barriers in place. She was too preoccupied to be bothered with Tempering, the lights were usually off, and they were certainly in physical contact. But she never sensed anything beyond the physical from him! Not that there was anything wrong with the physical.

She added this question to her growing list, but felt too awkward to ask Linda about it. She obviously couldn't ask Kat. Every Sunday, Elena made the now-familiar drive to the Kowalskis', telling her parents a series of innocuous lies to keep it believable. She looked forward to the meetings, both because they allowed her to cross questions off her list, and because Linda was a calming person to be around. Still, she felt nervous every time she rang the doorbell, but fortunately, Kat never answered. While the obvious avoidance hurt, Elena eventually accepted that the situation kind of made sense; it protected Kat and her both. After all, what would the Herd say about her hanging out with a Beautiful Person?

She had an idea what they'd say. During lunch on the first day back in January, Elena blurted something about talking with Kat over break, and things got weirdly quiet. Addison messaged her immediately after school to get the whole story, and Elena concocted a lie about she and Kat taking the same yoga class. Later, Addison called to let Elena know where her loyalties should lie.

"In elementary, Kat and Kayla were best friends," Addison said. "Then, in sixth grade, Kat dropped her for no reason, completely cut her off, and Kayla was all alone for a year. When she finally became friends with us and told us the story, we agreed that Kat was dead to us."

Message received. No friendship with Kat Kowalski.

In contrast, Elena's and Kayla's friendship was common knowledge, among students and teachers. Mrs. Vickers held Elena back after calculus one day, pointedly telling Kayla to go on ahead.

"I have good news, Elena," Mrs. Vickers said. "You've been accepted to the institute!"

"Thanks!" said Elena, automatically happy to win. Then she remembered the conflicts. "When do I have to let them know by?" she asked.

"Let them know by?" the teacher repeated, her coral-smeared lips falling.

"Whether I plan to go."

"Is there a chance that you won't?" she asked.

"I'm not 100%," Elena said.

"I wish I'd known that, Elena, or I might have made a different choice."

"What do you mean?" Elena asked.

"The University changed its policies and is allowing only one student per school. They had both you and Kayla ranked quite highly, so they asked me to choose between you."

"That doesn't seem fair . . ."

"It is unusual. However, they valued my observations of your work in my class. They are looking for people who work well in groups, so I chose you as the more outgoing."

"Did you tell Kayla?"

"No, and I'll hold off for now," Mrs. Vickers said, annoyed. "Please tell me by the end of the month if you decide not to accept, as I think the spot would still be available for her. That being said, I really think this would be good for you, given your desire to pursue biomedical engineering."

"Yes, definitely. It's really good news," said Elena, realizing that Mrs. Vickers must have read her biomedically-embellished application essay. "My parents will be excited."

"They should receive an email today. Congratulations again," the teacher said, moving toward the door.

Maybe the email would go to their spam folder and Elena could just not tell them, at least while she figured out what she wanted. Just add it to the growing list of parental omissions.

•   •   •

By February, Elena was relaxed heading into her every-other-week visit with Dr. Johnston. She carried her notebook, in case the therapist wanted to see evidence of her work. Dr. Johnston reassured her that she never would read her journal, but Elena brought it along to demonstrate her overachievement.

Between the journaling and her Talent, she was realizing all sorts of new things about people. For example, Mom was oblivious to people's feelings unless told of them directly. Elena noticed that her dad adapted to this, and frequently gave her mom little updates about himself and the kids. Elena began providing her with tons of "I'm okay" data, too. She fed her a steady diet of good grades and friend updates. It seemed to help keep her off Elena's back.

She was surprised that the journaling thing worked. She always knew that lists were her thing; years of filled notebooks couldn't be wrong. Now, the free-flowing words led to new insights, which she committed to memory in case the teacher, er, therapist, asked for a report.

The appointment went well, and Elena anticipated that, when her mom came in at the end of her session for and update, she and the psychologist would agree that everything remained great with Elena. No changes, no tests, see you in a couple weeks.

"Ladies," said Dr. Johnston, "I've enjoyed getting to know both of you over the past couple of months."

Elena and her mom exchanged satisfied smiles.

"And I think that this is a good opportunity for you to be honest with each other."

Elena looked up in confusion, her mom's face mirroring her own.

"I suspect you both are holding back regarding recent events," she said with a disappointed look.

Elena squirmed, unaccustomed to disappointing authority figures.

"It's normal for mothers and daughters to begin leading very separate lives during adolescence. However, for you to move toward a more mature version of your relationship, you must learn to communicate even uncomfortable feelings. I am not here to judge or take sides, merely to facilitate. Why not take advantage of the moment?" She looked encouragingly over her glasses between the two. "Meghan? I believe that you have some concerns about Elena's friend that she had coffee with?"

"Ummm," her mom said awkwardly.

Elena felt defensive. "Who, Kayla? Stephen?"

"No, honey, not them," her mom said. "Dr. Johnston, I don't appreciate being put on the spot like this . . . "

"I imagine so."

Her mom sighed. "Elena, do you remember the day after your winter dance?"

"Yeah…" replied Elena, beginning to panic.

"You went out to meet some friends for coffee, right?"

Elena nodded, blood pounding in her ears.

"I went through the Starbucks drive-thru and saw you there. And I know you weren't with friends."

Elena froze, her mouth sawdust-dry. Mom spied on her?

"I saw you there with Dad's Aunt Mary. I never said anything, because I didn't want you to think I was spying on you."

Elena nodded, studying her ragged cuticles.

"Even though Aunt Mary assured me that nothing weird happened—"

She talked to Aunt Mary?

"—I don't understand why you met her. And why you lied about it," she finished.

"I didn't lie, Mom, I said that I was meeting a friend, and I did!"

"Elena," interrupted Dr. Johnston, "do you think that when you told your parents that you were meeting a friend that they assumed the friend was an estranged relative?"

"No, but . . ." Elena's mind raced. She had to explain Aunt Mary's presence with a non-Spuren story.

"Meghan," Dr. Johnston continued, "in addition to confronting Elena regarding her deception, do you think that perhaps you owe her an apology?"

Her mom furrowed her brow. "I'm not sure what for."

"Might you have communicated better?"

Her mom looked chagrined.

The doctor continued. "Might you have shown more trust by raising your concerns directly with Elena?"

"That might have been better," her mother agreed. She took a deep breath and turned to Elena. "Elena, I'm sorry that I didn't tell you about seeing you there. I made assumptions and snuck around by writing a letter to Aunt Mary. I didn't even mention it to your father. I apologize." She glanced at Dr. Johnston.

She gave a small nod of approval. "Elena?" she prompted.

"I'm sorry that I wasn't honest about who I was meeting," Elena muttered.

"Let's talk about why this particular person, Aunt Mary, was of particular concern for your mother. Do you have any thoughts?" Dr. Johnston asked.

Elena shifted the pillows on her chair and ad-libbed. "Dad doesn't like Aunt Mary, and they probably wouldn't want me to see her. But!" she continued, warming up. "I also know that they were worried that I was having a breakdown like Aunt Nell. And they never even told me how she died! I was trying to get information!"

"Oh, Elena," her mom said, looking devastated. "I had no idea how much this weighed on you. I feel awful."

"Yeah. So, when I found out that a girl at school knew Aunt Mary from camp, I had to contact her to learn the real story. You guys are so secretive," Elena finished, lobbing the blame ball back to her mom.

"Fair enough," she said. "It sounds like we both need to work on being more honest with each other."

"I guess," Elena said. Dr. Johnston was annoyingly good.

Having achieved her therapeutic goals, Dr. Johnston leaned back, rearranged her legs, and gave the pair an approving smile. She then spent the rest of the session helping them unpack the Aunt Nell elephant in the room that was finally being acknowledged.

Later, her mom was the first to break the silence in the car. "Since we're being honest, were you planning on telling me about the engineering scholarship? I found the email in my spam folder. Congratulations!"

"Oh, yeah, thanks," Elena said. Of course her mom checked the spam folder.

"Make sure to tell Dad about it tonight. That's good news."

Elena nodded, silently.

"So," her mom continued in an annoyingly chatty tone. "It looks like we both know Aunt Mary now."

"Yup," Elena replied, determined to stay annoyed.

"I've only written to her. The last time I saw her was before you were born. She was very…solid."

"Mom!" Elena said, shocked. "How rude."

"I don't mean fat, although she is on the huskier side. She just was very, I don't know, Midwest practical."

"Hmmph," Elena said protectively. But Mom was right. From the knit cap to the shoes to the purse to her whole demeanor, Aunt Mary was solid practicality personified, with the whole Spuren thing thrown in for good measure.

"She was very athletic! Always reminded everyone how she was a varsity athlete in high school. She's something else. I always enjoyed her company back when we all got along."

Elena couldn't resist. "Let me guess. Bowling?"

She and her mom cracked up and shared Aunt Mary observations the rest of the way home. Kindly.

Stephen weirdness
- *No Spuren info=Talent kryptonite?*

Chapter 33
Meghan

"How's Elena doing?" The question came from a colleague who used to see Elena for an egg allergy. These days, the allergist and Meghan only ran into each other at the mandatory monthly faculty meeting into which they now headed. "I miss seeing her in clinic."

"She's great," Meghan replied. "I wish I could say I miss the allergy clinic, but we were glad when she outgrew it."

"I get that a lot," the woman answered with a smile. "You moved this summer, right? New school?"

"It was a little rocky in the fall," Meghan said, "but she's back on track. We found out yesterday that she was accepted to a super-competitive summer engineering program."

"Wow, congratulations!"

Meghan smiled her thanks and zoned out as the department chair spoke on patient satisfaction, clinical revenues, and call schedules, none of which concerned a pathologist. Her department would always be needed, as long as there was sickness and death, regardless of budget cuts.

The old Elena was back, Meghan reassured herself. The email from the engineering institute was a real bright spot the previous afternoon, dousing Meghan's worry fire for a few hours at least. But why hadn't Elena mentioned it yet? Did their awkward therapy conversation accomplish nothing? The old Elena would have come straight home from school, crowing over her win. Instead, she didn't get home until nearly 9 the night before, having spent the evening studying at Stephen's.

Stephen. He really was a lovely kid: polite, nice to Ava and Jacob, got good grades, appeared to treat Elena well. He was the ideal first boyfriend. This assumed that "first boyfriend" was a milestone to be celebrated. Meghan wasn't so sure; the baby books irritatingly stopped listing "firsts" around age five. How was she supposed to think about this guy? Meghan always assumed she'd be one of those parents who was supportive of her children's relationships, but that was before she actually had to be. These days, she saw the appeal of her parents' shame-filled approach in which ignorance was, apparently, bliss.

Time to rein Elena in, remind her that family and school were most important. Maybe they should re-institute the required Sunday family meal? Too bad her parents lived in Florida. A little bit of mandatory grandparent time never hurt. There was always Great Aunt Mary, she supposed. But that begged the question: who was the true wolf in sheep's clothing? The old lady, or the teenage boyfriend, or Elena herself?

CHAPTER 34
KAT

When Elena was coming over to meet with her mom, Kat tried to be gone. She wasn't sure who felt more awkward about their pseudo friendship, or whatever it was. Probably me, Kat thought. Elena wasn't having any problem acting normal at school, she had a good group of friends and a boyfriend. From across the commons, life looked good for Elena Tannin.

Not so much for Kat who was beginning to suspect that she didn't belong with the BP, and not just because she wasn't beautiful. Being a judgmental bitch was exhausting. Talking to Val used to be enough to restore her mood, but not anymore. Kat felt like a wrung-out dishrag most days.

Worse, Kat suspected she was actually envious of Elena, who was skinny, smart, nice, and even funny. It wasn't fair for one person to get all those things. Plus, Elena was figuring out Spuren life easily. She knew it was petty, but Kat secretly hoped to see her struggle a little bit more.

As she walked home from the library, Kat looked through her and Elena's text conversation. They still messaged a couple of times a week, so there wasn't a total wall between them. Elena always responded, but Kat was the one who started the conversations.

Kat snuck inside and found Elena and her mom sitting at the kitchen table with steaming mugs of tea and a packet of Milano cookies. Ugh, she was still here. She must have missed Elena's car along the snowy curb.

"Hi, guys," Kat said, trying to sound casual.

"Hi," her mom said. "Sit down and have a cup of tea. We were just talking about Communing. Elena mentioned that you two did that already. Amazing!"

"Why is it amazing?" Elena asked.

Kat sat down across from Elena and the cookies.

"Well," her mom said, "usually you have to really focus, and be in a low electricity environment. But you two pulled it off spontaneously in a room full of fluorescent lights!"

"Sorry I told her about the dress store, Kat," Elena said. "I hope I didn't say anything I shouldn't have."

"It's fine, Elena," she said, with a smile soaked in apology. "We Communed so easily because I was a disaster area that day. You know how I am about trying on clothes, Mom." Kat hoped that Elena only mentioned what happened at the mall, not the Winter Dance. Mom still had no idea about how bad things got with Ty.

Linda nodded. "I stopped shopping with Kat long ago. Too much drama. I think she looks beautiful in everything, and she takes that as a personal insult."

"So, because Kat was upset . . . it was easier for us to Commune?" Elena asked.

"Mmm hmm," Kat said, swallowing a bite of cookie. "And you seem to have pretty good control of your Talent naturally."

"I don't know about that," Elena said. "I was a mess before winter break. I was convinced I was going crazy. My parents even had me start seeing a therapist."

Linda started clearing the table. "I'm not sure how it'll be with your family, Elena. For now, Mary wants your mom out of the loop." Kat sensed disapproval in Mom's voice.

"Speaking of family," Elena said, "did you know my aunt, Nell Tannin?"

"She was a few years older than me," began Kat's mom hesitantly.

"Don't worry, I know what happened," Elena interrupted.

"What?" Kat asked, looking between the two. She didn't like them sharing secrets.

"My aunt was Spuren, and mentally ill," Elena said, "and she committed suicide."

"I'm so sorry," said Kat, trying not to let her face reveal the horror she felt.

"I didn't know her," reassured Elena, "but when I started getting exhausted from my Talent—"

"Spiraling," corrected Linda.

"Spiraling," Elena said, "my parents worried that I was headed the same direction as her."

"I'm glad you figured out that it was your Talent," Kat said.

"That's just it," said Elena, leaning on her elbows. "I still worry it's not *just* my Talent. People have been comparing me to my aunt for years."

Kat nodded in synchrony with her mom. "Well, you seem sane right now," she faltered.

"On that serious note," Kat's mom said, "I think we're done. You have your Tempering practice—"

"Sitting in the mall food court?" asked Kat, smiling at Elena who offered a smile flicker back.

"Did you download that meditation app?"

"Yup," said Elena, looking at her phone.

"All right. Good work today," Kat's mom said and walked out of the room in her perennially bare feet.

The silence was super awkward. Kat wondered who would be brave enough to break it.

"So," Elena said.

"So," Kat replied, "what's new?"

"Since when?" Elena asked with an edge to her voice. "Oh, that's right. January, the last time you actually spoke to me in real life." Elena's mouth looked funny.

"Are you biting your tongue?" Kat asked.

Elena shook her head, but stayed silent.

"Never mind, sorry I said anything." Kat started to stand up.

"So that's it?" Elena burst out. "You're just going to walk away? You can't even talk to me in your own kitchen? Is it going to be this bad if I go to Zedernwald? Or are you only a bitch in Belvedere?"

Kat's stomach knotted up. "I'm sorry! I just don't know how to launch a new version of me, Elena," Kat said, her voice rising. She hovered in that dangerous territory between anger and sadness. "You're lucky. You got to start over at a new school and didn't have to bring along years' worth of baggage. You just waltzed in and could be your perfect Spuren self."

Elena snorted. "You think that I *waltz* around all day, being some sort of natural me? All I think about is how people are going to react to me, trying to not blurt the wrong thing. And now I'm trying to do a crash course on Tempering on top of it all. Yeah, really easy."

"You have no idea what I've been through with my Talent, who I've hurt."

"Besides yourself, you mean?"

Man, Elena could be really mean when she wanted to. "Kayla, actually. Back in sixth grade."

"I heard that you ditched her. What does that have to do with your Talent?"

Kat glanced at the door through which her mom exited. "I hid my Talent coming on from my mom, so I didn't have control of things for a while."

"Wait, I thought you knew you were Spuren since, like, the beginning? Why'd you hide it?" Elena asked.

"I don't know. My mom was always so awkward about the Talent, periods, everything. I just didn't want her to bake me a celebration cake like she did when I started wearing a bra."

"You're kidding."

"Nope," Kat replied with a sigh of chagrin. "So, I started picking up on stuff from Kayla, and I misread her emotions and accused her of liking me as—more than a friend." Kat never admitted this to anyone, and now that she started, she couldn't stop. "It was middle school. I didn't know what anything meant, all I knew is that I didn't want to be teased, especially not about being gay. So, I dropped her and froze out all that confusing stuff. And I've been doing it ever since."

Elena shook her head. "That was shitty. Plus, Kayla's not even gay."

"Hey," Kat said, tipping toward anger, "you would still be going crazy if it wasn't for me, remember? I'm the one who connected you to Mary and Zedernwald and all this!" She wasn't sure what she expected to happen after her confession, but definitely not being called shitty.

"Maybe you're a different person at Zedernwald. Who knows if I'll ever find out," Elena said.

"What do you mean, *if*?" Kat demanded.

"I won this engineering scholarship for summer," Elena said, sighing, "and I can't do both. So, who knows if I'll be at Zedernwald?"

"No pressure, but you really need to get to camp this summer. Like, really."

"I know. But I'll let down a whole lot of people if I give up the scholarship,"

"Being Spuren is important too, even if it doesn't have a scholarship!" Kat said. She realized how much she was looking forward to tending their fragile friendship in a safe space.

Elena nodded. "It's just hard. People have so many expectations of me."

"Tell me about it," said Kat, glancing at her phone and seeing dozens of missed social media notifications.

Elena noticed Kat's glance and took the hint. "Okay. Well, I'll think about it. Thanks for telling me that stuff with Kayla. I won't say anything." And she left.

Kat went to her room. Maintaining one's social media presence took time. She scrolled through her feed, pausing at Ty's face. Although she blocked him, he still showed up in friends' pictures.

In this instance, he appeared with Bailey's sister. Paige, a freshman, was an underclass Beautiful Person. The Puberty Fairy had been ridiculously kind to her. She got the benefits of a narrow waist and big chest without the drawbacks of stretch marks and acne. Her carefully curated feed was a thing of beauty.

Paige posted a pic of her sitting on Ty's lap. It made Kat think of a bird perched on a crocodile's open jaws.

How could Bailey not tell me? Kat thought she was out of the woods after squashing lies about their breakup. But now, there would be pitying stares and hopeful rumors about girl drama between her and Paige.

Even more worrisome, Paige was too innocent to deal with Ty. The youngest in a family of girls, Paige was protected and indulged. She didn't have the jaded armor necessary to survive him. Kat had to warn Bailey and, by extension, Paige.

Kat called, irrationally feeling that every second counted.

"Hey," said Bailey. Her hair was wrapped in a towel.

"Hey, um, so Paige and Ty?"

"Yeah, I felt awkward telling you."

"Uh huh," said Kat.

Bailey leaned toward the mirror to pluck her eyebrows. "It's not like he was going to stay single forever."

Panicking, Kat tried a direct approach. "I never told you, but Ty was kind of abusive to me. I feel like we need to warn Paige."

"Abusive? What do you mean?" said Bailey, pausing.

"Like, he constantly put me down, for one."

"Put you down how?"

Kat gulped. "Well, mostly that I was fat and ugly."

"Asshole," said Bailey. "You aren't the skinniest, but you're no Lara," said Bailey, referencing a fat girl that Kat feared becoming.

Kat knew that she was expected to play along. "Some of us aren't blessed with good metabolism."

"I doubt he'll say anything like that to Paige, she's a stick," Bailey said, resuming her plucking.

But I deserved it? thought Kat. Instead, she said, "It wasn't just words, Bailey. He was—aggressive."

"He's a football player, Kat. What are you saying? That he date-raped you? I don't remember you ever complaining."

Kat was shocked by the words coming out of her friend's mouth. Didn't they sit through the same health classes all through elementary and middle school?

"Anyway," Bailey continued, oblivious to Kat's horror, "it'd look pretty bad if you started accusing him now, like you were jealous or something."

"I'm not jealous, Bailey," Kat said. "It's just that someone needs to protect Paige...." Kat stopped to swallow some tears.

Bailey finally looked up. "Oh, my God, Kat! Calm down! I'll watch out for my sister! I just don't think we should scare her with your jealous-ex-girlfriend drama."

Kat stared at Bailey in disbelief.

"Kat. I'm your friend. I would never say anything publicly to hurt you. I'm just trying to watch out for you."

"I know," Kat said in a resigned voice. Bailey valued reputations above anything else.

"Good. I want to paint my nails tonight before bed. Byeee!"

Kat felt gutted. She didn't use the word "assault," but Kat doubted it would have changed Bailey's reaction. She considered calling Val or Elena for advice, but feared what they'd say: be done with them. Break up with them, just like you did with Ty. But if Kat wasn't a Beautiful Person, then who was she? Sure, she'd been living a lie for all of high school, but it was a lie of omission, the most innocent kind. She was omitting herself, not hurting anyone else.

Kat let her mind wander back to her pre-icy self, back in the early days of middle school when she was still best friends with Kayla. That was the last time she let her Talent hurt anyone else, back when Kayla still trusted her, and she still trusted herself.

CHAPTER 35
ELENA

By March, everyone gave up on making winter palatable. The custodians half-heartedly swabbed the school hallways, but the entire world remained cast in a dirty gray pall. Elena walked through the school doorway and began her usual routine, avoiding the gray meltwater that puddled the halls despite industrial rugs at the entries.

Elena applied lip gloss and Tempering walls before starting the day. As usual, Chris was next to her. She sensed his unique energy before she saw him. It was a vague olive green and ripply.

"Hey," he said

"Hey," she replied. "How was your weekend?"

"I worked on the car all weekend. I'm surprised you didn't see me."

Elena smiled and looked confused. "Where, at the tech ed shop?"

"No, in my garage! Next door to the Kowalskis? I saw you leaving yesterday. It's good that you're hanging out with Kat," he said, jumping to a logical conclusion. He slammed his locker shut and wandered away to mystery tech land.

Crap, they'd been spotted. Elena panicked all day that Chris would start a rumor about her and Kat being friends, thereby pissing Kat off. Weirdly, ever since Elena confronted her a couple weeks before, Kat was slightly more open. She smiled at Elena a couple times at school and hung around when Elena was at the house the day before. Elena didn't want to screw up and ruin whatever progress they made.

To be safe, at the end of the day, she cornered Chris and asked him to keep her and Kat's friendship on the down low. His "Sure, whatever," was delivered with such disinterest that Elena knew she could trust him. The Belvedere social currency of juicy gossip was worthless to him.

She grew more reassured a few days later. Chris showed up with his hair freshly shaved, less than ¼ inch of dark stubble dotting his scalp. When Jacob got his hair buzzed, she loved the feeling.

"Nice hair," said Elena. "Won't your head get cold?"

"Nah," Chris said. "I wear shorts all winter, I'm okay."

"Can I touch your hair?" Elena blurted.

"Sure," Chris said with an amused shrug, crouching down.

Elena stupidly hadn't prepped her Temper, so she received a blurry snapshot of the book of Chris through the fuzzy stubble. It was more like a peek at the dust jacket, since electricity coursed through the fluorescent bulbs lining the hallways, dimming her Talent. But, like with Kayla, she was shocked by the information that touch transferred. She pulled away.

"Got your fix?" Chris laughed and walked away. "See ya," he called, as Elena silently nodded.

Chris's head was filled up with memories of him and Kat: the two of them running in the sprinkler, playing video games on his couch, and her leaving for dances as she grew more beautiful with age. The memories were rendered with the composition of a loving photographer. Elena knew that the scrapbook full of Kat stuff in Chris's head meant one thing.

Chris liked Kat. Like, really liked her.

He'd never do anything to hurt her, so their secret was safe with him.

• • •

A few weeks passed since Elena found out about the scholarship, and Mrs. Vickers kept reminding her that she needed a decision soon. Her parents seemed to assume it was a done deal, abandoning all conversations about the Cabin. But it wasn't a done deal to Elena, who filled pages of her notebook with pro and con lists, coming to no conclusions in the process. She finally decided to talk it out with Stephen, someone who could neutrally help her with the pros and cons. She couldn't be 100% honest about why Zedernwald was so important to her, so she told him that the camp was a family tradition that she never had time to do before.

"…so, that's about it," she finished, over a table at McDonald's. "I have to decide soon whether to take the engineering scholarship or not. My parents don't even know that I'm considering *not* doing it. What do you think?" she asked, stopping to take a drink of soda.

"Since both options mean you'll be gone for most of the summer, I don't like either," he said.

"Stephen. You're going to be working most of the summer. Gimme a break."

"Does either allow visitors?"

"I'd have to check," said Elena, her mind leaping ahead to the beach and a shirtless Stephen. "All I know is, either way, I'll be disappointing someone."

"Elena, in all the stuff you've said, you never talked about what *you* want. There was lots of stuff about your parents, Kayla, some great-aunts, teachers, but nothing about you. No offense, but you worry too much about what people think of you."

This was the first time that Stephen critiqued her. She did not like it. "Thanks?"

He came around to her side of the booth, forcing her to look him in the eye.

"You are the most intriguing, ambitious person I know," Stephen said, his face inches from hers. "Which has nothing to do with what classes you take, or what honors you get. Whether you go to this thing or the other thing, you'll still be amazing."

"You're just saying that since I'm your girlfriend," Elena squirmed.

"You're my girlfriend *because* of those things," he said. "Why do you think I started to like you in the first place? Because of your GPA? Because you stood up to me and my big mouth on the first day of English. It was totally hot."

She was stunned. He liked her because of her blurting, her worst habit. "You knew I was an outspoken, opinionated weirdo this whole time?"

"Pretty hard not to notice," he said.

"So…even when I'm a disaster area, you're still okay with me?"

"Yup. I like when you accidentally let your armor slip. I know you don't let many people see the real you, Elena. But I love the real you," he said with the briefest pause over the loaded word.

Elena instinctively blurted, "I love you too."

This was so big that Elena let him kiss her in the middle of the restaurant, riding a wave of out-of-control-ness. "I don't think I'm going to accept the scholarship," she said as she pulled away.

"Sounds good," Stephen said, squeezing her hand. "Ready to go?"

A freak March snow sprang up while they were inside, and she grabbed a scraper to help Stephen clear the windows of his Toyota. Her gloves quickly grew soggy and her shoes took on water, but she was too distracted with this change of events to notice.

•   •   •

"Mom, Dad, can I talk to you?" Elena sat in her kitchen studying chair. As she gained better control of her Talent, she resumed studying there almost as often as she did in her room. The twins were in bed, and her parents cleaned the kitchen.

"Sure, honey," her dad said, taking a pot to dry from her mom. "What's up?"

"So, you know the engineering institute?"

"Yes," her mom answered, perking up.

"I've been thinking about it a lot. And, well, I decided not to go."

Her mom raised her eyebrows dramatically. "Really," she said, crossing her sudsy arms.

"Yes, and I'll tell you my reasons," Elena said. She rehearsed the list and was anxious to get it out there.

"I hope you put 'removal of amazing college application item' on the list of cons," her mother said.

"Let's hear her out," her dad said, sitting down.

"First, it's basically two months of more school, and I don't want to spend the last summer of high school studying all day," Elena began.

"Okay," he said. "What else?"

"Second, I'm not that interested in engineering. The more time I spend in upper level classes, I realize that I don't enjoy math and science, even though I'm good at them. I like *being* good at them, but not the actual subject matter."

Her dad nodded. Her mom listened silently.

"And last, I would hate to take the spot when there is someone who deserves it more: Kayla. She's interested in engineering and is better at math," Elena concluded.

"Can you just transfer the scholarship to her?" her mom asked. "That's not usually how these things work."

"I asked," Elena said, remaining calm despite waves of maternal disapproval. "And Mrs. Vickers said that they gave her the final choice between me and Kayla. If I don't take it, it'd go to her."

"What would you do this summer instead?" her dad asked.

She anticipated this question. "My advisor says I can take a couple of college pre-req classes online for free by enrolling through the high school. Then, I can start advanced classes right away in college."

Her mom's eyebrow wrinkle diminished.

"They're online, so I could take them anywhere. That's good, because I want to go to a summer camp."

"It sounds like a decent plan," said her dad.

"The online classes sound okay," her mom said hesitantly. "Obviously, not as rigorous as the university engineering institute. I'm surprised that you suddenly gave up on STEM. I thought that was your plan?"

"It was," said Elena, "mostly because it sounded good. I'm a girl who's good at science, I say I want to go into a STEM field, people praise me, positive feedback loop begins. Who knows?" Elena continued quickly. "Maye I'll settle on engineering eventually, just not yet."

"So, what is this other camp and how much will it cost?" Dad asked.

"That's the amazing thing," Elena said, nervousness climbing up her throat like a toxic caterpillar. "It wouldn't cost anything because I—we—know the owners."

Her dad went pale. He stood up and walked to the island, taking her mom's previous cross-armed position.

"Do you mean Zedernwald?" her mom asked, less surprised than she should have been. As though stage-directed, she took Dad's abandoned spot next to the chair.

"Yes. A girl at school goes there—Kat—and she was telling me about it," she said. "I'd like to try out this camp that is actually part of our family. I would like to work on college credit. And I would like to have a little fun. I could see you guys when you come up to the Cottage, maybe even more. And I'd be doing something to help out a friend, Kayla." Elena spoke as though giving a closing argument to a jury of two.

"Obviously, we aren't going to force you to do anything against your will. However, we'll have to talk about whether Zedernwald is an option," her dad said.

"Are you saying it's okay that I decline the engineering institute scholarship?" she asked.

"I agree with Dad. We aren't going to force you to do anything," her mom said. "I just feel badly that you've pretended to love science and math all these years. I really tried to avoid the tiger mom thing…"

"I didn't pretend, it just took me awhile to figure out. And Mom, you are the biggest tiger mom ever, but I'm the same way."

Her mom smiled. "I guess we're cut from the same cloth. I have a feeling that I better learn to lighten up for the twins." She glanced toward the corner of the room where a heap of dress-up clothes and rocks lay.

"I think they may be more…left-brained," Elena said diplomatically.

She and her mom laughed the laughter of the relieved, having passed through a minefield conversation intact, albeit unsure of exactly where they all stood.

As she fell asleep, Elena envisioned Mrs. Vickers telling Kayla about the scholarship, and Kayla's unadulterated happiness. She tried to imagine herself at Zedernwald with Kat and Aunt Mary, but that was still a blur.

Stephen weirdness

- *No Spuren info=Talent kryptonite?*
- *Stephen loves me. Gulp. I guess I love him too? Right?*

Chapter 36
Meghan

Me: Hi, it's Meghan, Anders' wife. Are you available to talk?
Mary (Aunt Mary): Sure. Do You Have My Number?
Me: Yes, I'm texting you
Mary (Aunt Mary): O.K. Call Me In An Hour Or So.

It was foolish of her to assume that the Aunt Mary and Elena situation was in the rear-view mirror, so Meghan wasn't really surprised when Elena brought up Camp Zedernwald. By the end of that conversation, Meghan could barely keep track of all of the new things to worry about, from whether Elena was screwing up her life to Anders finding out about her and Elena's secret contact with Mary.

Panic made Meghan controlling, and she first wanted to control the Mary situation as much as possible. She anxiously watched the clock tick down the hour "or so." What on earth could Mary be doing on a Thursday that was so important? Maybe she was in a meeting or a doctor's appointment. Or maybe Mary was at home and just wanted to keep her waiting.

An hour and ten minutes passed, and Meghan dialed.

"Hello?" a voice boomed. Meghan held the phone away from her ear, turning the volume down.

"Hi, Mary?" she asked.

"Speaking."

"Hi, Aunt Mary. This is Meghan. Thanks for taking the time to speak to me," she said in one rushed breath.

"Oh, sure," Mary replied. "I was just finishing up card club at my friend, Nancy's. How've you been?" She sounded as though they chatted the other day.

"Oh, fine. Work has been busy," Meghan replied. When in Rome…

"I looked you up on the Google and see that you're an associate professor now," Aunt Mary said.

So, Mary was keeping track of her. "I was promoted a couple of years ago. Anders started staying home with the kids around that time."

"Yes, how are the children? Elena is doing well in school, I suppose? And the twins? What are their names?"

"Jacob and Ava," Meghan said, smoothing her creased list of talking points. "They're three, so very busy. They keep us on our toes."

"It's a wonderful age. I was never blessed with children myself, as you know, but I always enjoyed children."

"I feel badly that we haven't kept in better touch."

"Well, now, that's something I've regretted too," Aunt Mary said.

"The reason I called, Mary, was about Elena," Meghan said, glancing down at her notes.

"All right."

"As I mentioned in that letter I sent awhile back, I had no notion that you and Elena were in touch," she said, getting to the awkward crux of the matter. "In this day and age, we can't be too careful, and she's been a little distant lately. I am curious if you can tell me what Elena talked with you about?"

There, she said it. There was a brief pause before Aunt Mary began.

"Let me remember, that was a few months ago now. Well, I know a friend of Elena's, Katherine Kowalski, through camp," Aunt Mary said.

This must be the friend that Elena mentioned; Meghan jotted down the name. Was Katherine in the Herd?

"And so, Elena reached out through Katherine with some questions about camp and family things," Aunt Mary said.

"Can you tell me more about your camp?" Meghan asked, taking advantage of Aunt Mary's chatty mood. "Is it the usual bonfires, canoeing, and lanyards?"

"Well, there's certainly plenty of that, but also focus on empowering females and leadership development."

Surprisingly progressive . . . "Did you talk to Elena much about camp? The reason I ask is, she's taken it into her head that she wants to attend."

"A bit, but I haven't been in touch with her at all since my note a few months back. I'd guess she's been talking to Katherine about how much fun she has there."

"Elena is dead set on going, so I wonder if you could send me some information? Or is there a website..." Meghan asked, predicting the answer.

"Oh, we aren't on the web. Let me tell you a few things. We follow a traditional model, lots of outdoor activities and team building, with a focus on building strong young women, ready to succeed in today's world. We've added new programming as the times require—we even have yoga classes now."

"What's the age range and how long are the sessions?"

"We start girls around 12, depending, and most attend through their first couple summers of college, transitioning to more of a counselor role."

"Do that many girls keep it up after high school?" Meghan asked, incredulous that an 18-year old would want to hang out with middle schoolers.

"Yes, we have a very strong following. Lots of legacy campers. You know, girls whose moms attended and such. As for sessions, we only run the one—mid-June through mid-August, before we break for the family Labor Day reunion."

"So, there's no option for a shorter stay?" She found that strange. Kids were so hyper-involved these days. How could they give up an entire summer?

"We've never had anyone ask for shorter sessions, so we haven't offered them," said Mary. "If it's money that's a concern, she would get the family rate, which is free!"

Meghan smiled. "No, that's not it at all, Aunt Mary. It would just be quite a change from the norm, and something that Anders and I will need to discuss. I'm concerned about her being ready for college applications next year. Anders' concerns are more—"

"Personal."

"Exactly."

"Tell me, does Anders know that I've been in touch with you and Elena?" Mary asked.

"No," Meghan sighed, happy to unload this emotional burden. "I'm nervous about telling him, he's so emotional about it all. I was such an outsider-looking-in when everything happened with your family and Nellie." Meghan removed her glasses. "Whenever I try to talk to him about it, he shuts down. Elena didn't even know how Nellie died until a few weeks ago, that's how secretive he is. I feel like a real traitor even considering this, but…"

"You want to ask me more about what happened?"

Whew. "Yes."

"I'm happy to tell you my version of things," Mary said, "but it would probably make sense to have a talk with Anders too."

"My main question is…why did you and Sylvie feel so strongly about Nellie's treatment?" asked Meghan, surprising herself with this particular focus. Rather than backtracking, she went with it. "Were Helen and Dick really that off-base?"

Mary heaved a huge sigh. "You have to realize that the women in our family have a very unique relationship. Especially us three sisters, running the camp together every summer."

"What did Dick think of that?" she asked.

"He loved it! He spent summers golfing and fishing with Anders, and they came for visits on the weekends and, of course, everyone stayed at Zedernwald for the big Labor Day reunion. Back then, the idea of 'summering' somewhere was more common. It was just the way things were in our family. All the husbands understood."

"What was your and Helen's unmarried name again?" Meghan asked, automatically sketching out a family tree.

"Schultz. Growing up, we were the three Schultz girls, and Mom took us to camp in the summers, too, while our dad stayed back and ran the store." Aunt Mary said.

"So, Dick never felt resentful of how close the three of you were? Or the other husbands?" Meghan drew a question mark next to Dick Tannin.

"Nope," Aunt Mary said. "The hard feelings only started when Nellie got sick in college. She was high strung about school, but Zedernwald always helped her recalibrate. After a summer at camp, she was tuned up and ready to go. By the end of the next school year, though, she'd have run herself ragged again. She was real strong academically."

"Who pushed her so hard? Helen and Dick?" Meghan asked.

"Some," Aunt Mary said. "Mostly herself, though."

Sounds familiar, thought Meghan. She glanced down at the family tree, where she subconsciously drew wispy lines connecting Nell and Elena. "Do you think her work ethic contributed to her breakdown at college?" she asked, dreading the answer.

"Yes, we all three did," Aunt Mary said. "Unfortunately, she didn't want to miss any school, and Dick went along with that attitude. He really thought that the best bet was to trust the fancy psychiatrists on campus. By the time we got her that summer, she was a mess. On so many different meds that she barely knew which way was up."

"To be fair," Meghan said, reflexively defending the medical profession, "it can take time to adjust psychiatric medications. It sounds like everyone was doing their best."

"Unfortunately, that wasn't good enough," Aunt Mary said flatly.

Meghan was shocked at the statement. "What good does it do to cast blame? Nellie was schizophrenic—her disease killed her."

"I guess there'll always be a question in my mind of how much was nature versus nurture, as they say."

"Hmm," Meghan said. She firmly believed in the chemical underpinnings of mental illness.

"After Nellie's funeral, Helen came to stay with me and Sylvie for a bit. She finally told us just how rigid Dick was about Nell, how he wouldn't even let Helen bring her to meditation, yoga, all the things that helped her out in the past."

There was a pause while Aunt Mary had a coughing fit. Meghan felt torn. She found Mary's story compelling, but her training nudged her to take her late father-in-law's side, just like Anders had.

" 'Scuse me. Went down the wrong pipe," Aunt Mary said. "I guess Sylvie and I didn't do anything to paint a different picture of Dick in Helen's mind."

"Helen died, what, six months later?"

"167 days later," Mary corrected. "She just faded away. They said it was pneumonia. Probably was, but there wasn't an ounce of fight left in her in the end. The rest is the usual story: Dick blamed us, we blamed him…"

"Now, *that* I remember. The episode at the funeral was…not pleasant." Meghan recalled the clutch of older people with raised voices, arguing behind the table laden with casseroles and sheet cakes.

"I can't think about it without feeling sick," Mary said. "The number of apologies we sent Dick, phone calls we tried to make." She sighed. "But he was just angry at us and the world at that point, and he took Anders with him."

"I think that he had some right to be angry," Meghan said, probing for a response.

"Absolutely," Mary quickly agreed. "Life gave him a double punch, and Sylvie and I just poured lemon juice on it, to mix metaphors. But I wish he hadn't taken Anders down that path of grudges."

"Family can be difficult," Meghan said, filling up the silence with an appropriate platitude.

"Indeed, but it's all we've got, isn't it?" Mary volleyed back. "So, to that end, Sylvie and I would love to have Elena at camp. It'd probably do her some good. Even we high-achieving types need to be able to unwind. I graduated second in my high school class and received the

John Philip Sousa award for euphonium, in addition to being a four-year varsity bowler. I understand competitive."

"You make a good point, Aunt Mary," Meghan said. It was hard to hold a grudge against this open, artless woman. On a whim, she blurted, "Maybe it would be helpful if you could continue to talk to Elena about family and stuff. You know, if she wanted to reach out to you again, I'd be okay with that."

"I'm happy to do whatever I can to help Elena," Aunt Mary said.

"Maybe it would help to talk with all of us together? You, me, Elena, and the, um, Kowalskis?"

"A fabulous idea," Mary boomed through the phone. "How about I set up a get-together?"

"Yes," Meghan said, briefly worried about what she'd gotten herself into. "And can you send me a brochure, please, and when does registration close for camp?"

"Tell you what, I'll send you some materials and arrange the get-together. You take your time and let me know in May. Sound good?"

"Yes. Thanks, we'll talk soon," said Meghan.

"Alrighty. Bye-bye."

Meghan looked at the penciled family tree, complete with x's to mark deceased members, and cross hatches to symbolize severed relationships. She drew a complex knot around the three Shultz girls: Helen, Sylvie, and Mary, and included tendrils connecting Nellie and Elena. In the online photograph of tribe of camp girls and Nellie, everyone looked so free, so happily enmeshed. Meghan had a few close friends, but none that traveled nomadically across the years with her as the Zedernwald girls seemed to do. It made her feel left out somehow.

·   ·   ·

There were a lot of great things about being married to Anders, but getting him to talk about his feelings wasn't one of them. Meghan didn't love unpacking emotional baggage either, but believed it to be a useful endeavor. Over time, she learned to play the dual roles of participant and amateur therapist during their thornier conversations. It was tricky, and she staged these forced dialogues carefully, and always in the car. Where no one could escape.

The evening after her phone call with Aunt Mary was just such a time. "Let's go for a drive," Meghan said casually. "The kids are asleep, we need to talk about Elena's plans for summer. Come on." She texted Elena to let her know they were leaving and grabbed the keys to the minivan.

As he followed her to the garage, she sensed that Anders' veneer of calm was thin. When he shut the car door, he let out a whoosh of breath, raked a hand through his hair, and balled the other into a fist.

Meghan glanced over from the driver's seat and assessed his tense body language. She pulled out into the night and started a long route that she could drive without thinking. This would take a bit.

"Seriously?" Anders said, breaking the silence. "A random girl at school just *happens* to go to the Zedernwald? And Elena just *happens* to hear about it from her? Knowing my aunts, they orchestrated the whole thing. Just when things were getting back on track with Elena, they somehow manage to interfere."

"It does seem strange." Meghan ad-libbed shared surprise. She bit her tongue against an analysis of his leap to nonsensical conspiracy theories.

"I'll say. If it were any other camp, I could go along with it. But after what happened between my aunts and my dad, I don't know if I could ever trust them with Elena."

Meghan saw her opportunity to play therapist. "Tell me more about what they did. Aside from the scene at your mom's funeral, I mean."

"They tried to control everything! Mom and her sisters, the Three Schultz Girls. It's, like, no one else's opinion ever mattered to them!"

"Were things bad before Nell got sick?" Meghan asked, focusing on the wedge of road captured in the headlights.

"Not really. Dad and I didn't mind hanging out alone in the summer while Mom and Nell were away. But isn't it weird that they went to that camp and we just came for visits?"

"It *is* different. But it's a girls-only camp, right?"

"Yeah. And it's not like I didn't do anything. I had baseball and football, fishing. Me and Dad kind of went with the flow."

"Sounds pretty nice for you two introverts."

"I guess. But after all those summers, my aunts were so wrapped up with Nell and Mom. When Dad tried to stand up for his views when she got bad, it's like no one knew what to do! He didn't know how *not* to be bossed around by them!" Anders' head shake reverberated through the darkness.

"It is hard to change established relationships," Meghan echoed.

"And somehow, this screwed things up with Nell's treatment."

"I've never understood that," she said, taking a right down a twisty country road.

"Mary and Sylvie asked too many questions and made Mom and Nell doubt the doctors."

"Treating mental illness is hard enough nowadays," Meghan said, "but it was worse back in the 90's. There weren't as many options. We're lucky that Elena didn't end up going down that path, knock on wood," Meghan said, and they both absentmindedly knocked the wood-veneered dashboard.

"Elena has too many similarities to Nell," Anders said. "And now wanting to go to camp and hang out with my aunts!"

"I wonder how much of this is you not trusting your aunts and how much is fearing that Elena will repeat Nell's life story?" she asked, proud of her astuteness.

"I try to not think about how similar they are," he said. "No, it's definitely more about my aunts. I trust Mary and Sylvie about as far as I can throw them, which, in Aunt Mary's case, is not very far."

Meghan sensed Anders grinning at his joke. "Maybe it's because I don't have a history with your aunts, but I'm leaning toward letting her go. I know," she said, holding up a hand in his presumably shocked face, "I'm surprised too. But this is something Elena came up with on her own. Pretty soon, she won't have us around 24-7. It's a good adulthood test drive." I am killing this counseling thing, Meghan thought, turning onto the highway.

"I still can't believe that Aunt Mary somehow wormed her way into Elena's head…"

Meghan took a deep breath. "I think I might be able to help explain that situation."

The highway's periodic lights brought Anders uncomfortably into view.

"I have a confession to make. I have been in contact with your Aunt Mary. I'm sorry I didn't mention it sooner, I didn't know how to."

"Wait, what? Why? How? I can't believe you'd do that, Megs…" Anders said.

She knew that if they weren't in the car, he would storm off. "Actually, Elena reached out to her first," Meghan explained. "Remember her new school friend who goes to the camp? This girl, Katherine, gave her Mary's information. Elena wanted to learn more about your family and Nell in particular. We really stoked her interest by not being up front from the beginning," she said, anticipating Anders' protest. "So, she did her own investigating. She called Mary and they met for coffee."

"Elena confided in you, about meeting her?"

"Eventually. I actually happened upon her and Mary accidentally, without Elena even seeing me. I confronted your aunt. I still had her contact information in my Christmas Card address book. I told her that it was inappropriate to meet with Elena."

"Hear-hear," he said. "When was this?"

"Just before Christmas, and she agreed and apologized profusely," Meghan reassured. "She had absolutely no idea that we didn't know; that secret's on Elena." And me, I suppose, Meghan thought. "I've been wanting to tell you." She put her hand on his leg, steering with her left. "I'm so, so sorry for keeping this from you. To be completely honest, I spoke to her the other day after Elena brought up camp. I was curious about the details, and Mary's version of events about Nell."

"What'd she say?" he asked, lacing his fingers through hers, a good sign.

"She admitted that she and Sylvie butted in and were inappropriate at your mom's funeral. She said she tried to reach out to you over the years, and that she didn't blame you for ignoring her. Honestly, she seems harmless. Did you know she played the euphonium?"

"I'm glad she admitted her and Sylvie's fault in the whole thing," he said, ignoring the attempt at levity.

Meghan sensed a chink in Ander's defenses. If anything could budge his grudge, it was the kids. "Can we let Elena be a bridge of sorts? Just to test the waters with your family? She seems really set on going to this camp," Meghan said, squeezing his hand hopefully.

"It's a lot to ask. But…why don't you find out some more information about it."

"All right, I'll look into it," Meghan said. "One good thing, we could show up at camp unannounced any time," she reminded him. "We pay some of the property taxes every year, after all."

"One step at a time," Anders said. "I need a brochure. And a beer."

"We're almost home," Meghan reassured. She'd wait a day or two to tell him about the get-together, as Mary insisted on calling it. She knew he would agree, but she also knew that challenging discussions with Anders needed to be handled delicately, with frequent breaks for Spotted Cow beer.

CHAPTER 37
ELENA

Now firmly decided, Elena moved quickly to control her summer's fate. She got to school early the following Monday to tell Mrs. Vickers she would not be her STEM golden child.

Mrs. Vickers gave a several-minute speech that was "Well, that's really disappointing," phrased in a variety of ways. Finally, with perhaps more than a bit of nudging from Elena's Talent, she said, "Fortunately, we will keep the award at our school. I will just tell the committee that I'm transferring my selection to Kayla. I think it would be best if we kept your declination between the two of us, not let Kayla know she was a second choice. Does that sound reasonable?"

Perfect. "Yes. My parents know, of course, but they won't say anything."

"Excellent. I wouldn't want anything to tarnish Kayla's success or my reputation."

"Absolutely," Elena said as students started coming into class. She worried through the entire hour that Mrs. Vickers would somehow screw up telling Kayla. As a friend, she didn't want to spoil Kayla's excitement. As Elena, she didn't want anything to snag her plan on principle.

So, Elena was massively relieved when Mrs. Vickers said, "Kayla, could you stay back?" at the end of class.

Perfect. Elena waited for her outside the room, and Kayla's giddy smile on exiting told her everything she needed to know.

"I got the engineering scholarship!" she squealed. "I'm sorry to be excited, you must be so disappointed. I wish you would have gotten it," Kayla apologized.

"No, I'm happy for you," Elena said honestly. "I already knew I didn't get it, I was just waiting for you to say something before I told you. Really, I'm so, so happy for you!"

Kayla's giddy grin returned. "One of 50 in the whole state! Gah!"

Elena gave her a hug. They linked arms and walked down the hall, each floating on a different, yet adjacent, cloud.

Elena prepared for how uncomfortable the rest of the day would be. She was usually the one having her name read at afternoon announcements for having won something or acting modest as her friends gushed. The Herd knew that both she and Kayla applied for the award and, by default, they knew that she lost to Kayla. Elena maintained a practiced, unflinching smile, like the non-selected nominees at the Oscars. Because she was genuinely happy for Kayla, this was surprisingly easy.

"Kayla," Addison said, "you'll be in Madison for *two months*! In the summer! Without your parents!"

"I know! I can't wait to visit the Capitol, eat ice cream on the Terrace—"

"Meet college guys!" Morgan interrupted.

Kayla blushed. "I don't know about that, but I'm really looking forward to the classes."

"I hope you're not too disappointed, Elena," Addison said. She glanced at Elena apologetically.

"It's fine," Elena said. "I'm happy for Kayla. Really, I am!" she insisted to skeptical faces. Her competitive streak was common knowledge, especially after nights of playing board games at Addison's. "Really," she insisted. "Now focus on Kayla, please!"

While the Herd's gaze turned back to Kayla, Elena's focus drifted. Eventually, her gaze settled on Kat. She sat at the Beautiful People table, but not in her usual spot; Kat usually was next to Bailey. Today, Kat sat a few seats down from the Waif, shifted from her usual power position. When did that happen? Why did that happen?

There weren't any obvious changes. The girls picked at their salads and diet sodas. They gossiped and frothed in a shell of popular invulnerability. Elena loosened her Temper and surveilled the table with her Talent, pretending to look at her phone. The only changes were subtle, available only to girls with Talent. When Elena tapped into that additional stream of input, she saw that Kat was miserable.

Elena searched for any clues of Kat seeming sad before today. She scolded herself for mostly ignoring her at school, despite the fact that Kat demanded that they keep their friendship secret. All their online exchanges were normal. However, Elena hadn't actually interacted with Kat in real life for days. The two classes they had together, choir and English, were distracting, thanks to the piano and Stephen. She had no idea what was going on with Kat, not really. Some secret friend she was.

"Can you hang out Friday, Elena?" she heard Addison repeat.

"Oh, I might have plans with Stephen," Elena answered reflexively. Plans that involved making out, obv.

"We're starting to feel a little neglected here Elena," Addison said in that joking-not-joking way of hers.

"It must be hard to balance having a boyfriend with everything else," Kayla said kindly.

"I can probably hang out, don't worry," Elena said. She really had been blowing them off. Instead of going home right after school, she'd been going to Stephen's. His parents were hardly ever around the gloriously empty house which afforded the opportunity to kiss Stephen in all sorts of interesting new places.

One afternoon, feeling daring and so very turned on, she asked to see his bedroom, and he led her up the creaky old stairs and through the door to his narrow bed. They snuggled and made out in the plaid sheets that smelled like him, her framed picture smiling inches away on the bedside table. It was so personal. Too personal, too easy. She didn't ask to go back after that one time, too risky.

But boy, did she want to, because she was physically addicted to Stephen. She knew what would happen if they kept going up the creaky stairs. And she knew that Stephen would be more than okay with taking their relationship to that level. He was so in love with her that the cliché worry that he might just be using her for sex didn't even cross Elena's mind. She never asked to go upstairs again because Elena was worried that she might accidentally be using him.

Ever since they said I love you, everything was more: more intense, more addictive, more time-consuming. She got home later, did homework later, and neglected her friends. His stares and goodbyes were more frighteningly vulnerable and intense. "Yes, I'll definitely hang out Friday," she repeated to the Herd.

"I know it's hard," Morgan said. She'd been with Isaac for two years. "You obviously want to spend time with Stephen. But don't forget us, 'kay?"

Elena vowed to be a better real *and* secret friend, starting with the secret friend bit first. After lunch, Elena rushed to choir. For the second time that day, she used her Talent with adults to help a friend. The director stood at his stand, sorting through music.

"Hi, Elena," he said. "You're early today. Need anything?"

Elena motioned to the piano music for their most challenging piece, a Hayden cantata, and turned on her patented charm. "I'm having a hard time managing the page turns on this one," she fibbed. "Do you think I could have a page turner?"

"Absolutely. Anyone you like," he replied, turning his focus back to his music.

"Can you ask the old page turner for me? Kat? I really don't care one way or another, and that way, it won't be awkward, like I'm picking favorites or something."

"Whatever you say." By this time, a few students started to arrive.

Elena sidled into to her seat on the piano, careful to avoid telltale eye contact with anyone. As the room filled, she studied her ragged nails intensely. When the director said something, she looked up.

He spoke over the din. "Miss Kowalski, could you come down here?"

Kat gave a half shrug and walked to the front. She listened to the director, glanced at Bailey, glanced at Elena, and shrugged again. She grabbed a chair and dragged it to the piano in the traditional place to Elena's left.

"Hey," Elena said.

"Hey?" Kat said. "Since when do you need a page turner?"

"Since you need rescuing, and since we can talk all through class." "*Right?*" she thought-said, bumping Kat's leg with her own.

Kat allowed the side of her mouth facing away from the soprano section to twitch into a grin. "*Right,*" she said. "*But first, let me be irritated.*" She made a big show of dramatically rolling her eyes. With that taken care of, the girls proceeded to talk through the rest of class. Since their knees touched, communing was ridiculously simple.

"*Smart,*" Kat said. "*Why didn't I think of it.*" She turned a page. "*It's pretty hard to go through an entire day feeling like I can't talk to anyone that I trust. Just don't tell any jokes. I'm not brave enough to have anything other than resting bitch face.*"

"*Noted. Oops, turn the page,*" Elena said. "*I have to concentrate on this section, so shut up for a sec.*"

That's when Elena learned that you can think laugh too. Kat's chortle filled Elena's head with her friend's pent-up anxiety and sadness and happiness and all the stuff that she should have been able to share with her so-called Beautiful friends.

Elena finished the difficult passage, then they got back to think-talking. Elena told her about the scholarship and camp, Kat told her about Paige and Ty. They talked about what they had for lunch. They talked about the director's hair. It was so normal! Elena wondered if she and Kat looked like how Bailey and Kat did, back before the Piano Debacle. But, of course, they didn't. They weren't whispering, they weren't glancing around at people, and there was far less scowling. Plus, Elena played all the notes correctly

Things to do with Stephen besides make out (need to try!)
- *Movies*
- *Go for a walk*
- *Go to a game*
- *Do homework*
- *Talk about making out*
- ~~*Make out some more*~~

Chapter 38
Kat

Kat: Do we have canoes at zedernwald
Val: Maybe idk why
Kat: Trying to make us sound normal

"It would be easier to design a website," Kat complained. "Formatting a document is a pain."

"Neither sound easy to me," her mom answered, peering at Kat's laptop. "But Mary said that Elena's mom specifically requested a brochure."

"Hopefully, this will convince Elena's parents to let her go to camp."

Ever since Elena went out on a limb for her in choir, their friendship took a hesitant turn toward the better. Graphic design was the least she could do.

"All of these hoops for poor Elena."

"Yeah, she's in a weird situation," Kat replied, dropping a photo of girls kayaking into a field of text. "Do you have any idea how she ended up Spuren, if her mom isn't?"

"Not a clue," her mom answered with a shrug. "But I don't understand how the whole thing works anyway."

"I'm a little worried that girls will be mean to her, ask questions and stuff," Kat said, furiously hitting tab.

"I'm sure it'll be alright," her mom said.

Kat hated that her mom refused to get upset about things, in contrast to Elena's always-worried mom. "I think that her mom is mostly worried about Elena's college applications being weak if she goes to camp. Her dad is just anti-camp Zedernwald."

"I found out some more about the Tannins' drama," her mom said. "There was a major disagreement around how her aunt's mental illness was treated. And then Elena's grandma died within months of her aunt, and there was a scene at the funeral."

"I'm glad we don't have family stuff like that," Kat said. Her mom had one sister and two brothers. The Talent automatically created a divide between the siblings, since her uncles were clueless about the Spuren world. Still, her mom's siblings remained close. "Do you ever wish that we had a bigger family?" Kat asked, glancing at the three placemats on the table.

"Nope," her mom replied. "We knew after you were born that we couldn't possibly love anyone as much as you, so why tempt fate? So, it's just the three of us, even though we got pressure."

"From who?"

"Grandma and the older Spuren ladies. They want to make sure we have 'enough female lines going to keep the Talent alive,'" she said, throwing in air quotes.

"Who cares about 'the lines?' Aren't we all related somehow anyways?" Kat asked.

"That's what they say, way back. I have a few Spuren third cousins. It's so far in the past, we're pretty much strangers."

"It's weird to think that way back somewhere, I'm related to Elena." Kat said, hitting print.

"That's probably true of nearly everyone in Wisconsin," she said.

"Makes dating anyone a risk."

"Speaking of dating, do you see Ty much at school?" her mom asked, glancing up and down quickly.

"Nope. He's dating Bailey's sister, Paige," Kat said.

"That must be awkward for Bailey."

"You'd think so," said Kat sarcastically.

"Oh, dear."

"I'm kind of drifting away from Bailey and them, but I'm not sure what I'm drifting toward," Kat said, hitting "save."

"Maybe think of it less as moving toward a truer version of yourself," her mom said. "Michelangelo said something about how he didn't so much create sculptures, but rather released the forms that were already there in the marble, hidden. You've been carrying around a lot of extra marble protection. Maybe you need to let some of it go, honey?" she said.

"I know, Mom. You told me this before," Kat said, feeling cringey. She closed her laptop forcefully.

Her mom didn't answer and got up to collect pages from the printer.

Kat thought about the past couple weeks. With Elena's encouragement, she was working on her Tempering, occasionally letting it drop a bit. Kat started to see the Beautiful People with Talent-tinged nuance. She noticed how fragile the group's veneer of perfection was, how carefully everyone measured their words and monitored responses, how anxious they all were. The Beautiful People were exhausting and exhausted.

"Finished," her mom said leafing through the pages. The result of their three hours' work was a tri-fold brochure for "Zedernwald: A Camp for the Women of Tomorrow." They shamelessly modeled their work on other camps; if Meghan Walsh comparison-shopped, she'd find many similarities between Zedernwald and other girls' camps in the area. This was what Mary requested: bland legitimacy.

"I think it's good," Kat said, stretching. "No mention of learning to break a Spiral or to avoid accidental Communion. All nature, exercise, and leadership skills."

"I'll look it over for typos, then print off a few copies to send to Mary. Hopefully, it'll be enough to reassure Elena's parents," her mom said. "By the way, Mary said something about Elena's mom wanting to meet to hear more about camp."

"Sure, if she thinks it'll help. We just have to be careful. There's no adult in that family to help Elena protect the Spuren secret."

"All the more reason I'm happy to help her. Should I invite them over or arrange to meet somewhere?"

"Meet somewhere," Kat answered quickly. "They're, um, picky eaters."

•   •   •

A dinner date was arranged for the following weekend. Aunt Mary stopped by Kat's house before dinner so that they could get their stories straight. It was the first time they were all together since Elena was identified as Spuren.

"Okay, gals, let's chat," Mary said, collapsing into the recliner.

As Mary spoke about Spuren secrecy and tactics, Kat tried to identify a resemblance between her and Elena. There wasn't one. Mary was solid and wide. She had thick hands and short-cropped, beauty parlor curls. Elena was willowy, anxious to the point of stubby nails, and had naturally wild curls that she hated.

"…So, since Meghan was kind enough to allow me to communicate with Elena again, we have to respect her boundaries, but still push for Zedernwald."

Mary was tough. Kat wondered if she was that tough with Elena or if she treated family more gently.

"It'll be like navigating a 7-10 split. Very little room for error," Mary concluded.

"So," her mom said slowly, "we should talk up camp, but mostly, try to be normal?"

"Yes," Mary agreed, nodding. "I'm glad we had this chat. Any questions before the get-together?"

"No, ma'am," Kat and her mom answered in prompt unison.

CHAPTER 39
ELENA

The restaurant's windows were open, letting in a freakishly warm breeze. Fifty-degree March days were the stuff of Wisconsin dreams. The world stretched off the cricks of a long winter, ignoring the crusty bits of blackened snow that still clung to shadowed corners. Summer was just around the corner, with important decisions still to be made.

Sitting around the table, studying their menus, were Elena's mom, Kat and Linda Kowalski, and Aunt Mary. Elena pictured herself as the center of a wheel, connecting all their separate spokes, with one goal: Zedernwald.

Elena knew that her mom was warming to the idea, carefully studying the brochure Mary mailed. She carefully prepped Linda and Kat on how best to seduce her mother: female empowerment, quality programming, lifelong friendships. Plus, Aunt Mary was there. If anyone could stand up to a Meghan Walsh interrogation, it was Aunt Mary.

"Can I get you ladies started with something to drink?" a waitress asked.

"Diet Coke," Elena said. She'd need the caffeine to stay on point.

"Brandy old fashioned, sweet, three cherries," Aunt Mary ordered without looking at the menu.

"I'll have a Lakefront Gluten Free New Grist," Linda said, pointing to her menu.

"Just water," Kat ordered.

"Can I have a white wine spritzer?" her mom said. After the waitress left, she took charge. "Well, ladies, thanks so much for meeting us tonight!" She closed her menu and Elena knew she'd get the scallops. "You all know each other already, so I guess that makes me the odd one out!"

They all smiled, an air of friendly secrecy shrouding the table.

"Seems like *I'm* the odd one out, coming from up north," Aunt Mary said. "Except for that one time I met Elena, I've never even been to Belvedere. Seems like a nice town."

"Yes, we like it," Linda agreed. "We tried living somewhere else for a while, but ended up back here. Feels like home, I guess. Plus, it has this place." She gestured at the supper club's wood-paneled walls and décor frozen in the mid-70's.

"*This is so cringey,*" Kat said, and her mom kicked her leg under the table.

"*No think-talking,*" Linda scolded.

Elena mentally logged off and paid attention to the actual conversation. Aunt Mary gave a barely perceptible frown as she scanned her menu. Elena glanced at her mom, her hands folded and huge smile on her face. She remembered how she felt at St. Veronica's, when she discovered that her friends planned to skip school and exclude her. It sucked being left out, but Mom simply couldn't know the truth.

"I'm so glad that you came, Aunt Mary," said Elena. "I really want to go to Zedernwald this summer, and hopefully, you all can help me convince my mom!"

"Typical Elena, cutting right to the chase," her mom said. "Thanks again, Mary, for getting me the brochure so quickly. I was impressed."

"We certainly aren't running some fly-by-night, no-paperwork style operation," Aunt Mary said.

The waitress arrived with their drinks and took their dinner orders. When she walked away, Aunt Mary cleared her throat. "Ahem. I'd like to propose a toast." Dutifully, all the women raised a glass. "To friends, new and old. Cheers!"

"Cheers!" they replied, clinking and glancing around to see who would speak next. A comfortable conversational rhythm had yet to be established.

Linda took a generous gulp of her beer and began. "So, Meghan, you work downtown?"

"Yes. I'm a pathologist, a doctor for dead people. So, no pressure! Sorry," she said, glancing nervously around the table, "hope my gallows humor doesn't offend you,".

"Not at all," Linda said, smiling. "I'm the activities director at an assisted living facility. If I didn't have gallows humor, I couldn't make it through the day."

"Speaking of," Aunt Mary said, "I've been looking into those senior apartments. Do you know, has anyone ever built one that includes a bowling alley?"

"My parents live down at The Villages in Florida," Meghan said. "If you want to talk active, they could tell you stories," she said, waggling her eyebrows. "Apparently, they're all *very* active."

The women laughed, while Elena and Kat rolled their eyes. It was so awkward, but at least they were getting along.

As they talked, the three women drained their drinks and nodded when the waitress pointed at their empty glasses. The girls rolled their eyes again.

"Is that the place that has the highest rate of STD's in the state?" Linda asked, circling back to her mom's comment about The Villages.

"I wouldn't be surprised," Meghan responded

"I'm not sure I consider that a selling point," Mary said. "I'm looking for peace and quiet. Plus, think of all the broken hips!"

They hooted with laughter.

So much for worrying about keeping the conversation rolling, thought Elena. She and Kat checked out of the conversation once the term "hot flash" came out, along with the second round of drinks.

"They seem to be getting along okay," Elena said quietly, turning to the side to talk to Kat.

"Yup. You better watch out, or my mom will invite your mom to join her book club, a.k.a., wine club," Kat said.

"That wouldn't be the worst thing, would it?"

"I guess not, but your mom is so proper and smart. I'm afraid Mom's friends would shock her."

"She wasn't kidding about gallows humor," Elena said. "My mom doesn't have a ton of friends, but when she has people over, this is what it sounds like."

"How funny is Mary?" Kat said. "I can't wait to tell the girls this summer."

"I hope I get to be there for that!" Elena said. "Should we steer the conversation back to Zedernwald?"

"Leave it to me," Kat said, turning back to the adults. "So," she said loudly, during a pause in which all three women removed their glasses to wipe laughter-tears from their eyes, "about Zedernwald."

"Yes," Mary said, replacing her glasses. "Zedernwald. Meghan, I know you're worried about Elena's college applications, but I've been talking to a friend of mine who used to work admissions at the UW, and she said that schools look for a well-rounded applicant with a variety of life experiences."

"And," Linda added, "I can't tell you how much attending camp enriched my own life. Some of my best friends to this day are women I met there. My husband and I have absolutely no reservations about Kat attending. It's simply the best."

"I have to admit," Elena's mom said, folding her hands under her chin earnestly, "it looks amazing. Sometimes I wish I'd taken time for such an experience, or even a gap year. There's plenty of time for year-round pressure later in life,"

"Hear, hear," Mary said.

"Does that mean I can go?" Elena blurted.

"*Slow down!*" Linda, Mary, and Kat all thought loudly.

"Weeeeeell," her mom said, swirling her wine spritzer, "as far as I'm concerned, it's a yes." Kat and Elena squealed and hugged each other. "But." They stopped. "It depends on your father too. I don't like to present a divided front, but in this situation, it's best that you know the truth. He's still on the fence. We have to convince him, somehow."

"Any ideas?" Elena asked. Dad rarely held grudges, so there wasn't a roadmap for this situation.

"I have a few ideas," Aunt Mary interrupted. "He's always been stubborn, but I think we can convince him. I'll work on a few things from my end and then, Elena, when the time is right, you have to come right out and ask him. I recommend—oh!" she interrupted herself as their waitress appeared with a tray laden with covered dishes. "Put a pin in that, looks like our food's here!"

They murmured words of appreciation at the supper club fare that attracted customers for over fifty years.

"Yes, let's eat and talk Anders later," Elena's mom said, picking up her fork. "These scallops look amazing."

Elena smiled as she cut into her chicken. Maybe her oh-so-predictable Mom had a few surprises after all.

Later that night, Elena received a text from Aunt Mary:

Dear Elena. I Think That Went Well. I Will Be Sending Your Dad A Package That I Think Will Help To Sway Him. After He Gets It Wait A Few Days Then Pounce. Sincerely, "Aunt Mary"

•   •   •

"And she's gonna be sending some sort of magical, I don't know, thing to convince my Dad. So now I just wait," Elena said. She and Kat were on the phone talking about what they decided was a really successful evening, overall. Aside from their moms' next-level embarrassing behavior. But, at least they were both embarrassing.

"Well, it better come quick. Camp's less than two months away."

"No kidding. Your mom's a great teacher, but, no offense, I'm ready for some honors-level Spuren learning."

Kat rolled her eyes. "You will have plenty to learn from everyone. Especially the other girls."

"What, like special Spuren make-out tricks?"

"You'd be surprised."

Elena suddenly had an opening to ask a question that'd been bugging her for months. "So, I have a question," she blurted, speaking faster than ever. "With everyone else, my Talent gives me tons of information, but with Stephen, nothing. I've never once gotten a read off him. Why doesn't my Talent work with him? Is something wrong with me? I mean we're obviously serious, sometimes too serious to be honest…" Elena trailed off, letting all of the vulnerable honesty hang thick across her phone screen.

A slow smile spread across Kat's face.

"What's so funny?" Elena demanded, embarrassed.

"Girl. This is a good thing. A very good thing."

"How?"

"You're Heart-Blocked. He's sending so many huge feelings toward you, that they somehow cancel out your Talent. We all dream of our first Heart Block!"

"Oh. My. God. Now what?"

"I guess you be glad that your mom wants you on birth control," Kat teased, knowing it was a sensitive topic for Elena.

Elena stuck out her tongue and quickly ended the call. Heart Block as an explanation made no sense and perfect sense, just like everything about being Spuren. It probably had something to do with the fact that she really never picked up anything from her family either, other than vague moods. It explained her uncanny connect / disconnect with Stephen, and why she probably was so physically addicted to him. She needed to be careful, she suddenly realized. Cuz, apparently, he was really, really into her—even when they weren't making out.

Stephen weirdness
- *Stephen=Talent kryptonite?*
- *He loves me. Gulp. I guess I love him too? Right?*
- *Apparently really, really loves me? (Heart block????)*

CHAPTER 40
MEGHAN

Meghan had bookmarked the picture of Nell at camp on her computer, and she went back to it obsessively the night after the supper club dinner. Every refresh convinced her of one thing: she wanted camp and its gang of girlfriends for Elena. The next morning, she set down her phone and turned to the unexpected wall of stubbornness that was her husband.

"Hey," she said to Anders over the twins' heads. They sat on the couch, watching the kids' favorite TV show, something about dogs wearing masks. "I wanted to tell you more about dinner the other night."

"You said everyone behaved and the scallops were good. Any juicy details?" he asked.

"Katherine's mom, Linda, only had good things to say about the camp. She went when she was a kid, and Katherine has gone for several years."

"Camp Zedernwald has a loyal following. How was Aunt Mary?" he asked.

"She's kind of a hoot," Meghan said.

"Yeah," Anders said, fiddling with some Legos that he dug from between the couch cushions. "She was always a big personality. The three of them—Mom, Mary, and Sylvie— really knew how to work a room."

"I wonder," Meghan said carefully, "if that's part of the reason you're still angry with them; that they overshadowed your dad?"

Anders stopped fiddling. "After Nellie and Mom died, it was just him and me, and I felt like I had to protect him, y'know? He seemed so small without Mom."

"You feel a lot of loyalty to him," she echoed.

"That's it. I feel like holding this grudge is somehow paying respect to my dad!" Anders seemed to have a breakthrough. "How crazy is that?"

They sat in silence. She thought about how, every spring, they went to the cemetery and planted flowers at his family's graves. "Do you think that your dad wanted this bitterness to be his legacy?"

"Maybe not. But I don't want Elena to start thinking that my dad was bad, either. I don't want Mary and Sylvie filling her head with nonsense."

"Your dad never struck me as vindictive," Meghan said. "I like to remember him sitting in his chair, watching people come and go while he nursed his Manhattan, in that plastic Bucky Badger cup."

"You mean brandy over ice, with a bottle of vermouth opened on the counter nearby?" Anders said, smiling.

"Drunk religiously during the 6:30 airing of *Wheel of Fortune*."

"I wonder what happened to those cups. We brought them home from UW football games." Anders looked down at his Spotted Cow resting on the coffee table, then glanced at the clock that read 6:25. He laughed. His laugh turned him into the young man at the house party where they met.

"So, maybe you'll consider it at least?" Meghan asked quietly.

"I'll consider it. Let me finish the taxes, and then I'll worry about the Zedernwald problem. Sound fair?"

She smiled at her husband over the kids' heads, pleased with the baby step of progress she made. Now to wait for the divine intervention that Aunt Mary promised, whatever that might be.

•   •   •

When Meghan went upstairs at 10:30, light still peeked from Elena's cracked door. It wasn't unusual for Elena to still be awake. What was unusual were the questions swirling in Meghan's mind. She knocked on the door.

"Come in," Elena said. She leaned against her headboard, writing in a notebook that she casually tucked under her pillow. "What's up?"

"Oh, nothing much. You're still an *Anne* fan, hey?" Meghan asked, noticing the well-worn copy on the floor.

"Some things never change," Elena said, shrugging and pulling her hair into a messy bun. Her fingernails were still the ragged stuff of a child, but otherwise, she looked old enough to get into a bar with a lax ID policy.

"So, Katherine seems nice. Her mom invited me to join her book club. Is Katherine a member of the Herd?"

"She goes by Kat. She's in some of my classes, but we have different friend groups," Elena replied. "Why?"

"I just like to know who you're hanging out with," Meghan said. "How weird is it that this random girl in Belvedere happens to go to Mary and Sylvie's camp, huh?"

Elena glanced up. "I know, right? I forget how it came up, but we figured out that we had that connection. What do you think of Aunt Mary?"

"The few times I've talked to her on the phone and now in person, I really like her."

"Few times? I thought it was just the once. Have you been checking up on me?" Elena asked.

"A little bit," Meghan said, trying to stay calm. "But I also wanted to talk to her about Dad's family. I wanted to get a few facts straight."

"What kind of facts?"

"Oh, who did what to who, when," Meghan said. "When you get down to it, most family quarrels are pretty boring. Sounds like it's the same with this one."

"Do you think it will ever get better? Between Dad and Aunt Mary and Sylvie?" Elena asked.

"I hope so, especially now that we've connected with her. All of this drama is getting to be a bit much," Meghan said. "Speaking of drama, Mary said something about you helping Kat with a bad boyfriend situation?"

Elena lay back, legs still crossed, and looked at the ceiling while she spoke. "I found her crying in the bathroom at the dance. I was the only one around, so I talked to her," she said slowly. "She was dating a real a-hole. I helped her think of a plan to get home."

"That's amazing," Meghan said, simultaneously proud and appalled. "We raised you to be strong, but remember that even strong women can find themselves in bad situations. You know you can always call us, no questions asked, if you feel stuck, right?" So many lessons to get in, so little time.

"I know, Mom," Elena sighed. "But you seriously don't have to worry about Stephen. I finally had to tell him to not open the car door for me. He's almost too gentlemanly."

"Watch out for him being overly controlling."

"He's *not*, Mom," Elena said.

"You really like him, huh?"

"I don't know," Elena said, squirming. She pulled the blanket over her head.

Meghan took the hint and stood. "I just wanted to check in, say I'm proud of you, and remind you that if any guy ever tries to force you to do something that you don't want to do, you should kick him in the balls."

"Mom!" Elena shrieked, sitting up and throwing the covers off with a shocked expression.

Meghan closed the door with a smug grin. While drifting off to sleep, she moved Elena and Stephen up her mental list of things to worry about. Things between the two of them seemed to be going worrisomely well.

•   •   •

A few days later, Meghan sat in a waiting room, stress-scrolling through Facebook. Elena was in with a provider. Alone. For birth control. Hence the stress-scrolling. Meghan wasn't sure how imminent the need was, but in the words of a mentor, "You'd rather be looking at it than looking for it."

She presented going on birth control to Elena as an automatic step rather than a response to the state of her and Stephen's relationship. Sophomore year? Get your license. Junior year? Get on birth control. She was proud of her frank, age-appropriate approach to sexuality throughout Elena's life. It was so unlike her own experience, which involved a prepackaged kit from Kimberly Clark and an admonition to 'save it for marriage.' She thought back to their conversation with a mixture of pride and mortification.

"Elena," she said, walking into her room the same way she had the previous night, "we need to have a talk."

Elena laid aside her textbook and sighed dramatically. "Yippee," she said. "Let's see, we've already done 'how babies are made,' 'the mechanics of intercourse,' 'tampons and you,' and 'no means no.' What super awkward topic do we have tonight?"

"Pre-planning for responsible sexual activity," she replied, sounding vaguely like an ad for a funeral home.

"Oh. My. God. Mom," Elena said, barely moving. "Is this really necessary? I am not having sex."

"Well, I'd rather know that when you were ready to do so, in a safe, mutually respectful relationship, you are prepared. What are the risks of sexual activity?" she quizzed.

"I dunno. Diseases," Elena replied.

"Excellent, yes," she said, ignoring the stubborness. "And how can we prevent acquisition of said diseases?"

"Condoms," Elena muttered.

"Every—"

"Every time, no exceptions, and there are condoms in the top shelf of the bathroom," she recited.

"And condoms prevent all sexually transmitted infections, correct?" she asked.

"No, that's why you should trust your partner and be in a monogamous relationship," Elena said in a singsong. "We've been over this."

"You're right. I was quizzing you," Meghan said. She spoke in a clinical fashion, the manner that felt most comfortable. "I'm glad you've been paying attention. The other thing that condoms can't reliably prevent is pregnancy, which is why we advise young women to choose a more reliable form of birth control well before the onset of sexual activity."

" 'Well before the onset' would be me, Mom," Elena said, getting red in the face. "Stop talking like I'm your student or your patient!"

"I know the topic of birth control pills came up after you had that fainting episode. Even though your anemia is better without them, it might be a good time to consider starting. You know, get things straightened out before you move off to college and sow your wild oats."

"Mother. This is so embarrassing. I don't want to talk to you about this," Elena screeched.

"Fine, but will you talk to another doctor? One who's not your mother?"

"Yes, anything, just get out of here!" she exclaimed, throwing a pillow at Meghan.

So, she got out of there and made the appointment.

When she told Anders, he said, "I trust you to handle this. Better you than me."

Meghan sighed and began planning for Jacob's puberty with a vengeance. Her attention jerked back to the present when Elena dropped a prescription into her lap.

"Here," she said. The P.A. wrote a script for a brand of pills which Meghan recognized. "Did they have to do an exam or anything?"

"Nope," Elena said, "thank God. Just pee in a cup. Can we go now?"

"Sure." Meghan was relieved. She knew that the P.A. would do a full exam if Elena said she was already sexually active, and Elena wouldn't lie to a medical professional. She still had the upper hand in a few situations with Elena, such as being familiar with medical management and the clues it provided. Unfortunately, the situations in which she had the upper hand seemed to be growing rarer by the day.

CHAPTER 41
ELENA

"I'm so glad your parents got rid of the no Sunday night dates rule," Stephen said. "But I don't like the whole 10 pm curfew and having to do this in my car."

"This" was messing around in the backseat, which wasn't nearly as romantic as it appeared in the movies. His parents were still up, watching TV inside, which is how Elena found herself squished next to Stephen in the car, instead of on the blue couch. They already made out in the parking lot near the park before driving home, but Elena couldn't resist some more in Stephen's driveway at the end of the night.

"It's okay, better than nothing," she said, arching her body against his in a way that she'd learned was particularly effective. Her clothes were on-ish, but her bra was unhooked, and the windows were fogged.

Stephen kissed the base of her throat and Elena closed her eyes. She almost missed the sound of gravel crunching, but not quite. She froze, popped her eyes open, and made the briefest, most humiliating eye contact with Stephen's father through the car window. He quickly looked away and hurried into the house.

Elena flung herself to the floor, squealing into her sleeve.

"What's wrong? Did I hurt you?" Stephen rolled onto his side and looked down at her.

"Your freaking dad just walked by and HE SAW US!" Elena whisper-shrieked. "This is so embarrassing! I thought they were inside!"

"Jesus, Elena, you freaked me out. He must've been out. He won't care. He's walked in on much worse, trust me."

"He's gonna think that we're having sex…"

"I'm pretty sure he already thinks we're already having sex, if the box of condoms that appeared in the bathroom means anything."

"And…I did start taking the pill."

"Did you go to Planned Parenthood or something? That's a big deal!"

"Nope, I had help. My mom took me to a clinic," Elena said.

"Wait, your mom knows?"

"Yeah, it was actually her idea…"

"Now we can both be awkward around each other's parents," Stephen said, kissing her ear and staring past her at their reflections.

They sat quietly for a while, the mood ruined, a window cracked to allow the fog to clear. Elena felt uncomfortably grown up, all the sudden. It was getting close to ten, and she didn't know what came next in this "serious relationship" plan.

"I need to get home," she said.

Elena started to scoot toward her door, but Stephen pulled her out his side first. He flicked on the headlights which blared into his now-darkened house, and pulled her into the spotlight.

"Elena Tannin," he pronounced loudly, "you are the best first love a guy could ask for, and I don't care who knows it," and he pulled her into what can only be described as a kiss from the pages of a cringey young adult romance novel.

• • •

"And, of course, we'll go to dinner at the Prime Quarter," Addison said.

Elena thought back to her charred steak from the Winter Dance. She couldn't believe that was almost five months ago, and that she and Stephen were together for nearly that long.

"Prime Quarter it is," Elena said. "Kayla, wanna ride with me and Stephen?"

Kayla nodded. "I normally wouldn't butt in, but since it's Spring Fling, I don't mind."

Elena worried she was ignoring Kayla lately, spending more time with Stephen and Kat. She tried to call Kayla a couple times to hang out over spring break, but she was always busy. If Kayla minded Elena's absence, she didn't show it; maybe she was working on a project or something? The spring dance was the perfect chance to make it up to her.

"It'll be great," Addison said. "Sorry, Elena, but Spring Fling isn't super romantic, in case you were hoping for a chance to make out on the dance floor with Stephen."

"I can barely hold his hand in public, let alone make out in front of the entire school," Elena said. Her stomach fluttered, remembering the Snowball. There were bits that she loved remembering, such as that first kiss in the car. The end of the dance? Not so much. And it felt like all the Herd could talk about lately was her and Stephen.

"*Hey,*" Kat said, her leg nudging Elena's as she started playing chords for warm-up.

"*Hey. We were talking about the Spring Fling at lunch. Are you going?*"

"*I haven't decided.*"

"*You're can come with us,*" Elena said. "*I'm sorry I didn't think of it sooner. But I just assumed...*"

"*That I probably wouldn't want to break up with the Beautiful People by ditching them at a dance? Correct. So don't feel guilty.*"

"*Well, I do. Addison said that it's the funnest.*"

"*It is. More dancing in groups and less making out on the dance floor.*"

"*You're the second person to mention that. I think it's a sign that I should absolutely never do it!*"

The girls laughed. Thought laughing was delightful. It was somewhat auditory, involving the sounds that a Kat laugh made, plus a warm feeling, like when you take a big drink of hot cocoa and it hits bottom all at once.

"Either way," Kat continued, *"I won't have to lose 20 pounds this time. Not that I don't need to."*

"You actually would do that?" Elena asked, incredulous.

"Yeah, I diet for every dance. It's not that hard, really. As long as I only eat 800 calories a day and work out for an hour, I can usually drop 20 pounds in about a month," Kat said.

"I think you look gorgeous," Elena said.

"I don't want to talk about it," Kat said, zapping the warmth of the previous laughter.

Elena went along with her request, but she didn't feel good about it.

•   •   •

The Spring Fling was on April 1, which is how Elena found herself standing with her parents and Stephen, listening to her mom talk about history. She felt Stephen's grip on her hand become strangling as her mom finished up. "…But the most likely explanation for April Fool's Day has to do with the change from the Julian to the Gregorian calendar." When Mom felt awkward, she lectured.

"Well, I'm sure you kids want to get out of here," her dad interrupted.

Elena smiled at him. "Yeah, we have to get Kayla before we go to the restaurant." Elena felt so much more relaxed in her outfit than she had in the Snowball dress. Her flowered dress from the back of her closet allowed for a bra, and her sandals were cute without being painful. She left her hair down and curly.

At the grill-your-own steak restaurant, Elena took control of the situation and stood next to Morgan's boyfriend, Isaac, at the communal grill. She didn't give Stephen a chance to massacre her steak, upending the ridiculous gender norms of the dated restaurant.

"I'm not going to complain," Stephen said to the group, shrugging. "My attempt last time was a disaster. Real men don't need to grill. Plus, they wear pink," he said, flipping his collar in Kayla's direction, who laughed.

Elena brought back respectable attempts at medium and medium rare steaks. She watched videos to prepare, so she wasn't completely clueless.

After dinner, the Herd and their dates caravanned to the high school, arriving just as the sun dipped below the horizon, sending optimistic pink shoots into the low-lying clouds. Elena took a deep breath and soaked up the moment; the earth smelled alive, Stephen's arm rested around her shoulders, her friends' laughter echoed, and a clump of hopeful crocuses huddled next to the gym door. She automatically worried that if she was too happy, she would jinx it. Maybe she should be worrying more about something. She decided to be happy anyway.

The dance was as fun as the Herd promised. Like the winter formal, it took place in the school gym. Unlike the formal, there were no fairy lights or gauzy swags hinting at romance. The only decorations were a few clusters of balloons. The DJ mixed popular hits and electronic dance numbers that kept everyone dancing. Eventually, someone propped open the outer gym doors to let in a cool breeze.

Elena barely left the dance floor. She went from dancing with Stephen, to dancing with the Herd, then finding him like magnets when the DJ played a slow song. In a moment of insanity, she let Stephen kiss her in front of everyone.

After a while, Elena relaxed her Tempering. Her Talent was mostly shut down anyway, thanks to the combined electric and acoustic onslaught from the DJ. She danced through a sea of teenage emotional energy, letting it wash over and through her. The feeling of surrender reminded her of when Stephen taught her to drive stick. At first, it was a battle of wills between the clutch, the gearshift, the steering wheel, and her brain. The car won every time, repeatedly stalling in the church parking lot where they practiced.

"You gotta stop overthinking this," Stephen said. "Just flow with the car. Let the car drive you."

"Oh, that sounds really safe," Elena said sarcastically.

"You wanna see unsafe?" Stephen said. "Close your eyes. All you have to worry about is the clutch and the gearshift. I'm going to steer. Now, close your eyes."

"What?"

"Yup. I'll steer us around this completely empty parking lot in the middle of the country. You just listen to the car and shift when it's time. Stop staring at the tachometer."

"This is ridiculous."

"Shut up," he kissed her, "and shut your eyes." She complied, after rolling her eyes first.

And his stupid idea worked. After panicking, she gave in and shifted the car up to third gear and back down before stopping.

Riding the feelings at the dance was like that afternoon, eyes shut, in the church parking lot. She didn't try to muscle through the emotional waves, she surfed along the top and let them pass through her, neither anticipating what would come next, nor fixating on any one thing, just observing and moving on. Maybe, like driving manual, this was something she'd eventually be able to do easily.

Around 10, Elena sensed that Kat arrived. She scanned the room and spotted her walking upstairs with a few Beautiful People. They gathered on the balcony overlooking the gym. Elena smiled at her and waved. Amazingly, Kat smiled back. The room was crowded and they were too far away to form a connection, but the huge public smile was more than Kat ever gave her before.

Annoyingly, anytime Elena connected with Kat, she felt guilty about Kayla, and vice versa. She assumed that her two friends would feel in competition with each other given their past, plus there was the added responsibility to tend to her shy, single friend's feelings, particularly at a dance where there were so many couples. Elena realized she hadn't seen Kayla in a little while, not since the other girl left to go to the bathroom.

"Have you seen Kayla?" she asked Stephen.

He shook his head, as did the other people she asked. She walked quickly to the bathroom, illogically fearing a repeat of the last dance, when she discovered an emotionally broken Kat in the stalls. "Kayla?" she said, opening the door. A group of vaping freshmen guiltily looked up. "Have you seen Kayla Klein?" Elena asked.

"She left," one of them offered, "I think."

Elena nodded and stepped back into the hallway. Should she go back toward the dance or down the deserted hallway toward empty classrooms? She quieted her mind and took a deep breath, listening with her Talent for the unmistakable sound of Kayla's emotional energy, flickering and steady at the same time.

She found it, pinging inexplicably from the darkened hallways. Something was off. Elena kicked off her practical, yet still impractical sandals and ran silently down the hallway to its intersection with the next, where she sensed Kayla was somehow trapped. She imagined the worst, and tried to remember basic self-defense maneuvers. Her mom's advice to kick him in the balls echoed in time to her footsteps.

As she rounded the corner, she saw Kayla bathed in the light of an exit sign. She was pinned against the wall! Elena took a deep breath to yell. Through some miracle, the sound caught in Elena's throat before she blurted a warning. On closer inspection, the trap in which Kayla was captured appeared intentional. Kayla reached to take the hand of her captor, a tall sophomore girl that Elena recognized, but didn't know by name. When the girl leaned down to kiss Kayla, Elena realized that she had it all wrong.

Elena tiptoed back down the hallway to her waiting sandals, mortified by her faulty assumptions: assuming that she was the main character in Kayla's life, assuming that Kayla told her everything, assuming that she read the book of Kayla correctly in the first place. So much for all-seeing Talent. Some best friend I am.

"Everything okay?" Stephen asked when she got back to the gym.

Elena nodded and leaned into his chest which smelled like cologne and sweat. She needed to hold onto something real, and for now, Stephen was that thing. Her Talent never worked on him anyway.

<u>Stephen weirdness</u>

- *Stephen=Talent kryptonite?*
- *He loves me. Gulp. I guess I love him too? Right?*
- *Apparently really, really loves me? (Heart block????)*
- *=real reason for cringey pink pill dispenser*

CHAPTER 42
KAT

Kat remained behind on the balcony overlooking the dance while the Beautiful Girls that she caught a ride with went down to the gym to join the others already there. With her newly-thawed Talent, observing the scene was like watching a field of athletes with play-by-play explanation, like when the TV announcer marked up the screen with a virtual pen to analyze a play.

She saw Elena return from the bathroom hallway and collapse onto Stephen in emotional exhaustion, while the rest of the Herd and their dates danced happily nearby. They were so goofy. Didn't they know how ridiculous they looked, doing those stupid dance moves? Kat caught herself automatically invoking BP criticisms and winced. Sure, the Herd looked goofy, but compared to the more sophisticated BP cluster with its anxiety cloud, they were shrouded in happiness. The Herd wouldn't stand out in anyone's social media feed, but Kat's Talent rendered the Herd beautiful, the BP unbearable.

Kat had to get out of there. She messaged the BP group chat that she wasn't feeling well and would walk home. She slipped out a side door, away from the Herd, the BP, and everyone else. She didn't drop a glass slipper, but she felt like she symbolically left something behind. She stepped into the night air, the door slamming behind her, locking her out of the gym.

Kat started walking home. As she slid between cars in the parking lot, the nighttime silence was abruptly shattered by the low rumble of Ty's emotional energy, a khaki cacophony that drowned out everything in its path. Kat spotted his car a couple rows ahead and started to make a sharp turn away. That's when she noticed the tinkling ping of energy chirping underneath Ty's yawps. She didn't recognize the source, but whoever it was needed help.

All she wanted to do was mind her own business, yet here she was, getting drawn back into Ty's bullshit! Furious, Kat stormed toward his SUV, which lurched concerningly. There wasn't much actual noise coming from the car, just the Talent-detected yelps of someone she suspected was Bailey's sister, Paige.

Stupid Ty never locked his doors, which is how Kat easily unveiled the grotesque scene. Paige lay on her stomach on the seat, Ty pinned her shoulders down with one hand, muffling her face against the seat. With his other hand, he fumbled with her flowered sundress. The torn hem strained against Ty's pale, hairy thigh.

"Hey, asshole," Kat said quietly as the illuminating dome light froze him long enough for Paige to squish her head to the side. The light from Kat's phone settled on his face.

Paige's muffled shrieks coalesced into one panted word. "Stop."

"You heard her, stop," Kat said icily. "Or I share video."

"Shut the fuck up, Kat!" Ty said wildly, trying to calculate a plan with his two functioning neurons while pulling up his pants. He stumbled out of the car, his fury lashing toward Kat.

"What will Coach think when he sees all this?" Kat said quietly, filming and neatly taking a step backward. "Nope," she said, holding her phone out of Ty's swiping grasp. "Automatic cloud backup, remember?"

He frantically looked between Kat in front of him and Paige behind, like a trapped opossum staring down headlights on a country road at night. Pathetic.

"When will you learn that, even if someone's shoved into the seat, no means no." Kat wanted to hurt him, to kick him in the balls or something. But she realized that, at that moment, Paige needed her more than she needed vengeance. She walked around the car and opened the opposite door, helping the younger girl out. Kat gathered her wrap and purse from the floor, but left behind the crushed flowers. Neither looked back as they walked to well-lit doorway, away from both the gym and Ty.

Kat sat next to Paige on the curb, sensing that she needed silence. Paige texted frantically, in between dabbing at her eyes and rearranging her hair. Kat was tempted to see who she was texting, but forced herself to look straight out across the parking lot, where Ty's headlights cut a hasty retreat into the darkness.

"Somebody coming?" Kat eventually asked.

Paige nodded. "Aunt. She'll take me home. I posted to my story that I got a migraine."

Kat understood her instinct to create a cover story. "I'll wait with you 'til she gets here."

Paige nodded, staring at her hands in her lap.

Kat knew she felt sad and embarrassed. "He pulled the same shit with me."

Paige gave her an astonished glance. "But you're a badass."

Kat was surprised to hear the younger girl's impression of her and searched for a reply. She thought back to the speech Elena gave her at the Winter Dance, but didn't think it would work in this situation. Finally, she simply said, "I'm sorry that happened to you."

Paige nodded and sniffled. "Yeah. Me too." She was quiet for a second and then said, "You won't say anything, right? Won't share that video?"

"Not if you don't want me to. I promise. I'm sorry I didn't say anything about Ty before," Kat replied.

"No one would have believed you," Paige said. She glanced at her phone. "My aunt's here." She stood up to walk to the curb to meet a car that pulled along the drive. She got in and didn't turn back to say anything more.

* * *

Kat: call ltr
Elena: K home in 10

"What's up?" Elena asked without preamble. She was in her pajamas with her makeup somewhat removed. "I saw you at the dance for a sec. Where'd you go?"

"Nowhere," Kat answered. "I left, but you'll never believe what happened."

Elena shook her head in disgusted silence as Kat told the story. "That effing asshole."

"I know. Do you think I should say something to, I don't know, someone?"

"Not about Paige, not if she asked you not to," Elena answered.

"Obv."

"But if you ever wanted to tell a cop or a counselor or whoever what happened with you, I'd support you."

Kat nodded, trying to imagine what that would be like. She wasn't sure, but her ideas about what she was capable of seemed to be changing by the day.

"Thank God you've started using your Talent instead of freezing it. You literally rescued Paige," Elena said.

"Yeah," Kat said, stunned. Talent as a force for good, what a novel idea. She had so much to tell Val.

Kat: Call when u have a sec ready to talk about ty
Val: OMG calling

CHAPTER 43
MEGHAN

Meghan compared this April weekend to that of the winter dance. That December night, Meghan was still awake at 10, when an unwell Elena slumped through the door. Last night, Elena stayed out until seconds before her 2 a.m. curfew and was giddy when she entered. On the December next-morning, Elena couldn't get out of the house fast enough, rushing to secretly meet with Aunt Mary. This morning, she wasn't in a hurry to leave at all. She sat in the comfy upholstered chair, occasionally talking to Meghan, who tiptoed around the unexpected friendliness, making breakfast. Rather than leaving the house altogether, Elena invited Kat over.

Meghan, plotting to keep the girls in the kitchen, threw together a brownie mix, dug some caramel sauce out of the pantry, and rescued a gallon of ice cream from freezer. She closely approached the girls only once, to provide un-asked for seconds. Kat initially refused, but quickly changed her mind. Meghan provided generous helpings and retreated to work at her laptop on the counter. She sat near enough to eavesdrop, but far enough away that it wasn't blatantly obvious. To complete the ruse, she sat with her back to them, with headphones in, but no music playing.

She caught bits and pieces of their cryptic conversation. The girls talked and then sat in mutual silence for longer than felt comfortable to Meghan. Maybe they were close enough friends that silence didn't feel awkward, or maybe it was the phones. Both were foreign to Meghan's recollection of adolescence.

"It was a very Talented evening," Elena muttered, smiling at her phone.

"Truth," said Kat.

What an odd way to describe it; there must have been a lot of good dancers.

"I didn't see that coming. Or maybe I did," Kat said several minutes later, raising her eyebrows. "I promise I won't say anything. Besides, no one's interested in gossip about Kayla."

"I didn't see it coming either. I feel so dumb," Elena said.

Meghan tried to figure out the juicy secret; they must have texted it to each other.

"I don't know how I'm *not* going say anything to her," Elena continued. "I mean, I want her to know I'm happy for her, but I don't want to make her embarrassed."

Maybe Kayla won another award?

"It's not your fault. You know that," Elena said sometime later, drinking the last bits of melted ice cream from the bowl.

Meghan was completely lost.

"Did you see Addison's pictures?" Elena asked. "I like this one of all of us." She passed her phone to Kat.

"That's gorgeous," she agreed. "You all look good."

"You should at least consider hanging out with the Herd sometimes. Maybe just one or two people? Kayla? Addison?"

Meghan was surprised that Kat wasn't part of the Herd.

"Addison scares me," Kat said. "What do you think she'd say if she knew I was here?"

"She's intense," Elena agreed, eating a spoonful of plain caramel sauce. "Honestly? She doesn't exactly seem like a big fan of yours."

"No," Kat agreed. "There's the Kayla thing. Plus, since I'm BP, I'm bad, which is actually unfair. It's like, as individuals, they're—we're—mostly okay, but the problem is when we're—they're all together."

"Mmm-hmm," Elena agreed. "Too bad we can't all just get to know people as *people*."

"Whatever, Elena."

"Did you ever see that old movie, *The Breakfast Club*?"

Meghan smiled to think of that movie being a classic. Sigh.

"Is that the one with the mom from *Riverdale*?" Kat asked.

Elena nodded.

"Yeah, my mom made me watch it," Kat said. "It was pretty good. But kind of unrealistic."

"I guess."

The girls went back to their phones again.

"And maybe, around the Herd, I could manage healthy Tempering better…" Kat murmured distractedly.

"Kat!" Elena exclaimed. Meghan glanced up and saw both girls staring at her anxiously.

"Thanks for the treats," Kat said, abruptly bringing her plate over to the sink.

"Let's go upstairs," Elena said, doing the same.

Tempering? Just when Meghan thought she had a clue, teenage social media trends smacked her down. She really needed to get on Instagram.

•　　•　　•

Anders' self-imposed April 15 deadline was quickly approaching. He already had the taxes in, but hadn't said anything about Elena and Zedernwald. Meghan resisted bringing it up, though, remembering Aunt Mary's supper club promise of an intervention before doing so.

The Monday after Elena's dance, Meghan got home from work around 5:30. The sun treaded water slightly above the horizon, offering a promise of longer summer evenings to come. Meghan sorted the mail, where a thick package stood out, and a glance at the handwriting told her who it was from. Anders' name and address were written in neat, Palmer-method script. The envelope itself was sealed with an excessive amount of packing tape and 16 mismatched stamps. Aunt Mary's intervention had arrived.

"Hey," she said, walking into the kitchen.

"Hey," Anders answered. "How was your day?"

"Good. Looks like you got something from Aunt Mary," she said nonchalantly.

Meghan left him alone with the package and found the twins coloring at a paper-covered table.

"Hi, Mama," Ava said. "We're making pictures for your work."

"They're gorgeous," Meghan said, kneeling to study the cryptic images. "Tell me about them."

"Here's our family," Jacob said, pointing to a cluster of circles with twig limbs. "There's me and Ava, and Daddy and you, and Lay Lay, and Stephen."

"Is Stephen in our family?" Meghan asked, interested in his nearly four-year old take on things.

"Yes," Jacob said. "Because they kiss like you and Daddy."

"Ew, kissing!" Ava said, and the twins giggled.

"When did you see them kissing?" Meghan asked. Elena and Stephen were generally reserved, thank God.

"At night, I got up to go to the bathroom, and I saw them downstairs kissing and wrestling," Ava said. "So, that means they will get married. But I don't put Stephen in *my* pictures."

Oy. She'd have to have a conversation about discretion with Elena, and make sure that she was taking her pills. "Elena and Stephen are many years from getting married. They might not marry each other at all," she explained.

"I'm going to marry Daddy," Ava announced.

"And I'm going to marry you, Mommy," Jacob added, enveloping her in a hug.

"Sounds like a plan," she answered. "I'm going to go talk to Daddy, okay?"

"Sounds like a plan," Ava said.

Meghan returned to the kitchen and found Anders sitting at the table in front of a pile of papers, wearing his reading glasses.

"What did she send?"

"All this," he said, motioning to the stack of papers. They were yellowed, creased, and covered in handwriting. To the side lay a worn leather bag. On top of the pile sat a note on familiar "Let the Good Times Roll" stationery.

"Old letters?" she asked.

"Yeah." He picked up Aunt Mary's note and read from it. "Left in Mom's room at Zedernwald. She says that these are the letters that my dad wrote Mom her last summer at camp with Nellie, that Mom kept all the letters in the bag, that she read them every night. They did this every summer, and apparently, he made this for her," he held up the leather satchel, "the first summer that she and Nellie went away." He shook his head.

Was he amused? Confused? Angry? "Can I see it?" Meghan asked, searching for a clue. He didn't *sound* angry.

"Sure," Anders replied, handing her the bag and gathering the letters into a stack. "I remember Dad being into leather-working one summer. We made knife holders. I never knew he made this, though."

Meghan picked up the bag, worn smooth with time. It had a brass hasp that, when closed, created a large, gusseted envelope. The inside was soft, with scattered ink stains. There were little loops and pockets inside with tooling. The pockets were labeled: "envelopes" "stamps" "pens" "paper." The main opening had a divider down its length. One side was labeled "from Dick." That must have been where she kept the letters that she received. There were two larger pockets sewn to the inside of the bag on that side. One was labeled "Anders" and the other "Me."

"Did you check in these pockets?" she asked.

"No, I've been just reading through the letters. They're amazing! I had no idea my dad wrote letters, let alone good letters."

"What a treasure," Meghan breathed. She lifted the flap on the pockets labeled "Anders" and reached inside. Her fingers encountered familiarly sharp edges that she couldn't identify until she pulled them out. "Polaroids!" she exclaimed.

"The Polaroid camera, I remember," Anders said, looking up and holding out a hand to see the pictures after she flipped through.

"These are all of you. You must be in high school, younger than when I knew you." She studied the lanky, less-chiseled version of Anders. He favored cargo shorts that summer, posing in front of the Tastee Freeze, in the vegetable garden, with a couple of buddies, in his baseball uniform. He looked annoyed in most of the pictures.

"These are all from the same year, I think," he said. "That would've been Nellie's last summer at camp."

"Your dad must have sent them along with his letters, kind of like an early version of Instagram. Pinholes in the top, see?" She pointed to the evidence in the white border along the tops of the snapshots. "She must have hung them up."

"Yeah," he said, with a growing smile.

"I wonder if there's pictures of him in the other pocket? It's labeled 'Me.'" She reached inside, but her hand encountered only a slip of paper. She pulled out a scrap of notebook paper, folded and refolded so many times that it threatened to disintegrate. She carefully opened it.

"'Absence makes the heart grow fonder. I guess I can learn to love you more. Dick.'" She read out loud. "Jesus, Anders, I had no idea your dad was such a romantic."

"Neither did I."

"Why don't you take this stuff into the office so the kids don't ruin it? I'll finish getting supper on the table."

"Good idea," he said, and gathered up the treasures in a reverie.

Meghan appreciated the wisdom in Aunt Mary's gift. Rather than simply insisting that Zedernwald was okay, she tapped into Anders' deeply-buried, positive memories. She evoked a version of his father that didn't demand grudges. The woman was good.

"Could I read the letters after dinner?" she called.

"Of course. They're mostly boring, the minutia of my parents' marriage."

"Boring is sometimes the most interesting," Meghan replied. "Speaking of marriage, the twins are planning to marry us and never leave home."

"Sounds like a plan."

CHAPTER 44
ELENA

Elena followed Dr. Johnston to her office. Instead of worrying about what she'd say to hide her abilities, Elena entered her now-monthly visit calmly. Since the focus moved on from voices, Elena enjoyed the woman and her orange notebook revelations.

During the session, Dr. Johnston sat in the same upholstered chair in front of the same bookshelf and cycled through the same series of bird-like postures. She wore her gray-streaked hair in a sleek ponytail low on her head. Elena realized that she and the doctor had similar physiques, and noticed how the woman's neat nails looked elegant on her long fingers. Life goals.

"How have you been doing this past month?" Dr. Johnston began.

"Okay, I guess," Elena said. "I still get irritated at my parents, especially about this summer. I want to go to this camp that my family runs, but I also got invited to this super competitive engineering institute. I convinced them to let me turn the engineering thing down, but my dad still hasn't said okay to camp. And it's May. And I'm annoyed."

"Is this your aunt's camp?" Dr. Johnston asked.

"Great-aunts', yeah. I know the scholarship thing is a big deal, but I realized that I don't really like math or science all that much, so I turned it down," she repeated.

"Why did you apply in the first place?"

"Because everyone expected me to. Cuz I wanted to win. I don't know, I guess I just like being the best at stuff."

"What would happen if you weren't the best at something?"

Elena's gut swerved at this impossible question. "When I started at my new school, I was so worried about being the smartest kid in the class. But sometime this year, I started to realize that maybe there are other things as important as being the smartest one in the room." Elena surprised herself with her own honesty.

"That's a big realization."

"I think it helps that I mostly compete with my friend, Kayla. I can't be too mad when *she* pulls ahead in class rank," Elena said.

"Who's in first right now?" Dr. Johnston asked

"Me," Elena answered quickly. Too quickly.

Dr. Johnston's expression remained neutral. "What if you weren't first? What if you were, say, fifth? And what if it were someone that you didn't care for who bested you?"

Elena tried to imagine that scenario and was embarrassingly unable to do so. She sat quietly for a bit before answering, one of the skills she learned from Dr. Johnston. "I can't imagine that happening," she finally admitted.

"Sounds like a good area to work on then," Dr. Johnston said with a gentle smile. "Why is it important for you to be the best?"

"I never really thought about it," Elena said uncomfortably.

"How does talking about this make you feel?"

"I don't like it," Elena said.

"That means we are on the right track," she said, making a note.

Elena knew she would say that. Ugh, therapy was hard work. "Okay. I think I partly do it for other people," she said. "Like, I worried for weeks that it would destroy my mom when I told her I didn't want to go to this engineering thing." She felt something loosen in her chest, the therapy doing its work.

"What happened when you told her?"

"She was disappointed, but she got over it," Elena said, remembering the fake brochures and supper club dinner. "She's okay with the camp thing. If I could just get my dad on board, I'd be set."

"What's going on with your dad?" Dr. Johnston moved her glasses onto her head and settled in for a story.

"He has this big grudge against his family and thinks that I'll be brainwashed or something."

"Did he forbid you from going?"

"Not exactly, but I'm afraid he won't say yes. Plus, I'm afraid of disappointing him and making him upset," Elena admitted.

"And what happened when you told your mom that you don't want to study engineering?"

"She eventually got over it. Dad probably would too," Elena said, sniffling.

"Sounds like you know what to do. Talk to your dad," Dr. Johnston said, putting her glasses back in place. Dr. Johnston rarely gave explicit instructions, so this directive glowed with clarity.

•   •   •

Elena called her mom after the appointment to report what Doctor Johnston suggested. On some level, Elena hoped that her mom would disagree and remove the burden of confrontation from Elena's shoulders. Instead, she agreed entirely, especially since Aunt Mary's divine intervention package had arrived a few days ago and the time was right.

While Dr. Johnston's suggestion sounded simple enough, the thought of confronting her father was daunting. When she got home, she avoided thinking about such a confrontation directly. Instead, she worked on homework, and ran the tricky third movement of a Beethoven sonata, letting her subconscious do the work of scripting something to say. By dinner, Elena had the words and a plan.

Thursday night dinners were popcorn and smoothies, and the twins owned the task of chopping fruit and pushing the blender buttons. Her dad hovered over Jacob and Ava, who stood on chairs and chopped bananas and strawberries with plastic knives. They focused on their task with amusing seriousness.

Elena attacked while he was preoccupied. "Hey, Dad, I wanted to make sure that you were on board with me going to Zedernwald this summer," she said, faking nonchalance.

"You were still planning on it, huh?" he said, using a classic a 'playing dumb' defense.

"Yes. I think Mom has it on the calendar," she countered

Whatever he said next was drowned out by the sound of the blender coming to life. Elena could tell that he was upset, though; his shoulders stiffened and his emotions went icy.

The blender quieted and Elena cleared her throat to fill up the gaping silence. Dad poured smoothie into cups with lids and straws and sent the twins away. "Go pick out a movie with Mom," he said as he lifted them down from kitchen chairs.

"*Air Bud*!" they hollered in unison

"Well?" Elena said after her siblings left.

"I was hoping you might have given up on the idea," he said with a sigh.

"Nope. I don't have any other plans for the summer, and I would like to go for my last summer of freedom before I have to start worrying about college," Elena said, just like she rehearsed. Then she added an unrehearsed bit. "Plus, it's *my family*. All these other girls get to go, and it only seems fair that I get to go to *my family* camp."

"I can't think of any logical reason to say no . . ."

"Does that mean you have illogical reasons?" Elena blurted.

"No—yes—well, maybe," he sputtered.

This was getting ridiculous. "Why can't you give me a straight answer?" she demanded.

He raked his hands through his hair and his zig-zag vein twitched wildly. But, instead of exploding, he melted. He closed his eyes and slowly smeared his hands over his face before leaning over the kitchen island at which Elena sat, transfixed. He didn't look up as he slowly began. "I never knew Nell as an adult, not really. She was out of the house by the time I was old enough to pay attention."

Elena held her breath, afraid to break the confessional spell.

"She was my irritating big sister. Irritating because she was so damn perfect. She wasn't always the nicest to me. When she went away to college, she cut herself off, and then she got sick. I guess I never realized how much I resented her until it was too late to do anything about it."

He took a deep breath and looked up. "But all I know is that you are cut from the same cloth as she was. You have the same overachiever streak. I used to worry about how you'd react if you failed. But you kept on succeeding, following more and more in her footsteps. I'm afraid of encouraging the similarities too much by letting you go to camp. I know it's illogical, but I guess I'm afraid to tempt fate. So, no, I don't have a good reason, and that's apparently why I can't give you a straight answer." He shrugged and looked at her sadly.

Elena didn't like her dad thinking about her in that way, what she might become and how she really was. It felt awkward and cringey, and besides that, "I'm my own person, Dad."

"I know. But at the same time, you're so Tannin-y."

"I know you're talking about Nell," she said. "But, up until she got sick, it sounds like she had a pretty good life. And, Dad, I'm not schizophrenic."

He shrugged and gave a reluctant nod.

"And the other Tannin women seem pretty amazing."

She sensed her dad's tension easing as the throbbing vein melted back into his lightly-lined forehead. He sat down, rested his chin in his hands, and looked at her. A wistful smile spread across his face. "You know, you're pretty smart. How'd you turn out so good?"

Yesssss. "Well, I had good parents to start with," she said, laying it on thick.

"I'm going to miss you this summer, though," he said.

It was all she could do not to squeal with excitement. Instead, trying to meet the moment, she mirrored her dad's position across the island, head in hands, eye contact hovering about eight inches over the surface. "Does that mean I can go?"

He sighed. "Okay, fine. I'll probably worry all the time, but it'll give me practice for when you go off to college."

"I'll text you every day," she promised.

"Facetime every day?" he countered, eyebrows raised

"Text every day, Facetime every Sunday?"

"Sunday Facetime, answer my calls, text at least once a day. Deal?"

"Deal," she said. "*Air Bud*?"

"*Air Bud*," he said, shifting back into normal mode.

Elena, though, couldn't be normal. She was for sure going to Zedernwald! She was going to be fully Spuren! She gave her mom a small nod as she sat down on the couch. Mom sent her a subtle thumbs up. She spent all 98 minutes of *Air Bud* frantically messaging with Kat. Ever since the Spring Fling, their friendship had taken a step forward. The shared experience of using their Talent in such monumental ways that night created an unshakeable bond. Kat even said hi to her in the hallways now, something she knew Kayla and the others noticed.

It wasn't until near the end of the movie, when Buddy the dog reunites with his owners, that she told Stephen, Kayla, and Aunt Mary. When she gave her phone a final look before bed, the last texts from the three of them stirred up all sorts of confusing emotions.

Stephen: that's good i guess...i'll miss youiI'm visiting every wknd....ilysm

Kayla: You sure are good at keeping secrets No wonder you weren't sad about engineering symposium :)

Aunt Mary: That Is Great News! I Will Let Sylvie Know So She Can Start Getting Herself And The Others Adjusted.

As per usual, Stephen was the perfect boyfriend. Annoying. And Kayla was one to talk about keeping secrets! Elena was dying to force a confession out of her, especially after she scoped out the person Kayla was kissing at the dance and determined that the tall girl was an unremarkable sophomore named Lauren. And what did Aunt Mary mean "adjusted?" Time to put all those therapy lessons to use and sleep on it, hoping her subconscious would deliver her some lovely insights by morning.

Zedernwald packing list

- *X long sheets*
- *Towels*
- *Toiletries*
- *Medications*
- *Spare notebooks. Multiple.*

CHAPTER 45
KAT

Val: u got this pay attention to ur inner voice
Kat: my inner voices so irritating tho

After the dance, and with Val and Elena's prodding, Kat decided to fully melt her icy shield, taking the worn-out training wheels off her Talent. She couldn't wait for her two best friends to meet at camp, but anticipated a lot of tag-team nagging if she didn't get her Tempering in order before then. With her Talent somewhat engaged, she picked up on mood clouds surrounding people and groups. It was like how the Peanuts character, Pig Pen, was drawn, with a scribbled mess cloud trailing him. Instead of dirt, she sensed people's emotional energy clouds.

Kat anticipated a fog of toxicity around the Beautiful People. Instead, the feelings were mostly the same as everyone else: self-doubt, hormones, moments of giddiness, with an added dash of anxiety. When she talked about it with Val, she knew her friend wanted to say, "I told you so!"

Instead, Val kindly said, "Yeah, the Talent lets in the good and the bad."

"I mean, it's not like my friends are evil, they're just a little …toxic," Kat said.

"That's maybe too harsh," Val said. "We're just teenagers, is all."

"So, I shouldn't be worried that Belvedere people are especially awful?"

"Nope, that's just normal stuff you've been blocking out this whole time. Nobody likes themselves at our age," Val said.

"Bailey seems pretty okay with herself," Kat said, scrolling through her pictures.

"All right, very few," Val corrected. "My mom says that the people who peak in high school end up being the biggest losers at the 20-year reunion. I think that's supposed to make me feel better."

It made Kat feel a little bit better. It was unnerving to contend with her newly-melted inner critic. But, she was reassured by similar clouds of self-doubt trailing her peers.

•　　•　　•

For awhile after the dance and the Great Melting, Kat continued going through the motions of being a Beautiful Person, unsure of how to make a clean break. Instead, she dutifully liked the BP's posts, responded to their messages, and sat with them at lunch. Instead of engaging in the gossip, she monitored for hints of people knowing about what happened between Ty and Paige after she quietly broke up with him, but detected nothing. Just another short-lived high school romance. Irritatingly, he would survive to assault another day.

None of the BP noticed Kat's subtle changes. When she stopped taking an active role in their day-to-day dramas, others gladly filled the void. And their leader wasn't into subtlety. Bailey tracked her friends' statuses by, literally, tracking their statuses. Kat continued to message her back, and only when she allowed their streak to break did Bailey ask whether something was up.

"I guess I'm not loving being single anymore," Kat lied.

Bailey sent sad emojis. Typical.

Kat waited until the weather was consistently nice to make her final break. She told herself that she waited because she needed to be able to eat lunch outside, and Wisconsin wasn't reliably warm until May. But really, she was chicken.

Finally, when the forecast called for highs above 50, Kat had no more excuses and made her move. After months of gray, the blaring sunshine lured people outside during lunch. Clutches of students sat cross-legged on the grass, not worried that the ground remained damp. Girls rolled their sleeves up to avoid farmer tans, and shoes were scattered in the hopeful grass.

Kat took a deep breath and headed toward a shaded spot. She laid her jean jacket on the ground for a seat. Even though she had no appetite, she went through the motions of normal lunch. She wondered if anyone noticed her absence inside. Eventually, a couple of people messaged, wondering where she was. She made up plausible excuses which must have worked, as the messages stopped and she focused on forcing down some of her lunch. Kat's phone chimed again.

Elena: You doing OK?

Kat: Yup

Elena: Want to come by us?

Kat: Nope

Elena: K lmk if you need anything

Kat: Thx

·   ·   ·

Kat survived three days of sitting alone outside. There were only a few weeks left til the end of school, she reassured herself, and she could do anything for three weeks, especially with distractions like a spring sky filled with clouds. They were the light, fluffy kind that skidded decoratively, posing no threat of rain. She lay on her back and traced the contours of a camel in one, when a shadow fell across her face. Her neighbor, Chris, walked into her field of view. If it were anyone else, she would quickly sit up and try to be cool, but she didn't bother with him. After all, he used to look for cloud shapes with her.

"See anything?" he asked, dropping his crinkly Kwik Trip bag and plopping down next to her.

"Camel," she replied, pointing up to her right.

He followed her pointing finger. "Yup." He didn't say anything else for awhile. Briefly, Kat was nervous, worried that the silence would let too much Talent leak out, or feelings leak in, or whatever. She took a deep breath, felt her shoulder blades on the ground, and rode it out. He emanated a whiff of calm friendliness, nothing else.

"Whatcha doing out here?" he asked.

"I'm changing things up," she said, carefully avoiding eye contact. She squinted up at the sky, despite the fact that the sun emerged from behind the camel with full force.

"Huh," he said. "I always eat at the table outside the Aux building."

"Huh," she replied. "Can you believe I've gone to school here for almost three years, and I've never once been in the Aux building?"

"It's an alright place."

Kat glanced at him and smiled. "What do you do there all day, besides class, I mean."

"Well," he said, clearing his throat as though preparing for a big announcement, "Mr. Stein let me bring my car in, and I work on it during my free periods."

"The Grand Am?" she asked. When he drove her home after the Winter Dance, the teal car seemed like it was about to fall apart.

"Nope," he said, sitting up, removing his phone from his back pocket and pulling up a picture. "I sold it to help buy one of these over Christmas Break. It'll look like this someday, at least."

Kat sat up to study the image. The green car looked old, but she didn't know enough about cars to render judgment. "1978 Dodge Charger," the caption said.

"Where'd you get it?" she asked, not knowing what else to say.

"Guy down by Rockford. It was his dad's and he gave me a deal if I hauled it away. My uncle brought his trailer down and I bought it. Used my saved money, plus what I got for the Grand Am, and then my uncle loaned me a thousand bucks. He says I don't have to pay him back, but I will."

"Does it run?" She could tell that this was important to Chris. His voice changed a lot since middle school.

"Almost. I'm hoping to have it running for summer, and then it'll mostly be interior work."

"That's amazing," Kat said, genuinely impressed. "I just learned how to check my tire pressure this winter, and I thought that was a big deal."

"It's not hard if you're willing to learn." He shrugged.

"I'm not surprised that you can do it," Kat said, worried that he misunderstood. Chris was always one of the smart kids in elementary, then sort of disappeared in middle school. "You've always been smart."

"It got to be hard for me to keep up with school once I started working at Kwik Trip and helping out at home," he said, "but this is something that I can work hard at without having to worry about grades."

"Is this what you want to do when you grow up?" she asked.

"Yeah, for sure," he said, glancing at her. "Next year, I'm only going to be in class here three mornings a week. The rest of the time, I'll be doing classes at the extension, and I just lined up an apprenticeship," he said with pride.

"Wow," Kat said, wanting to ask more. But of course, the bell rang. As they stood up and brushed the grass off, she said, "Can I see your car?"

As much as was possible for Chris's ruddy face, he blushed a little. "Sure," he said. "Meet here tomorrow at lunch, and I'll take you down to the Aux."

"Sounds good," she said. "See you then."

Later that night, she told Elena about Chris. "I can't believe that he is doing all these adult things!"

"He's really ahead of us," Elena said. "Like, he's probably not going to college—"

"But that doesn't matter!" Kat said, a little too quickly.

"Agree. I'm glad it worked out," Elena said. "Bye!"

Glad what worked out?

.   .   .

After that, Kat ate outside with Chris every day. She learned about his plans for next year, about the car, and about how he got interested in cars to begin with.

"I picked this one because my dad had one." He pulled up a faded snapshot on his phone. A thin man with hip-hugger jeans and a mustache leaned against the hood of a red, shiny version of the car up on blocks in the Aux garage.

"Wow, Mitch really looks different," she said, referencing Chris's father.

"Oh, that's not Mitch," he replied, looking at the photo. "That's my dad, Ted."

"Wait, isn't Mitch your dad?" Kat asked.

"No, I thought you knew that," he replied, putting his phone away. "My dad died of cancer when I was three. Mom married Mitch a few years later. I don't really remember my real dad, always called Mitch 'Dad.'"

"So, your brothers are actually your half-brothers?" Kat asked.

"Yup. That's why there's a gap between me and the three of them. When the little guy started school, Mom went back to work, and I had to do a lot to take care of them after school and stuff. I was twelve, and technically legal to babysit. I can't believe we didn't destroy the place though," he said with a laugh.

The younger Nolte boys were well-known marauders in the neighborhood. They rode bikes through yards and left boyish debris scattered across lawns, waiting to get caught up in lawnmowers. She never realized that Chris was in charge during their reign of terror. Middle school was around the time that Chris slowly drifted out of her classes.

When she told Elena about eating with Chris, Elena smiled in a knowing way, like there was something more going on. That was ridiculous. Chris was like a brother to her. She ate with Chris because it was convenient. Plus, the car was amazing, even though the interior was in rough shape and it needed a paint job. She rode in a convertible once before and remembered the joy of wind rushing past her ears. Buzzing in the ears meant effortless Tempering.

Her advanced Tempering challenges were going okay, too. She imagined melting progressively larger holes in the freezer where she kept her Talent and emotions. As she removed the Talent walls, the rest of her mental compartments tumbled, too. It was like a scary game of Jenga. Now that it wasn't locked up, her inner voice was constantly there, criticizing. "That was a stupid thing to say. You look fat. Nobody likes you. Ugh." The voice was so ubiquitous that Kat gave her a name: Marjorie. Stupid Marjorie. Marjorie never let her imagine that Chris might see her as anything more than a friend.

•　•　•

"So Elena is coming to Zedernwald for sure?" Val asked. Camp was only a bit more than a month away.

"Yup, her dad finally agreed," Kat said. She and Elena still weren't out as friends at school. How would it feel to be totally outed at Zedernwald?

Of course, Val sensed her discomfort, even over the phone. "Are you worried about her coming to camp? It'll be fine. She knows you, she practically knows me, she's related to Mary and Sylvie."

"Yeah, I'm just thinking how awkward it will be to all the sudden be friends with her this summer."

"I thought you *were* friends?" Val asked.

"Yeah," Kat said uncomfortably. "But not many people actually know we're friends."

"Have you been pretending not to know her or something?"

Kat's silence served as an answer.

"Not to be mean, but that kind of sucks."

"Um, okay, well, talk to you later," Kat said. She had to end the call quickly because she needed to do something she hadn't done in years—cry. She cried for all the time she'd wasted being fake and frozen and scared of Marjorie.

CHAPTER 46
MEGHAN

Meghan enjoyed the settled feeling that came with having the summer planned out. Almost as soon as *Air Bud* finished that night, she officially registered Elena for Zedernwald. It was amazingly simple, requiring only a phone call to Mary. She didn't even remember to request Elena's vaccination records until Meghan reminded her! What a batty old lady. Hopefully, Sylvie was in charge of record-keeping.

The twins were signed up for a variety of day camps, and she and Anders even planned a weekend away together. They'd take their two weeks at the Cottage in August as usual. She'd wait until closer to the date to suggest visiting the old lady aunts at the Lodge. Obviously, the Labor Day extended family reunion still remained out of the question this year. Baby steps.

Meghan discovered that Zedernwald campers were allowed to have visitors. She overheard a conversation between Elena and Stephen in which he planned to drive up on weekends when he wasn't working. She wanted to ask where he planned to stay, but decided that she really didn't want to know the answer, not really.

Stephen was a lovely kid, very polite and seemingly smitten with Elena. He was just what a mom would want for her child's first boyfriend. It wasn't him specifically that gave her pause, but the concept of boyfriend in general. There were the emotional and physical complexities of such a relationship. But, even more concerning was the central position that Stephen now held in Elena's life.

Even though Elena's car sat in its usual spot in the driveway as she pulled in that evening, she knew that she wasn't truly home, not in the way she used to be. Much of at-home Elena was actually engaged in ongoing conversations and a whole separate life with Stephen, her friends, and who knew who else.

When Meghan went inside, she found Elena lying on the living room floor, playing Little People with Ava. She watched them quietly, afraid to interrupt the scene.

Ava loved to assign characters for her adult playmate to "be." Elena was "being" the mom and the chicken.

"But Mama, Mama," Ava said, being the baby, "I don't wanna go to bed!"

"You need to get a good night's sleep to grow up big and strong!" said Mama Elena. "Cluck, cluck," Chicken Elena agreed. "I'll sing you a song and tuck you in."

"Okay, hop, hop, I'm going on the roof to sleep!" Baby Ava said.

"Chicken will stay with you. What song should I sing?" Elena asked.

"I see da moon!"

Elena pulled Ava into a hug and swayed back and forth, singing the lullaby that Meghan used to sing to her.

I see the moon, the moon sees me,
Under the shade of the old oak tree,
Please let the light that shines on me,
Shine on the one I love.

Just when she worried that Elena drifted hopelessly out of her orbit, she delicately nudged herself back in.

CHAPTER 47
ELENA

Sundays after 11:00 a.m. sucked. It no longer felt like the weekend, more of a preamble to the school week. Despite this, Sunday 'Learning with Linda' were a break rather than a burden. Linda preferred to focus on Tempering techniques and Communing, but Elena still got a lot of theoretical questions answered. What Linda couldn't handle, Mary managed in her stilted texts. For example, Mary explained that Tempering around one's family wasn't strictly necessary, given that familial affection somehow messed with the Spuren signals. That was a relief. Elena's coded notebooks became cluttered with information on top of her usual lists and therapy assignments, filling up more quickly than ever before.

Writing about the Talent was difficult; there weren't adequate words to describe this sixth sense. Instead, she used words from other senses. Sometimes, she thought of the bits of emotion that people trailed behind them as scents sprayed by a perfume lady in the mall. Other times, she experienced people's energy as a change in temperature, sometimes as one of those word clouds built by assigning words sizes based on their frequency of use.

And, some of the time, it was voices, those auditory glimpses into people's inner monologues. Those moments of starling clarity didn't happen as often anymore, not like back in the fall when she was a Spiraling, un-Tempered disaster area. Now she generally only heard her Talent with adults when it was quiet, or if she touched someone at just the right time. Of course, she regularly heard Kat's voice when they

Communed in choir or at her house. She and Kat grew so skilled at Communing that they talked silently throughout class, even without their legs bumping up against each other, even when everyone was singing or talking. All this made the fact that she still received nothing via her Talent from Stephen all the more startling.

A few weeks passed since Kat abandoned the BP lunchtable and started spending time with Chris, for which Elena gave herself partial credit. Everyone felt buoyant when they gathered on the Kowalskis' back deck in the May warmth. Kat always joined in Learning with Linda now, and she bragged to her mom about her and Elena's Communing skills. "It's like we barely even need to try anymore!" she finished.

"Impressive," Linda said. "Wanna show Elena some distance Communing?" she asked Kat, who nodded.

"She's ready," she confirmed.

Elena blushed with the false modesty of a top student. "Distance Communing?" she asked.

"It's just seeing how far apart we can Commune, in good areas with no electrical interference," Kat said.

"When we're up north," Linda explained, "it's easy to find good places. It's trickier around here, with all the power lines and WiFi, but there are a few spots, like the Bong," she announced.

"The Bong Rec Area?" Elena asked. Driving into Wisconsin from Chicago, you passed an exit for the Bong Recreation Facility. Whenever they went by her dad made a joke. The sign was often missing, stolen to decorate dorm rooms.

"Good old Bong," Kat said. "It's not nearly as interesting as it sounds."

"Nope. Just wetland for miles. This will be sort of like a final exam slash celebration before we head to Zedernwald," Linda said, standing up. "Put on good shoes and a jacket and, Elena, check with your parents."

"They'll be jealous to hear that I'm going to Bong," Elena said. She texted to let them know her plan and both simultaneously responded, "Jealous!"

They took Linda's Subaru south, the surroundings growing flatter and less densely populated with every mile. Linda pulled into a parking area that, despite the gorgeous weather, had only one other car in it.

"Probably birders," Linda said, pulling on her jacket. "Leave your phones in the car, and let's go."

They walked for about ten minutes into knee-high grass. Elena was glad she borrowed hiking boots. Every step caused a pool of water to form around her feet.

"All right, this looks good," Linda said.

"So, we stand with our backs to each other," Kat explained, "start Communing, walk apart, and see how long we can keep it up. When you lose connection, turn around and see how far apart we are. Are you ready?"

Elena shrugged and said, "Sure." She wasn't, but she loved a challenge.

"Backs together, no more talking, starting—*now!*" Linda said. "*Start walking!*"

Elena walked toward the western horizon, the midday sun on her left shoulder. She breathed in and out slowly, dropping her Temper. She was determined to be the last one standing. She knew that the other two were more experienced, but she thought she had an advantage because she wasn't distracted by birds.

"*Okay, here we go,*" Linda said. "*So, what should we talk about? Tree Swallow!*"

"*How about Chris?*" Elena asked innocently.

"*How about Zedernwald?*" Kat shot back.

"*We have to get through exams first!*" Elena said. She focused on the horizon and the disembodied voices.

"*She gets like this every spring,*" Linda said. "*Anxious to get back to Zedernwald.*"

"*And Val,*" Elena blurted. She usually avoided talking about Val, so Kat wouldn't pick up on her jealousy.

"*What's your deal with Val?*" Kat asked. "*You'll like her. I know you think she's some kind of professional Spuren, but she's not.*"

"I'm just nervous about camp. I know everyone's going to be suspicious of me since my mom isn't Spuren," Elena said, taking a big leap over a puddle.

"Elena, you have to find a way to make peace with that," Linda said. *"None of us know how the Talent works, Blue-Winged Teal, so we probably won't ever have a full explanation."*

"Elena has a hard time not having all the answers. Canada Goose. That's kind of her brand," said Kat.

"Yeah," Elena said, chagrined. *"Plus, it's been kinda hard to not talk to my mom about my Talent."*

"That must be so hard. I lie to Kat's dad about being Spuren, but that feels natural, since everyone else does too. But I always had my mom. Pied-Billed Grebe!" Linda said.

"Yeah. It's like no one knows the total real me," Elena said, squinting up at the sunshine. It was getting harder to focus.

"What about me?" Kat said.

"Well, the whole secret friend thing makes it tricky—"

"What?" Linda interrupted.

"Oops," Elena said, not really meaning it.

"Thanks, Elena," Kat said sarcastically.

"Sounds like you two need—-come to Jesus," Linda said. *"Do you want me —- Mary?"*

Linda's voice began to cut in and out.

Elena redoubled her efforts to focus. *"No, I'll just keep my Spuren secret buried, like all the rest of the secrets in our family. It's kind of our brand."*

"— secrets," Kat said, *"— — tell the Herd - we've been friends? I — if you're — it kind of defeats the purpose."* Kat's voice rang more clearly than her mom's, perhaps because of their daily Communing practice.

"I didn't know that this would be so hard!" Elena said.

"Conversation. — we're doing pretty well on. Stop a sec. How — — feeling?" Linda said.

Elena assumed that everyone was starting to have problems and turned around. *"We've gone so far! Pretty good, huh?"*

"*Yes— Elena! For — Commune, that's a big distance.*"

"*Yeah, good job,*" Kat added. "*Mom—- to keep going?*"

"*Sure. Elena— mind just waiting? — do whatever. —you notice us turn back — we're finished— five minutes or so? Now Kat, What Chris - Elena — about?*"

Elena watched Kat and her mom continue to walk away, still connected.

"*That's fine. I'm fine,*" Elena said, disappointed. She ignored their receding voices and listened to the wind in the tender grass. She would look ridiculous at Zedernwald; weird for her lack of a Spuren mom, weirder for her preschool level abilities. But mostly she felt lonely, lonely in a way that no amount of making out with Stephen later would erase.

Eventually, the other two turned and started to walk back, meeting up partway to Elena. Linda pointed out a bird to Kat, who nodded. Elena waved and started walking, setting a course to intersect the pair as they trudged across the pale green expanse.

•　　•　　•

Driving home, Elena couldn't help but blurt from the backseat. "Okay, fine, I admit it, I'm jealous."

Her outburst interrupted the spa-like music that Linda always played in the Subaru. She glanced in the rearview mirror and Kat turned in the seat to give Elena a funny look. "How could you not be jealous? This reasonably priced SUV is truly the height of luxury," Kat said with sarcasm.

"Ha ha. No, I mean, I'm jealous that you have a mom that you can ask about, you know, stuff. Spuren stuff," Elena replied.

"Oh, honey, you know you can ask me anything," Linda said, maintaining a worrisome level of eye contact in the rearview mirror as she careened down the highway.

"I know, I know," Elena said, flustered at her inability to explain the loneliness she felt watching the Kowalskis Commune in Bong. "It's more, like, if something just sort of comes up, I can't automatically mention it to my mom. She's so extra into explaining everything else about life—"

"-some would say awkwardly so-" Kat interjected.

"Oh, absolutely," Elena responded. "But it's kind of got me trained to forget about asking about certain, well, things."

"Like..." Linda prompted.

Elena sighed in embarrassment. "Okay, fine. Like Heartblock."

"Oh, honey, is your boyfriend Heartblocked?" Linda said. "That's so special."

Special, being an awkward word, caused Elena to blush even more than she already was. "Yeah, Kat explained Heartblock to me, and I know for a fact that he's in love with me. But what I want to know is, well, how do I know if I'm in love with him? From the Talent, I mean?"

"Not that easy, unfortunately," Kat said.

"What do you mean?"

"Heartblock can tell you something about how your partner feels about you," Linda explained, "but you have to figure the rest out just like everybody else. There's no Talent shortcut."

"Doesn't that suck?" Kat exclaimed.

"I've told you, Kat, it's actually kind of a good thing," her mom continued, now thankfully fully focused on the road while she spoke. "Otherwise, we might just end up committing to the first person who Blocked us and bought us dinner," Linda said.

"Oh, God, she's going to talk about Chad," Kat groaned.

"Yes, Chad," Linda said. "My college boyfriend, my first Heartblock."

"First? You can be Heartblocked more than once?" Elena asked.

"Sure. There's not just one chance at love, Elena. But Chad was my first, and he said all the right things, was immune to my Talent, and he was blonde and drove a Jeep. So, I figured he was the one. Fortunately, I remembered what my mother told me and paid attention to the other things, the normal relationship things that non-Spuren women have to pay attention to. Eventually, I realized that while I loved many things about him, I didn't love the whole him. More the idea of him. Despite the Heartblock."

"Huh," Elena said. This all sounded a bit too familiar.

Kat picked up what must have been an oft-told story. "And then, at her first job out of college, Mom met Dad who was assigned to do her IT training, and the rest is history."

"As they say," Linda agreed. "Hope that helped, Elena."

"Yes, it did…" Elena said, her voice trailing off and a worrisome knot forming in her stomach. She planned to hang out with Stephen that night.

•   •   •

Because the weather was so nice, Elena suggested they go for a walk along the bike path that skirted the edge of town. It ended at a small county park that emptied of children at dusk. This left Stephen and Elena free to make out in the pavilion under the cover of near darkness.

"You're so beautiful," Stephen said, as they walked hand in hand back to his car a few minutes before Elena's curfew. "I love your hair. Promise you'll never cut it short."

"Thanks," she said, feeling the same discomfort she always did when he praised her appearance. Clearly, he was completely infatuated. How else could he make such a statement when she hadn't washed her hair in three days and had a stubborn zit on the end of her nose? "You're pretty good looking too," she said, knowing what a good girlfriend should say.

As they drove home, she glanced repeatedly at his profile. He *was* as good-looking as the first time she saw him, and she still loved his body. But she never seemed to say it first. In fact, lately she never said any of the girlfriend-ey things first. But Stephen never seemed to wane in his dizzying affection for her.

As he reached for her leg over the center console, she suddenly couldn't wait to be home with her guilt in her own bed.

Stephen weirdness

- *Stephen=Talent kryptonite?*
- *He loves me. Gulp. I guess I love him too? Right?*
- *Apparently really, really loves me? (Heart block????)*
- *=real reason for cringey pink pill dispenser*
- *Teeter-totter level of lopsided love. How's he not falling off???*

Chapter 48
Kat

Kat and Chris ate lunch together for almost two weeks before she started to wonder what, exactly, was going on with Chris Nolte. Those 25 minutes were the best part of her day. One time, they rushed into the auto shop when it started raining and Chris briefly put his hand on her back. Her stomach dipped, and she was aware of her lower back for much longer than normal. Did that mean she liked him? Her only previous boyfriend was Ty, who was a series of heady highs and disastrous lows. She didn't have either of these with Chris, just undulating pleasantness. Could it be "like" without the drama?

And how would she know what Chris thought about her? He didn't use social media, so there were no clues there. They didn't share any friends in common. She knew better than to try and figure him out using her Talent. After all of her mom's warnings about the risk of trusting in Heartblock, she was afraid to even check for it. It certainly had never been there with Ty. So she kept her Talent gently Tempered when with him to avoid being disappointed by getting a read off of him. All she knew was that his eyes were cornflower blue, and she'd never noticed that before. She contemplated his eyes when her thoughts were interrupted by a question.

"So, are you free?" he asked, putting trash into a Kwik Trip bag.

"What?" she asked.

"For a drive? Tonight after school? Because the car's ready?" he said, with his eyebrows raised. "Did you hear anything I just said?"

"I was daydreaming," she admitted. "The convertible's ready?"

"Yeah. The interior still needs work, but the exterior looks good, and she's running. Wanna go for a ride tonight before the sun goes down? Hit up that frozen custard place over in Waterford?"

"You had me at frozen custard," she said.

"Cool. Come over at 5."

"Cool," she said, trying to be nonchalant as they walked their separate ways: Chris to the auxiliary building, and Kat to the main building where she would space out the entire afternoon. She was too busy thinking about what would happen on this outing/drive/date.

Since she didn't know what it was, Kat had an awful time figuring out what to wear. It was warm, but she didn't want to go short-shorts. But she didn't want to wear what she wore to school either, leggings and an oversized t-shirt. She settled on a look somewhere between not caring at all and caring too much: torn jeans, a V-neck crop top, and a jacket. If it seemed like a date, she'd take off her jacket. If it was just a buddy thing, she'd keep the jacket on and make sure the neckline of her shirt didn't droop too low.

The last bit to figure out was her hair. They'd be in a convertible, so she needed to secure it back. She didn't want to do a tight pony, though. In the end, she borrowed a scarf from her mom. She wrapped it over her head like the movie stars did. She added sunglasses and felt pleased. Normally, she'd run her outfit by someone, but she didn't tell anyone but her mom where she was going.

"That's nice," Mom said innocently. Too innocently. Elena knew she was drawing all sorts of conclusions after Elena blurted Chris's name out at Bong.

Kat cut through the hedges separating the Kowalski and Nolte yards. When they were kids, the gap was by a constant flow of traffic. It might have made more sense to go around and approach through the driveway, but that felt too official. When she caught sight of the convertible, her jaw dropped. Last she saw, it was rusty in places, with mismatched paint jobs. Now it was a sleek, uniform green. With the top down, it was eye-catching. She was glad she did her hair.

Clearly, Chris felt the same. "Hey," he said, smiling and walking over to her. "Whaddya think?" He wore tight black jeans and vintage T shirt advertising a local bar. He never wore anything this form-fitting at school, and she admired him when he turned and motioned to the car.

"It looks amazing," she said truthfully. "I can't believe this is the same car!"

"It's not the same color as my dad's, but I chose this green cuz it's my favorite color."

"Cool," she said, smiling like an idiot. She felt like a fool, but he gave off the same vibe, so she went with it. "I like your shirt," she added.

"Thanks. It was my dad's."

"Cool," she said again. The T-shirt fit tight across his arms, and she realized that he must lift weights. "Can I get in?"

"Sure," he said. "Let me open the door, the handle's tricky." She felt glamorous sliding onto the wide bench seat. He closed the door with a loud thump and she swung a startled glance in his direction. They briefly locked eyes and she knew that, yeah, this was a date.

Even though the seat was massive, she felt close to him without a console between. The drive-in scenes from old movies suddenly made a lot of sense. She buckled a flimsy lap belt that seemed like something from a carnival ride.

"I added those. The car didn't have seatbelts originally," he explained.

"That's so weird!" She felt an odd pressure to say something witty, but, luckily, he pumped the gas pedal a few times, turned the ignition, and the car roared to life. Literally. It was very loud, and the smell of burning fuel hit her.

"Ready?" he asked over the car's engine.

She nodded.

"If you need to get my attention, just hit my arm," Chris said loudly.

She nodded again and leaned back as he eased the car into reverse and out of the driveway. As they headed out of town, people looked up and smiled. Convertibles and motorcycles were a welcome sign of spring.

Chris made a questioning face when they got to the intersection for the county highway at the edge of town. "Okay to go this way?" his expression asked.

Kat nodded and mouthed, "Yes."

Once he pulled onto the road and eased the car up to 55, Kat relaxed fully. The breeze was chilly, but the late afternoon sun was warm, and the combination was intoxicating. Between the physical sensation, the stultifying rumble of the car, and the presence of an unexpected Chris Nolte, she was content.

The trees had rounded the bend from "bare, with a hit of green" to "definitely leafy." She caught a sense of movement and spotted a pair of cranes up ahead. She tapped Chris's arm and pointed in the direction of the lanky birds. He glanced over and raised his eyebrows in appreciation. He was excited to see a couple of cranes, just like when they were little and collected toads together.

A moment later, she felt a tap on her forearm and followed Chris's pointing finger to some kids with a lemonade stand in their front yard. He laughed, and so did she. It was funny that these kids thought they'd stop highway traffic with 25 cent cups of lemonade. What was even funnier was that, after the moment passed, Chris's hand returned to her forearm. She looked up to see what he wanted to show her, but his eyes were fixed straight ahead, and his hand was maneuvering hers. He flipped it over, and then slipped his fingers into her upturned palm.

Kat shifted closer, she didn't want to make it awkward for him to drive, with his arm craning across the seat, she told herself. That slight movement caused him to glance over and smile. Maybe she should have worn the short shorts after all.

"We'll stop for lemonade on the way back," he yelled.

Chris eventually pulled into a custard stand in the next small town over. They held hands for only ten minutes during the drive, but it felt like forever. Eventually, he had to let go to turn the steering wheel into a parking spot.

"No power steering," he said.

Kat nodded as though she understood. They walked up to the window on the outside of the red building.

"Do you still like mint chocolate chip?" Chris asked.

"Yup," Kat said, delighted that he remembered. He ordered them both double scoops. In her head, Marjorie suggested she insist on a baby cone, but Kat ignored her.

They sat on a blanket next to the car, watching the sun as it sank low in the sky. It was warm without the breeze of the drive to balance the sun, and Kat took off her jacket, baring her pasty arms.

As they licked the custard with "the highest butterfat percentage in Southern Wisconsin!" as the menus proclaimed, they talked about school and their families and funny things that happened when they were kids. There were moments of silence, but they didn't feel awkward. Chris quietly slipped his arm around her shoulders. She clenched, considering whether it was gross to touch her flabby upper arm. He must have felt her stiffen, because he took his arm away.

Before they got back into the car, Kat had Chris pose for pictures with the car, then he took some of her. She considered taking a selfie of the two of them together, but worried what that might imply. She moved to open the car door, forgetting his warning about the handle. She threw her jacket and phone into the back seat and used both hands to wrench it open with a dramatic grunt.

Chris laughed as he walked around to the driver's side. "It's just as hard to close. Be careful."

She slid in and noticed a third seatbelt in the middle of the front seat. "I just remembered riding in my grandma's station wagon. I'd sit in the front seat, up on the armrest, between her and my mom. Can you believe that we used to do that?"

"Same. I put three sets of seatbelts in for authenticity," he said.

Feeling daring, Kat shifted to the middle set of belts. "Okay if I use this one?" she asked.

"Fine with me," he said, "but I'm going to have to find somewhere to rest my arm."

They drove home with his right arm snugged over her shoulders. Since she threw her jacket into the back seat and the sun was setting, she needed some extra warmth. Eventually, she tucked her legs up to the right on the seat in order to lean in and absorb his warmth more fully. Even after they stopped at the kids' lemonade stand, she ignored her jacket and returned to the same position.

When they got to Belvedere, Kat wasn't sure she wanted the neighborhood to know that she was on a date with the boy next door. She abruptly sat up and unbuckled her seatbelt, pretending that it was important to grab her jacket at that exact moment. Chris probably understood. His younger brothers were playing catch in the front yard, watching everything. Their presence resolved any question about what would happen next. Chris and Kat exchanged a friendly hug and she disappeared back through the hedges, the rumble of the engine still ringing in her ears, the warmth of his arm weighing on her shoulder.

Later that night, scrolling through her pictures, Kat started to worry. Would it be weird tomorrow at school? She stopped at the picture that Chris took of her sitting against the side of the car, her sunglasses lowered as she gazed over them. He zoomed in so that the glinting green of the car's paint job formed a seamless backdrop behind her face. The color exactly matched her eyes.

Perhaps the opinions of others didn't matter so much after all, she thought, as she made the photo her profile picture. Within seconds, Elena liked the picture and was calling.

"Where's that picture from?" Elena demanded.

Kat couldn't wait to tell her all the details, so she did. Elena squealed at all the right places. After she hung up and started to call "VALBFF" as she was listed in her phone, Kat realized with satisfaction that Elena was her best friend, too.

CHAPTER 49
ELENA

It was the talk with Linda that did it. Or that night in the park. Or her non-Talent instincts. Or maybe it was seeing how Kat was with Chris. Or all of it.

Whatever it was, it made no logical sense. Stephen was the perfect boyfriend. Cute, such a good kisser, attentive, smart, funny, charming…everything that he always had been. But somewhere along the line, she had started to grow weary of how unfailingly *into* her Stephen was. At first, she thought that maybe she was just confused by the lack of supporting Talent data to justify the lopsided affection, but that wasn't it. Not really. On some level, she'd known for a while that she needed to take a break with Stephen.

It didn't make logical sense, but it made emotional sense. Non-Talent emotional sense, even. She journaled and journaled about it, eventually realizing that breaking up made sense. She was using him- initially as a distraction from her spiraling Talent, and then because she just loved being with him physically so much, and the security of having a boyfriend in general. And he never questioned her reasons, apparently because he loved her too much. The Heartblock never let up. It was terrifying. When she imagined his waves of Talent-canceling affection, she couldn't help but envision drowning. This truth-bomb gave her the worst sort of guilt ever.

She felt sick, thinking about how to break up with him. She settled on the following Friday evening, waiting for a weekend to hide from the fallout, like a chicken. Even wimpier, she wouldn't have to see him at all during the day Friday, since she had a choir field trip. The field trip day would be a countdown to that awful time. In twelve hours, it'll all be over, she reassured herself. Leaving her car that morning, she looked guiltily at the pile of Atomic Firecracker candy wrappers piled on her center console. He never missed a day. This was going to suck.

·   ·   ·

Elena sat in silence, counting down the minutes to awfulness as she rode in a van back from the choir field trip. There were too many music students to fit in a single school bus, so the director picked nine students to ride in one of the district's passenger vans. She and Kat were crammed in the back seat with a baritone named Lloyd.

The director drove, three freshman girls sat on the first bench, and Bailey and a BP named Brooklyn sat in the middle seat with a sophomore assigned to the van due to his food allergies and pushy mother. They traveled to the district's elementary schools and performed in enchilada-smelling cafetoriums. Then, they rode 45 minutes south to a college campus for a performance and tour. The already long day was made especially long because, at the last minute, the director made them leave their phones at school, out of fear that they wouldn't pay respectful attention. People muttered about their parents being pissed if they couldn't contact them, but he didn't really care; he planned to retire soon.

"Oh, dear," the director suddenly said. The van slowed down and eased off the busy county road, gravel crunching.

"What's going on?" asked the allergy boy, whose name was Hunter.

"I think we have a flat," the director replied.

Everyone groaned.

"Should we get out?" asked Brooklyn, reaching for the door.

"Sure, be careful," the director said.

The kids walked onto the shoulder and gathered under a shady tree.

"Bad news, kids," the director said, striding over. "It's a flat. Someone will be here in an hour or so to fix it."

"We won't get back before the end of school?" Hunter said. "You better call my mom or she'll freak out."

The director sighed. "Anyone else's parents need a call?"

The freshman girls nodded. One of them asked, "Would it be faster if we started changing the tire?"

"Um, well, it's been a while," the director mumbled.

"That's okay, I can do it," the chirpy freshman announced, and returned to the van with her friends.

The director appeared indecisive until Kat said, "Don't you think you should put out cones or something? You know, make sure they're okay?"

He sighed again and walked away muttering something about pensions.

The remaining six glanced at each other warily.

"Say something," Elena said to Kat. *"This is so awkward!"*

"So," Kat said stiffly, "what's everyone doing this summer?"

Bailey lay down on her back, draping one lithe arm over her eyes, ignoring Kat. The rest scooted into a loose circle.

"Good job," Elena said, smiling at Kat. "I'm going to camp up north."

"My parents never felt 'comfortable' sending me to sleep away camp," Brooklyn said, glancing at Bailey, presumably for signs of disapproval. "This summer, they're letting me get a job. It's in my dad's office, but that's better than babysitting my brother."

"Luckily, my parents never made me do that," Elena said, relaxing a bit. "I have twin four-year old brother and sister. My dad stays home with them."

"Living the dream," Lloyd said, not looking up from his gaming device. "I'm hoping to find a sugar mama to support me until my Twitch stream is profitable."

"My dad doesn't just sit around all day," Elena said. "Kids take work."

"Never having 'em," Lloyd replied. "I'm doing a camp in July. Coding. I'm not really into coding, but it's the only thing my parents would agree to that relates to gaming."

"I wish I could go to camp," Hunter said. "My mom barely lets me come to school. I'm only applying to colleges out of state."

"That sucks," Kat sad. "I can't imagine—"

"I went to camp once," Bailey interrupted. She stayed on her back, arm over her eyes. "Fat camp."

"What?" Kat gasped. "When?"

"Fourth grade. It wasn't called fat camp, but that's what it was," she said. "Ever since, I sign up for summer school so they can't pull that again. Not that my BMI has been above 20 since, obv."

"*Obv*," Kat and Elena thought in unison. "*Can you believe this?*" Elena hissed.

"But what did they actually do at the camp?" Kat asked, seeming grotesquely intrigued.

"Limited our food and had us exercise all day," Bailey said.

"That doesn't sound too awful," Hunter said, eyebrows raised.

"Plus weighed us every morning and posted it publicly, searched our bunks for contraband, and sent our parents weekly updates. I got to stay for the extended session," she said flatly.

"That's screwed up," Lloyd offered, glancing up. "My parents are psycho, but not that psycho."

"I don't remember you ever being overweight," Kat said.

"She wasn't," Brooklyn said sharply.

"I was."

"You weren't, you still aren't, and your mom is nuts," Brooklyn said. "New topic."

"I can't believe those kinds of places still exist," Elena said, reveling in the weird sharing. "Not since people started talking about eating disorders."

Hunter interrupted. "You want to talk about eating disorders, my mom literally wipes down food before she brings it into the house. I haven't eaten in a restaurant in over four years."

"What happened four years ago?" Kat asked.

"I went to DQ with some friends and got a blizzard, and there must have been peanut dust somewhere. I blew up like a balloon. She's cooked every single one of my meals since."

"I can see why you want to go away for college," Brooklyn said. Elena sensed she was relieved to no longer be talking about Bailey. "Are you going to camp again, Kat? I wonder if it's near the one that she's going to," she said, glancing at Elena.

"It's the same camp. We're going together," Kat said hesitantly.

"I didn't know you two were friends," Brooklyn said.

"We've been friends for a while, Christmas at least," Elena blurted. After a moment of panic, Elena's mood shifted, like the flip of a switch, to something approaching nonchalant confidence. "And Kat's one of my best friends," she finished.

"*Sorry if I overshared,*" Elena said.

"*All good,*" Kat said. "Same."

"That's cool," said Brooklyn, who seemed to mean it. "Is that who you've been eating lunch with? Elena?"

"*That's the first time I ever heard a Beautiful Person other than you say my name,*" Elena said.

"No, I was being honest when I said I was eating alone," Kat told the tightly bunched group. "Well, at least at first," Kat said. "*Should I say it?*"

"*Be brave.*"

"Until I started eating with Chris Nolte, who I'm kind of seeing now."

"Wow," Brooklyn finally said. "You've had a lot going on, Kat. Why didn't you tell us?"

"I—we— didn't really tell anyone," Kat said, shrugging. Elena wasn't sure whether she was talking about the relationship with Chris or her.

"Lucky us, first to know," Lloyd said sarcastically, turning back to his game.

"You *are* lucky, Lloyd," Elena blurted, drunk with honesty. She turned to Brooklyn. "What would you all have said if you found out that Kat and I were friends?" Elena said, glancing between her and Bailey. "And Chris Nolte? An Aux kid? I can't imagine the BP putting him into their Instagram stories."

Brooklyn looked down at the grass, plucking at strands. Bailey remained motionless on her back, and Hunter looked nervously back and forth between the two groups of girls.

"What's up with you today?" Kat said. She joined Hunter in glancing back and forth.

The only sounds were the freshmen working on the tire, an occasional passing car, and the red winged blackbirds. Finally, Brooklyn spoke, in a cloud of awkwardness. "It all sounds so stupid when you put it like that," she said. "Especially when we're out here, away from everything."

"Yeah," Kat said. "But realistically, if we had our phones, we'd all be ignoring each other and messaging people about everything that happened."

"Which we will do anyway when we get back to school," Bailey said, suddenly sitting up and facing the others. "Because that's just how it is. I'm not interested in being some sort of change leader or something."

"Well, things are pretty good for you and your friends already," Hunter said, with a touch of hostility. "Why change, right?"

"True," Brooklyn said. "We're popular. But I don't know if that's necessarily the best thing."

"Try being me for a day and let me know," Lloyd said. "People shit on me all day long. You'd have to try hard to convince me that things are that bad for you all."

"Oh, they're mostly good, as long as you don't look too hard," Bailey said evenly, focused on the horizon. "Meanwhile, we're on so much Zoloft that we can barely see straight and afraid to reveal anything ugly that might ruin the perfection."

Just as quickly as she opened up, Bailey's mask fell back into place, and she lay back down. She wasn't finished talking, though. "If you think we're going to go back and be BFFs again, Kat, it's not going to happen. But. I'm not going to be a bitch about Elena or Chris or anything else. You never did anything but try and watch out for me. And Paige. And you were right."

"*What was that all about?*" Elena asked, as everyone stared at Bailey's impassive form. Everyone except the freshmen who took selfies in front of the changed tire.

"*Paige and Ty, I think,*" Kat said.

"*She must have found out,*" Elena said.

"*Yup,*" Kat agreed.

"Well, I hope it'd be okay if I at least nodded in the halls when I saw you," Hunter said to the group.

Everyone exchanged looks, shrugging. Lloyd glanced up and said, "You'd be the first, so okay with me."

"Of course, Hunter," said Elena.

"Same," Kat followed.

Brooklyn shrugged.

And just as quickly as the bubble-fragile moment formed, it popped. A school district truck arrived, and the trio of freshman girls led a man in coveralls over to inspect their work.

The strange grouping in the grass stood up and walked slowly back toward the van. Bailey led the way.

"*I feel like an 80's rock song should be playing,*" Elena said. "*Like that movie we were talking about, The Breakfast Club?*"

"*You're so weird,*" Kat replied.

"*Yeah, but that's why I'm your best friend.*" Elena was grateful for the momentary distraction, killing 30 minutes in the countdown to the awful thing she had locked away in her mind, away from Kat's roving Talent, ashamed to tell even her best friend.

· · ·

Elena felt sick as she walked the now-familiar steps to Stephen's back door Friday night. She considered knocking, but that would be a dead giveaway. They hadn't knocked at each other's houses for months. She took a deep, shuddering breath and stepped inside. The house smelled like Stephen. She was going to lose her nerve. He was standing right across the room.

"Hey," he said, pulling her in for a hug. He kissed her.

Elena didn't resist, but she ended it early. She tried to file the memory away, knowing it might be their last kiss ever. He really was a good person to kiss.

"Can we talk?" She felt out of her body, listening to the fateful, no-turning-back-now words.

"Uh-oh, did I do something wrong?" he asked, his reliable smile momentarily flickering.

They sat next to each other on the blue couch. The same blue couch in front of the TV on which they watched innumerable movies over the winter. The same couch on which Elena barely maintained her status as a 'technical' virgin with a sweet boy who repeatedly called her beautiful. The same couch on which she would say, "I'm not sure how else to say this, so I'm just going to say it." She stared at her hands. "I'm breaking up with you."

She finally looked up and hated the way his face had shifted.

His lower lip started to not exactly tremble, but just to sort of go weak. The blood rushed from his face "I could tell that something was up with you," he said, pulling his hand away from her leg, "but this is out of nowhere, Elena. Was it something I did? Something I said? I love you, Elena."

She hated herself and was tempted to backpedal. But she needed to stick with the plan, despite those hazel eyes. "No, it's not you, it's just me." She felt so lame, and his face creased into a grimace, as though her words actually hurt him. She knew she was being painfully trite, but, in this case, it was true. "I just—I just really need to be on my own for a while, Stephen. I've loved being your girlfriend, it's been the best 7 months and 2 weeks of my life. Honestly."

"I just can't believe this…" he said, standing up and pacing the room.

"I know," she said, following. "In some ways, I can't believe it either. But it's happening. And I'm so, so sorry." She reached out and put a hand on his shoulder. Maybe she could sink in for one last hug.

He gently removed her hand, without turning to face her, and said, "I think—just go, please." And she went. It was over.

Too sad, no lists.

CHAPTER 50
KAT

Not surprisingly, word traveled fast after the Breakfast Club-style revelations outside the van Friday afternoon. True to her word, Bailey didn't start speaking to the Herd. However, she didn't add any fuel to the tentative fires that kids tried to build up around the news that Kat Kowalski had left the Beautiful People, become friends with a Herd member, and started seeing an Aux kid.

And, just like Kat had guessed, Paige must have spoken up about what happened with Ty. No one knew anything for sure, but he was seen being pulled from class by the School Resource officer, benched from Track that night, and absent from the remainder of the school year. People assumed it had something to do with drinking or vaping. Neither Kat, Bailey, nor Paige indicated otherwise, but Paige's pinging emotional strength newly asserting itself was apparent to Kat's Talent. Good on ya, Paige.

"I know you know more than you're telling me," Elena said, referencing the Ty situation that weekend, "but I suppose I can stop asking. I'll talk about something else. I've convinced the Herd that you're, well, safe."

"Was it hard?" Kat asked.

"Not really. I mean, we've all changed since middle school. And they were a little confused how we started hanging out, but I used the yoga excuse again. So, remember that you're into yoga."

"Got it. Downward dog."

"And I thought maybe it would be a good idea if you apologized to Kayla, but they said that would be awkward, so maybe just talk to her to let her know things are okay?"

"When is that supposed to naturally happen?"

"I'm hoping you'll come to my place along with the Herd the last day of school. And maybe you could, I don't know, hang out by me before school for these last few days? Just to break the ice?"

"Fine, fine. But since you're creating awkward social situations for me, I might as well tell you. After you were all lonely at Bong a few weeks ago, Mom called Mary, all worried about you not having anyone at home in on the Spuren thing. I think Mary's considering trying to tell your mom."

"Shit," Elena said. "Shit."

And having met Elena's mother, Kat couldn't exactly disagree.

•   •   •

Kat knew it was the least she could do to apologize to Kayla, and Elena, for that matter. But all this honesty was getting taxing. Marjorie was going bananas. In addition to all of the other fallout from Friday van ride, there was her panic, having labeled the Chris thing as "seeing each other." In the moment, Kat felt fine sharing her Chris information with the weird gathering on the side of the road. But for the rest of the weekend, the perpetually negative Marjorie yammered nonstop. Was there really a Chris thing? Was she merely one in a long chain of meaningless nothings to Chris? Why would any boy, let alone someone as together as Chris, be interested in her? Elena broke up with Stephen, an apparently perfect Heartblocked boyfriend! Was there even hope for her?

The following Monday, she tentatively joined the periphery of the Herd before school, sneaking into a seat next to Elena. "Hey," she said to Kayla. "I like your shoes." Kat had rehearsed this lame comment all the way to school, and she delivered it with the driest throat possible.

"Thanks. I wanted to get them in white, but they were sold out," Kayla replied.

It was the most words they'd exchanged in years. Elena practically glowed with approval.

Having used up all of her bravery for the day, Kat made up a headache-related excuse to miss Chris at lunch. After school, Kat watched talk shows, ate Cheerios, and swirled down a shame spiral. As she reached for the box to top off her remaining milk, Chris called.

"Hey," he said. "I feel like you avoided me today. Did I do something to piss you off?"

She simultaneously asked, "Hey, why did you ask me to go for a drive those two times? Are we, like, hanging out hanging out?"

"Whoa, whoa, whoa," he said. "You're not mad?"

"No, I'm not mad. I'm just anxious! I know that guys don't like to have labels, but I guess I'm kind of just wondering what this is," she said, motioning to his image on her phone, and then back to herself. "If it's anything," she quickly added. "Cuz if it's not, no big deal."

"This is stupid," Chris said.

"Oh, sorry," Kat said, beginning to burn with humiliation. She imagined the whole thing, just like Marjorie said.

"No, not you. You're not stupid," Chris said. "It's stupid that we're having this conversation on the phone when we live, like, 100 feet apart. Meet me at the secret passage," he said and hung up.

Kat took a deep breath and walked slowly to the secret passage, preparing to face humiliation and a tiny bit of heartbreak. The secret passage was their childhood name for the gap in the backyard fence between their yards, where a huge lilac grew on Chris's side. When they were eight or nine, they removed a couple of the boards, the gap being largely hidden by the lilacs. They felt so sneaky. She later learned that, of course, the parents knew about it. They were probably just glad to have the kids busy and out of their hair.

Perhaps by summoning her with the phrase "secret passage," Kat felt compelled to obey. Like if someone yelled, "One, two, three, four, I declare a thumb war," you have no choice but to participate. She slow-walked to the secret passage, rehearsing nonchalant opening lines. As she pushed aside the lilac bush, she was ready to say, "Let's just keep hanging out and see what happens." But before she had a chance, her inward breath melted into a gasp.

Chris Nolte stood there, the scent of ghostly lilacs heavy in the air, and reached for her clammy hand. "I don't want to just hang out. I want to be your boyfriend. That's what I want to call it." As he spoke, he leaned closer and closer, until his forehead rested against hers. She was mesmerized and, for once, at a loss for words. Instead, she allowed a slow grin to spread across her lips and nodded.

Not that the grin lasted for very long. She soon was fully distracted kissing Chris Nolte, her boyfriend, in the middle of the secret passage.

CHAPTER 51
ELENA

Elena's breakup with Stephen came with just over a week left of school, and they were the worst, most painful days of her life. They were even worse than that last year at St. Veronica's. Even though she was relieved that she broke up with him, she still wanted him to love her. So, it made her sad and yet gratified to see him avoiding her or looking at her sadly from across English. It made her really, really mad to see him laughing with other girls between class or after school, the few times it did happen. It was all very confusing.

Belvedere High School was collectively confused by the breakup. There weren't any dramatic reasons for it, and Elena wasn't particularly helpful in defining a narrative. The Monday after it happened, every conversation went more or less the same:

Random person: I heard you broke up with Stephen. You were such a good couple!
Elena: Yeah, we were. I just wasn't feeling the relationship anymore.
Rando: Weird. You two were totally into each other.
Elena: I still like him as a friend.

The Herd pressed her for more details. Did she like someone else? Did he cheat on her? Was she nuts? Some moments, Elena feared that she was. She still loved Stephen somehow, but she couldn't ignore the fact that she started to mildly resent the time that she had to devote to the relationship, tending to his intensity. She *knew* she did the right thing, and not being able to explain it didn't matter. Right?

Elena knew that even Kat, with her extra Spuren information, wasn't sure what to do with Elena's irrationality. "You were Heartblocked!" Kat's confused glances seemed to scream. Elena felt on the verge of emotional danger, like back before she knew about her Talent. She again felt like controlling her thoughts was like controlling a car on a slippery highway. To survive those last days of school, Elena adopted Kat's old, clumsy Tempering method of going through life's motions behind thick emotional barricades.

When she told her parents, they were surprised, but not nearly as interested in the details, thank God.

"So, Stephen and I broke up," she mentioned nonchalantly a few days after it happened.

"I'm sorry to hear that, honey. Breakups are hard," her dad said, giving her a hug.

"Who broke up with who?" her mom asked, before quickly trying to reel the comment back. "I mean, of course it doesn't matter. But you're a catch, honey!"

"Mom. That was about the worst thing you could have said," Elena said with irritation. She saw her dad give her mom a look before quietly slipping out of the room.

"I'm sorry I'm such an idiot," her mom said, trying to give her a hug.

"And now you're trying to force me to make you feel better!" Elena exclaimed, pushing her away. "For your information, I broke up with him. And, no, he didn't do anything horrible. And, no, I don't want to talk about it anymore."

"Okay, okay, sorry. But before you go storming out of the room, one more thing," her mom said, holding up her hands in defeat. "Aunt Mary's coming over day after tomorrow. Can you make it a point to be around after school?"

"Fine," Elena growled as she ran up to her room. She was relieved to have an excuse to rush away. She was fully annoyed with her mom and couldn't wait for a summer away from her. But she was even more worried about how much Aunt Mary would try to tell her. She didn't like her mom needing to know all her secrets, about what may or may not have happened with Stephen, about Spurenhood, about what she was thinking and feeling and, just, all of it.

Which made Elena feel really guilty about an idea she'd been toying with. Ever since Kat told her about her dieting hobby, Elena had been compiling observations about the other girl's behaviors. She was starting to worry that Kat might have some kind of an eating disorder. But should she tell Kat's mom? That's what the pamphlets in Dr. Johnston's office suggested: tell a trusted adult. But feeling the way her own Mom just made her feel? Elena wasn't sure what was in Kat's best interest.

Why I did it
- *Wasn't feeling the relationship any more*
- *Stephen too intense*
- *Distracted by other things, school, Zedernwald*
- *Felt out of control*
- *Panic*

CHAPTER 52
MEGHAN

Meghan took Friday afternoon off, giving her time to make coffee, tea, and bake frozen cinnamon rolls for Aunt Mary's visit. She was so pleased at the warming of relations with Anders' family, and subconsciously congratulated herself on shepherding the advancements along. Elena arrived home from school shortly after Mary arrived.

"Thanks for stopping by," Meghan said, for the third time.

"Worked out perfect," Aunt Mary replied, groaning into a chair. "I had to meet up with a gal in the area for Senior Bowling League business." She plopped a teabag into water and eyed the pastries.

"Well," Meghan said. "I'm so glad Elena's going to Zedernwald." She glanced at Elena who smiled nervously.

"Maybe, when you're up for your time at the Cottage, you and Anders and the kids can stop over for supper? Like I've been asking him all these years?" Mary said, moving a cinnamon roll to her plate.

That was news to Meghan. "I had no idea you and Anders were in contact."

"I always sent an invitation at the beginning of summer, but he never got back to me."

Apparently, corresponding on the lowdown with Aunt Mary was a Tannin family tradition. "You know what?" Meghan said, reveling in her diplomatic prowess. "From now on, we need a group text. That way, there won't be any more secrets. We can all be on the same page."

"Sure," Mary said, unwinding her cinnamon roll. "Only I don't know what a group text is."

Meghan explained while she set up Mary's phone.

"Didn't you forget someone?" Mary asked after studying it.

"I don't think so... me, you, Anders."

"What about Elena?" Mary said, glancing at a silent Elena. "Shouldn't you should be on this too?"

"Suuuure?" Elena said hesitantly

She's acting so strangely, Meghan thought. Even weirder than after she inexplicably broke up with Stephen. "Good idea. No more secrets, right, Elena?"

Elena glanced back and forth between Meghan and Mary. "Speaking of secrets," Mary said, looking at Elena over her glasses, "there's something we'd like to discuss with you."

"What now?" Meghan asked uneasily, glancing between the two.

"Meghan, I wonder if you ever noticed what a special girl Elena is?"

"Of course! I know how bright and thoughtful and creative she is." Meghan caught Elena's eye and smiled. Elena smiled back tepidly.

"Do you ever think there's something a little bit, well, *different* about her?"

"What do you mean?" Meghan asked defensively. In medicine, you never wanted to be different.

"Here goes," Mary muttered, then cleared her throat and sat up straighter. "In our family, women and their daughters share a special gift. Somehow, Elena inherited this gift, despite her link to our family being through her father."

"Do you mean the camp?" Meghan asked, completely befuddled. What on earth was Mary going on about?

"Indirectly," Mary said. "We go to camp *because* of our gift. We sense emotional energy in a powerful way. That's our gift, and it passes from mothers to daughters, but Elena somehow inherited it through Anders." She stopped and stared at Meghan, clearly assuming that her comments made perfect sense.

Meghan blinked. Mary's words did not make perfect sense. In fact, the woman sounded asinine.

Perhaps sensing her skepticism, Mary continued. "This gift is something that we learn to manage at Zedernwald. However, Elena also needs the support of people in her home as well. We're hoping that, even though you lack the gift, Elena will find strength and support now that you understand. Of course, no one else can know."

Meghan sat, dumbfounded. Aunt Mary was practicality personified, but this was sheer nonsense. Was she having a stroke?

"Mom, I know it sounds crazy," Elena interrupted, touching her arm, "but it's no big deal. Just a little bit of additional sensory data that I have to learn to manage."

Meghan groped in the recesses of her mind for an explanation for these fluffy assertions. "Are you talking about empaths? People who believe they're particularly attuned to others' feelings or whatever? I'm surprised you're interested in something like that, Elena." What did she agree to with this camp? "Is everyone at Zedernwald into this empath, woo-woo stuff?"

"It's not woo-woo. We learn very practical skills," said Aunt Mary. She finished her cinnamon roll and wiped her mouth for emphasis.

If anyone was the antithesis of wishy washy, it was Aunt Mary. Still. "I'm beginning to understand why Anders' father had a falling out with you all," Meghan said, knowing how caustic her words were before they even finished crossing her lips.

"But Mom, he never even knew about the Talent," Elena said.

"No," Aunt Mary agreed. "The men never do. That's why we're telling you, not Anders."

"Don't worry, Mom," Elena interrupted, effectively silencing Aunt Mary. "I'm still going to college, I'm not going to start using drugs. This Talent thing is just a way of thinking about social skills, that's all. No big deal."

"Hmmph. I don't love this new agey nonsense," Meghan said, clinging to Elena's more palatable explanation. "Elena, could you give us a moment?"

"Sure," Elena said, clearly happy to leave. "Bye, Aunt Mary!"

When she was out of earshot, Meghan laid it out for Mary. "We've had Elena in therapy this year for anxiety. Things were really bad a few months ago. If this "empath" approach helps her, great. But if I see *any* sign that she's slipping, it's off. Camp, Zedernwald, this," she said tersely, motioning to the cozy table of tea things.

Mary nodded in grave acknowledgment. "Yes. I concur that Elena should have the best of both worlds."

Meghan gave her a quizzical look, hoping that whatever that meant aligned with her ultimatum.

"By which I mean," Mary continued, "both Zedernwald and academia."

"The best of both worlds," Meghan echoed with a sigh of resignation. "It's been a hard year for me, giving up the plan I had for her."

"Like my mom always said, a parent's job is to provide guidance and then let go," Mary said. "Ultimately, it's their life to lead."

"Easier said than done," said Meghan defensively to the childless woman. "It's not like kids have an indicator light for when they're able to manage themselves."

"I didn't feel totally independent until I didn't have a choice," Mary said. "I called my mom every day until she died. Elena will always need you," she said, patting Meghan's hand with her own solid one. "You're not losing her. We'll take good care of her at Zedernwald. And not let her go all woo-woo."

Mary didn't stay long after that, citing the need to get on the road before dark. Before Anders got home with the twins, Meghan needed to talk to Elena. She found her in her room.

"That was strange," Meghan began. "How long did you know about this hippy dippy stuff?" She regretted her approach and steeled for a sarcastic response.

Instead, Elena was surprisingly contrite. "I know, it's a bit much. I'm more interested in the kayaking, TBH. Aunt Mary can be a little weird."

Meghan was relieved. "Enough talk about this empath nonsense. And please don't mention it to Dad."

"Agree," Elena said, reaching for a teal notebook and pen.

·   ·   ·

Meghan replayed the surreal conversation as she tried to fall asleep that night. Obviously, it was all malarkey. A trait inherited by women only? That would be an odd inheritance pattern. If this so-called Talent came from Anders, shouldn't Ava have it too? She tiptoed into the twins' room and lay down next to Ava. Her weight on the toddler bed set off a series of creaks.

"Hi, Mama," Ava said, batting open her thick lashes with the unsurprise of a secure child.

"Hi, sweetie. Sorry I woke you up."

"S'kay," she whispered conspiratorially.

"Ava, can you tell how Mommy is feeling right now?" Meghan whispered.

"I'm hungry. Are you hungry?"

"No. Here, let's hold hands and lay quietly," she said, squeezing Ava's chubby fingers. "Is Mommy feeling happy feelings or sad feelings?"

"I don't like this game, it's boring," Ava said. "Can I have a snack?"

So much for some sort of Tannin ultra-sensitivity gene, Meghan thought smugly as she tiptoed downstairs for a handful of goldfish crackers and thinking up a plausible cover story to keep the woo-woo Aunt Mary conversation from Anders and his completely unremarkable gene pool.

·   ·   ·

"Where's Elena?" Jacob asked the following day, slamming a cupboard. Sometime over the spring, she stopped saying Lay-Lay. Jacob still held on, though.

"Probably with the Herd," Meghan and Anders said in unison. They decided not to tell the twins about the breakup with Stephen unless they asked. Out of sight, out of mind. Meghan cooked dinner and Anders sat, reading his tablet.

"I started following Elena and some of her friends on Instagram," he said. "Did you know that her friend Kat started dating someone?"

She briefly glanced up from rolling out a crust before returning her focus to the tricky task of transferring it into a pie tin. "Maybe I'll have to get on Instagram. Since Elena bargained down to once a week calls this summer, it'd be a nice way to keep track of her." Meghan didn't find out about Elena's breakup with Stephen until several days after it happened, a fact which still chafed, despite her resolutions about letting it go.

"It's gonna be weird to not have her around," he said, scrolling. "I volunteered to coach T-ball to keep myself busy. Right, Jacob?"

"Yup, we're the Purple Narwahls," she said. "Can I go play outside?"

"Yeah, Ava's already out there. Stay in the backyard."

"Okay, bye," he said, dropping a wrapper on the floor.

Meghan began crimping the pie dough. "Those two will fill up the Elena vacuum."

"They might overfill it," Anders said, tossing Jacob's trash.

"I can't recall any time with the twins being as hard as this past year was with Elena, even when they were babies."

"You think? I mean, for me, it was hard because of all the stuff with my family. But I don't know, she wasn't that bad," Anders said.

"It's different for moms and daughters."

"Maybe," he said.

"Definitely. I remember how I felt at her age. I thought that my mother was the most out-of-touch individual in the world, I was obsessed with my first boyfriend, and I wanted to scream every other minute. But remembering didn't make it any easier to be on the receiving end of all Elena's drama."

"I suppose you two have shorter fuses for each other, but I figured it was normal."

"It is normal," Meghan said, exasperated at his blissful ignorance. "It's also exhausting."

"You have to learn to pick your battles," he said.

"Okay, Mr. Fifteen-Year-Family-Feud." Meghan offered a sickly sweet smile and watched him decide to back down.

"Maybe it's nature's way of making it easier to kick them out of the nest," he said. "If teenagers were delightful 24-7, no one would ever want them to leave." Anders pulled a Spotted Cow out of the fridge and any thought of a real argument was dismissed with platitudes and a beer.

"Maybe." Meghan heaped grated cheese into the pie shell before laying in blanched asparagus spears. She prided herself on her fresh asparagus quiche. Before they moved to the country, she bought fresh asparagus at a farm stand. Now, she picked it wild from along the property line.

"What'd Aunt Mary have to say when she stopped by yesterday? I'm kind of sad I missed her," Anders said. "Okay, not really."

"Nothing much. She was in the neighborhood and just stopped by," Meghan answered, whisking the egg mixture with a fork.

"No agenda?"

"She did mention that she invites you to the Lodge every year and suggested that this might be the year to stop by. I set up a group text to eliminate any further confusion," Meghan said with faux innocence belying her actual omission.

"I'll think about it. Maybe." Anders said.

"Mmm-hmm," she said noncommittally while focusing on pouring the eggs into the pie shell and adding a dash of nutmeg.

●　　●　　●

Work the next day was rough. Meghan reviewed two surgical specimens from the Children's Hospital, both confirming cancer in previously healthy kids. She made the mistake of pulling up the first child's electronic chart. Meghan usually avoided learning the stories attached to the slides that passed through her hands. Not getting involved let her sleep at night.

But, that day, she opened the chart. The patient, a 15-year old girl, came in with knee pain. Within three days, she went from preparing for track regionals to possibly having her leg amputated, thanks to the evil, round blue cells under Meghan's microscope. In the patient's picture, the girl had a beaming face with a messy bun on the top of her head, just like Elena.

Meghan added the seductive storyline of a healthy teenager dying young to the maternal worry fire dedicated to Elena, who was becoming more distant by the day. At least once a week, she was at the Kowalskis and all she could talk about was Zedernwald. Mary, Linda and Kat were lovely people, but they weren't Meghan's people. Her people spent summers worrying about their resumes, not their inner feelings. And then, of course, there was Stephen, or whoever the next Stephen would be. When Elena told her about the breakup, a shameful scrap of Meghan felt relieved. Seeing Elena's sadness elevated the shame scrap to a full-fledged shame trophy.

Elena's world now existed almost totally outside of Meghan's sphere of influence. Ever since Elena was born, Meghan feared losing her. From the fear of sickness, to that of Nell's mental illness stealing her, to fear of a new boyfriend, and the reasonable fear of losing Elena to life in general. And there wasn't a damn thing she could do about it.

Meghan best demonstrated her fierce love through extreme presence. During Elena's early childhood, Meghan was in residency, working well over 100 hours a week. Even during those impossible days, she was determined to never let Elena down. She arranged elaborate on-call swaps so that never missed a lisping preschool concert. She baked whatever birthday cake was requested, from Elmo to Dora to Minecraft. Even recently, when Anders became the stay-at-home parent, she memorized Elena's schedules and grades and never missed a reminder to add money to her school lunch account. But now that Elena barely needed her, how would she know that Meghan loved her so much, it hurt?

CHAPTER 53
ELENA

Mary called Elena a few days after her "impromptu" visit. "How'd you think it went?" she asked.

"About how I expected," Elena said. "As much as I may've wanted my mom to know the truth, there was no way she'd ever believe it."

"I was a little surprised that she didn't ask any questions, just kind of blew the whole thing off."

"Mom's a doctor," Elena said protectively. "If you gave her a research paper or a test result, maybe she'd believe it. But—"

"—there isn't such a thing. Not that we'd ever want a Spuren blood test, God forbid."

Elena thought that a simple lab test would have been helpful in her situation.

"I'm worried I might have made things worse for you," Aunt Mary said, an unexpected sheepish tone creeping into her husky voice.

"Nah," Elena said while secretly agreeing. "I'll just pretend the conversation never happened. It should blow over. And if she freaks out for some delayed reason, and I end up missing camp, I'll just make it work."

"Elena, you absolutely can't miss camp," Aunt Mary said sternly.

"It wouldn't be the end of the world, would it?" Elena quickly grew nervous in response to Aunt Mary's uncharacteristically gloomy demeanor.

Aunt Mary remained eerily silent before resuming. "I wasn't going to tell you this anytime soon, but in light of what just happened, you need to know. Honey, your Auntie Nell didn't commit suicide because she had schizophrenia."

"Was it an accident? Or murder?"

"No, she *did* kill herself," Aunt Mary said. "But she lost her mind because she stopped tending her Talent."

"She…Spiraled to death?" Elena said, horrified.

"Now don't panic," Aunt Mary said quickly. "The Talent is a good thing. But left unchecked, it can become a problem."

"Why would someone ignore their Talent?"

"For most of us, being Spuren is more than enough for a full life. But for someone like Nell, with so many other gifts, the temptations of the non-Spuren world were irresistible. No, hon, you need Zedernwald. It'd be downright irresponsible to leave you and your Talent unattended."

"Has this ever happened to anyone else who ignored their Talent?" Elena asked, verging on panic.

"Only stories, but as you know, we don't write anything down," replied Aunt Mary cryptically.

Elena was skeptical. "How can you know for sure that's what happened inside Nell's mind?"

"She left behind diaries, for one."

Elena glanced warily at the stack of spiral bound notebooks neatly stacked on her bookshelf. "Well, I guess we just hope Mom doesn't change her mind."

"Don't worry. You're not your Auntie Nell. You'll be fine."

Elena hoped she was right.

• • •

One late May afternoon, Elena went to her last monthly session with Dr. Johnston, who promoted her to every-other-month meetings with the summer off. She'd long since stopped censoring herself (too much), but decided keep the Stephen breakup a secret. Enduring the litany of questions from her mom was painful enough, especially since she didn't have any neat answers to the inevitable "why?"

Luckily, Dr. Johnston didn't ask any boyfriend questions this time. "It's been six months since we started working together," she said toward the end of the hour. "Looking back, what do you think?"

Elena paused. "Even though I didn't want to come here at first, I'm glad I did."

"Why were you resistant?"

"I thought my parents were blowing things out of proportion," Elena said.

"Anytime someone hears voices, a physician fears the worst," Dr. Johnston said. "Combine that with your family history, and it doesn't surprise me that your parents sought a professional opinion."

"But I never heard voices," Elena said carefully. She never admitted that to Dr. Johnston. Did she?

"Hmmm," she said, giving Elena's chart a cursory glance.

Elena truly believed that Dr. Johnston accepted the lies she crafted back in December. "Did I tell you I heard voices? That doesn't seem right…"

"Elena," Dr. Johnston said, kindly, leaning toward her. "I know that you like to control everyone's impressions of you, but I'm trained to observe. I could tell that you weren't sharing the whole story when we first met."

Elena felt mortified heat bloom up her neck.

"Plus, I had notes from the Emergency Department. You told the resident that you heard voices, something which your mother also mentioned."

The resident's stupid notes.

"However, I quickly determined that you were *not* delusional, that your voices were benign. Some people experience vivid internal narration, and you happen to have a particularly strong inner voice," Dr. Johnston said, with a genuine smile. "Many high achievers have them, myself included."

Elena nodded, dumbfounded. This woman saw right through her without even having Talent. The whole time. Did other adults see through her too? "Why didn't you mention it before?" she asked.

"There wasn't any therapeutic advantage in doing so," Dr. Johnston replied with a shrug. "You weren't ready to accept that you *can't* control everything. But you've made progress!" She closed Elena's file and stood to replace it in a cabinet.

It was true. The silly writing exercises and conversations helped. While the doctor's back was turned, Elena voiced the germ of fear that remained, ignored, from those dreary, Spiralling days. "Could I still become like my Aunt Nell? With crazy voices?"

"I can't make any predictions," Dr. Johnston said, returning to her seated pose. "But, it's reassuring that your father is unaffected."

"Yeah, he's the most mentally healthy person I know."

"Interesting," Dr. Johnston said, handing her a new list of journaling prompts. "See you in two months."

Elena took the back roads home. She needed extra time to untangle swirling Nell thoughts that resurrected like a whiff of moth balls locked in a trunk. Nell was just a bit older than Elena when she started falling apart. What made her unravel? Was it straying from the Spuren community or garden variety mental illness? How much were the two things intertwined? Despite Aunt Mary's and Dr. Johnston's hollow reassurances, Elena knew she would continue worrying.

If the Talent and schizophrenia were both inherited, why not both at the same time? She still couldn't explain the freakish inheritance thing that happened with her Talent, despite trying to find answers on Google, and everywhere else. The topic was overwhelmingly complex. It was impossible to apply articles on mitochondria and X-chromosomes to the spoken-word tradition shared by the Kowalskis at their formica table.

She doubted that she'd ever know, since the Aunt Mary's world and that of Dr. Johnston were hopelessly separate. Look what happened to her family when the two worlds collided: it tore the Tannins apart for almost 20 years! By the time she pulled down the gravel driveway, she hadn't found any answers, instead realizing that she'd have to learn to live with uncertainty.

Fabulous.

One thing she *was* certain of was the absolute necessity of the summer at Zedernwald to get her Talent in order. A summer of Elena. A summer to focus on herself. She'd done the right thing, breaking up with Stephen, she reassured herself. She just couldn't continue to meet Stephen's level of devotion (was she ever truly meeting it anyway?) while saving herself from her aunt's fate that summer.

Worst case scenarios-Zedernwald
- *Bad housing assignment*
- *Sheets don't fit*
- *Aunt Sylvie hates me*
- *Stress constipation*
- *Val is perfect, Kat abandons me*
- *Poison ivy*
- *Poison oak*
- *Food poisoning*
- *Homesick*
- *Discover not really Spuren-big mistake*

Chapter 54
ELENA

Elena quickly flipped to the decoy Top 40 station, locked her door, and steeled herself for the last day of school, the last day to accidentally bump into Stephen, which was both thrilling and horrifying. But, of course, just like she made it through the first day, Elena made it to the last bell on the last day of school intact. Last hour, and she found herself back in English, carefully avoiding Stephen by talking with her favorite teacher, Mrs. Stanton. She even asked the teacher to sign her yearbook, the only thing really being accomplished in the waning minutes before summer.

"Thanks for a great year," Elena said, truthfully, as the teacher handed back the book. She'd transitioned to Birkenstocks in anticipation of summer, Elena noticed.

"It *was* a great year," Mrs. Stanton agreed. "And I'm glad to see you signed up for my creative fiction class next year," she said.

"Really?" Addison asked with surprise. Most college bound students took AP Literature senior year.

"I do so much writing in my journals, I thought it would be interesting," Elena tried to explain.

"You've probably already read most of the AP Lit curriculum anyways," Mrs. Stanton reassured. "This will challenge you in different ways."

Elena smiled as her teacher walked away in her sandals and linen overalls. She never fooled Mrs. Stanton a bit, she realized.

The bell rang and all hell broke loose. Elena weaved through the halls, dodging flying debris and the same make-out couples that weirded her out on the first day. They were part of the background now, like the recycling bins and fire extinguishers. She removed the last bits of personality from her locker, filling two tote bags.

Next to her, Chris laughed. "I travel light," he said, holding up the blue notebook and pen, along with the magnet and car picture.

"Kat told me your car's running," Elena said.

"Yup. Maybe you can come for a ride this summer."

"That'd be amazing," Elena said and gave Chris a brief hug. "I'm glad about, just, everything, you know, with Kat."

"Yeah, me too," he said. "Thanks again for the tip about lunch. See ya."

Elena walked out of school on the last day in the midst of the Herd and Kat, solidifying plans for the glorious first night of freedom. She practically skipped down the steps, weaving through the throng of jubilant students carrying the dregs of the year in plastic bags. When she got to her car, she felt a familiar crinkle under the handle. It surely wasn't an Atomic Fireball; those stopped abruptly the Monday after she broke Stephen's heart. Instead, it was a piece of notebook paper folded up, paper football style.

Her heart pounded in her throat and the blood rushed to her ears as she got into the car, clutching the paper in sweaty palms. Even though she was sure of her decision (she reassured herself numerous times a day), she missed Stephen so much, and somehow still longed to be the object of his affection. Her irrational hopes were answered. In the center of the unfolded paper sat a cellophane-wrapped candy, and the paper bore his familiar, slanted handwriting.

Dear Elena, I'm still not sure how I'm supposed to get over you, but I guess I'm learning, and maybe it will get easier eventually. Whatever happens, I hope that you remember our 7 months and 2 weeks together as the best you ever had. Remember the times we laughed together. Remember our English class arguments. Remember the Snowball.

Remember my kiss. Because I know I'll never forget you, and I don't think I would want to anyway. Love, Stephen

And, finally, after denying it for weeks, Elena cried for her newly-scarred heart.

•   •   •

"Should I order the pizzas for six o'clock?" her dad asked.

"Sure," Elena said. The Herd was coming over for a bonfire that night, and while she appreciated her parents' efforts, she was worried they'd be too present. "And I know you'll be around when we're in the house, but can you promise to give us some privacy when we're by the firepit?"

"Why, what do you have planned?" her mom asked.

"Mom. Nothing. I just don't want you annoying us," Elena said.

"Besides, Megs, if they were planning to have some Miller Lite, would you really want to know about it?" her dad teased.

"Yeah, right?" Elena echoed.

They wouldn't be doing anything all that awful. Morgan was bringing some champagne left over from her grandparents' anniversary party, but that was about it. Elena made her promise to also bring trash bags to collect and remove the evidence. Her parents always offered her a small glass of wine at special dinners, but this was different, and she didn't want them to start giving her a curfew. Elena was only allowed to change so much in one year, after all.

The girls arrived and the party started with pizza on the deck. The twins weaved wildly between the equally excited girls. Everyone was giddy with the promise of an entire summer stretched out before them. Social media showed that similar parties were happening all around Belvedere, some milder, and some larger and considerably wilder.

Eventually, they moved to the firepit, armed with green bottles of mosquito repellant. Elena's dad built a fire, and then left them with a wheelbarrow of wood and instructions to come and get him when they were ready to abandon it. They settled in, comfy in well-worn lawn chairs and old quilts. Elena relaxed her Tempering and let the waves of succulent emotion wash over her.

By the time the last bits of sunlight snuffed out, it was going on 10:00. Frog calls filled the air and the scent of dying lilacs hung heavier in the dark. The uproarious laughter part of the party died along with the sun. They shifted into chill mode and Morgan popped the champagne with suspicious skill, pouring it into red plastic cups.

"To summer," Addison said before drinking.

"To summer. And I'm not drinking this because of peer pressure," Kayla insisted, as she took a timid sip of the champagne.

The glowing embers created an intimacy unique to campfires. Everyone looks beautiful in firelight, Elena thought. She couldn't remember where she heard that quote, but it was true. All her friends were gorgeous: Addison with her curves in a halter top and yoga pants, Morgan with her carefully applied makeup and sleek hair, Kayla's delicate wispiness, and Kat's no-longer-mysterious dark beauty. And, Elena supposed, me and my riot of curls and skinny legs.

Kat must have felt the fire's seductive power, too. "A year ago, I would have been at Bailey's party," she said.

"Do you miss it?" Morgan asked. "Being popular, I mean."

"Parts of it, to be honest. It's easier to hide in that crowd." Kat held her cup out to Morgan, who poured more champagne.

"But you don't feel like you have to hide around us, right?" Kayla asked.

"I still do, a little," Kat confessed.

Elena monitored the conversation with the intensity of a parent dropping off their child for a first play date. She so wanted this to work, for the Herd to permanently adopt Kat.

"Yeah, that makes sense," Addison said. "A year ago, we wouldn't have thought you'd be here either. We would've been making fun of your Instagram story, along with the rest of the Beautiful People."

"A lot changed this year," Kat said. "Mostly for the better. There's you guys, plus, I'm not with Ty anymore, thank God."

"What was he like?" Kayla asked.

"Handsy jerk most of the time, complete ignoramus the rest," Kat answered.

"Can I confess something so embarrassing?" Morgan asked. "In middle school, I had the hugest crush on Ty. I planned my entire day around running into him in the hall."

"I can top that," Addison said. "My first kiss was…Chris Nolte!" Dramatic pause. "In the lunch line. In first grade."

Everyone laughed. "It's like I was meant to join the Herd or something," Kat said. "Confessions about my ex and my boyfriend both?"

"Wait, it's official?" Elena blurted excitedly.

Kat nodded and smiled, Morgan squealed with delight.

"Guys," Kayla said slowly. "Umm, I have a confession to make too…"

OMG, Elena thought. Is she finally going to say something?

"I've kind of been seeing someone too…"

As thought by unspoken agreement, no one spoke, sensing the fragility of Kayla's bravery.

"And, um, they're a she. I'm, um, well, I prefer girls." She looked up, her eyes darting wildly between everyone, as though awaiting sentencing.

"Kayla!" Addison said, jumping up to hug her. "I love that for you! Who's the lucky girl? She needs the Herd seal of approval!"

"Wait, aren't you even a little surprised? I've been working up the courage to say this all year!"

Everyone exchanged glances, and Elena thought back to the now completely understandable Book of Kayla, The Issue, and the Spiralling incident in Chemistry.

"Um, no, Kayla, we're your best friends," Morgan said, rolling her eyes. "I kind of guessed, but I figured you'd tell us when you were ready."

"Same," said Elena. "I'm just happy you trust us. So, who is it?" She congratulated herself on the epic tongue biting that the past two months required.

Kayla started telling her friends about the sophomore named Lauren, who Elena already investigated and approved shortly after the Spring Fling.

"So, I was right back in middle school about Kayla-and still the worst kind of asshole ever," Kat thought, staring into the fire.

"You were 12. Give yourself a break," Elena said.

"Things really have changed," Morgan said. "But kind of stayed the same, you know?"

"Maybe Elena had something to do with all the changes?" Kayla said with palpable relief now that her secret was out in the open. "I mean, she's the only thing that's new."

"All my magical, people-influencing powers?" Elena joked for the sake of everyone but Kat.

"You said that being able to influence teachers *was* your superpower," Kayla said.

"I was in Civics with Elena," Addison declared, swirling her cup knowingly. "The teacher was a disaster area, and Elena basically ran the class."

Elena blushed. "Was it that obvious?"

"Ummmm, yeah! But thank God you did," Addison said. "If it weren't for you, he would have spent the entire year trying to figure out the seating chart."

Elena laughed along, but wanted to get out of this conversation that felt dangerously Spuren-ish. She'd had two cups of champagne and might blurt anything. "I have to use the bathroom," she said, standing up.

"I'll come," Kat said.

The girls left the warm firelight and walked across the lawn toward the house. The setting dew was cool on their sandaled feet. Even though the magic of the firelight was broken, the early summer darkness still invited secret sharing.

"You know what I said back there? About Ty?" Kat asked.

"Yeah."

"Well, that wasn't the whole story." Kat took a deep breath. "He was *abusive*, Elena."

"I kind of know," Elena said carefully. "Remember the Winter Dance."

"Yeah. That was kind of the tip of the iceberg."

"Do you want to talk about it?"

"Maybe. I'm thinking after what happened with Paige, I might need to say something too. Maybe."

Elena carefully considered her words, sensing the gravity of the moment. "Whatever you decide, I'll support you."

"I know. Thanks. I never told you that he showed up at my house after I broke up with him. Over Christmas break."

"What happened?" Elena said, fearing the answer.

"He came over to 'watch the game' with my dad. And then all a sudden, he was by me, and we were in the basement, and he was super apologetic and kind. And—I'm so mortified. I actually almost forgave him, almost had sex with him. He was that much in my head."

"How'd it end?" The girls stopped walking, under a tree in the near-total darkness.

"I thought of you, weirdly enough," Kat said.

Elena laughed and then immediately tried to stifle it.

"No, it is ridiculous," Kat said. "I thought of you and the girls from camp, and I got brave enough to kick him out. My dad heard me yelling at him to stop, to leave. And I think Ty only left because of my dad. If he weren't there, who knows what would've happened. Dad kicked him out without his shirt."

"In December?" Elena asked, laughing fully now.

"Yup. I still have it. I use it to clean the hair out of my sink."

"Nice," Elena said.

As they resumed walking to the house, Elena saw her mom silhouetted in her bedroom window before she quickly stepped away when Elena looked up. She shook her head at her mom's predictability.

They reached the back porch and the motion-activated light blared to life. The magic of the evening was quickly shattered through LED lights and Elena's dad dozing in front of a *Law and Order* rerun. It was weird to walk into the normalcy after hearing Kat's story. Elena supposed that the messy bits of life had to fit in with the mundane ones.

• • •

Elena smelled the ghosts of the previous night's campfire before she opened her eyes. The sky was taking on a hint of gray, but the sun wouldn't fully be up for an hour or two. Realizing she forgot to shut the curtains on the basement windows, Elena carefully tiptoed between the sleeping bodies of her friends strewn across the floor. The room thrown back into darkness, she slid back into her sleeping bag, hoping to will herself into a few more hours of sleep.

"Elena?" she heard the whisper from nearby and saw the faint outline of Kayla's head popping up over Morgan's mouth-agape form.

"Hey," she whispered back. "Need something?"

"No, I'm good. But I wanted to thank you for giving up the scholarship for me. Don't try and deny it, because I already got Mrs. V. to confirm it."

Stupid Mrs. V. "How'd you find out?"

"Your name was listed on the housing assignment sheet instead of mine. I've known for awhile, I just didn't want to say anything. I mean, you must have kept it secret for a reason."

Elena longed to make a pot / kettle comment, but resisted. It was too soon. "I didn't want you to feel awkward," she said. "Besides, it wasn't some big sacrifice. I really, really didn't want to go."

"I did feel awkward at first, like maybe I should try to get them to change their minds, like that's what a friend should do…" Kayla spoke over Morgan's light snores. "But then I figured that maybe the best way to be a friend would be to accept this as a gift. So, thanks for the gift, Elena."

"It's not like you didn't deserve it. We were tied, and Mrs. V recommended me over you because of my class participation, even though most of the time I just repeat answers you give me."

Kayla couldn't deny that.

"Plus, Kayla, I *really hate math*."

"Duh," Kayla said. "I've known that for awhile."

"Seriously?" Elena said. "I didn't really realize it 'til, like, winter!"

"That's why we're friends," Kayla said, laying back down to signal the conversation was ending.

"Best friends," Elena blurted.

"Yup," Kayla whispered back. "And it's okay with me if you have more than one best friend."

Elena lay back down too, staring at the ceiling. Before she drifted off, she thought, I really lucked out, moving here.

Best case scenarios-Zedernwald
- *Figure out what Aunt Nell really died from.*
- *Learn to live with myself*
- *Learn to live with Kat*
- *Learn to live without Stephen*
- *Homesick, just a little*

EPILOGUE

"Do you think your mom could drive us to Piggly Wiggly?" Val asked Elena, peering over the edge of the top bunk.

"Yeah, of course," Elena replied as she neatly arranged the blanket on her bottom bunk. At camp, she became obsessive about making her bed. When you share a small cabin with three other girls, you had to keep your own space under control. "They'll probably want to take us out to dinner, too," Elena added, referencing her three cabin-mates: Kat, Val, and another girl from Iowa named Mallory.

"Ya think?" Kat said sarcastically. "Elena's mom is super helicoptery."

"Should we be worried?" Val asked, jumping down from the top bunk.

"No, they're pretty normal," Elena said. "My mom just doesn't know anything about all *this*."

"That must be so weird," said Mallory from above Kat. "I know you told us all a million times, but I can't imagine my mom not knowing."

"True," said Elena. "But, it's not like your moms know everything about you, right? I mean, that's kind of the point of growing up."

"My mom still has no idea what was going on with Chris before I left for the summer," Kat said.

"Or during the summer," Val said, *"in the convertible when he came to visit,"* she added. Val was an expert at the Communal-afterthought-zinger.

"Shut up, Val," Kat said, blushing, but radiating happiness. Chris drove up once that summer and she was practically giddy for days after.

"And you aren't exactly the poster child for parental honesty either, Mallory."

"Thank God my mom follows a strict no-Communing rule at home," she said, glancing down at her phone and whatever gossip was brewing.

"Even though my mom's not Spuren," Elena said, "she still has all those extra Mom powers. Sometimes I think she can read my mind, even though I know it's not possible."

Elena picked up her toiletry bag and left the cabin, heading to the shared bathroom. While the cabins were rustic, the bathroom was fairly modern. Sure, there was only one shower for every eight girls, but they developed a system for sharing, and it worked out fine.

In fact, everything worked out just fine. Did Elena love every one of the 53 girls at Zedernwald? Absolutely not. But she didn't feel the need to pretend that she did. Some Spuren girls were annoying, but that didn't mean Elena couldn't take a yoga class with them, or practice crowd reading with them during a trip into town. And, unlike at school, cliques never developed at Zedernwald. Talent undermined the emotional subterfuge on which high school society was built.

Even though her days were filled up with camp activities, Elena found time to be alone. She worked on completing her online courses, just like she promised her parents. By the end of summer, she would have college credits in math and English. She also read a bunch of poetry books that she bought at a small used bookstore. She never used to like poetry—too wishy washy. But somehow, it was growing on her.

She filled up her own notebooks, too. They still contained a lot of lists. But more and more, she let her mind and pen wander beyond the confines of the bullet points, and occasionally wrote something that made her smile.

She kept in touch with the Herd. Addison was a font of information on all the Belvedere gossip, and Kayla was having a magical time in Madison. Elena guarded against jealousy as she gushed about her accomplishments and new friends. Elena wondered if she was still seeing Lauren, but Kayla never mentioned her, so she was left in the dark. She couldn't use her Talent over the phone; this and so many other teal notebook questions were answered daily, much to Elena's relief.

Stephen called her a couple of times, too. He looked sad the first time, and stubbornly okay the second. Elena felt awful for breaking his heart. Even more, she really, really missed him. But not enough to do anything about it. Not yet at least.

This was the first day of her family's vacation in the Cottage, almost half a mile away along the shoreline path. Her parents and the twins arrived late the night before. Elena got the text from her mom around 10:45, and they agreed to see each other in the morning. Elena planned to walk over and join them for the traditional first-morning breakfast of pancakes cooked in the cast iron skillet that hung in the Cottage.

This year, Anders, Meghan and the twins would visit the lodge. There were loose plans for supper with Aunt Mary and, by extension, Aunt Sylvie, although she steadfastly refused to commit to anything. Sylvie had such steely control of her Talent that Elena couldn't get a whiff of her true intentions. She still didn't know what Sylvie actually thought of her, exactly. As opposed to Aunt Mary's comfortable warmth, Sylvie remained cool and controlled.

But before the potentially awkward reunion, Elena would have time to spend with just her own family. She hadn't decided whether to sleep at the Cottage. As she repacked her toothbrush and face products into the flowered bag and flip-flopped out of the bathroom, she leaned heavily in favor of spending a few nights there. Being able to leave her bathroom supplies in one place sounded nice. The company sounded nice too.

Elena wandered toward the shoreline path, entering the cool cedar woods, still damp with morning dew. As her eyes adjusted, she saw a figure sitting on the bench next to the water. Spuren or not, she knew exactly who it was, even from that distance. As though pulled by a fine, gossamer thread, Elena dropped her bag and ran toward her mom, who smiled and opened her arms.

Acknowledgements

This book started with the musing of a true nerd about mitochondrial inheritance and the very cool concept of Mitochondrial Eve. Do a little digging, it's fascinating! This was my first book-length project and was interrupted by many things, including an unavoidable nonfiction memoir, but Elena is finally in print. I hope you love her and all the women in the book as much as I do. And, yes, _____ is me. They are all me, they are all a little bit all of us.

Kathie Giorgio, my writing coach and friend, and the AllWriters community in Waukesha, Wisconsin gave me the audacity and confidence to make this happen! What a gift you have given me, Kathie. Thank you.

There were many people along my crazy journey who gently nudged me along. From a massage therapist who left an encouraging voicemail to my therapist- therapist who helped me out of medicine, to the many enthusiastic commenters on my blog. You all dropped little pebbles into my cup of writerly water until it overflowed, Aesop-like, into a book. Thank you.

Thanks to John McSweeney, one of my most enthusiastic pebble-droppers, who helped me land on Spuren as a good word to capture what, exactly, was going on with the Talented women in this book. All credit for inspiration is his, all blame for misuse of the German language is mine. Despite my last name, I, like Aunt Mary, only know how to inquire after drinks and toilets in the language.

I wonder if my fellow journeyers in the Write Your Novel in a Year workshop will even recognize the iteration of this novel? Thank you for your insights and all of the laughs and encouragement. I'm still going to get that drawing of Nona's gliders pulling up at the midair light for a little light flirtation into commission.

My book club friends are my first and best beta readers! I worry sometimes that they are too enthusiastic, but hey, a little wine-fueled enthusiasm never hurt anyone. Thanks to Vicky, Michelle, Denise, Leah, Patty and Julie.

And, finally, thanks to my Jimmy, who greeted my announcement that I thought I was done with medicine with "you only live once and deserve to be happy." Thanks for never casting aspersions on my pursuits and encouraging me to pursue my seemingly nonsensical dreams.

Finally, thanks to my daughters, Natalie & Evie, for allowing me to gain Meghan's voice and insights. I'll always be waiting at the end of the shore path to give you a hug.

ABOUT THE AUTHOR

Angie is a former pediatrician, a mother, and a Wisconsinite from birth. Her interests run the gamut from genealogy to the obsessive collecting of perennials, from Pilates to creative napping. *Voices* is her second book. The first was a work of nonfiction genealogical mystery titled *The Accidental Archivist*. She is a student of AllWriters Workplace & Workshop and a member of the Door County Published Authors Collective. She lives between Franklin and Gills Rock, Wisconsin, with her husband, two daughters, and two dogs.

NOTE FROM ANGELA BIER

Word-of-mouth is crucial for any author to succeed. If you enjoyed *Voices*, please leave a review online—anywhere you are able. Even if it's just a sentence or two. It would make all the difference and would be very much appreciated.

Thanks!
Angela Bier

We hope you enjoyed reading this title from:

www.blackrosewriting.com

Subscribe to our mailing list – *The Rosevine* – and receive **FREE** books, daily deals, and stay current with news about upcoming releases and our hottest authors.
Scan the QR code below to sign up.

Already a subscriber? Please accept a sincere thank you for being a fan of Black Rose Writing authors.

View other Black Rose Writing titles at www.blackrosewriting.com/books and use promo code **PRINT** to receive a **20% discount** when purchasing.